SHADOW CASTE

THE MELDERBLOOD CHRONICLES
BOOK 2

E.A. WINTERS

DRAGONLEAFPRESS

Paperback ISBN: 978-1-958702-21-5

Hardcover ISBN: 978-1-958702-22-2

DragonLeaf Press, imprint of Snowfall Publications, LLC

To the doom and accountability writers:

You have made your mark on me and my writing, encouraging me, challenging me, and pressing me forward with an above and beyond community.

Thank you, from the depths of my heart and keyboard.

SOCIAL MEDIA

Connect with me on social media! [1]

- Website and newsletter: https://www.eawinters.com
- Facebook: https://www.facebook.com/ eawintersnovels
- TikTok: @eawinters
- Instagram: @e.a.winters

---

1. Warning: connecting on social media may lead to exclusive content, behind the scenes snapshots, and joining a community that is way more fun than your daily to-do list. Engage with caution.

1

Plastered smiles, dancing townspeople, a gilded cage —the processional symbolized every miserable lie Aviama's life had become. The canopied howdah she now occupied dripped with gems and shining filigree, a beautiful shell gently swaying in the breeze on the back of the bahataal. Naturally, Radha had chosen the highest transport animal possible. Shiva had said it was for visibility so as many people as possible could see the spectacle of the betrothal announcement. But Aviama knew choosing a habitually slow creature that stood three meters high was also a wise deterrent for jumping out of the howdah and fleeing for her life.

The bahataal's soft fur lifted in the natural wind in tufts, welcoming enough that she wished she could bury her face in it and block the world away. Its large flat nose lifted this way and that to catch the scents of the city, and its wide, circular ears lifted and swiveled in every direction. The crowd pressed in on either side, shouting, throwing flowers and handfuls of colored grain, and craning their necks for the romantic young couple. The bahataal's long limbs reached to the ground of the streets of Rajaad in long, smooth, deliberate strides.

"You aren't eating."

Ah, yes. The best phony of them all, the bane of her waking hours, her ever-present, ever-manipulative fiancé. Prince Shiva. Aviama reached across him into the cup of nuts and dried fruit attached to the front of the canopy, waved a handful in his face, and dropped several pieces into her mouth.

"Yes, I am."

He glared at her. "In general. You're not eating. You grow weak."

"An astute observation, my prince."

It was true, of course. She'd hardly had a bite, except food from common trays set out for palace guests to share. Food the queen couldn't be sure would go to Aviama.

Shiva sighed. When he turned back to the people, it was obvious why they were taken with him. Not to say there weren't growing factions of anti-Tanashai family sentiment. But the gorgeous young prince oozed charisma wherever he went, and his support base was not small. Even now, Aviama could see three giggling girls *ooh*ing and *aah*ing over him from behind the line of guards keeping the more overeager observers at bay.

Permanently sun-kissed skin wrapped a muscular frame and a face decorated with dark umber eyes that captured the attention of men and women alike. Men wanted his respect. Women wanted his love. And all begged for his ear.

Shiva smiled, waved, and slithered his arm around her shoulders as if they were the happiest couple in all the land, jauntily going over their hopes and dreams for the future.

Except that Shiva wasn't *in* any of Aviama's hopes for the future. Though her hopes were more of a pipe dream at this point.

Aviama gritted her teeth and waved to the sea of people

below. Laughing children ran alongside the processional. Draped in silks or shrouded in rags, every soul in the city seemed to have come out for a peek at the latest palace drama. It had been over two decades since the last royal wedding, and after the return of magic caused chaos throughout the world just three years ago, people were starved for distraction. For hope.

She wished she could reserve some of that hope for herself. Or that her betrothal to their charming prince offered some promise of a better future, rather than a looming deadline filling Aviama's nightmares. If she didn't escape before the wedding, she'd truly be trapped forever.

The question was, would the queen find a way to assassinate Aviama before she found a way out of the palace? And how exactly would Shiva force Aviama to provide information on melders like her that would give him an edge in controlling the neighboring kingdoms? Would the king soon mobilize his forces to invade Jannemar, now that they knew about a substance with the power to make magic melders sick and helpless? Even if she escaped, if Radha waged war on Jannemar, would she have a home left to escape to?

Okay, so there were actually quite a few questions.

"Stop looking so sour."

Aviama flinched at the sound of Shiva's voice so close to her ear. "I don't look sour. Hours and hours of my childhood were spent being polite to people I don't like. I can smile and wave just fine, thanks."

Hammering home her point, she lifted her chin and flashed a beaming smile at a woman tossing colored grain. The woman nearly squealed when they made eye contact. A young boy darted behind her and back into the throng, and when he disappeared, so did whatever was in the woman's purse. She turned in dismay, and a less-than-delicate slit down her satchel served as punishment for her fascination with the prince and princess. Events like these were a pickpocket's dream.

The king and queen's bahataal and howdah swayed in front of them, mounted guards surrounding the royal family. Five carriages, one with Shiva's younger siblings, the rest stuffed with nobles, followed King Dahnuk and the crown prince. Even the nation's emblem inspiration, the massive, colorful pakshi birds, were featured in the front, each one bearing a royal guardsman. Their plumage was beautiful, but their beady eyes still gave Aviama the creeps, just as much as they had when they'd pulled her on the sand sled across the desert from the beach to the palace just six short weeks ago.

Shiva dug his fingers into her shoulder. "It doesn't have to be this hard. You're making yourself miserable for no reason."

"Really? I thought *you* were making me miserable by blackmailing me, threatening my family, and generally forcing me to be in your presence."

A vein in his neck bulged as he clenched his jaw and looked out upon his adoring people. Were they adoring? Or were they as much a part of the charade as she was?

He turned back to her suddenly, seizing her waist and pulling her toward him, kissing her on the mouth, then her neck, letting his lips linger at her ear. Aviama gasped and froze, revulsion washing over her at his closeness. His breath tickled her neck as he murmured against her hair. "You grow bold in public. Do you expect me to forget your behavior when we are behind closed doors again?"

A chill ran down her spine, and she started to pull away, but he snaked a hand up to the nape of her neck and yanked her against him, kissing her once more. "Play the game, Lilac. If you insist on acting like a hostage, you'll force me to treat you like one. And useless hostages die." Shiva pulled away, on *his* terms, and smiled. But his eyes were hard. "And start eating again. We can't have you looking like a street rat."

Aviama's chest tightened, and power pooled in her palms —eddies of wind, bated breath, begging for a command. A wisp of her wavy blonde hair blew back from her face in the opposite direction of the natural wind. The air around them tingled along her skin, charged with unspent energy.

Shiva shot her a look and seized her fingers. Was that a flicker of fear across his face, or had she imagined it? He pursed his lips. "Watch yourself. We're almost back through the gates. Our archers are everywhere. And if you act up, your siren friend will suffer."

Heat flushed her cheeks, and she ripped her hand from his grasp in the privacy of the howdah's shell. He let her go, and she turned to wave out the opposite side. Aviama leaned over the edge, and her stomach lurched at the sudden drop beneath her. Three meters was no short fall, and watching the bahataal's rolling shoulder blade under a shroud of fur brought her attention to the straps of the howdah. How securely was the thing tied on?

She wondered how Makana was doing. Aviama hadn't been allowed in the menagerie since the arena. The queen had tried to spin things to look as if their three-year house-guest, Prince Chenzira of the island nation of Keket, had been romantic with Aviama. It wasn't true, though as it turned out, the two of them were both spying on the king, were both melderblood, and both despised the Tanashai family as a whole.

As bad as it was, the queen's lie was better than admitting to espionage and conspiracy to commit treason. The king had charged Chenzira with some sort of spying, but the evidence was shoddy, and he knew it. The two of them had been sent to the arena to be made examples out of, but no one expected a surprise alliance between Aviama and the siren mermaid Makana. Aviama was as shocked as the rest of them when Makana decided to save rather than kill her. She owed the siren her life.

Aviama reached to catch a tossed bouquet, but the throw fell short. She smiled her apology as the processional wound around the final corner, and the House of the Blessing Sun came into view. The palace was enormous, far larger than Shamaran Castle back home in Jannemar. Vermilion red met the horizon with a shock of vibrant color, melting in a gradient of sunset shades from coral to candlelight yellow. The sight of it had left her awestruck when she'd first seen it. Now it only made her sick.

"What will you do when you run out of people to threaten to keep me in line?" Aviama murmured.

Shiva leaned back against the cushioned seat, and she could feel him looking at her, though she refused to meet his gaze. "We never will. You're a soft-hearted thing, Lilac. It's what drew me to you to begin with. You would attach to a stray squirrel."

You mean it's what made you think I could be controlled.

But she had been controlled, hadn't she? After all, it was her own idiocy that landed her on the howdah next to Prince Shiva. Nobody forced her to trust him. She'd been summoned to compete with three other neighboring princesses for his hand and therefore for an allegiance, but her brother King Zephan had only sent her to avoid snubbing a powerful nation when Jannemar was recovering from war and low on coin—and to spy.

Spy she did, too, but no good spy would have turned over sensitive secrets to the enemy. She was such a fool. She'd truly believed Shiva might change things in Radha, might be more welcoming to melders than his reputation had claimed. That they might work together, form a real relationship of trust and love, that there was hope for the political and the personal to meld.

Aviama supposed they did meld. His betrayal had felt personal. The queen demanding that she seem disinterested in her son, forfeit the contest, and leave before she had to murder someone to prevent the great Tanashai line being tainted with melderblood—well, that had felt pretty personal too. Being tossed into an arena to fight for her life against various monsters hadn't helped matters.

Aviama turned back to the gold-wrapped illusion beside her. "Do you have squirrels in Radha?"

Shiva shook his head. "No."

He was, unfortunately, just as attractive as he'd always been. She just wished her name wasn't on the list of naïve women his looks had tricked into trusting him. Aviama looked back out over the crowd, the people cheering for a future where she was trapped with a bloodthirsty tyrant forever.

"They're smart. They learn from their mistakes. And I learn from mine."

"Good. Then you'll earn your stay in comfortable lodgings rather than a dungeon and lay your pretty head down at night with a clearer, less bloody, conscience."

A wisp of breeze escaped Aviama's fingers and wafted over Shiva's face. He slipped his arm tight around her waist again, with far too great an air of familiarity, and dropped his voice low as the gates to the palace swung wide. "Play the game. Kiss me, darling. Step one of your new role is complete. We have much to celebrate—and much to look forward to."

Aviama swallowed. She'd accepted Shiva's offer of marriage to save her own skin in the arena. She'd signed up for this. But her public displays supporting the lie of their relationship would end the instant she found an escape.

If she found an escape.

She leaned in and kissed him, firm but quick, though he lingered on her lips before letting her go. Whoops and hollers went up from the crowd amidst flurries of colored grain in a wild celebratory finale, fueled into a frenzy by their kiss.

Aviama fought the urge to wince at the frenzied excitement of the crowd and turned for a farewell wave as the king and queen's bahataal passed through the gates ahead. The memory of Shiva's lips on hers still hung over her like a cloud, his strong arm encircling her and gripping her hip, as a movement caught her eye by the gate.

A commoner with double axes on his back.

How had the guards let him so close to the entry? But Aviama would have known the man's short, well-kept beard and ruddy, perfect skin anywhere. The cut of his jaw, the glare of his eyes. He may have been dressed in rough spun wool, but he moved as if he expected a legion to answer his call.

Chenzira.

Their eyes met, and for a fraction of a second, the world stopped as the reality of his presence sunk in. But his eyes were scathing, harder than she'd ever seen them. Her stomach dropped.

Whizzzz. Fwup.

An arrow buried itself in the canopy just above her head, and Shiva knocked her to the howdah floor.

2

Aviama stirred the food around on her plate with her fork, her brain whirling in endless circles. Her forearm still ached from where she'd hit the floor of the howdah. Shiva had lain on top of her until the gates shut behind the processional. It wasn't until they'd sat up that they noticed the parchment hanging from the arrow lodged in the canopy.

> *House of Blessing, House of Blood*
> *The name Tanashai is in the mud.*
> *The day you take a melder wife,*
> *You both shall face the end of life.*

The streets were searched. The gates secured. Witnesses questioned. The result was three inconsistent descriptions of possible subjects, the details too jumbled up and vague to be of any help.

Shiva had insisted on dining with Aviama when they returned and had spoken to no fewer than seven officials coming in and out of the prince's private sitting room over the course of the meal.

"It's Darsh. The extremists want to be the only place for melderbloods to go. They want power, not peace. And he's willing to kill his own to gain control."

The latest official nodded fervently at the crown prince. "Quite possible, Your Highness. The king's men have already arrested four known melders, but they all deny connection to Darsh and his radicals."

Shiva shook his head. "Not good enough. Petition my father to storm the west end, in their last known hang-out spot. Interrogate the owner of the pub and the bakery. If they don't give up names, kill them."

"What if they don't know names, Your Highness?"

Shiva drained his goblet to the dregs and drilled the official with a cool stare. "They know."

The official bowed and made a hasty retreat out the door.

Aviama twirled a white starchy substance with her fork before setting it down and raising her glass to her lips. She didn't drink a drop of it.

Shiva set down his goblet hard and turned his glare on Aviama. "I thought I told you to eat."

"Not hungry." Traitor that it was, her stomach growled. Loud.

The prince rolled his eyes and arched an eyebrow.

Danger had yet to remove her appetite. If anything, it made her hungrier. Aviama pursed her lips. "You seem quite invested in keeping me alive, after today's scare."

"So?"

"I'll tell you when we're alone."

Shiva side-eyed the servants standing in attendance and jerked his chin toward the service door. They left without a word.

Aviama didn't particularly relish time alone with Shiva, not after all that had happened. But the queen had her web of listening spiders all through the palace, and it would behoove her to get rid of any additional sets of ears in the room before disclosing anything sensitive.

The door closed, and the tension of the silence was palpable. Aviama shifted in her seat. Shiva cocked his head. "Speak."

Her gut twisted, and she hesitated. Then, without a word, she stood to reach across the wide table and steal Shiva's plate for herself. Roasted game, onions, vegetables, and whatever the white starch was filled her nostrils with beckoning spices and mouthwatering juices. She stabbed her fork into the meat and barely chopped off a piece with her knife before wolfing it down.

Shiva's eyebrows soared. "You really do think you're going to be poisoned."

Aviama stuffed another chunk of game in her mouth, hardly caring for propriety in her hurry. "After today, do you blame me?"

"No, but you've been like this since the arena."

"Yes, well, the arena was only the most recent time your family has tried to kill me." Aviama scooped up a bite of vegetables next. "Your mother takes to the halls with her ruby hyena every chance she gets. Why do you think that is? It's for my benefit."

Shiva leaned back in his chair and crossed his arms. "That's quite an accusation."

Aviama shrugged. "She tried to kill my guard. When he disappeared, she still told me she'd killed him. And she threatened to kill my handmaiden."

The prince's eyes narrowed. "Where exactly did Murin get to, I wonder?"

"So terribly sad, her disappearance." Aviama tsked and shook her head with a show of mournful sadness, but when the façade dropped away, the lump in her throat was real. "I miss her. I miss having servants who don't hate me, just in general."

Shiva reached across the table for Aviama's plate, picked up his fork as if he were about to eat from her plate as she ate from his, then paused and set it aside. "You can't know for sure she tried to have Murin and Enzo killed."

Aviama gestured with her knife in the direction of her abandoned plate. "And you can't be sure she didn't. If I were trying to kill myself, starvation is the last way I'd go about it. I can hardly last a day without eating, as it turns out, and it makes me twice as irritable going without food when I'm already irritable about being engaged to you."

The corners of his mouth turned down. He probably wanted to address her dig, but at least she'd said it in private. He let it go. "She threatened you since the arena?"

Aviama shook her head and stuffed her face with another bite. "Didn't have to. She did plenty of that during the contest for the wildly enviable position I find myself in now."

This time, his fist came down on the tablecloth. The table settings leaped from their places with a clatter, and she jumped. "That's enough. I've put up with more than enough disrespect from you today. Say your piece and be through."

An annoyingly fair request, however evil she might think him. Aviama took a deep breath and let it out in a rush. She swallowed the last of the meat and looked him dead in the eye. "My mail was intercepted. The pigeons I brought from Jannemar were exchanged for ones that fly a few yards back home to their dovecote on the grounds of the palace here. Your father knows your mother wants me dead. He said so, in your hearing. You knew it too, before the arena. Did you really think a betrothal would make her abandon course? This is her greatest fear. The great, pure bloodline of her family tainted with melderblood."

The image of Queen Satya's face hovered in her mind's eye like a living nightmare. *I will not have an abomination wed to my son.*

"To be fair, none of us planned on you having access to outgoing messages. But you've made your point."

Aviama grimaced at his cavalier admission of curtailing her communication—any chance of getting word home for help. For all Jannemar knew, the contest was still going on, and should be wrapping up soon, and she'd be sent home to them shortly. Of course, it was a three-month trip home, so even if she did manage to get a foot messenger out, it would take them longer than she had.

Aviama could only hope that when she'd caused the distraction that let Murin, her lady-in-waiting, escape, that she'd made it out safely. The plan had been for Murin to find the defected guard from the palace, get him to help her locate Darsh, and tell him his suspicions were correct—Aviama was a melder and was willing to help his cause against the Tanashai family. But that was before she'd gotten engaged to the Tanashai prince. Had Murin made it out, and Darsh ignored Aviama's message? Or had she been caught or killed? Aviama chewed on her lip.

Shiva tapped his fingers on the table, pulling her from her thoughts as he seemed to work through his own. "You will dine with me every night. No one will know which plate will be yours, and which will be mine. Neither will we, until the plates are before us. We'll make some arrangement for breakfast and the midday meal, but you will eat. Acceptable?"

More time with Shiva was not exactly her favorite option,

but starving was worse. And he was being almost tolerable at the moment. She gave a short nod. "Acceptable."

"Good. Finish what you want and get out. I have criminals to catch."

It shouldn't have hurt. He'd gained her trust, weaseled out her secrets, and planned the onslaught of her home and the potential death of her brother and sister-in-law, the invasion of her homeland. But it still did.

Aviama pressed her lips together and swept two dinner rolls into her napkin. "There's the charm I fell in love with."

"There's the snark that almost got you killed three times today. Want to find out if four is your lucky number?"

He tilted his head in that lackadaisical way of his, and Aviama imagined what it would feel like to unleash her wind and blast him against the wall. Those defining cheekbones, haughty, piercing eyes, muscled arms he put so much trust in —all chucked to the back of the room like a sack of produce. It would expend a decent amount of energy, but it would be worth it.

Until her head landed in a basket.

Aviama cringed and headed for the door, then turned as a thought struck her. "I want to go to the menagerie. The *magna* on the walls curtails my melder powers, so there's no need for a host of guards and servants to glare at me there. I'd like to be alone somewhere other than in my room."

Shiva stood from the table, strode to the desk, and pulled out a stack of papers. He didn't bother looking up. "Is there a question in there somewhere?"

Aviama swallowed hard, but the cost of her silence was a bitter dose of resentment that clung to the back of her throat, begging to be set free. *Gee, genius, do you think?* "Can I go to the menagerie tomorrow?"

"Thank you for asking." He shuffled some papers, then

paused just long enough to glance up at her. "No."

Aviama stared at him, shock rippling through her as though she'd been slapped in the face. This was his hope for the future? Patronizing her, toying with her, humiliating her until it suited him to drag her out for public displays to prove what an adorable couple they were? Using a melderblood queen as a power play to gain the trust of the melders in Radha and weaken the influx of new members flocking to Darsh?

Her cheeks flushed hot. Yes, that was exactly what he expected. Until he decided what else exactly to do with her. She spun on her heel and reached for the door handle when his voice cut across the room again.

"Don't forget—we still have that wedding planning meeting tomorrow over brunch. My mother will be there, but the food will be shared. Don't be late."

If it wasn't for Aviama's commitment to keeping down the food she'd finally managed to acquire, she might have thrown up. Wedding planning. To the man potentially plotting her family's murder.

She turned the handle and slipped into the hall, tears welling in her eyes. Shiva was just as bad as she'd feared, only appearing more human in spurts when it served him to play the role. Radha was still bent on bending melders to their will or destroying them completely, with a preference for the latter. And even the radical group leader, Darsh, had rejected her plea for aid.

In the House of the Blessing Sun, the enemy of her enemy had just another angle on why Aviama should die. And the only option that wanted her alive painted a dismal picture of their future together.

The door clicked shut behind her, and she fled down the passage to her own lonely quarters.

3

As lonely as she felt her quarters were, Aviama's rooms were three bodies less empty than she'd hoped. Sai, Bhumi, and Durga milled about, fluffing already fluffed pillows and straightening already straight food platters that had been sent up for her supper.

Aviama stifled an inward groan as she stepped through the doorway. "Help yourselves. I already ate."

She shut the door firmly behind her, blocking out her view of the guard outside her room, and crossed to the bed. Eyes in the halls, guards at her door, shadows everywhere she went. But the eyes in her own chambers worried her the most.

Aviama belly-flopped on the bed and kicked her shoes off, silently begging them to just disappear for once. But her luck couldn't be that good. Not in Radha.

"How was the processional, Your Highness?"

Sai. The servant she'd accidentally knocked sideways on her first day in Radha. The one she'd sort of forced to be an accomplice when Aviama dove into her laundry cart to get out of her room before this whole betrothal business.

Her tone was soft and sweet, matching her petite frame

and round face. She was short, though not overly so for a Radhan woman, and her almond skin glowed with health, her arms strong from her various menial tasks. Nothing in her voice betrayed any bitterness toward Aviama, but it was Sai who had kept the throwing knives hidden for Aviama before the arena, wrapping a note from Shiva in her clothes.

Sai was Shiva's girl. His eyes, his ears. She wasn't here for Aviama.

And the throwing knives had been confiscated immediately following the engagement. Not that she was particularly skilled with them, but she was probably better than the average person after her ex-assassin sister-in-law's tutelage. The only things of her own that remained were portions of her wardrobe, the rings she always wore, and her jewelry box —though she'd once come back to find the pieces out of place.

Aviama rolled onto her side and plucked at the bedding. "Precisely as delightful as I expected."

"Would you like to go over tomorrow's wardrobe, Your Highness?"

Aviama's lips flattened as she shifted her attention to Durga. Beyond Durga, Bhumi didn't quite stop herself from a reflexive grimace. Servants who spent their lives waiting hand and foot on people should know when a girl just needed to be left alone to cry. At least Bhumi seemed to grasp the concept.

Bhumi was the youngest of the three, the least experienced, and the most infrequently present. But that only made Aviama think the girl might not know much of what was really going on, and had been placed there to honestly fill the gaps of work the other two were not required to attend to as they scampered to their masters with whatever scraps of information they'd gathered in a day.

She hoped she made their reports short and boring.

"I would not. I'm confident we'll figure it out in the morning, and I won't be left traipsing through the palace without any clothes."

"Can we draw you a bath?" Bhumi asked.

"No. It's been a long day, and all I really want is just one person in these rooms instead of four."

Bhumi drew back, and Aviama's stomach dropped. *Biscuits.* The girl was only trying to help, and now she'd let her own misery pass on to Bhumi.

Durga folded her hands in front of her, a seemingly benign gesture Aviama had come to interpret as a curse. She did it whenever Aviama wasn't doing what she wanted, despite the fact that Durga was supposedly the servant and Aviama the princess.

"Your Highness, perhaps some writing or drawing materials would ease your mind. Shall I bring some refreshment for the evening, since you've already dined? The king and queen are having a new cream custard tonight. It smells divine."

Custard sounded incredible. Even better if it were served cold. The day had been hot, the processional long, and dried sweat left an unpleasant feel to her skin. But though Durga's words were honey, there was an edge to them as sharp as the girl's nose.

Aviama's gaze drifted to the untouched platter of food on the low table in front of the sofa in the adjoining room. "Thank you, Durga, but I had plenty to eat from the howdah, and then supper. I'm completely stuffed." Aviama wasn't convinced she'd ever been stuffed a day in her life. Sated, sure, but stuffed?

The women turned to go, Durga last of all. Sai might be Shiva's girl, but Durga was the queen's. Aviama was sure of it. Where did Bhumi's loyalties lie?

"On second thought, Bhumi, I'd love a bath. Thank you."

The girl turned back and beamed. "I'll get it prepared, Your Highness! Right away."

Sai gave a small smile and a curtsy, and Bhumi hurried to copy the gesture. Durga offered a barely perceptible dip before the three of them filed out into the hall.

Alone at last, Aviama buried her face in the pillows and let the tears flow. They came slow at first, as the built-up tension of another day of pretending worked its way up through the anxious knots in her stomach, the ache in her heart, the fear set deep in her bones. And then they overflowed, respectable one-off tears down the cheek transitioning into shoulder-wracking, body-rocking sobs.

Shiva had Sai. The queen had Durga, and her spiderweb of spies, and a man-eating hyena. Who did Aviama have?

Briefly, she wondered if Bhumi was the king's spy. Did the king even care what went on with Aviama, as long as Radha got to use the union for political gain? Besides, it was Sai she'd occasionally caught glimpses of heading to and from the royal residences at odd hours. Durga was more discrete with her disappearances to report to the queen.

Perhaps Darsh had gotten a hold of Bhumi, or would, given the chance. Considering the threatening note driven into the howdah, he clearly believed he had all the access necessary to penetrate the palace. He'd done it before.

Eventually, the door reopened, and all three of her servants returned to set her bath. Of course. The prince's girl couldn't let Bhumi be alone with Aviama. And the queen's girl couldn't leave Bhumi and Sai.

Aviama rolled away from them, snuffling back the last of her tears and wiping her face. An embarrassingly large damp spot stained the pillow where her face had been. Durga set hot tea on the table by the sofa, unasked and unwanted. But the tub filled with beckoning, steaming water, and soothing lavender and eucalyptus scents eased pleasantly throughout the room.

Could soaps and lotions be poisoned? Perfume? If so, wouldn't anyone who applied it be poisoned too? But she'd taken plenty of baths since her betrothal to Shiva and wasn't dead yet, so she let the women undress her and help her over the side.

She sank into the water, grateful the women went through the motions without interrogating her with unnecessary questions or agenda items. Sai massaged her scalp, the heat of the bath clearing her head from the pressure collected there after her long cry. Aviama closed her eyes and slipped beneath the surface, trying to imagine she were back home in Shamaran Castle in Jannemar instead of the cursed House of the *Blessing Sun*.

Whatever she was experiencing, it wasn't blessing. And if she didn't want to keep on having things happen *to* her, Aviama was going to have to find a way to go out and make better things happen on her own. *Easier said than done.*

Her lungs started to burn, but she wasn't ready to come up yet. She didn't want to face the world. She didn't want to die. That was, of course, the problem. Everybody but Shiva seemed to want her dead, but life with Shiva wasn't something she could bear. Especially after he and his father invaded Jannemar and emptied its throne.

Under the water, a hand tapped her on the arm, first gently, then more firmly.

Leave me be.

Two hands gripped her by the arms then, but Aviama swatted at them and swirled her hand, palm up, at the surface. Currents of air buffeted the smooth bathwater into little waves lapping at the edges of the tub. With a single jerking motion, Aviama drove a forceful pocket of air straight through the water and down toward her face. She took a breath and almost smiled.

Small victories. They were all she had anymore.

She tried not to think about Shiva's obligatory public kisses, the anger lighting his eyes at her missteps, the way he so seamlessly shifted from the jovial man of the hour to casting threats like darts behind closed doors. It was a shame her only experience of a kiss had been with a man like Shiva. Even worse that he'd duped her into honestly caring for him when they'd first met.

What a fool she'd been. Aviama had always hated when people called her naïve growing up. But she hated it so much more when they were right.

Aviama finished her bath, and her servants, who were not really hers, dressed her in a light rose-petal night dress and braided her hair. After that, they left her alone, and she sat on the sofa staring at the walls, thinking through her dilemma. The sofa she sat on faced a twin couch on the other side, flanked with matching chairs the same shade of emerald green. Cream marble floors with jasper red swirls flowed between the bedroom and sitting area and into a scalloped alcove, on one end sporting curtains, tall windows of delicate lattice paneling, and a gilded wooden bench. Green and gold intertwined up the walls, ornate details branching out and reaching across the ceilings.

She ignored Durga's tea, poured herself a glass of water, and took a sip before wondering why she'd never considered water could be poisoned just as easily as food. But Aviama couldn't avoid drinking water, and she'd already had three glasses since returning to her room for the evening. So she drained the glass anyway and set it back on the table.

The small flame of a candle wavered next to the neglected tea set, a bead of melted wax running down its side. The last of the sunset dissipated across her ever-darkening rooms, and the first of the stars cast weak pinpricks of light through a hazy night sky.

A rattle came from the alcove.

Aviama jolted upright but overshot the movement so badly that she tumbled right off the sofa. Her heart hammered in her chest. The alcove of her room was three floors up, the lattice windows looking out over an enclosed courtyard.

Another rattle, followed by a low scraping sound. Aviama remained on the floor in front of the couch, half under the low table, the cool marble sending a chill up her arms. She held her breath.

The edge of one of the lattice side panels wiggled, then popped free and swung inward. A shadow blocked out the dim starlight beyond, and a foul wind wafted through the chamber, extinguishing the candle on the table with her untouched tea. A shadowy figure slipped through the window and landed in the blackness, a knife blade glistening in his hand.

4

"He told me you were jumpy."

At least I didn't squeal.

Aviama snapped back to her feet, pulse still pounding double-time in her ears. "Not my fault. You're awfully loud for somebody trying to be sneaky." She reached out for the wind, gathering it toward her chest, and blasted it at the newcomer.

The man threw his hands up, and two streams of power met midair. His counter-wind was strong, and she strained against it, the two of them locked in a sizing-up venture that seemed to last an eternity. He stepped forward, just slightly favoring one foot, revealing the last piece of the puzzle to confirm the identity of the man intruding in her chambers. Darsh Mushkil, criminal leader of the melderblood radicals in Radha.

Aviama jerked her chin at his foot, not letting go of the wind forming a horizontal column between them. "Still not healed from the arena?"

Darsh's silhouetted outline shrugged. "Being careful with it is mostly habit now. Our healers are excellent."

She doubted it was just habit, after the ciraba had gotten a hold of his ankle in the sand pit. But it probably wouldn't be wise of him to admit a current injury in front of a potential enemy.

Darsh's energy waned with hers until the two of them dropped their wind, chests heaving.

Aviama took a deep breath. "If you're here to kill me, I'm afraid you'll have to get in line."

"Whether you live or die is entirely up to you, Princess."

Aviama shifted her weight, sidestepping around the sofa as he slunk two steps forward. "Ah, well, that's easy enough. I choose to live. Thanks for stopping by."

Darsh laughed. It was not a reassuring sound. "Enzo is with us. Murin, your girl, came with Arjun."

Arjun must have been the name of the palace guard who wanted to defect to Darsh's extremists. The one with the scar on his hand that Murin had told her about. Aviama pressed her lips together, and Darsh continued.

"As you can imagine, you've created a rather uncomfortable situation. You're a melder. Congratulations. But that doesn't make you a friend. And you just betrothed yourself to the family we plan on obliterating."

Aviama swallowed. "If it makes you feel better, I'm confident I feel worse about that particular situation than you do. If I trusted you, I'd ask you to take me with you, and I'd unbetroth myself real quick."

"It's a shame. If I trusted you, I might even accept." Darsh shook his head. "We have a deal for you. But we won't tell you here."

Alarm bells rang in the back of her mind. Her sister-in-law, Semra, had taught her never to let an assailant take her anywhere. She should fight with all she had right where she was, with the understanding that the relocation was likely simply to torture or kill her more conveniently or efficiently.

But was Darsh an assailant? So far, he'd scaled three floors, broken into her room, had the gall to call her *jumpy,* and defended himself with wind just as she had. If he was going to kill her, why hadn't he? But on the other hand, if he wanted her to feel safe, why was he threatening her about options of living and dying and talking about annihilating the royal family?

He told me you were jumpy.

The thought had come to her mind before, but now it refused to give way to other distractions. Chenzira. "Why does Chenzira hate me?"

The words were out of her mouth before she could stop them, and their softness surprised her. A lump formed in her throat, and she blinked back tears. *Biscuits, you're a moron. Chenzira is free. You are not.* And he only had his life, his very ability to despise her, because of the choice *she* made in the arena. Because of the deal she struck with Shiva, accepting his marriage proposal in exchange for Chenzira's freedom and her own conscience.

So that she and Chenzira didn't have to fight to the death.

The only way they could both live.

But the way he'd looked at her today in the streets...

Darsh snorted. "I tell you we're prepared to wipe out both you and the Tanashai family, but we're going to offer you a deal to determine whether or not you survive the carnage, and —and all you can ask about is why the Keket boy hates you?"

Aviama's jaw dropped, and she stumbled backward as Darsh strode toward her. Darsh lifted his hand, and Aviama raised her palms in defense. But Darsh only lifted a sealed envelope from his vest and set it on the teacup saucer still sitting on the table. His eyes, barely visible at this angle in the dark, never left hers.

Aviama racked her brain trying to remember what crimes he'd been charged with in the arena. Destruction of property. She knew he'd blown up a portion of the guardhouse, among other attacks on the palace, but she didn't know specifics. That charge had likely expanded by now to include collapsing the tunnels to the pit before its expansion into the arena as it was today, not to mention attempted kidnapping and attempted murder of the prince, if not the king. And, of course, murder. Probably in the service of *the Shadow*, as his radicals were informally called.

"No, that's not what I—it's just I saw him today by the gate. At the processional. And the way he looked at me..." Aviama's voice trailed off, and her chest hitched. Then it hit her. What Darsh had just said. "Did you just say *carnage*?"

"Is there a better term?"

She lifted one hand, and Darsh mirrored her movement, but neither called the wind. Darsh stepped again, and Aviama countered him from the far side of the sofa.

"Rumor has it that your beloved sister-in-law is an expert in carnage. Dragonlords tend to be good at that sort of thing. But she was good at it before the dragon, wasn't she? The assassin queen of Jannemar. Quite the bedtime story. Is it true you were close?"

Aviama gritted her teeth. "We *are* close. She's still alive. And she's not an assassin anymore."

Darsh laughed again. "Assassins never get to be *ex*-assassins. That's a comforting lie people tell to let the normals sleep at night. And do you know what else lets people sleep at night? Peace. But peace is often paid for in blood. Even in Jannemar. Perhaps, if you take our deal, you'll feel right at home."

"You've gone through all the trouble to break in. Just tell me now."

"Oh, it was no trouble. I was in the neighborhood." Darsh flashed a wicked grin.

Aviama's heart stopped. "What did you do? Did you kill the king?"

Darsh wagged a finger at her. "I'd hate to spoil the fun. Find out for yourself."

If the king died, Shiva would take his place, and the wedding would be scooted up so his heir-production-factory wife could fulfill her queenly duties. Aviama's stomach rolled. "You can't. Shiva's no better than Dahnuk is. Killing him won't help you."

Darsh arched an eyebrow. "Not anxious to be queen, eh? Even with the power, the influence, the *utility* of that position?"

Aviama opened her mouth, but no sound came. Blood drained from her face, and her eyes only made a silent plea. *Please.*

The extremist leader pursed his lips. "Interesting. Very interesting." He gestured at the parchment in the tea saucer and backed his way to the lattice-paneled window through which he'd come, his features lost to the shadows of the alcove. "Read that and burn it. Order tea for a stomachache after sunset tomorrow. The guard will be taken care of. Get in the basket on the south terrace. We'll do the rest."

Aviama glanced down at the parchment on the saucer. When she looked up an instant later, he'd already disappeared, swallowed by the fog-ridden starlit night.

She spun her rings. Semra's warnings about secondary locations warred against the chance to escape the palace walls, to find Enzo and Murin. To hear Darsh's deal.

Darsh seemed genuinely surprised that she had no

interest in being queen. Did he hope to kill the king so he could promote her to be his melder puppet queen? What strings did he think he could pull to control her from outside the palace, while Shiva did his best to control her from within it?

But he'd also said he planned to destroy the entire royal family. If that were true, promoting her to queen would do no good. With Shiva dead, she would no longer be queen. She'd have no tie to the Radhan throne.

Aviama froze. Shiva had three younger sisters. Children, really. They couldn't inherit the throne in Radha, but the thought burned in her mind. What would happen to them? Would the radicals murder children to wipe out the Tanashai line?

And if that were true, why was Chenzira with him?

The night passed slowly, and Aviama hardly felt she had blinked by the time the sun crept up over the horizon and filtered in through the latticework. The latticework that had so kindly opened the way for an intruder last night.

Everyone in Radha knew she was a windcaller now. Servant interactions were either polite and overly formal, or they gave her a wide berth in the halls. Judging by the melderblood slurs she'd overheard and the dark looks cast her way, her abilities hadn't exactly won everyone over.

Which meant that no matter how much danger she felt she was in, her abilities should be used wisely rather than recklessly. But she had zero hand-to-hand combat capability, and her best weapon-wielding skill was moderate at best— with throwing knives she didn't have. On the other hand, if Darsh had broken into her room, so could anybody else.

If it came down to life and limb, Aviama knew she'd have no choice but to protect herself by whatever means were necessary. But if anybody watched her do it, there would be repercussions. Dungeon and chain-related repercussions. A cage lined with magna repercussions.

Something unpleasant, at any rate, if the king determined her worthwhile to keep alive at all. Because the name of the game was precisely what Darsh had indicated: utility.

Was she useful? If her use outweighed the problems she created, she kept her life. If the problems outweighed her usefulness...

Aviama pulled out the parchment Darsh had left her and scanned it for the third time that morning, which made for a total of seven times since last night.

I'm not sure what Darsh expects me to say.

Something to get you to come to the meeting, I guess, as if you've ever done something because I suggested it.

Maybe I should be saying thank you. Maybe I owe you.

Or maybe you shouldn't have thrown your life down the drain to delay the inevitable. Maybe you only made him stronger by giving him what he wanted.

It doesn't matter now. Be there tomorrow night, and I'll be there to meet you.

But if you don't show...

Sand and sea, if you don't show, there's nothing I can do for you.

That "inevitable" I mentioned is heading your way.

P.S.—I'M not signing this.

If you don't know who this is, you're an idiot.

The door latch turned, and Aviama yelped. *Biscuits, Chenzira was right. Jumpy.* She grimaced and spun toward the entryway, stuffing the note under the covers of her bed and slumping into the pillow just as the door swung open.

5

S ai slipped through the door. Shiva's girl. She was early, which was odd, and she hadn't knocked, which was even more odd. But something else caught Aviama's attention—a dark bruise on the girl's arm that she'd obviously tried and failed to cover up with powder. Her sleeve had slid up her arm as she moved, but after closing the door, Sai tugged the edge of her sleeve down to cover it.

Aviama stared at her, crumbling the note in her palm beneath the blankets.

Sai stared back, feet shuffling awkwardly as if she'd slunk into Aviama's chamber against her better judgment.

Aviama furrowed her brow, trying to decide what to do, when Sai floated to the side table, poured Aviama a glass of water for no reason, and tucked a stray hair behind her ear. Multiple stray hairs, on the primmest, most proper person Aviama had ever met. She cleared her throat, bored a hole in the floor with her deep brown eyes, then raised them furtively to meet Aviama's gaze. "Can I ask you a question?"

Aviama blinked. Sai never asked questions. None of them did, not personal ones. And they never *asked* to ask. They simply stated what would or would not be occurring that day, and confirmed this dress or that, or Aviama's preference for one boring activity over another.

"Of course. But first—can I ask *you* a question?" Aviama lifted her hand and sent a gentle wisp of breeze to lift Sai's sleeve, revealing the bruise once again. She kept her voice low and soft and straightened in the bed to peer into Sai's face. "Did Shiva do that?"

Sai blanched and snapped her sleeve back down, clasping the cloth against her skin to shield herself from Aviama's power.

Aviama dropped her hand. "Sorry. But I have a right to know what kind of marriage I'm entering, don't you think?"

The girl was around Aviama's age, maybe nineteen, her eyes growing rounder by the second. "No, no, Your Highness. It was not Prince Shiva."

Something twisted in Aviama's gut. She opened her mouth to ask what had happened, but thought better of it. Better not to interrogate her the first time she decided to ask some sort of honest question.

The crumpled edges of Chenzira's note poked against the palm of her other hand, its mere existence like a knife to Aviama's throat. She should have burned it last night. Why hadn't she? Aviama's chest tightened. *Or maybe you shouldn't have thrown your life down the drain to delay the inevitable...*

What was she supposed to do? Kill Chenzira to save her own skin? Did the man have a death wish? Or would he rather have overtaken her, killed Aviama himself, and left the arena victorious, rather than defeated by a woman?

Not that she had any delusions of being able to beat him hand-to-hand. She'd only won because he'd been loath to use his quakemaker abilities, and she'd revealed her windcalling. Chenzira would absolutely destroy her hand-to-hand if it came down to it. But Aviama had no real sense of how powerful he was as a melder.

A rustle of cloth brought her back to the present as Sai shifted awkwardly in front of the bed. Aviama snapped her head back up toward her and swallowed. "You had a question. Go ahead."

Sai twisted her hands, then clasped them behind her back. "I've always heard how chaotic melderblood power is. How... wild. Dangerous. But yesterday, in the bath. And just now, with my sleeve. You have a delicate, precise touch. You can do the big stuff, like in the arena, but you have control. Is that normal? Are all melderbloods supposed to be able to do that?"

Aviama squirmed. This was not the sort of question she expected. Was Shiva fishing for information on her magic, and using Sai to do it? Or had it been a melder who left a bruise on her arm—a melder without control?

Radha's history with magic was long and sordid, and had not ended well at The Crumbling. Somewhat understandably, the kingdom had not exactly welcomed Jannemar bringing magic back. After all, it was one of Radha's own who had made the destruction of magic necessary in the first place.

Still, answering Sai's question could do no harm. If Shiva knew melders could learn to control their powers, maybe he could talk to his parents, and Radha could learn not to fear them so much. Wasn't that half the point of marrying Aviama? To bring melders out from the shadows, to weaken the radicals?

Though, admittedly, Aviama didn't know how genuine the gesture was. He'd told her openly he wanted to control magic and melders in general, and he felt that Aviama was the key to doing that. Shiva's end goal was power. And if melders had more power than he did, or his father King Dahnuk did, they were in danger of annihilation.

Hence Darsh's strong response to the crown and its requirement for melders to register. Most melders hadn't done it, keeping their powers a secret or living in hiding instead. Aviama cocked her head, scanning Sai's earnest features. Could it be that she was asking for herself?

"All melders have the capacity for control."

Aviama lifted her hand and called the wind, letting soft fingers of air lift the edges of her hair and swirl around her head in a vortex. It had taken her ages to learn to create anything other than devastating havoc. But under Frigibar's tutelage, the last of the Keepers of Magic, scholar of those rare surviving ancient texts prior to The Crumbling, she had come to understand her abilities and hone them not only to be safe, but to be precise.

She fluttered her fingers to one side and gestured in Sai's direction as if conducting a symphony, dancing the breeze across to play with the hem of Sai's servant's tunic dress. Sai glanced down and swayed this way and that, noticing how the wind clung to her at Aviama's instruction as she moved.

"In Jannemar, we're working hard to train melders so they do not hurt themselves or others. It's only been three years since The Return, and few of us are skilled enough to learn our own abilities, much less instruct others. But Queen Semra is infused with dragon magic and has had a bit longer to practice. She's even instructed by her own dragon, Zezura, at times.

"When magic sprang back to the world, it shocked all of us. I never knew I had melder in my blood. After six hundred years, how could any of us know? When my power erupted, it was like a volcano. I was dangerous." Aviama swallowed, trying to protect herself against the barrage of memories. Swirling wind like a hurricane, the roof of the smithy breaking apart, the hammer flying through the air and driving into the temple of Liben, one of the servants working on the outer ward. His body on the ground.

Aviama blinked hard against the gathering tears and cleared her throat. "Semra and Zephan knew I would be a target, so to protect me and everyone in the castle, I spent months training in a safe space."

"Just on your own?"

"I had a trainer."

"That...that would help. Having a trainer." Sai crossed to the vanity and started pulling out cosmetic powders, brushes, and hair accessories, but her focus was still on the conversation. "Was it Queen Semra who trained you?"

Aviama pursed her lips. She didn't like to lie. But Frigibar was a private man, and the last thing he wanted was attention from foreign royals. Or, frankly, for anyone to know he was alive. "Yes, Semra did train me."

It wasn't untrue. Semra did often help. She just wasn't Aviama's primary trainer during those first months, as she was off putting out fires—often literally—throughout the land.

Sai moved to the wardrobe, and Aviama slipped Chenzira's note out from under the sheets and glanced at it one more time while her back was turned.

Maybe I should be saying thank you. Maybe I owe you...

That didn't sound like he hated her. Though he certainly made it clear that he wasn't *actually* saying thank you, and the next line reeked of bitterness. But what did he have to be bitter about?

And toward the end, he implied that if she came to the meet, he'd be trying to help her somehow. But by the time he got to the P.S., he was back to calling her an idiot. Was he mad at her, or not? Was he trying to save her, or insulting her?

Sai rifled through dress after dress. "Did you need a lot of empty space to train, or just use a—violet dress like this one would suit your eyes just right!"

A knock sounded more of a warning than a request for permission, and the door swung inward. Aviama stuffed the note back under the covers at the same time Sai switched topics from banned magic to daily attire, just as Durga strode in carrying a tray of breakfast teas everyone knew would go untouched. Bhumi trailed her with a vase of fresh-picked flowers, and Aviama reached for the water Sai had poured earlier.

With the arrival of Durga's sharp nose, adept at sniffing around in everybody else's business, all chances of interesting conversation died away. Aviama stole glances in Sai's direction, but she was the picture of dutiful subservience. Durga shot her some dirty looks when she didn't think Aviama was looking, but Sai pretended not to notice, and Bhumi seemed genuinely oblivious.

Aviama let the women twine her hair up in an elegant half-up style flowing out in blonde curls, her mind wandering back to the note she'd stuffed in her bodice the moment she'd had the chance.

Maybe you only made him stronger.

Had she really made Shiva that much stronger? After all, he was still crown prince rather than on the throne, and so far he'd only used her as arm décor for public appearances. Darsh had said Aviama would choose whether to live or die, presumably promising to kill her if she didn't take whatever deal he planned on pitching to her. If that were the case, Darsh was no different from the Tanashai family—except Darsh and his minions had melder powers to aid their violent causes.

He'd also said that Enzo and Murin were with him. Had they joined him, or were they hostages? Had she made a mistake sending Murin to Darsh?

Aviama's heart sank, and she spun the rings on her fingers. This wasn't what she'd hoped would happen.

If you don't show, there's nothing I can do for you.

But if the radicals were set on destroying her, what could one foreign prince do? Or did Chenzira simply mean join or die, and Darsh's extremists were her only chance at survival?

There was only one way to find out. Now the question was, could she escape her multiple spies in time to get to the south terrace come sunset?

6

A viama rejected Sai's violet dress choice in favor of a sage green one. She'd hated purple for six weeks straight, and she didn't expect the loathing to let up any time soon. By the time the latest guard on her detail marched her across the palace to brunch, she was powdered and coifed and utterly famished.

Shiva greeted her at the door with a beaming smile and a kiss on the hand. Her grumbling stomach soured, and she tried not to wince before returning a tart smile. The prince ran a hand through his dark hair and snaked his arm around her waist, tugging her against him hip to hip. "Good morning, Lilac."

Aviama pressed a hand to his chest, trying not to notice the feel of it under her fingers as she flashed green eyes up at him. "I despise you, Your Highness."

It would have looked like sweet nothings to the modest collection of people waiting for them inside, but Sai's mouth twitched in Aviama's peripheral vision. Durga was already scowling, but no more than usual.

Odd. Shouldn't Shiva's girl be offended for him, and the

queen's girl be glad to see conflict? Maybe Sai didn't enjoy her assignment.

Shiva spun Aviama away from the door and guided her toward a table set for eight under a sparkling chandelier. Bold color choices graced the ceilings and walls. His fingers dug into her ribs as he leaned in to brush his lips against her ear. "You're late."

"I'm early."

"The time was moved up. No one told you?"

Aviama's lips parted. She swallowed. "And who would have told me?"

Shiva's jaw clenched just a hair as he tucked her arm in his and directed her towards their seats. "I took Ishaan off your detail. I'm doing what I can to make life decent for you. It doesn't have to be like this."

The queen's favorite snitch, Ishaan, had been recalled from Aviama to another assignment by order of the king almost immediately after the arena. Aviama wasn't sure what strings Shiva had pulled to make sure his mother's man was placed somewhere else, but whatever the case, she'd take what she could get.

Secretly. Shiva had to have an ulterior motive. He probably didn't want more of his mother's snoops around his melderblood fiancée—or maybe he was more concerned about the queen's intentions toward her than he had let on. In any case, it was nothing to be outwardly grateful about. Not to him.

If only he'd had as much luck with Aviama's attendants. Bhumi had been released to attend to chamber pots or some other such unfortunate responsibility, but Sai and Durga hovered by the door, pointlessly rearranging objects and pretending Aviama had any use for them at all as servants over brunch when the meeting room itself was already well staffed.

Aviama smoothed the fabric of his embroidered tunic and smiled at those already seated at the table—three noble-women, two men. And the queen. "You didn't have to threaten my family, but here we are."

The waiting brunch guests nodded back with polite smiles of their own, four with the forced diplomatic kind, and two with what might have been sincerity. Queen Satya patted the seat beside her, and Aviama almost choked on the strangling panic reaching for her throat as Shiva pulled out the chair for her.

Biscuits. Spectacular. Of all her prospective killers, the queen was top of the list. Not by her own hands, of course. Aviama's gaze drifted to Satya's dainty hands and long, bejew-eled fingers.

Aviama curtsied. "Your Majesty. So good to see you."

Satya waved her off and leaned in to greet her with a kiss as she took her seat. "Naturally, the pleasure is mine. My son is gaining a wife, and I am gaining a daughter. The Tanashai family will be stronger than ever."

Shiva took the chair on Aviama's other side without a word. Did he hate that patronizing, cooing voice of hers as much as Aviama did? He reached for his goblet. Aviama pursed her lips to suppress a smile. Oh, he hated it. At least as much.

Queen Satya fluttered her fingers in the direction of the rest of the table and proceeded to introduce the other brunch guests. Their names were about as forgettable as the historical dates in Frigibar's old texts, but Aviama did get the gist: one of the noble-women and one of the noblemen represented the rest of the court to ensure the interests of the kingdom were served in the production of the wedding. The second man was a high-ranking military official, ensuring all plans would offer reasonable security options. One of the women was in charge of style and aesthetic, with gardeners, tailors, and the like under her purview. And the last woman was what the queen called an *exotic capabilities advisor*.

Aviama arched her eyebrow at the woman, and she smiled again with a gentle dip of the head. Frigibar had said he was the last keeper of magic. Were there others he didn't know about, or was this *advisor* little more than a grasping at straws for expertise in a field that had been utterly useless for five hundred and ninety-seven of the last six hundred years?

White-gloved servers lined the wall. Four easels of sketches stood to one side—dress designs, seating arrangements, military honors, menagerie displays. And a pile of furs lay at one end.

The word *exotic* came to mind again. This wedding was a gloat to the world, a chance to boast of wealth, put on a show, and demonstrate to every nation in striking distance just how overflowing were Radha's coffers. *See our might. See our power. Observe our new melderblood pet.*

Shiva had insisted on Aviama's usefulness, and the queen had found a way to make it so. In her own way. One that relegated her to arm candy and diplomatic showings before being stuffed back into her corner out of the way. Perhaps whatever other ideas Shiva had for her were unnecessary now or had been overruled by his parents. Perhaps this was all Aviama would be expected to live for.

The pile of furs yelped and growled, and Aviama jumped. Shiva put his hand on her knee beneath the table in silent warning, but it was too late. Queen Satya was already grinning.

"Mrtyu has been so cooped up, you know. He loves to come with me wherever I go. I hope none of you mind that I brought him. He dreams of his favorite kills when he sleeps, but he will always obey my command."

A second glance revealed the pile of furs was, in fact, a pile of furs, but with the enormous breathing body of a ruby hyena sprawled on top. Sai had told Aviama it was so named because of the rust-red color of its fur around the head and neck, as though permanently stained from messy hunts. The beast snorted and rolled, and this time Aviama caught the slight stiffening of the nobles in contrast with the queen's slithering ease. They were nearly as uncomfortable with Mrtyu as Aviama was. And the queen enjoyed setting them on edge. Power and control. The hyena's presence had her drunk on it.

Platters of food came out, individual portions hand-delivered to each place setting at the table. Shiva flashed a piercing look at his mother. "This is beautiful, Mother. When did you change the brunch arrangements?"

Satya laughed. "Darling, leave the hosting to me. We are not barbarians. We do not reduce our esteemed guests to *self-serve*." She glanced around the table and shook her head with an amused *tsk tsk*. "Men! They mean well, but we know they don't know a thing about hosting with flair. That is why I have hand-chosen each and every one of *you* to be here. Men of standing to inform us in their expertise, and women to inform us of *their* expertise."

Aviama lifted her goblet to her lips, letting the dark liquid touch her mouth but not enter it, and swallowed. Pudding topped with glistening berries and a metallic silver drizzle winked up at her under the cascading light bouncing down from the chandelier. Her stomach twisted.

It was a stunning culinary display, and she was hungry. How long would it take for the poison to set in, if the queen was bold enough to have her targeted while sitting right beside her?

Shiva gave a jovial shrug. "Right as always, Mother. You can never quite trust a man to be genteel." To the horror of the guests, Shiva stuck his finger straight into Aviama's pudding and into his own mouth.

Aviama gasped. Satya froze. No one moved. And then he winked at the noblewoman gaping at him across the table and traded puddings with Aviama.

"But at least we do our best to make up for our mistakes when we make them, hmm?"

Aviama shook off her shock and leaned into him, breaking into a charmed giggle. "I can't very well complain. It was his sense of mischief that drew me to him."

The queen gave a thin smile, and Aviama dipped into her replaced pudding, as a strange, contorted mix of emotions battled in her chest. Aviama almost hated the sliver of warmth that warmed her heart at his gesture. Shiva was surely only protecting his own interests in the power play between himself and his mother. But he'd risked being poisoned himself to make the point to his mother.

Queen Satya could change the plan. But Shiva could adapt to every twist she threw. The queen was not an island to make decisions without restraint. And he would respond to her threats.

A truly dazzling array of pastries, lunch meats, and sweetbreads followed the pudding, breaking up debate over dresses, performances, decoration, guest list, timing, and all manner of spectacle. Shiva occasionally sampled or traded Aviama for her portion of something, claiming he preferred one food over another, or that he knew the item he'd been given was her favorite.

Discourse swirled around the table for a full three hours before breaking for the day, each expert charged with a litany of to-dos and don'ts. But Aviama only came away with one:

escape the palace after sunset. Get in the basket on the south terrace.

Movement at the door caught Aviama's eye as they all stood to leave. Ishaan, Queen Satya's favorite and most incorrigible bodyguard, appeared in the doorway. His lips barely moved, but they moved—though he wasn't looking at anyone in particular.

Aviama smiled and nodded at each of the guests as they made their exit, casting a glance in Ishaan's direction just in time to see Durga clutch at her stomach and shuffle to the door, disappearing down the corridor. Sai watched her go, but said nothing, and busied herself with refolding a stack of linens on a side table.

"I look forward to seeing you tomorrow evening, darling."

Aviama tore her gaze from the door toward the queen, expecting to see her addressing her son. But no. *Biscuits.* The woman had that intense glaring thing going that Shiva had obviously inherited from her and was directing those eye-daggers straight at Aviama.

"Excuse me?"

"You've made your public foray into the streets with my son. It's time you were formally presented to the court, and the...wonderful benefits of your union celebrated. Our kingdoms grow stronger together, wouldn't you say?"

Aviama's mouth went dry. She lifted her chin. "I believe Jannemar is as valiant a friend as they are perilous as an enemy. There are many wonderful benefits to appreciate. Speaking of unity and alliances, when will my family—your new in-laws, the king and queen of Jannemar—be officially informed of the engagement and invited to Radha?"

Satya's eyes narrowed just a hair, so slightly Aviama almost questioned whether it had happened at all. The queen patted her on the arm, and the corners of her lips twisted upward.

"Oh, not to worry. Messengers are already on their way to King Zephan."

Shiva slipped his arm around Aviama's shoulders and kissed Satya on the cheek. Aviama's parting smile to her came with a pinch in her gut that didn't let up until the woman snapped her fingers at her hyena and both disappeared down the hall.

Sai waited by the entrance with several other servants as Shiva and Aviama stood side by side in the center of the room. The silence stretched between them until Satya's footsteps and the hyena's nails clacking on the floors faded away.

Aviama shifted her weight. "Is the queen a better mother than she is a liar?"

Shiva sighed. "She has her moments."

Aviama turned to go, and Shiva pulled her back to his side. "You did well today. *We* did well today."

"I think we adequately fooled a few nobles and kept your mother on her toes. And—" Aviama grimaced. Gratitude wasn't what she wanted to feel for how he'd taken care of the food issue over brunch with the queen, but it would also be wrong not to acknowledge it. "The pudding." It wasn't a real sentence, and she stopped talking in an awkward way that shouted *uncomfortable* even more than her shifting eye contact did. But she let it lie anyway. He'd gotten the message.

Shiva tilted his head and peered down at her, searching her face. "I meant what I said. It's true your...freedoms have been curtailed. And you don't have to forgive me. I don't really expect that. But if you can accept your position here, and work with me, we might be able to be a team. If we can do that, life will be far more pleasant for both of us."

She stared at him. "A team?"

"Yes. A team." He tucked a strand of hair behind her ear, and she stiffened. "Try not to hate me when I make the announcement tomorrow night. You don't have to like it, but there are definite upsides. For one, it'll send Mother into a rage. And for two, it'll make life around here a bit more interesting for you."

"I'm supposed to accept my position without knowing what it entails?"

Shiva dipped his head. "Exactly. I expect enthusiastic consent tomorrow evening. Otherwise, I'll know you've made your choice. We'll still be getting married, and you'll still do what I ask, but your life with me in Radha will feel precisely as tyrannical as you push me to become."

7

Aviama gritted her teeth all the way back to her room. If Shiva became a tyrant whenever things didn't go his way, he was a tyrant to begin with. She couldn't *make* the man into an oppressor any more than she could make a canary into a horse.

How dare he put the blame on her for his own behavior? For the behavior he *knew* was wrong and used as a weapon for threats? Did he really expect her to believe this teamwork nonsense when he couldn't survive a single interaction without ramming his authority—and her hostage status—down her throat?

Daydream visions of showing him up and proving her independence cycled through her mind as she marched through halls splashed with ornate designs of every color. She would go to his dinner. She would let him make his announcement. And when he did, she would lay a hand on his arm, flash a beguiling smile that charmed everyone who saw it, and launch into a motivating speech about unity, freedom for melders, freedom for all, and an era of peace and prosperity. Shiva, the king, and the entire court would be enraptured, and pledge a true faith alliance with Jannemar, withdrawing any plans of invasion. The queen would be exposed for her blackmail and backhanded dealings. And Shiva would admit their engagement was a sham and beg her forgiveness in front of everyone.

Or maybe she would convince Shiva to let her walk through the menagerie just before the dinner. All the animals of the menagerie, every beast and bird, even the trolls, would somehow innately feel her goodwill and kind intention and offer her their allegiance. They would break through their cages, bear her up among them, and carry her off away from the palace.

Men would shout. The guards would give chase. But Princess Aviama of Jannemar would be long gone, blasting them back with a wall of air beyond anything her strength had yet supported. No one would dare come after her then. And her great escape and saving of the melders would be told for generations to come.

How exactly her escape would save the melders, she hadn't quite sorted out. But in the daydream, it definitely solved the problem.

Aviama marched down hall after hall. Sai had to break into a jog to catch up after rounding the first corner, but now she progressed through the halls with Sai several paces behind one elbow and the latest guard on rotation behind the other. Every step she took brought her closer to her prison of a room, where she would stay pent up until called for, like a dog. Or before Shiva demanded she show off her powers for the gloating rights of Radha, in a room full of nobles and dignitaries, like a juggler or dancer.

Like an exotic animal on display.

Aviama stopped in her tracks so suddenly that Sai bumped into her. Ahead, the door to her chambers loomed—

a place of baths, perfumes, and other trite distractions, but
certainly having nothing to do with matters of state. Shiva
wanted her to cooperate. He wanted her easy to control. Well,
she'd show him! She'd refuse to be his puppet!

Her face flushed with heat, and her hands clenched into
fists as she spun on her heel and swept back down the hall
from whence she'd come. *I'm not your Lilac, Shiva. And if
Jannemar is to fall, I will not stand by quietly and watch, as if I
were a willing party to my family's destruction.*

She reached the end of the hall and turned down a new
corridor. She'd always been horrific with directions, but she'd
become a bit more familiar with the palace in the last six
weeks. This one should lead to—

Aviama stopped again, and the shadowing footsteps of
Shiva's spy female servant and the latest guard stopped
precisely when she did. Her throat clenched. What good
would a confrontation do but get her tossed in the dungeon?
The dungeon wouldn't be good for appearances, but Shiva
would surely see to it she was cleaned up for public events.

Her stomach turned. A cage here, a cage there. But in the
cage here, above the ground, Darsh had a plan to get her out
that very night.

Don't be stupid. Play their game. Aviama pursed her lips and
took a deep breath. *And play your own game while you're at it.*

Aviama frowned, spinning the rings on her fingers. If she
were to play her own game, rather than only Shiva's or Darsh's,
she'd need allies. Far more allies than the zero she currently
counted.

With an internal groan, Aviama steeled herself, wheeled
back around, and walked back to her room. She stared at the
smooth bronze handle of the door. *Going in isn't defeat. You
won't marry him. You'll satisfy your appetite for freedom tonight,
after sunset.*

Aviama turned the handle and slipped inside. Sai followed and closed the door, and Aviama twirled back to face her. "I wanted to thank you for this morning."

Sai furrowed her brow. "Your Highness?"

"For asking questions. Human questions, not stiff stupid ones like you all have to ask me every day when we all know there are right and wrong answers dictated by this or that Tanashai at every turn."

The girl blinked, then her features softened, and a sliver of the professional veneer, the impassive servant, slipped away. For a moment, she could have been the girl who let a princess stow away in her laundry cart without alerting the queen some weeks ago.

"You're welcome. It was my honor."

"I like you. I want to trust you. But you can imagine I'm in rather a spot." Aviama crossed to the bed and belly-flopped onto it, kicking off her shoes in the process. "Ugh, something from the brunch did not agree with me." Better to start building her stomachache story early. Aviama rolled on her side and dropped her chin in her hand.

Sai was lovely. Small frame, with the dark hair and eyes typical of Radhan people, but wiry arms from years of labor and keen, bright eyes set in a round face. Sai's delicate brows knit together again, this time in concern for her health, but Aviama waved her off.

"I'm sure it's nothing. Like I said, I need someone to talk to, and you're a someone, and the someone I'd like to trust more than the rest. You trusted me with a question, and I will trust you with a question, and I sort of figure perhaps if we go on slowly trusting each other with little snippets, maybe we will get somewhere. What do you think?"

"I'm grateful you think highly of me, Your Highness. I am happy to hear anything you feel the desire to share."

Aviama pressed her lips together. It was a start. "You know more about me than most. You know I fled my room those weeks ago. You know I've had training as a melder, not just the haphazard guesses of how to control powers that most new melders have. And you know—well, I suppose you don't know for sure, but I think you know—that I don't like hurting people. Radhan or otherwise."

Sai said nothing, only attentively waiting for her to continue. Aviama sighed. "True, or not true?"

"Oh! True, Your Highness."

"I ran that day because of the queen. She wanted me dead even back then."

Sai said nothing, but it wasn't a shock. She already knew.

"Do you know what Ishaan told Durga at the end of the brunch today?"

Sai's lips parted. "No, Your Highness."

"But you knew they were working together."

The girl hesitated, then nodded. "Yes."

Aviama sat up. "What do you know?"

"Only that she doesn't like me alone with you. Whatever drew her away to allow us to speak as we are now must have been important."

Like Darsh paying someone an unexpected visit?

Aviama winced against an imaginary pain in her stomach and laid back down. "I'd love excuses to get away from Durga. Does she set your teeth on edge like she does mine? Find out what we can do that might keep her away. Is she allergic to horses or something so that we could go to the stables?"

The corner of Sai's mouth twitched. "Not that I know of, Your Highness, but I'll look into it. She does tend to have an effect on people."

"Yes, well, please do. And can I get my easel and charcoals

back? With all this wedding planning, I've decided I could use some sketching."

Sai curtsied. "Of course."

Aviama dismissed Sai, and she slipped out to gather the easel and charcoals and pretend she hadn't already been looking into everything having to do with Durga. How much did Sai really know? Did Shiva confide in her or only use her for basic information?

Aviama genuinely liked her. It was a shame she had to dupe her that evening to get away. She'd revel in escaping from Durga, but she hoped Sai wouldn't get in too much trouble. Maybe she could leave and come back fast enough not to cause a fuss. Darsh said there was a plan to get her out. Was there a plan to get her back in?

A sudden thrill ran down her spine. Maybe she wasn't coming back in. Maybe this was goodbye. Maybe, somehow, informant or not, Aviama could get Sai out of the palace too—and away from whoever had left that bruise on her arm.

The rest of the day passed like molasses, slow and miserable. Durga made no appearance at all that entire day, but the guard was posted outside, and Aviama had been holed up in her room. The easel and charcoals did arrive as Sai had promised, and Aviama drew up some basic sketches of dresses with a more modern Jannemari flair to them than the traditional Radhan garb the queen planned to truss her up in.

Granted, the garments were beautiful, but Aviama was not Radhan. And the purpose of the union, at least allegedly, was to bring two kingdoms together—not have the stronger one swallow the other. Jannemar would *not* be forgotten.

Though after tonight, there would be no need for wedding planning.

The thought brought a shiver of delight to her bones. By the time she was summoned for supper with Shiva, she was antsy, and by the time she left, she had nearly given herself the stomach upset she was about to pretend she had. Supper was uneventful, and Shiva seemed distracted, which served her purposes just fine.

Aviama didn't claim stomach pains around him, lest he suspect poisoning and double her guard or send a healer. But as quick as she'd tried to be, the sun was already setting when she arrived back in her chambers. Aviama called for tea, complaining of stomach upset and a headache, and hopped awkwardly from one foot to the other in the privacy of her rooms. She twisted the rings on her fingers and chewed her nail before ripping her fingers from her mouth again. The gesture reminded her of her capricious older sister. Avaya chewed her nails when she was anxious. And Aviama was *not* a desperate, power-grabbing woman like Avaya had been.

She was not Shiva.

But she *was* triple-blackmailed on all sides, first from the queen to stay away from Shiva (which she'd obviously not done), second from Shiva to play pretty dress-up as his pawn fiancée, and third from Darsh to accept whatever deal he planned to offer tonight.

The tea arrived, delivered by Bhumi, and a moment later she was alone again. The torch lighter came down the hall as the sun set on the horizon, spilling vivid oranges and reds through the latticework of her window. Aviama cast a long glance around the room, and her throat tightened.

Today might be the last day she would see it. She wouldn't miss it, though, not really. Aviama's heart pounded in her chest, and she took a deep breath to steady herself before crossing to the door and flinging it wide.

The guard was there, standing, staring. Her stomach dropped like a rock to her toes. Wind swirled in her palms, but she dismissed it with a wave of her hand as the guard slowly wavered and slumped back against the wall.

His eyes still stared, his knees still locked, but his eyes stared at nothing and his knees would carry him nowhere. Aviama's lips parted. Was he dead? Did Darsh kill a man to get her out?

Just then, the guard fell sideways from his slumped position and clattered to the marble floor. The crash of it rang down the corridor, and Aviama did the only thing that came to mind.

She ran.

8

H er soft shoes hit the marble floor with a soft pattering sound, only half drowned out by the rustling of her sage green gown as she flew down the hall. She skidded to a stop only half a second later, pulse still pounding against her temple. She'd left the door open next to the fallen guard.

Aviama's stomach dropped. *Idiot! Semra would never have made a mistake like that. Chenzira would never have made a mistake like that. You're going to get yourself killed, and you'll endanger everyone you work with while you're at it.* Not that she had anyone to work with. Yet.

There was nothing for it. She had to go back. Aviama retraced her steps and winced at the sight of the guard staring up at the ceiling, unmoving. He was only doing his job. What did he know of all of this?

Maybe a little. Maybe a lot. But the man was only a pawn. Aviama wondered if one day soon she too would be staring into the nothingness, another dead pawn among a laundry list of other victims. She wasn't even sure who would get the chance to kill her first, and it was likely that all the possibilities had plenty of experience killing people. Or ordering them killed, which was essentially the same thing.

Aviama softly closed the door to her chambers and whirled back down the hall. Torchlight filled the halls with moody reds and sallow yellows, spinning the bold colors to more somber tones as the deepening dark increased every shadow with every step. Semra's tutelage took root in her brain as she moved, warning her of ringing alarm bells for everyone she passed.

Slow is smooth, smooth is fast. If she didn't slow down, she'd draw attention and be dead as a doornail by morning. But if she didn't go fast enough, the guard outside her door would still be dead, but her chance to escape from the palace would be gone.

She settled for a brisk walk and turned another corner, mentally reviewing Darsh's orders for the night. *Order tea for a stomachache after sunset tomorrow.* Check. Though sunset was passed, and time was not exactly on her side. *The guard will be taken care of.* Check. Though "taken care of" seemed a rather gentle way of putting it.

Get in the basket on the south terrace.

Aviama dipped into a service stairwell and took the steps to the third floor. *We'll do the rest.* How exactly Darsh planned on doing whatever *the rest* entailed was weighing heavier and heavier on Aviama's mind by the second. But there was only one course of action left for her now.

She had to get to the south terrace.

Swish, swish, swish. Aviama grimaced. As it turned out, she also should have chosen a quieter dress. At least she'd chosen green instead of red or violet or some other glaring color.

Men's voices floated toward her from just beyond the landing. Aviama clutched at the growing pit in her stomach and pressed herself flat against the curve of the spiraled stone staircase, just out of sight.

"...doubled the guard on the north side for the second time in two weeks. It's not sustainable. But if His Majesty had wanted my opinion, he'd have asked for it, and I'm not holding my breath."

"Her Majesty knows the load has increased. She is grateful to you for your diligence. Your work will not go unnoticed. Double the north towers as commanded, but do not leave the south unmanned."

The pit in Aviama's gut twisted like a knife. The second voice wasn't a guard's as she'd expected. It was Durga's.

A low, throaty laugh from the guard answered her. "With what men, exactly? Does Her Majesty keep an extra legion hidden in her skirts?"

"Watch yourself. Your disrespect will cost you. Does Mrtyu look too thin? Should we feed him tonight? You have the men. But they are lazy. They are given too much time off. Alter the times of the guard changes, and offer shorter shifts in exchange for more frequent ones. Total time working will increase, but breaks will happen more regularly, and if your men are faithful and loyal, Her Majesty will reward you."

"And this is for the security of the kingdom, not the fact that Her Majesty lives in the southwest wing?"

The voices passed by the hall above her, and Aviama squeezed her eyes shut. All this slow walking, waiting, hiding —with the sun well past set, and the guard dead as a doornail outside her door—*biscuits*. She was getting a headache. And Queen Satya lived in the southwest wing? Wasn't that the hall behind her?

She had to *move*.

Her eyes snapped open, and she forced herself to wait two full minutes before easing out onto the landing and down the hall in the opposite direction from the voices. Two guards sharpened their weapons in the guard room to her right, but neither looked up. Coral designs wrapped around the walls and ceilings, and she knew one of the doors had to lead out to the south terrace. But who would be waiting for her if she opened the wrong one?

The small click sounded behind her, and Aviama glanced around. Nothing. Maybe it was the guards cleaning weapons or closing a door down the corridor. But her breath still quickened as she scooted around the corner and reached for the first door handle on her right.

It had to be a door on the right, facing the outside of the palace. She turned the handle, and the door swung inward, revealing lavish sitting rooms painted in emerald and accented with gold leaf. Aviama swallowed. The king's quarters were on the northern end. Were these the queen's rooms? Did they extend this far?

She shut the door, skipped the next one just to be safe, and opened the third. Why one room made a difference, she didn't know, but if the last room *was* the queen's, Aviama saw no harm in trying a door further down.

The handle turned. The door swung. A room lined with shelves of books, two tables, and carved wooden chairs greeted her, with a shocking lack of the bold colors so common to the House of the Blessing Sun. Four windows lined the wall, but no exit to a terrace.

Aviama stepped inside and gently clicked the door shut behind her. If she could see the terrace from one of the windows, maybe she could tell how to get to it. Her nose itched as the dust of the neglected room filled her nostrils. She wrinkled her nose. *Biscuits, not now.*

She held her breath and crossed the room, past the empty tables and rows of books, and stepped to the window. The moon was bright tonight, set in a clear sky and illuminating the palace walls. Directly beneath her, the walls fell straight down three stories to the ground. But to her right, a terrace welcomed the moonlight on its smooth stone floors and balustrade.

Aviama clenched a fist in silent victory and turned back to the door. She'd skipped the room she needed. But it was only one door over from the study she was in now.

She doubled her pace to get to the door. She was so close. Aviama ripped the study door open. And came face to face with Durga.

Her mouth went dry. Durga's eyes bored into her like daggers.

"Moonlight stroll?" A smirk took over the girl's sharp features, and Aviama's stomach soured.

Aviama shifted her weight. "I couldn't sleep."

"You're never asleep this early."

"You're never so argumentative."

"Your Highness, you are trespassing."

Aviama crossed her arms and arched an eyebrow. "On the contrary, I'm told this is my home now, and you were appointed to serve me. I'm sick of drawing and need some new reading material. I heard there was a library. So here I am."

She hoped the confidence in her tone would offset the nausea in her stomach. Durga didn't look convinced, but the smirk disappeared.

"Shall I escort you back to your room?"

"No. You're taller than me. If you want to be helpful, you can reach up to the shelf I need and get a book down for me."

"This library is not for you."

"Who is it for?"

Durga opened her mouth with fire in her eyes, but whatever snide remark she'd been planning she kept to herself.

After a pause, Durga started again. "It's time for bed, Your Highness."

She clearly wasn't getting anywhere. Aviama sucked in a breath and nodded. "Right, quite right. Okay."

Aviama stepped into the hall and pulled the study door closed behind her with a soft click. Down the hall, the two doors she'd passed before now stood on her left—the one with the sitting room at the far end, and the one she'd skipped in the middle. The one she needed.

She hesitated by the study door, eying the distance to the door, spinning the rings on her fingers. "Are you having a... pleasant evening?"

"You've never asked me that before."

Aviama gritted her teeth. "You've never been this openly annoying before. I suppose people change." *Biscuits, Durga, I've never hated you more than I do right now.*

Durga set her jaw and swept her hand toward the corridor. *You first, Your Highness.*

Ugh. Gross. As if the formality mattered now, after their hostile interaction.

Aviama's heart pounded in her chest, and she wiped sweaty palms on the skirts of her dress as she turned from the study door and slowly set out down the hall. Ten paces until the door. Five paces. And Durga was at her right elbow, just behind her, shadowing her every move.

She couldn't just go back. Not with the dead guard at the door. Not after *trespassing* in the queen's quarter. Not when this was her one chance to escape the palace.

Chenzira's words from the note rang through her mind like a haunted call: *sand and sea, if you don't show, there's nothing I can do for you.*

She bolted for the door.

Her left hand clutched at the handle just as Durga's nails

sank into her right wrist, yanking her back. Power pooled in her palm, and this time, she didn't hold it back, but delivered it straight into Durga's gut. The girl stumbled backward, releasing Aviama's wrist, and Aviama wrenched the door open and flew inside.

A long table sat to one side, swept clean and spotless, and a series of scalloped columns formed archways leading from the dining area to a sitting room opposite it. Straight ahead, double doors flanked with a long row of latticework windows on either side led out to the terrace. Aviama lunged for the far side of the room.

Her fingers closed over the cool brass of the handle. She lifted the latch, but it didn't budge. Her feet slipped backward toward the hall, and her hair blew back behind her—in an indoor space with no breeze.

Aviama's breath caught in her chest, long tendrils of fear working up through her belly to strangle her. Durga was a melder.

9

Not just any melder. Durga was a windcaller, just like her.

Aviama tripped on the wind wrapping her ankles and spun toward Durga. The girl's sickening smirk oozed with satisfaction. Aviama threw up her palm, socking Durga in the gut and knocking her hard on her rear.

One thought cut through the air thick with animosity in the room: *unlock the door.* Durga was back on her feet. Aviama sent a thin wisp of air into the lock, trying to feel for the tension within it, the shape of the metal as the wind wrapped itself around the obstacle. But just as its form started to come together in her mind, a blast of air pitched her sideways.

She hit the marble floor with a smack and skidded into the column of the first archway. A ringing in her ear mixed with explosive pain as her head made contact with the unyielding surface of the column. Aviama rotated toward Durga, hand raised, two great currents of air meeting in the middle in a swirling ball. Tapestries fluttered from their restraints on the walls, and a hollow whistle rattled against a window as

Durga's stream shook from its steady course and targeted the doors behind Aviama with a crack.

Durga's eyes widened, and she dropped her hand in surprise as a piece of the delicate door latticework broke off and skittered across the terrace on the other side. Aviama glanced from the door to the servant girl and scrambled to her feet.

"You've done it now."

Durga swallowed. She raised her hands again, and Aviama mirrored her movement. But Durga never called the wind. She worried her lip. "I can't let you go through that door."

Aviama's stomach twisted. *She's scared.* Yes, but that wasn't Aviama's problem. *Durga* was Aviama's problem. And if Durga was scared, Aviama might be winning, which was good.

So why did she still feel so sour inside?

Aviama shifted, her back to the door, and twisted a hand behind her to twirl another tendril of wind into the lock out of Durga's sight. "You won't be blamed. You tried your best."

Spittle flew in Aviama's direction as Durga spoke through a snarl. "You wouldn't survive my best."

Her eyes darkened, and her lip curled. Hate swirled in Durga's deep auburn eyes. And the confidence in her voice— there was no question that Durga believed those words.

The little snake of wind bumped up against the locking mechanism in the door. Aviama lifted the palm of her free hand ever so slightly, claiming Durga's attention with it, and tilted her head at the servant girl. "How do you know? Is that what happened to you at The Return?"

A cloud passed over her face, her features half-obscured by the shadow of the lattice in the starlight of the windows. Durga glanced down.

Don't look down. Look at me. Don't think about my hands, or where they are, or what they're doing...

Aviama cleared her throat and spoke again. "Does the queen know what you are?"

Durga scoffed, and a fresh current of wind flew across the floor, lifting the hems of their skirts and threatening a malicious, growing energy. She leveled Aviama with a spiteful glare. "Why do you think I'm assigned to you?"

The lock clicked free. Aviama took a step backward, and the hand behind her gripped the handle. Durga's gaze drifted down to Aviama's hands. Realization struck.

Durga threw up her hands and sent a cascade of air toward Aviama just as Aviama flung open the door. Durga's blow sent Aviama through the door and tumbling onto the terrace. She was strong. Really strong.

Aviama lifted both hands and slung them in Durga's direction, knocking her off her feet. She scanned the terrace. It was empty. Where was the basket? Who was supposed to pick it up? How could she get inside a basket, and be transported somewhere, with Durga sicced on her like a hound?

Her heart sank. She was too late. There was no basket. No help was coming. She battled with a melder servant of the queen on the terrace late at night, with a dead guard outside her room, and a looming wedding to a man who swore to show her the true meaning of tyranny if she stepped a toe out of line.

Durga gathered her feet and threw another blast, but Aviama called to the wind, and it enveloped her in a swirling vortex. Aviama strained in the effort to keep her shield in place as Durga shot blow after blow, moving out further onto the terrace. The vortex held.

But she couldn't see through the swirl of wind distorting her vision and her own long hair whipping about her face. Aviama dropped the vortex, her shoulders slumping forward as she released the energy keeping it alive. Durga shot another gust at Aviama, but she threw up an answering gust, absorbing its power.

Sand and sea, if you don't show...

Aviama ran toward the rail on the far side of the terrace. A mighty blow hit her from behind and her speed doubled as she slipped along the slick floor. She hit the balustrade full-on in the gut, doubling over at the waist and only barely stopping herself from pitching over the side and falling three floors to the ward below.

The dim silhouette of the outer wall mocked her from the terrace railing, the city of Rajaad enveloped in the night beyond it. Something cold hit her cheek. *Biscuits.* Of course. Of course, it had to *also* be raining.

Aviama clutched at the railing to steady herself as she stared down into the dark below. No starlight reached the ground below. Gently falling rain stained the wall a darker red than the salmon already coating the outside of the top floor of the palace, creating little rivulets of crimson dropping into blackness.

One of the drops fell on something beige in the corner of her vision. Not crimson. Beige. Aviama turned her head. A large basket sat suspended on a line running from the terrace to the outer wall, rigged to the cable with a wheel.

Her stomach churned, and her breath ticked up a notch. What kind of sick joke was this?

No one was here. No one but Durga. And nobody lurking around would dare stay with the queen's melderblood lackey dumping out her ire on the terrace. Her ticket out was the basket swinging lightly in the breeze beneath the balustrade, an extra tie binding it to the railing to keep it from rolling down the cable.

Durga's footsteps sent warning bells through Aviama's brain as she approached. Aviama's heart leaped into her throat and she whirled, throwing a vicious blast at Durga. Durga let out a cry as the blow sent her into a gathering puddle, slipping and sliding her way to the other side of the terrace and toppling over the rail.

Aviama squealed and reached out instinctively in the direction of the disappearing girl, clutching at the air and yanking her arm back as if by mere desire she could bring Durga back from over the ledge. But that was precisely what happened, as the wind bent to her will and blew an answering gale from the other side, knocking Durga back to the terrace with a whiplash effect. The girl collapsed on the terrace floor, and Aviama sent another sweeping current of air to slide her back across the terrace and through the open door into the queen's sitting rooms.

With a few flicks of her trembling fingers, Aviama shut the door between them with a final gust and shot long tendrils of air into the lock to turn the mechanism again, sealing Durga inside. The rain kicked up into a downpour, leaving Aviama trembling, chest heaving from exertion, on the flat of the terrace. She wiped her face with her hands and ran to the railing.

A faint pounding interrupted the sound of rain pelting the stone. Durga hadn't mastered the finesse required for the lock, but hadn't given up on getting to her through the door. How long before she called in reinforcements?

Aviama glanced over the balustrade at the basket swinging on its tether. Her stomach flopped. *This is the worst idea you've ever had.* She gritted her teeth, hiked up her skirts, and swung herself over the railing before she could think too long about it.

One foot found purchase on the outside of the railing, and the second swung helplessly in the air, slipping against the stone, before settling into a spot three inches above the lid of the basket. The basket that was totally safe and probably wouldn't kill her, despite its significant swaying and the light creak she could hear from its fibers even now. *Biscuits*.

The thing had a lid on it. *Why did the thing have a lid on it?* Aviama reached out one foot and nudged the top of the basket. The basket rocked twice as fast, but nothing happened. Aviama groaned, clutching at the railing. She kicked at the lid again, hoping to open it just enough to slide it over, but it didn't budge. Her arms started to ache.

Aviama steadied herself on the rail with one hand and lifted the other to send wind at the lid, but it was wedged down on the basket. The basket swung wildly, but the lid stayed on. Aviama bit her lip. The pounding at the door stopped. Durga must be going for guards.

She swung her foot out off the ledge at the basket. The toes of her shoe caught the lip of the lid, and she kicked it. The lid slipped off the basket, and Aviama winced as it fell without a sound to the ground three floors below. She tried not to imagine it hitting a night guard archer on the head, but the images came anyway.

Now or never. Aviama swung her foot out again, caught the side of the basket and angled it toward her, and dropped into it. Her breath caught as her weight transferred from the balustrade to the basket, its woven sides creaking under its load, the rain still dumping down on her face from the sky.

The instant she settled into the basket, the tie to the railing broke free, and the wheel over the basket started rolling along the cable. Aviama let out a squeal, gripping the sides of the basket, grateful for the sound of torrential rain to drown her out. The wheel rolled along the cable. The rain drove against her face. And the basket picked up speed.

Aviama's eyes widened, and her breath caught in her throat as she rocketed toward the outer wall. She was almost halfway across now. And then she passed the halfway point, and her speed dropped off, and she lost momentum—and started rolling backward, until finally coming to a lurching stop, swaying in the pouring rain three stories from the ground, in a basket soaked through.

She was stuck. She peeked up out of the basket and back toward the terrace. It was still empty, but surely not for long. Even now the queen could be roused from bed and marching to see her prey for herself, suspended in midair and delectably vulnerable. Aviama swallowed. A glance at the outer wall told her she had another twenty to thirty meters to go. And though she couldn't see the end of the cable, it was apparent now that it didn't run to the top of the wall.

Aviama followed the cable connected to the basket, running her hands up to the wheel and over to the cable on the side toward the outer wall, and tugged. The basket swayed but didn't move. She repositioned onto her knees in the basket, holding her breath as it swung precariously from its single connection point on the cable and reached up again. This time, the basket shifted toward the wall.

Inch by inch, the basket made its way toward the outer wall, as she pulled herself hand over hand toward whatever dead end awaited her there. She cast one last look behind her, just in time to see the door on the terrace burst open and Durga emerging once more. Aviama yanked on the cable, but inching along was too slow. Repositioning once more, she released the cable, lifted her palms, and called to the wind.

The rain splatted against the basket and hit her back like a wall as the gale she summoned pulled the downpour with it. Freezing cold water ran down her spine. But the basket was on the move. The wind pushed her along the cable toward the outer wall.

Aviama looked back again, but Durga's hands weren't up

towards her to call the wind as she'd expected. They were hovering by the end of the cable fixed to the terrace balustrade. And the blade of a knife flashed in her hands.

Panic seized Aviama by the throat, and she threw herself into the effort, leaning into the power she drew around her and funneling it with every ounce of energy she had toward the outer wall. She hadn't a clue what she'd do when she reached the wall, but she no longer cared. She had to get there.

The cable shook, and her wind pushed her along the cable closer and closer to her goal. Ten meters. Five. The cable wavered, and the wheel squeaked. Durga had set into the cable on the terrace end.

Three meters. Aviama threw a final gale into the basket she inhabited, and at the last moment, noticed the hole in the wall awaiting her arrival. Durga cut through the cable, and the basket fell just as it teetered on the brink of the hole in the outer wall. Aviama dropped with the basket, landed inside a dark room with a thud, and spilled out of her confinement.

She sprang to her feet, breathing hard, and took stock of the room. A cot in one corner, made up neatly with blankets. A table and chairs, with a water pitcher and stack of dirty dishes and cloth napkins left out from an evening meal. Basic supplies lined shelves along one wall, and a coat of armor hung on the other. She'd swung in through the window of some guard's break room or dwelling in the wall.

Aviama abandoned the basket and padded through the doorway to another room with four more cots. In the dark, she couldn't tell if anyone was in them. It didn't look like it. But what really caught her attention was the window on the opposite end and the rope fixed to a hook in the wall and coiled on the floor.

Her aching muscles screamed at her, begging for reprieve.

But she had one last task. Aviama seized the rope and tossed the end out the window. She gripped the rope, but it was rough, and she had three stories to go. Aviama ran to the other room, wrapped a cloth napkin from the table around each hand, and disappeared out the window.

10

Aviama skidded, slipped, and snagged her way down the rope and dropped to the ground outside the palace. She hesitated, blinking in the rain, and wiped the water from her face before a fresh layer replaced it an instant later. The city of Rajaad spread out before her in the night.

A dark fog clung to the palace. An invisible force pushing her down until she felt she might be crushed or strangled. But here, outside the walls, even as her heart lodged in her throat, she felt alive.

Not safe. But free. For however short a time.

Victory settled in her chest, a sense of liberation she hadn't felt for ages. The street was empty. For the first time, it seemed like the House of the Blessing Sun and its pile of problems might become a nightmare of the past, rather than a plague of her present.

But the street *was* empty. And Chenzira wasn't there.

What was supposed to be waiting for her, if she'd gotten to the terrace alone and unhindered, closer to sunset than the fullness of night? Aviama shifted her weight. Had Darsh given up waiting for her? Had Chenzira?

She swallowed and glanced this way and that, but nothing moved. Not yet. But Durga had tried to cut her down, and one way or another, whether an alarm sounded or they searched in silence, men would be on her heels any minute.

With a deep breath in, she took off down the street. Large buildings and gated estates cropped up at the fringes of the palace grounds on the south side. Her skirts made the distinct swish of *money* that she'd never noticed was quite so loud until only three blocks down, where the wealthy district gave way to slums. But the rain weighed them down with every step, and the swish deadened to a sort of sluggish sound instead until she finally pulled up short, breathing hard.

Aviama scanned the boxes on boxes of living quarters, patched together with mud, sticks, and straw, accented by the occasional sheet or tapestry, and bordered by two-story buildings in the distance. Before her, slums with people who might not take kindly to the rich. Or might not mind getting their hands on anything of value she possessed. Behind her, the rich—and, probably, sympathizers of the crown that had made them rich.

A chasm spread between the two sections, tall and ornate, archways and gates, versus short, packed in, and run down. Spacious stone walkways turned into narrow alleys, cobbled roads into dusty streets. Aviama bit her lip. She didn't know a soul in Rajaad. And with her blonde hair, she'd stick out like a sore thumb. Radhans didn't have blonde hair.

Biscuits. How had she managed such a massive oversight? A mantle would have hidden the finery of her clothes, at least a little, and a hood would have concealed her hair.

"My lady?"

Aviama spun.

Smack!

A dark blur rocketed across her vision ten paces away, knocking the silhouette of a man from his place at the gate of the last house in the wealthy district and flat on his back. A guttural roar ripped from the tangle on the ground as the blur slowed long enough for Aviama to register the form of a second man, the assailant pummeling the other in the face, and the victim reaching for the sword on his belt.

Aviama squealed, clapped a hand over her mouth, and darted across the class chasm and into the slums. The wealthy side was losing desirability fast. The House of the Blessing Sun—the supposed-most-glorious palace under the eye of the heavens—and attacks on the street were commonplace just three blocks away? What divisions caused well-to-do men to wander about and jump each other in the dark of night in Rajaad?

A form moved in the abyss of a doorway just three paces over as she flew into the slum. She cringed away from the opening and threw herself forward past two more houses and around the bend. Her foot connected with something on the ground, and she tripped, her hand plunging into the rain-packed dirt next to a broken bottle and single sandal that had seen a few too many summers.

A lull in the downpour revealed the sound of pounding feet thudding in the dirt an alley down from where she lay. They were getting closer. Aviama yanked herself up with a grunt, gasping for air, the night breeze wafting through her fingers asking her to play. Power ran along her skin like a current, but she dismissed it. She couldn't risk attracting even more attention, and would be better off convincing her legs to carry her further and further toward—toward what, exactly?

Aviama brushed herself off. Semra wouldn't run just to run. She wouldn't waste her energy without even knowing someone was chasing her, with nowhere to go, no direction. She'd have a plan. Aviama needed one of those.

She took a steadying breath, then eased her way down the dirt path and ducked down another alleyway between yet another row of residences. Could she find Murin, maybe stow away on a ship bound for Jannemar? Was Radha even sending ships to Jannemar anymore? Whatever happened to the Jannemari ship and crew she'd arrived on?

The running footsteps had stopped. Her chest tightened. How long ago had they stopped? Aviama pressed herself against the wall of the closest house and twisted to slowly peer around the corner down the pathway she'd just abandoned.

Something wrapped around her waist and yanked her backward, a hand clapping over her mouth just as she started to scream. Aviama writhed in the iron grip and moved to stomp on the foot of whoever was holding her, but her captor lifted her clean off her feet and dragged her into the dark doorway of the nearest box of a house. Height and strong arms twice the size of her own told her it was a man, and as she lifted her foot to stomp again, he whirled her against the wall of the inside of the house, hand still clamped over her mouth.

The torrential downpour had lessened to a pattering on the dirt outside, and the mist of rain drifted through the open doorway, pressing in around them. They stood in the deep dark—no lanterns, and the bulk of the moonlight blotted out by clouds. Neither of them moved, frozen in time, waiting. Aviama wasn't sure for what, but she waited nonetheless. Once she thought she heard something outside, another runner, perhaps, but she wasn't sure.

Her ribs ached under the crushing weight of the man pinning her against the inside of the house. Aviama tried to suck in air, but her mouth was still smothered by a hand that smelled like dirt and iron, and her lungs still burned from exertion and pressure as a human sandwich between a wall and a solid body.

The man seemed to notice her struggle, and slowly the hand dropped away. "Nice to see betrothal hasn't changed you. You still scream."

Aviama's mouth dropped open. She knew that voice. Chenzira Bomani. Her relief nearly overpowered the sour taste that came with a reminder of her engagement.

"You still..." Aviama floundered for a retort, but couldn't find one. "Attack people..." She winced.

A beat of silence passed before he spoke again. "I thought you weren't coming."

"I didn't think you'd wait."

"I almost didn't."

Aviama spun the rings on her fingers. He was here. He'd waited. She was safe. The tension in her muscles eased, and she sagged against the wall. A lump lodged in her throat, and she swallowed. "I tried to get out. I did everything he told me. But do you know where the south terrace is? Do you know? Darsh sent me—"

"Shhh. Don't say his name. Not here."

"Fine. *He* sent me to the *queen's rooms*. And Durga, her little spy assigned to trail me everywhere, is a windcaller."

Chenzira straightened in the dark. "Can't be. The queen hates melderbloods."

Aviama clenched her jaw and drilled him with a glare that was too dark for him to appreciate. "My mistake. I must have been dreaming when she broke the lattice with her invisible sword and tossed me across the terrace without touching me. I'm sure I'll have imaginary bruises in the morning too."

Chenzira swore. "How'd you get away?"

"She's a windcaller, and she's strong. But she seems only

able to create large-scale chaos. No finesse. I got her back inside and locked the door between us from the outside, and she couldn't unlock it."

He felt for her arm in the dark, ran his hand down it to her wrist, and gripped it, his fingers overlapping as they closed over her slender wrist. She'd never felt more like a fragile twig in all her life. Chenzira tugged her back out into the rain and into a maze of dirt and mud between row after row and house after house of the slums.

"I forgot you can unlock doors. That's impressive."

Aviama shrugged. "It's nothing. Just about applying pressure in the right place at the right time. Sort of like placing a current, and keeping it flowing, and then shooting a missile of air through it to punch it at the right angle. That probably doesn't make sense."

A shiver rippled down her body as the cold water dripped back into her damp hair and down her spine. Chenzira glanced in her direction, doubled his pace, and settled into a brisk walk when he noticed her jogging to keep up.

"What are you wearing? You didn't consider a mantle?"

"I did consider a mantle. I just didn't wear one."

"Not your smartest move."

"Yes, well, I didn't consider it until *after* I'd left my room, with a dead guard outside it. Did you know he was going to kill someone?"

Chenzira pursed his lips. "He does that a lot. Don't worry about it."

"Don't *worry* about it?" Indignation rose up in Aviama, and she drew back, searching his face in the dark, but she couldn't make out an expression. A man was dead. A man just doing his job.

Chenzira shook his head, his tone sharp when he spoke again. "Are you aware that you are the most important thing in that palace, the leverage for alliances and wars? That you were paraded through the public streets for all to see just days ago, and that you're quite possibly the only blonde woman in Radha? Did it ever occur to you that you could use a little more discretion?"

Aviama stared at him, dumbfounded. "Chenzira..." Her stomach flopped and then soured. She twisted a ring on her finger. Was he protecting *her*, or an asset?

"Did anyone see you?"

She nodded. "Durga, obviously. But there was no one waiting for me to help with the basket. I had to get myself across." Aviama grimaced and steeled herself to admit her mistake. "The, um...the lid fell. Off the basket. Down onto whatever is below it. And—"

"There's *more*?"

Aviama flinched. "Yes, well, if I had had someone to meet me, maybe none of this would have happened! Durga came back out with a knife to cut the cable down. I got through the window in the wall just before she got through it."

Chenzira pulled her around another corner and down three steps before ducking under a series of sheets spread like an awning between two houses. "What else?"

Aviama resented his assumption that there was more, but he was also right, so she plunged ahead. "In the rich part of town, closer to the palace. A man addressed me as my lady, but he didn't see my face. Someone...tackled him..."

"Yes, you're welcome. Because you were *going* to show the fool your face if I hadn't taken care of it. Anyone else?"

"Um, no. That's all."

Chenzira snorted. "Sand and sea. *That's all.*"

"Listen, I'm sorry, but if you wanted somebody like Semra, you got the wrong girl."

"Who?"

"Semra. My—" Aviama cut herself off and sighed. "Never mind."

"Oh, your assassin sister-in-law."

"Ex-assassin."

"Yes, yes, ex-assassin, current dragonlord. Got it. Now stop talking, stand straight, and be—well, watch yourself. We're here."

11

I   f she was supposed to *watch herself,* she would have very much liked to know how Chenzira was recommending she do it. Stop talking, stand straight, and be—attentive? Bold? Quiet?

Chenzira led her through the opening of one of the huts, through the dark of what seemed to be an empty room, behind a tapestry hanging on the wall, and into a connected room where lanternlight illuminated Aviama's surroundings once again. An elderly woman holding the lantern met them at the door. She smiled at Chenzira, a big, toothy grin that exposed a gap in her bottom teeth. A threadbare wool tunic draped across her bony shoulders, and Aviama noticed for the first time that Chenzira was wearing equally common Radhan garb that had clearly been through a few years of wear. Chenzira hugged her, and Aviama thought a little extra color filled her cheeks. Maybe a trick of the light.

Aviama offered a weak smile as another shiver rocked her body, but the woman only answered with a narrowing squint as if Aviama had just stolen her last ounce of flour and was fixing to snatch the sugar next. Aviama arched an eyebrow, and Chenzira shot her a sideways look. She fixed her face. And the older woman did too as soon as she turned her gaze from Aviama back to Chenzira.

"Welcome, Ramta. They've already started. We worried you would not be coming."

"I was delayed, but you know I would never miss an opportunity to see you."

The woman beamed again, then shuffled off toward a small table with a tray of clay cups and returned with the tray. Chenzira handed her a cup, and its contents smelled of a delicious blend of spices. Whatever it was, it was steaming hot, and Aviama wrapped her hands around it gratefully. The rest of the room held two large clay vases, a woven basket, and a young boy asleep on one of two beds made up on the floor in the corner, a motheaten blanket draped over him.

Aviama leaned in to whisper to Chenzira as he steered her toward the second bed, which was little more than a pile of blankets. "Ramta?"

"Yes. Darsh is the only one who knows the other name, and I'd appreciate you not sharing it."

The famous missing prince of Keket slinking around the slums of Radha certainly would raise eyebrows. Aviama nodded. "Ramta it is."

Chenzira downed the tea and returned it to the tray. Returning to the unoccupied bed, he pushed the side of the blankets, and they swiveled sideways on a board she hadn't noticed before, exposing a steep, rickety, wooden staircase. Aviama swallowed and stepped forward. Chenzira tapped her on the arm and gave a slight shake of his head, then stepped down the stairs first and lifted a hand up toward her. She took it, and he guided her into the dark room below. She stumbled once, and he caught her elbow and held her up. And then they reached the bottom.

The room was moderate in size compared to the energy it housed, perhaps six or seven meters square, with fifteen people engaged in heated debate and a man collapsed on the dirt floor with cuts and bruises across his face and arms. A muddy, scuffed set of armor had been tossed to one side, its pakshi bird emblem barely visible in the light of two torches set on the walls.

Aviama sucked in a breath. A palace guard. Chenzira stepped in front of Aviama, shielding her from view, and tapped a young woman at the edge of the argument on the shoulder. She spun toward him, eyes still blazing, then started as she registered who it was. Chenzira leaned in toward her and whispered something in her ear, and the woman's gaze flicked from Chenzira to Aviama. She looked Aviama up and down, and her expression sobered. Aviama shifted her weight and busied herself staring into the swirling tea in her cup.

The woman took off a hooded mantle she was wearing and handed it to Chenzira, who wrapped it around Aviama's shoulders and tugged the hood up over her still-damp hair. Aviama dipped her head in silent thanks and turned her attention back to the argument consuming the room before her.

"He was a dead man the moment he stepped foot into Waif's Garden." A broad-shouldered man with a thick beard slammed his knuckles into the palm of his opposite hand, eyeing the guard on the floor. "He's no defector. And he's seen too much."

A short, spindly man jabbed a long finger toward the guard. "He arrested three of us just last week! Roftim is dead because of him. Let his blood be on his own head. A life for a life!"

Voices rose in the dark, dirt-walled room, arms waving, fingers pointing, eyes glaring. Aviama could only pick out a few of the things they were saying.

"We could use him. He has a family he cares about, and we need someone else inside the palace."

"We have people in the palace."

"Well, we definitely can't let him live now, loudmouth."

A firm voice cut through the tangle of voices, and at the sound of it, the room hushed. "No need to fuss. We'll put it to a vote, as we always do, and move on to more important matters."

Aviama's throat tightened. She knew that voice. And as the man stepped forward, the dim light of the torch confirmed it as the flickering orange and red fell upon his grave face: Darsh.

The guard on the ground stuck out a hand to stabilize himself and moved to sit, but the broad-shouldered man socked him in the jaw, and he fell back to the earthen floor. Darsh clucked his tongue, and the sound grated in Aviama's ears.

"Patience is a virtue, sir. Have no fear, we'll not dilly-dally in determining your fate. Sit tight, or we'll skip the vote and I'll let Arjun here do whatever seems best to him."

The guard glanced up at Arjun. The man grinned, bone-white teeth flashing. The guard winced and sank back to await his fate.

Aviama held her breath, knuckles white on the cup she was holding. She stood in the belly of the radicals. She knew where they met. She'd seen their faces. How did the Shadow take votes? If she refused whatever deal Darsh planned to make her, what would they do to *her*?

Darsh held up a hand, and someone handed him a small glass box. Darsh snatched one of the torches off the wall and knelt on the floor. A water pitcher was handed to him, and the soft sound of the water pouring into the glass somehow filled the room as every soul fixated on the ritual. He pulled a small bowl from his pocket, set it afloat on the surface of the water, and stepped back, removing the light as he did.

One of the men started stomping on the dirt floor, a rhythmic beat like a drum. One by one, the others joined him. One by one, each person moved forward and leaned down before the glass bowl. The guard moved once, but a gesture from Arjun stilled him.

Aviama leaned toward Chenzira. "What are they doing?"

"Voting," he whispered back. "The stamping drowns out any sound, so no one knows who votes what. Each person puts a pebble in—either into the water, to stay execution, or into the bowl, to kill. If the bowl floats at the end, he lives. If it sinks..."

Aviama's mouth went dry. Chenzira gave her arm a light squeeze before following the others, moving forward to the glass bowl and casting his vote. She craned her neck, squinting in the darkness, straining her ears, but she heard only the thud of stomping of feet and saw only the solemn expression on his face as he made his decision in secret.

She tapped her fingers on the edges of her cup, her stomach twisting more and more with each vote. What would she choose if she were asked?

They'd said he had a family. She'd find another way. But no one asked. She wasn't one of them. But Chenzira had voted. Did that mean he was truly a radical?

Aviama knew what she would choose. She couldn't be responsible for another death, not after Liben, the stable hand she'd killed when her power first awoke in her blood and overtook her. Being a melder carried more weight than mere ability. It was dangerous. Like how she'd almost killed Durga earlier that very night, by a wind just a hair too strong carrying her over the railing.

A heavy weight. Darsh's crew were all melders, weren't they? Did they not feel that same weight? Was it not time to protect life, rather than take it?

The thudding stopped, only to take up residence on a loop in her mind to battle the uncomfortable silence that followed. No one spoke. No one moved. Then Darsh stepped forward, planted his feet before the glass, and lifted the torch in the air. "The Shadow has spoken. Let there be no debate."

With that, Darsh thrust the torch down toward the glass container. Aviama gasped. The bowl was gone. The surface of the water glistened under the torchlight. And then she saw it —the bowl resting at the bottom, laden with pebbles too great a burden to bear.

Darsh gave a curt nod. "Death."

The guard threw up his hands to defend himself from Darsh, but the blow came from the side. Arjun swung a battleaxe and chopped clean through the neck and spinal column, severing head from body in one clean, heavy-handed stroke. Aviama let out a sound between a yelp and a screech, and clapped both hands over her own mouth, dropping the cup to the floor and spilling its contents.

Blood soaked the ground at the neck of the corpse as the guard's head rolled toward her feet and came to a stop. The eyes blinked up at her twice before glassing over. Bile flew up her throat, and it was all she could do to keep from retching on the decapitated head and adding insult to injury. Though he was rather beyond injury by now.

A second man stepped forward, and the fire from the torch seemed to multiply and leap, two balls of flame enveloping the two parts of the guard's remains. Chenzira appeared beside her then, looping his arm around her waist and tugging her back toward the wall just as the dirt floor opened up and swallowed the guard, along with Aviama's cup, a meter to one side.

12

Aviama stared at the floor where the guard had been. Her breath came in gasps, chest heaving. His family would never know. No one would, not for sure. Not without a body. And with firebloods and quakemakers working together, it was untraceable. Not to mention if anyone spoke of what they'd seen, surely they would meet the same fate.

No wonder they used an underground room made of dirt. A quakemaker only had control of the natural landscape, not buildings.

"*This* is the Hope of the Shadow?"

The condescending tone snapped Aviama's attention from the floor to the woman who had handed over her mantle. She drilled Aviama with a cool stare, eyes narrowing as she spoke Aviama's apparent new title. Aviama winced.

A man in the center of the gathering stuck a toothpick between his teeth. "The Hope of the Shadow squeals like a pig."

Chenzira released her, and she wavered on her feet before

stabilizing. Aviama scanned the group, beady eyes boring into her. How much power did this room contain?

Darsh held up a hand. "You haven't seen her in action. I have. Do you doubt me?"

The group shifted under his piercing gaze and became silent. Darsh sat on the floor, propped an elbow up on one knee, and stretched the other leg out in front of him. The rest followed suit, and Chenzira gestured for her to do the same. Aviama took her seat beside Chenzira on the dirt, tucking her skirts neatly to one side. Darsh nodded at Chenzira.

"Ramta. Tell us again what you witnessed in the arena."

Aviama's brows soared as she turned toward Chenzira.

He glanced at her, then pressed his lips together and ran his hand through his beard, angling away from her to focus on Darsh and his radicals. "I was in the arena. I had slunk in that morning, set up my alias, and saw everything from the audience."

Of course. That way, he could still have witnessed everything he really had seen, but as an observer of the contest rather than a participant, thereby protecting his identity. He continued. "She was—ah—well, the odds were stacked against her, to say the least. The foreign prince has some experience with battle, so I'm told, but the princess had none. No sane person would have placed bets on her by looking at her, if you know what I mean."

Grunts of assent rippled through the listeners, and Aviama pursed her lips. *Biscuits, how flattering.* The worst part was how obviously correct he was. Sitting beside him now made it all the more blatant—Chenzira with his strong, muscled arms and chest, relaxed posture, and confident demeanor. Next to Aviama, the spindly weakling princess who squealed when there was danger, started at passing beetles, and had primarily spent her days doing only those activities that could be accomplished with elegance while wearing skirts. The sort of thing that went on in ballrooms and feasting halls.

Chenzira ran his hand through his beard again, then dropped it. "She displayed courage with the monstrous serpent in the mud in the first obstacle, and though I was serving the nobles at the end of that portion of the contest, I heard that she waited until its mouth was open to attack and threw a knife straight into the back of its throat."

All eyes turned toward Aviama, and she grimaced. Memories of the hideous snake monster in the mud pit still sent shivers down her spine. Her aim hadn't been great, but a little windcalling nudge had done the trick.

"Against all odds, she survived the python, the cirabas, and the hyland trolls. And through all of them, she'd managed to keep her identity as a melderblood a secret." Here Chenzira leaned in, and everyone in the room instinctively leaned in toward him as he dropped his voice and lifted a finger to illustrate his point. "But the siren—the siren was when things got interesting."

Darsh smiled, as Chenzira had clearly reached his favorite part of the story. Aviama glanced up at Chenzira, but he didn't look at her as he told the story. He shifted under her gaze, aware of her presence, and she wondered how often he'd told this story in her absence. The story of Ramta, Darsh's radical pawn serving as a fake Radhan servant for the day, watching from above what Prince Chenzira had experienced himself.

"She captivated the siren. It did not strike. It did not threaten. They were silent, each one sizing up the other, as lines of guards armed with harpoons stood at the ready to stop the siren from killing everyone in attendance with her death lullaby. Do you know what happened next?"

One of the men eyed Aviama with interest. "They say she sang. That she sang with a siren, the first human ever to sing together with a death daughter of the sea."

Death daughter of the sea. Aviama had never heard sirens called that, though that's certainly how the mermaid had seemed to her when they'd first met. When Shiva snuck her into the menagerie to show her his father's private collection of exotic creatures, when the siren's lavender eyes had filled with hatred. When her strong arms and makeshift seaweed rope had snatched Aviama off her feet and up against the aquarium glass, leaving a mark around her neck to this day.

But the hatred had been directed at Shiva, not Aviama. She'd thought Aviama was in league with Shiva. Although, Aviama supposed she was even more connected with him now than she had been then. But now she knew the most dangerous beast that had been in the menagerie that day had been Shiva himself rather than anything in those cages.

The siren had seen that. She came to understand, as Aviama did, that they were both captives under King Dahnuk and Prince Shiva's thumbs. That they were both conduits of *tabeun* magic. And that Radha was an enemy to them both.

At long last, after they defeated the guards, she'd even told Aviama her name. An ache set deep in her chest at the thought of it. *I don't know how, but I will save you, Makana.*

Darsh laughed, a jarring sound bringing Aviama back to the dirt room around her. "They didn't just sing, my friend. The siren did not sing the lullaby of death, but of friendship. They were bound together that day in a wordless alliance. Princess Aviama is a friend to the siren. And sirens have great magic."

"They say it was the most beautiful sound ever to grace the House of the Blessing Sun."

"The House of the Blessing Sun!" Darsh shook his head. "Curse the House. The most hauntingly beautiful song to grace Radha! Would you not say so, Ramta?"

Aviama squirmed in her place, staring down at her hands and spinning her rings. Chenzira's fingers tapped against his arm, and he hesitated.

"Come now, Ramta. Does the princess make even a man like you so shy?"

Aviama jerked her head up to look at him. *He* was shy? Because of her?

He cleared his throat and licked his lips. "It was as our fearless leader says. Stunning. She is indeed friend to the daughter of the sea, in a manner never seen or heard of in well over a thousand years."

Her stomach flopped in a strange fluttering sensation, and she bit her lip. He turned his head as if to look at her, but she quickly dropped her attention back to her hands, tracing one finger along the dirt at her feet.

"Would you sing for us?"

Aviama looked up in surprise. It was Arjun who had asked, but every eye was on her. She shook her head. "Um, no, thank you."

"Go on," said another. "We don't bite."

She almost snorted. *We don't bite. We just murder people, set them on fire, and command the ground to eat them.* She swallowed. "I haven't sung since the arena."

Nor was she in the mood.

"Let's not pressure our guest." Darsh was less interested in a show and more interested in whatever agenda he had planned. An agenda Aviama was growing more and more nervous about with every passing minute. "What of her power, Ramta?"

"Strong. She pulled air from above the surface down into the water to breathe. I've never seen any windcaller do that. She took out a slew of guards, defended against a zegrath, and sent the Keket prince flying across the sand. She stood up to the Radhan prince, used the leverage at her disposal, and made him an offer. It might have been a stupid offer, but she saved herself and the foreign royal in one fell swoop. Shiva was desperate to marry her and took her deal."

Aviama sketched the smooth, graceful lines of a mermaid's tail in the dirt. This was a bad idea. She got out of the palace, yes, but she wasn't free. And the way they looked at her now—they looked hungry. Greedy. This wasn't the kind of attention she wanted.

"I can't say I would have done the same in her shoes." Chenzira paused. She looked up at him, and he turned and looked her dead in the eyes. "But I've never seen anything like it."

Heat flooded her cheeks, and her lips parted as she stared back at him. His eyes were softer than she'd ever seen them, and it made something inside her flip-flop upside-down. Was this the same man that had said three seconds ago that her offer to Shiva was stupid? The man who'd said she may have only made Shiva stronger?

Sand and sea, if you don't show...

The torch flickered in Darsh's grip as he surveyed the room. "Shiva was and is desperate to marry her because he knows she is the key to a new era. The world is changing, and changing fast. If he married one of the other trussed-up normals, he'd have done as Radha has always done. But even a kingdom as great as Radha cannot afford normalcy now. Not in the aftermath of The Return. And the Shadow has seen to it that the House of the Blessing Sun knows just how irrelevant it is about to become."

Darsh turned toward Aviama. Something about his casual demeanor, lounging there on the floor against the wall, set her teeth on edge. "You were late in coming here. Yet you managed to escape the palace without assistance with the basket. How did you do it?"

Aviama opened her mouth, then closed it. The question demanded an answer, but her gut told her not to spill all the details. "Forgive me. I was delayed. But I climbed into the basket and got myself across with a mixture of manually pulling myself along the cable and windcalling."

Darsh's gaze flicked to Chenzira, and Chenzira let out a breath. "It seems the queen has a strong windcaller of her own who saw Av—who saw the princess and fought against her on the terrace."

Murmurs flew around the room, and Darsh's eyes widened. Aviama glared at Chenzira. A muscle tensed in his jaw, but he refused to look at her.

Darsh held up a hand, silencing his audience, and cocked his head. "We will deal with this new information in good time. We are fortunate you have brought us such news, as our own eyes and ears in the palace to date have failed to uncover this." He shot a daggered look at someone in the gathering, though Aviama didn't see who. Darsh turned back to Aviama. "How did you defeat this *strong windcaller*?"

"I caught her in a gale of wind and sent her back through the door. I locked the door, and she couldn't open it."

"You...you..." Darsh trailed off, caught off guard for the first time. Aviama winced. Darsh grinned. "From the outside? You locked the door from the outside, using *wind*?"

"Um...yes."

He clapped his hands, and the harsh sound made her jump. Beside her, Chenzira smirked just a smidge, and she wished she could punch him.

"Our selection was wise, was it not, friends? Shadow, what makes a *shadow* silent?"

The answer came in an awed hush, a roll through the listeners. "Skill and finesse."

Darsh spread his hands. "And what do we need to gain these?"

The group responded again as one: "Training."

Darsh nodded as if he himself were a sage instructor of many years, approving the acquired lessons of his pupils. He draped his arm over his knee again, zeroing in on Aviama. "And here we come to the reason we've invited you here today, Your Highness."

"Don't call me that. Not here." The edge to her voice surprised her even as the words burst from her mouth. She wasn't even quite sure why she'd said it. It just seemed wrong, somehow. Her title had done her no favors—an unfortunate qualification to a marriage with a man she did not want.

A thoughtful smile crossed Darsh's face. "I like that. You are more than your title. And used to being relegated only to a woman filling a role, a faceless position of obligation. Am I right?"

Biscuits. He wasn't wrong. Aviama's eyes narrowed, but she gave a slow nod.

He held up a finger and wagged it in her direction. "No more. Because today, the position you hold is not one of *any* princess. It's a position only you can fill. It is the bringing together of royal blood, melderblood, and drive. You strike me as a woman of conviction. And now you are afforded the power and the support necessary to make that conviction come alive. *Influence,* Your Highness."

Oh no. Here it was. The offer. Aviama sucked in a breath.

Darsh leaned back, bearing all the confidence of a leader men might follow. He let the anticipation build, looking in the eyes of each person sitting there with him before returning his focus to Aviama's face. "You are the face of a new government in Radha. You are the face of melderblood freedom. You are the eyes and ears and influence we need to effect change. Princess Aviama. As a melder, you will be our instructor. As a royal, you will be our queen."

13

"Don't worry. We will help you. You won't be left to rule alone."

Aviama cringed at the cooing, slithering quality of Darsh's voice. He misunderstood the hesitation on her face. She'd seen behind the curtain long enough to read between the lines. She wouldn't rule at all. She'd be ushered to power and do what she was told, or die.

She blinked back at Darsh, dumbfounded. Was the Shadow really just another power grab, another bloodbath? A coup wrapped in the trappings of a cause? Shiva and King Dahnuk described him as a criminal. What if they were right?

"Do you know how tight of a prison the palace is? I just got free. I'm not going back. I'm not marrying him."

Darsh's features darkened. "You swore to marry him. I was under the impression you were a woman of principles."

Aviama bristled, pulling her shoulders back and sitting up straight for the first time. In the streets of the slum, in the rush of the rain, in the frenzy of escape, she'd been only a scared girl on the run for her life. But now, no matter how heavy the weight of her name, she would inhabit every ounce of its meager authority or crumble.

"Perhaps you find me too simple, Darsh. I am a woman of strategy, and in the arena, I achieved my goal and bought myself time. I saved the life of a man I thought worth saving— whether or not he seemed to agree."

Chenzira stiffened, but said nothing. Her last comment was a dig, maybe, but she didn't regret it. She'd saved Chenzira's life. Maybe he *did* owe her, like he'd said in his note. Maybe he should have given her some slack for the decisions she made in an impossible situation. Maybe he should be helping her escape tyranny, instead of thrusting her into the belly of tyranny of a new sort. She lifted her chin.

"You promised to offer me a deal. I'm not interested in being a puppet. I've been a puppet long enough. And I see nothing of value that I get in return for being the face—and therefore the target—of your revolution. For a man of your reputation, sir, your negotiations leave something to be desired."

Half the melders leaped to their feet, tension rolling off the other half in waves. Aviama sprang to her feet in kind, and Chenzira rose at her side. But was he *on* her side? Or only Darsh's?

The corner of Darsh's mouth twisted up, his posture still casual as he leaned back against the wall. "That spirit. That fire. *That* is the heart of a warrior, Princess. *That* is why you are the perfect leader for our people."

Our people.

Yes, she'd heard a promise of unity before. A promise of leading a people together, making changes, bringing a new age to Radha. She felt sick.

"I admire your passion for melders, Darsh." Aviama breathed in a long, steady breath, and let it out. "I believe in freedom for us. Shiva knows this, though I'm confident he doesn't care. The Tanashai family hates melders, though I learned tonight that doesn't make them above using us to even the playing field when they feel disadvantaged. And those melders are as much pawns in the grand scheme of the web of lies in the palace as any of us."

"Then we agree."

"No. I won't marry him. And I'm not going back to the palace. And I disagree with the flippant way you kill. The easy way you take life. I'm going home to warn my people of the poison that is King Dahnuk Tanashai—and Queen Satya Tanashai, and Prince Shiva Tanashai, and the twisted mangle of polluted morality that is this land."

Darsh set his jaw, the first sign of frustration he'd allowed himself thus far. He took a breath and leveled her with a cool stare. "What was your awakening like?"

"Awakening?"

"When you first realized your powers. Your windcalling. Come, we all have a story. For many of us, they are traumatic, terrifying stories that keep us up at night. What is yours?"

Aviama's chest tightened. Familiar visions of Liben overtook her. The winds howled, the sky grew dark, and the air gathered might with each revolution around her and the smithy. Debris flew into the current. Tools flew off the hooks on the wall. The hammer slung through the air at top speeds, driving into the servant's temple as he went about his duties.

He dropped like a stone. His kind eyes stared up at her, glossy, dead—just like the Radhan guard the dirt floor had swallowed only minutes ago. Not to mention the one outside her room in the palace.

Aviama spun the rings on her fingers before remembering her rings were just another sign of wealth that could have been left behind. She folded her arms, tucking her jeweled fingers tight against her body, and looked away from Darsh. And into the eyes of Chenzira.

Bitterness boiled in her heart. Heat swept through her body. Energy swept along her skin, pooling in her palms with the promise of power.

What had he done? If she only gave Shiva more power by entering into an engagement, what had Chenzira done that was so much better? From the pot to the fire. One tyrant for another.

This had been a mistake. She never should have come. She was on her own. Again. "We're done here."

She hardly choked out the words before whirling for the stairs. A lump rose in her throat, tears welling in her eyes, when a firm hand seized her by the wrist. Aviama spun back, eyes blazing, even as a sob hitched in her chest. Chenzira's fingers overlapped around her slender wrist, and she didn't bother pulling. Something in his face looked strained. Pained, even. She didn't know what it meant, the way he looked at her, but whatever it was seemed to carry more weight than she was prepared for.

A single tear betrayed her, slipping down her cheek as she glared back at him. Her lip curled and her brow knit together in pain as the pressure mounted in her chest. By the time she spoke, it was nearly a whisper. "How dare you?"

"Let her go. She's not a hostage."

Darsh's voice. Aviama was sure it was the first of many lies from his mouth. Chenzira released her, and she fled up the rickety wooden stairs. Her fingers searched the wooden plank sealing her in at the top, stumbled across a lever, and yanked it. The board swiveled open again, and she stormed out.

The older woman turned at her approach, and the boy on the makeshift bed on the floor turned over in his sleep. Aviama wiped tears from her eyes and offered her a stiff nod as she marched out the door and into the rain-soaked, muddy street.

Street was a generous term in the Waif's Garden slum. The rain had stopped, but little rivers of brown water made their way through the dirt under the stars. How much time had passed? How many people would Durga have told about her absence? Had they found the dead guard?

No matter. She wasn't going back. She only needed a way back to Jannemar.

Despite looking completely different from anyone in the country, having few street-smart abilities, having no idea where she was or how to get where she wanted to go, and being dressed like a princess while sludging through a muddy slum. Aviama threw her hands up and let out a groan. *Biscuits.*

The sound of heavy footsteps trudged behind her. Aviama gritted her teeth and whirled to face them, palms up, the wind whipping through her fingers and playing with the corners of her hair. Darsh, Chenzira, and Arjun filled the alley. Darsh held up his hands, and Aviama shot a slim burst of air square at his chest. A warning.

Darsh summoned a wind of his own, a reminder that she was not the only melder—and outnumbered. He dispersed it with a clap of his hands and dropped his arms. "You must be anxious to get home. One question. How exactly do you plan on getting there?"

Aviama eyed him, but said nothing.

Darsh shrugged. "I'm sure you know all about how trade has suffered. How King Dahnuk has sealed the borders, and the new measures in place to examine everyone going in or out. I'm sure you've thought about a believable disguise, alias, and route from here to Jannemar, complete with provisions, lodging, and transportation. These are dangerous times, Your

Highness. And you don't even have your handmaiden to accompany you."

Her throat tightened, and her jaw clenched. His easy demeanor, the sly quality in his voice... "What have you done with her?"

"Not a thing. She came to us with Arjun. It seems you have made a habit of sacrificing yourself for others—first for Murin to get out of the palace, and then for Chenzira. The question is, why do you draw the line now, when you could save thousands?"

Aviama's attention snapped to Arjun. Well-muscled, quick to follow orders—it made sense that he was the guard who defected to the Shadow. She glanced at his hands, and a crescent-shaped scar circled the meat of one hand. It was true. He'd been Murin's contact.

Looking at him now, he didn't look angry with her. He simply looked like a guard, awaiting orders. But Arjun's gaze was also laced with interest. The princess he'd heard so much about. Did he also place his hope in her? In this plan of Darsh's?

Chenzira took a step forward, but Darsh stopped him with a slight shake of his head. Bitterness broiled in her chest again at his obedience. He set his jaw, and she knew then that Chenzira wasn't so used to following orders as Arjun.

What did Chenzira think of Darsh depicting her as the sacrificial leader?

Maybe I owe you. Or maybe you shouldn't have thrown your life down the drain to delay the inevitable...

It might have been a stupid offer, but she saved herself and the foreign royal...

Chenzira swallowed, but his eyes never left her face. What was he thinking? What did he think of *her*? And why was she so relieved to be near him, when he would only frustrate and irritate her in the end?

If she ran, would she ever see him again?

Darsh cleared his throat. "I don't mean to interrupt whatever moment you two are having, but I'm going to cut to the chase. Murin came to us willingly. That said, she's not going back with you to Jannemar. I'm really doing her a favor—if I let her go, you'd both die. But if you want to see her again, you'll follow my directions. Next time we get you out of the palace, I'll make sure you see her."

The lump in her throat was back, tears stinging her eyes. It wasn't the strong exterior she was going for. Somehow, Aviama doubted Semra had been a snotty, sobbing mess during any of her important encounters with enemies. Her shoulders sagged, and she dropped her hands. She could never leave Murin. Not like this. And Darsh knew it.

Darsh's voice softened to a softer, more diplomatic timbre. "You are wiser than I gave you credit for. Forgive me if our welcome felt trite. We truly believe you are the key to our salvation. We can do it without you, but with you—with you, our success increases one hundredfold. Our support, the people's acceptance of a new government, the transition of power, perhaps even the relations with the Iolani people of the sea—nothing matches our potential with you at the helm."

"Me as the *face* of the helm, you mean."

Darsh waved a hand. "Your authority will be real. Every leader needs advisers. You will need a court. And we will provide it, along with every other necessity. We will get our hands dirty where yours can be privileged to remain clean. Think of us as an extension of you, doing in the night what you cannot do in the day, so that you go to sleep in worry but wake in safety, never once having set your hand to the plow yourself.

"Right now, we are the shadow caste. The despicable, the hated, the dirty. The invisibles, whom the Tanashai family have taught the kingdom to blame for all its problems. We are a caste of outcasts, Your Highness.

"But how can Radha ignore us with a melderblood in The House of the Blessing Sun? How can they look down on us when you sit on a throne, looking down on *them*? Even now, Rajaad is shaken. They are taken with you, Your Highness. Every home is split by the shifting sands of change as one embraces a new age, and another rejects it.

"There is plenty to do in the day, Your Highness, and the day is a realm from which our people have been shut out. Day and night, Princess. Be our link. Be our gateway, our union. Be our future. Think on it."

14

Aviama gave a short nod and turned away, trudging down the alley. The queen's guard would be sweeping Rajaad any moment now. They probably already were. She'd wasted enough time.

We are the shadow caste.

Just how much activity had the Shadow undertaken already? How many people did they have in the palace? Was there any line they would not cross to get what they wanted?

Darsh hadn't said her authority *would* be real if she chose to go along with his plan. He said it *will* be real, as if her participation was already decided.

Three sets of footsteps followed her. Aviama stopped and turned, and Darsh gave a sheepish grin. "A thousand pardons. I should have been clearer. When I said you should think about it, I didn't mean you would do so while wandering in circles through Rajaad. You're going back to the palace tonight whether you want to or not. I'd rather you be alive to consider our offer, rather than dead by dawn, which you absolutely will be if you stroll Waif's Garden alone."

Aviama stared at him. The man's expression left no question. He was serious. And with three melders against one, without even knowing what Arjun's power was, she hadn't a prayer. But Darsh didn't understand. Her face flushed hot, and she balled her hands into fists. Aviama stormed up to Darsh, refusing to look at Chenzira or Arjun, and lifted her chin to drill the radical leader with her darkest glower.

"You left a dead guard outside my door. Durga saw me, caught me, and fought with me. She's one of the queen's spiders, and she'll have crawled back to her mistress by now. The lid of the basket fell when I tried to get in it, and Durga cut the cable just as I got to the other side. The palace will be swarming. I'm surprised I haven't seen guards out already. If you want me alive, you're going to have to do better than sending me back."

"If you're going to try to put me in my place, Princess, you're going to have to have all the cards." Darsh straightened. He wasn't particularly tall, but he was broad, and Aviama had to steel herself to keep from shrinking back. "The guard isn't dead, and he should regain his faculties by morning. We've blackmailed him, and he's unlikely to be an issue. Your blunders are unfortunate, but we have people to clean up messes. How kind of you to give them extra practice tonight. And I think you overestimate Durga's loyalty, and underestimate the queen's desire to see you strung up by your toes. Durga failed her mistress. And she might be so terrified of the queen's ire that she keeps the whole matter to herself."

Aviama pursed her lips. "That's a lot of guesswork. You're going to hang the face of your revolution on guesswork?"

Darsh shrugged. "Guesswork is better than what you get if you stay on the streets or try to go home alone. If you go it alone, certainty over your fate fills in to one hundred percent. I'll be sure to send my condolences to your family."

"If you let me go, that is. Which you won't."

"Correct."

"And you expect me to thank you for it."

Darsh arched an eyebrow. "After tonight, I'm not sure if I can expect you to be reasonable, so no. *Expect* is not the word."

Aviama's lips parted. She needed a retort. A good one. Nothing came.

Darsh took hold of her arms as if she were a child and placed her in front of Chenzira. She stumbled into him, and Darsh nodded at the prince. "I have a feeling she won't run from you, so you'll accompany Arjun taking her back to the palace."

Back to the palace. Her mouth went dry.

Chenzira frowned. "I think you've overestimated our relationship. Again."

Darsh glanced between him and Aviama. "No, I don't think I have. Make sure she doesn't do anything stupid. And see if you can get her head on straight."

Darsh pulled Arjun in close, spoke to him for three wildly uncomfortable minutes as Aviama and Chenzira stood together to one side, and then Darsh disappeared back down the alley.

Aviama glanced up at Chenzira. "You aren't seriously going to take me back there, are you?"

Chenzira winced, but it was Arjun who spoke.

"We look forward to working with you and learning from you, Your Highness. We'll have you out again soon. I promise."

The young man was annoyingly earnest. He offered her what he clearly intended to be an encouraging smile and gestured ahead of him for her to walk first. Chenzira groaned and shook his head. "She's not a princess, and you're not a guard. Get it out of your head. Blend in."

He reached to grab Aviama's arm, then hesitated, and

slipped his hand in hers instead. Less a hostage, more a stroll. A tingle shot up her arm at his touch. She glanced up at him, and he dipped his head at her in an awkward nod before turning to Arjun. "We only have a few hours until daybreak. Let's go."

Arjun looked them over, nodded, and led the way through muddy street after muddy street. The dark of night covered them, obscuring most everything but the dim silhouettes of houses and buildings. Once, Aviama ran straight into a damp hanging shirt on a clothesline she hadn't seen. After that, Chenzira pulled her in a little tighter to his side and guided her through Waif's Garden with enough familiarity that it could have been his own home.

The slum dropped away eventually, giving rise to the wealthier areas as they got closer to the palace again, but they didn't approach the same way she'd come. They seemed to be circling northeast, toward the main gate.

They progressed in silence for over an hour before Arjun took the path from dirt to cobblestone and wound them through the business district, where shop after shop lined the street, all closed for the night. Arjun led them around the back of one of the stores, told them to wait for him, and knocked on the back door. A moment later, the door opened, and Arjun disappeared inside.

Aviama's heart hammered in her chest, and a bead of sweat rolled down her forehead into her tangled hair. Chenzira still held her hand, and it both comforted and angered her. Comforted, because Chenzira had protected and helped her in the arena. Angered, because he was delivering her back to her prison.

And angered *because* his touch comforted her.

Chenzira passed her to his other side, holding her other

hand as he positioned himself on the outside, and her against the wall, facing the alley. He took a breath, then paused. "I know you don't like Darsh, but he's right. About this, at least. If you left on your own now, you'd never survive. And if you went to Jannemar and told them of the danger in Radha, it could mean war. A war Jannemar would lose if they invaded, by the way. You said your coffers were decimated by the war with Belvidore, and they're only now recovering and putting out fires within their borders after The Return. They'll be lucky to fend off Radha on their own turf, much less here."

Aviama's jaw dropped. "Are you saying I should be thanking you? That I owe you?" His own words from his note mocked her here in the presence of the man himself. She ripped her hand free. "What gallantry! What protection! Feed me back to the man I sold myself to, for—for *you*. A prince who apparently did not appreciate the sacrifice. You would rather be dead, is that it? If it were up to you, I would have killed you, taken the deal to escape, and gone home."

Chenzira drew back as if he'd been slapped. He put a hand up to stop her, to quiet her, but she'd already noted her uptick in volume. She shook her head, lowered her voice, and plunged ahead. "I used to dream of adventure. I hated being shut up in my room like a prize goose every time something dangerous or exciting or meaningful happened. I guess I'm not cut out for it. I guess everyone back home stuffing me into a box had the right idea, now that everyone seems so set on tossing me out in the open to the dogs. But now...now, I would like very much to be home."

Aviama turned away and wiped a tear from her eye. Dumb tears. Stupid emotions. Chenzira stood in silence, and she spun one of the rings on her fingers forty times a minute. Her hands slipped in their haste, sliding against the smooth metal of the ring until she regained her hold. Weight settled in on her chest like chains, bearing down on her, rooting her to the cobblestone street.

Her fingers froze. She turned back to Chenzira. "What was your vote?"

"What are you talking about?"

"The vote. The pebble. The guard. Did you vote for his death?"

Chenzira leaned away from the shops to peer down the alley for the third time in sixty seconds. "If I tell you my vote, it ruins the integrity of the vote."

She pursed her lips. "That's a cheap cop-out and you know it. Tell me."

"No."

"Why not?"

"Because you're angry and unreasonable."

Aviama opened her mouth, then snapped it shut. *Angry? You want to see angry? Are you saying I don't have a* right *to be angry with everything that's happened to me just in the last twenty-four hours?* "Angry, yes. Unreasonable, no." She stood there, stewing, for a solid minute. The events of that night replayed in her mind, the decapitated guard's glassy eyes staring up at her, the reminder of Liben. Fire springing to the corpse, and the ground opening up...

Aviama gasped. "You buried him. You moved me out of the way and made the hole in the ground. It was you."

"No." His voice was firm, angry even. Loud enough that she jumped. "I moved you because they're not always precise with their work. Last time, Juni's leg was buried along with the dead guy, right up to the thigh. It took some time to get him free, and we were lucky nothing worse happened. They have no training. They don't have the control we do."

"If you have so much control, train them yourself."

"I can't."

"Why not?"

"I just can't."

Aviama stepped up close to him, peering into his face. Something in his voice checked her, some unspoken pain. But she had plenty of her own pain, and she hadn't been afforded the luxury of using it as a shield.

She jerked her chin up toward him and stabbed a long finger into his chest. "Where is Chenzira? I might not have gotten to know him very well, but I respected him. Did Ramta kill him? Is he dead? Is the pawn of a radical criminal all that is left? You're a *prince*. Act like it."

A muscle in his neck twitched, and fire sprang to his eyes as he looked down at her. His voice was a rasping whisper, so low she barely made out the words. "He's not dead."

Aviama stared back at him, and her throat closed up again. Her chin quivered, and she took in a shaky breath. An emptiness in her middle seemed to rip open into a great chasm, an unshakeable ache, an impenetrable loneliness. She swallowed, but her voice still shook. "Then why has he abandoned me?"

The door to the shop opened, and Arjun peered out. "It's time."

Aviama ignored him, searching Chenzira's face. *Give me something. Anything.* But though he met her gaze like a man wounded, she could not tell what it might mean. Pity? Regret? Self-loathing? None of them did her any good. She'd still be in Shiva's arms the next night for whatever announcement he had planned, with Darsh expecting her to play his game or die as his enemy.

She was still just an orphan girl, outnumbered and surrounded on every side, threatened, blackmailed, and crumbling—before the one person left whom she'd hoped might care.

Aviama turned for the door as the first hot tear trailed down her cheek. Chenzira's hand shot out and caught her wrist, spinning her back to him. He caught her with an arm wrapped around her waist, pulling her in close enough to whisper in her ear, his breath sending goosebumps down her neck. "I won't let you marry him."

15

Chenzira released her, and Aviama staggered backward. She backed toward the door, eyes still locked on Chenzira, until she nearly tripped on the step and finally turned to follow Arjun through the opening.

The sensation of his strong arm catching her about the waist. The tingling of his breath on her neck. The rasp of his voice in her ear. All of it lingered in her body as she followed Arjun into the back room of a shop. He had a lantern with him, gently swinging it as they passed a row of crates and a smattering of fallen feathers on the floor. Chenzira followed, and Aviama hoped he couldn't see the goosebumps still prickling the skin of her arms as she walked.

She folded her arms, rubbing them as if to ward off the chill of night, as they slipped into a second room filled with cages of pigeons. Floor to ceiling, all along one wall, the birds seemed to wake in a flurry of fluttering wings and warbles at their approach. The smell of dust, birds, and uncleaned cages hit her like a wall, and she wrinkled her nose. Sacks of grain stacked the second wall, but a set of folded clothes captured Aviama's attention on top of a crate to one side.

Aviama leaned in toward Arjun and whispered, "Did you talk to someone here?"

Arjun lifted a finger to his lips. "Say nothing from here on out. They don't want to see or hear you, and you won't see or hear them. You were never here." He handed her the clothes, and she confirmed they were what she suspected—the uniform of palace servant women. "Put these on and leave the clothes you're wearing in their place. I'll take care of them. We'll stand right outside, and when you're done, knock twice on the door. Then we'll get you into the wagon."

Arjun and Chenzira stepped out and shut the door, and Aviama peeled off her damp, muddy dress and borrowed mantle and slipped into the servants' garb laid out for her. She raked her fingers through hopelessly tangled tresses, folded the dirty clothes as best she could before setting them back on the crate, and knocked twice on the door as instructed.

The door opened, and she sucked in a breath as she came almost nose to nose with Chenzira. He was standing closer to the door than she'd expected.

I won't let you marry him.

What did it mean? Would he betray Darsh? Convince him to change course? Would he really stop the wedding—and *could* he stop it, even if he tried?

Arjun gestured for her to step aside, and he moved into the room to collect her sodden clothes. He returned a moment later and indicated she follow Chenzira back through the first room and out to the door. Chenzira opened the back door, exposing a wagon hitched to two black horses she hadn't heard rumble up to the building while they were inside. Chenzira walked down the couple of steps to the cobbles and lifted a hand back up to help her down.

She wasn't wearing heavy skirts or swishing gowns. He could hardly have expected her to need assistance down the few steps. And a commoner from Waif's Garden would never have offered his hand to a palace servant as they both went about their menial daily drudgeries, up and down the busy streets of Rajaad, with their unending list of errands.

But a lord would offer his hand to a lady.

A prince would show courtesy to a princess.

The question was, if he was showing deference to her as a princess...would she let him be a prince?

Her own words came back to haunt her. It had been *her* idea that he act like a prince, after all. She'd implied she didn't respect Ramta. He'd passed her an olive branch.

Part of her wanted to storm down the steps. Part of her wanted to leave him and his judgments and Shadow dealings in the dust in her wake as she let bitterness catch her up in its wave.

I won't let you marry him.

She took his hand.

Chenzira looked startled, but smiled, and she found herself smiling back.

Biscuits, she'd lost her mind. He'd betrayed her and was shipping her back to Shiva. But as she allowed him to help her down the steps and up to the wagon, she almost didn't want to let go.

Arjun shot Chenzira a look. Aviama wondered if it was a reminder to *blend in* as Chenzira had demanded of Arjun only an hour or two ago. Whatever its meaning, Chenzira didn't care, and he helped her up into the wagon with just as much effortless grace as before.

Arjun jumped up on the wagon and pulled back the boards. The wagon had a false bottom. He offered her a hand to get down into the narrow space, but she ignored it and hopped down into the hole herself. Arjun handed her a balled-up sack and indicated she could cushion her head with it, so she stuffed it into the hole under her head and laid down. He knelt on the boards beside her and spoke in a hurried whisper. "When you get there, wait until everyone is gone, then get in the laundry cart. Good luck, and we'll see you again soon." He turned to go, then leaned back down once more. "I'll tell Murin you're safe. She'll be glad to hear it."

Aviama opened her mouth to speak, but Arjun replaced the boards on top of her before she could say anything. The wagon creaked as he moved to the side of the wagon and jumped off the side, back to the street. The burlap sack scratched her face, and she shifted onto her back so its coarse surface dug into her hair instead. Her knees bent sideways, cramped against the edges of the small space. Receding footsteps told her Arjun and Chenzira had left her alone in the alley in the compartment of an unmanned wagon.

Two minutes later, several sets of footsteps approached, and the wood boards creaked under their weight as they loaded crates, sacks, and cages overhead. Birds cooed and warbled, and the musty scent of straw and pigeon poop and feathers itched at her nose again. Several more trips went on and off the wagon, and Aviama knew she should be staying alert, but now that she was in one place, unmoving, with the dark pressing in around her, fatigue tugged at the edges of her mind.

Her eyes drifted closed, and she pinched herself to stay awake. Someone sat on the seat and snapped the reins of the horses, and Aviama noticed for the first time how none of the men loading the wagon or the driver had spoken at all. No good mornings, no instructions to move this here, or load things this way or that. Then the horses pulled, the wagon moved, and against her every effort, the rumblings of the wheels and steady rhythm of the horses' hooves rocked her to sleep.

AVIAMA WOKE with a start as someone jumped on the wagon, their heavy boots landing three inches from her nose. She gasped, but the creaking of the wood and soft warble of the birds covered the sound. Pricks of early morning light peeked through the slats of the wagon, and the rustle and heave of sacks and crates and cages told her men were already unloading.

Had she slept through the gate? Were they inside the palace, or had the carrier pigeon delivery been accosted for search? Aviama held her breath and shut her eyes as dust and dirt shook through the cracks down onto her face.

The wheels of a cart rumbled nearby, coming to a stop maybe two meters from the wagon. The swish of horses' tails mixed with the grunt of men and talk of a few servants as they went about their morning duties.

"There's a new dovecote for these birds. Keep them separate from the others. Not like that—gently! Were you raised by wolves?"

"Old man, if you want it done differently, then do it yourself. I've got better things to do."

"You paid for delivery, and they're delivered. I'll be on my way."

"Are these birds where they belong? Is the feed where it belongs? I didn't think so. I'll show you up to the roof."

Someone dropped a sack on the ground, and the wagon rocked as the driver got down off the seat and grumbled off with whoever had been doing the unloading. A moment later, all was quiet. Aviama froze in the compartment beneath the wagon floorboards, pulse beating in her ears. Was she supposed to get out now? If she did, and there was someone waiting, she'd be captured. But if she didn't, and now was her chance, she'd miss her escape route and stay stuck in the wagon. Escape route was probably the wrong phrase. Could she really be escaping, if she was going back to the place she'd just escaped *from* mere hours before?

Her muscles ached, and a cramp was building in her calf. She didn't hear anyone, and she was dressed in servants' clothes. Better now than never. Aviama reached up and pushed the lid of the compartment up and over, squinting as hazy early morning light spilled down on her.

The wagon was staged in a courtyard next to three stacked crates and a bucket. Three servants were visible at the far end of the courtyard, busied with tasks of their own, but it seemed the palace was not yet fully awake. The sky retained some gray from the night, with streaks of pinks and purples drifting up in the east to announce the imminent coming of the sun. And next to the wagon, a laundry cart.

The laundry cart was becoming somewhat of a habit, but Aviama didn't dare complain. She pulled herself up out of the compartment in the wagon, replaced the lid in the floor, and slipped over the edge, across the grass, and dove headfirst into a massive pile of laundry. Aviama jerked to a stop in the base of the cart, a pair of pants falling in around her head, her feet still kicking uselessly in the air. Heart in her throat, she yanked her legs in after her.

Except one foot was stuck. Something near the surface of the clothes pile had caught her ankle, leaving a human foot sticking out of the top of the cart to wave at any passerby. Dread washed over her. Aviama clutched at her leg in the sea of cloth, tossing tunics and whatever else to the side in her haste. It didn't budge.

Biscuits. This is *not* the way she wanted to die! Although, on second thought, it was probably better to be executed by a guard than have her throat ripped out by the queen's hyena. Unless the guard brought her to the queen, and the queen sent her hyena after her anyway. Maybe the king would have her beheaded. Maybe Shiva would devise another round in the arena, but one she wouldn't survive...

Firm hands seized her ankle. She nearly screamed. And then the hands ripped something off her foot, threw weight against her body, and shoved her further into the cart. Aviama let out a stifled grunt and curled her legs tight to her body. The laundry moved on top of her, rearranged to hide any sign of her. And then they were moving.

The cart wheeled out of the courtyard, rocked back once as it hit an obstacle, and then shoved forward over a ledge with a bump. But the courtyard meant the ground floor, and Aviama's room was now on the third. No way was the cart going up a spiral staircase. Maybe there was a pulley system or dumbwaiter apparatus for large, heavy things. Or maybe the wrong person had picked her up, and they were driving her straight to the throne room for an unpleasant, uncouth dumping onto the floor before death by hyena.

Aurin's spear. She really couldn't get the hyena out of her head.

Rumble, rumble, rumble. Aviama braced herself inside the cart. Any moment now, someone would reach in and snatch her out, or the cart would stop and she would be abandoned, left alone again in a room full of snakes. Not literal snakes, but still. Honestly, she'd been left in a mud pit of literal snakes before, and she would probably prefer it to the Tanashai family right about now.

The cart stopped. Wheels creaked. Something itched on the back of Aviama's head, and she reached up and realized the burlap sack she'd used to cushion her head in the wagon had caught in her hair and was along for the ride.

Shifting feet. The sound of metal clinking against stone. *One, two.* Footsteps. A moment later, someone rapped twice on the outside of the laundry cart. *One, two.* More footsteps.

And then silence.

Here we go again.

Aviama took a deep breath, shoved the burlap sack to the bottom of the cart, and pushed her way up through the laundry. As she got to the top and took stock of her surroundings, she noticed the cart was full of servants' uniforms. Aviama blended in perfectly.

To say Darsh knew what he was doing was an understatement. The contrast between his forethought and her own haphazard hope for luck as she stumbled through the treacherous sands of the House of the Blessing Sun could not be overstated. Aviama grimaced at the thought, then pulled herself up through the rest of the laundry.

The hall was empty, but that was likely arranged. It wouldn't stay that way forever. And the cart had been left directly in front of a spiral staircase. Aviama kicked her leg up and over the cart's edge, landing on the marble floors with a rather unceremonious thump before taking the stairs two at a time.

She loved beautiful gowns. She loved them with her whole

heart. But Aviama had to admit, at times like these, the lighter garments of a long tunic and pants had their benefits.

The spiral staircase was empty, and she flew up two stories fast enough to leave her breathless at the top—and a little dizzy from the spinning. But the hall was familiar, as she'd been positioned at the closest staircase to her own chambers. Aviama flew down the hall and reached her door in record time.

Her *unattended* door. No guard, dead or alive. She turned the handle and stepped inside.

A gasp stole her breath as she shut the door behind her. Her room was immaculate, save for the tea tray by the bed and her sketches from the day before still sitting on the easel in the sitting area. But it was the steaming bath that captured her heart.

No servants. No witnesses. No friends, either, but her loneliness only weighed heavier in the presence of people she could not trust. After the peril of the last twelve hours, the bath was a balm to the soul.

Aviama stripped free of the servants' clothes and stuffed them in a ball under her pillows. It occurred to her then that she needed some secret space to stow things if she were going to be forced to continue living here and would be called upon to engage in shady dealings from time to time. And then, glory of glories, it was time to wash the grime and mud and tension and terror of the night from her mind and body.

She yelped at the heat of the water when she first stepped in, but she couldn't afford for anyone to see her in her current state. And the sunrise was already smiling at her through the window. Slowly, Aviama sank down into the water, grabbing the bar of soap and running it along her skin like a hungry dog catching its first scrap from a table of cooked meat. Her stomach grumbled. She needed to stop making food-related analogies in her head.

The heat of the water eased into her muscles, breaking up some of the tension throughout her body, soothing her stiff arms and legs. She reached up to her hair and snatched her hand back. A bird's nest! Had it been this matted when she was with Chenzira, after the rainstorm? Or only after the wagon ride?

Idiot. He's sold himself out to Darsh. He doesn't care. It doesn't matter what you looked like.

It was true enough, right? But the last words he spoke were frozen in her brain.

I won't let you marry him.

What did it mean? Chenzira had still voted to kill the guard. He hadn't admitted it outright, but that must have been his choice. And he'd still followed Darsh's orders, joined the Shadow, and delivered her back to the palace. Even if he wanted to stop the wedding, without Darsh on board, he likely had few more resources than she did.

And just because he didn't want her to marry Shiva didn't mean he cared about her personally. Maybe Chenzira recognized he owed her his life, or he had his own agenda he was willing to get her out for. Regardless, he'd betrayed her. Abandoned her. Aviama had no guarantee that she could trust him. Why did she so desperately want to?

Because you're an idiot.

A knock came at the door. Aviama quickly dunked her head underwater and tried to work her fingers through the tangles of her hair. Her fingers immediately caught a snare too severe to work through. The door swung open, and Bhumi appeared.

"Your Highness! Forgive me, I didn't realize you'd called for a bath so early. I should have been here."

Aviama waved her hand with as unconcerned an air as she could manage. "Nonsense. I told them to let you sleep. I—I had another nightmare and thought the bath would help ease my mind."

The ease of the lie surprised her. Worried her, too, a little bit. But it was a believable lie, as Aviama's nightmares often involved embarrassing screaming that any servant with ears could hear. Everyone in the palace knew she had them.

Bhumi washed Aviama's hair and worked a comb through its mass of tangles, gripping the hair in small chunks and working her way up to the scalp until it was smooth once more. More than a little bit of hair was left in the comb by the end. What did Bhumi make of it? Perhaps the girl thought the princess with wind powers had gone crazy in her room. Would she suspect anything more?

But if Bhumi did have any suspicions, she made no indication of it. After Aviama was clean, Bhumi wrapped her in a towel and pulled a gown from the wardrobe, draping it over the back of the sofa.

"You're seeing Prince Shiva tonight for the diplomatic dinner. He requested you wear purple for the occasion, but I'm afraid your purple gown has a stain and has been sent out for repair. I'll send your condolences to His Royal Highness. Perhaps this blue one would suffice?"

The glint in the girl's eyes did not escape her, and Aviama grinned. Gratitude wrapped her chest in warm ribbons. Aviama had not exactly been subtle about her despise of wearing anything related to the lilac nickname Shiva had given her. The dress probably never even had a stain.

"What a shame. But this blue one is beautiful." Aviama ran her finger along the shimmering gold embroidery of the fitted bodice, the bold cobalt setting a deep contrast. "I think the prince will appreciate it."

And if he didn't, she really couldn't care less. She lifted her chin and pulled back her shoulders. She was Princess Aviama of Jannemar. And if she was a pawn in everyone else's game, she'd have to find a way to play on a new board. First, she needed friends. Sai was still an option, but Aviama would hold her at arm's length and build that relationship up slowly. As of now, Sai was still Shiva's girl. But if Aviama could turn Sai, she'd be in the perfect position to feed Shiva what Aviama wanted and be an informant. A spy *for* her, rather than a spy *on* her.

And she needed to get into the menagerie.

Bhumi moved to straighten Aviama's bed. Aviama's tongue stuck to the roof of her mouth, and she threw a hand out toward the servant girl. "Bhumi, wait!"

She turned, but then the door opened. Durga and Sai burst into the room, both breathless.

Aviama gaped at them, and they stared back. Sai's brows knit together in worry, but Durga looked positively murderous. Aviama collected herself and tugged the towel tighter around herself. "If you don't mind."

Sai shut the door, and Bhumi continued with straightening the bed, Aviama's getaway servant clothes still stashed under the pillow. Aviama cleared her throat, forcing herself to keep her attention on Sai and Durga.

"Is there a problem?"

Sai curtsied. "We only regret that we were not here sooner, Your Highness. We hadn't realized you wanted an early start to the day."

Aviama cocked her head at Durga. "Is this your concern also, the reason for storming in here like a pair of jackals were after you? Leaving unattended the princess you are sworn to serve?"

"The very same, Your Highness."

To her credit, Durga's curtsy was flawless, and her voice was measured. But her lips were tighter than a noblewoman's corset.

Bhumi's hands hesitated on a pillow in Aviama's peripheral vision. Aviama crossed to the sitting area and grabbed the gown off the sofa, lifting it up for Durga and Sai to see. *Look over here, you spies.* "What do you think of this? For tonight. I thought the gold would hint nicely at the coming union and compliment the prince nicely. I presume he will be wearing the royal color, maybe yellow with gold."

"Oh, lovely!" Sai gushed. "But didn't you wear blue recently?" She crossed to the wardrobe and rifled through the dresses. "Where is the violet gown?"

Bhumi pulled the pillow back, then laid it back down and smoothed the sheets and blankets. Aviama let out a breath and waved a hand. "It had a stain."

Sai dipped her head. "An excellent substitute, then, Highness."

Aviama managed a small smile. "Perhaps something a little less stifling for the daytime, though."

Durga pulled out a flowy dress in sunset orange and held it up. Aviama nodded, and Sai and Durga helped her into it. Durga yanked a sleeve into place.

"Ouch! Durga, if you don't watch yourself, my entire wardrobe will be sent off to repair, and I'll be left with nothing but my nightclothes. Let Sai do it."

"Forgive me, Your Highness. Just trying to be efficient."

"I'd rather it not come at the cost of my skin."

Sai paused on her other side. "Are you all right, Highness? You have scrapes on your arms."

"My nightmares are getting worse."

"We did not hear anything last night, Highness."

Aviama licked her lips and swallowed. "I dreamed I was

paralyzed, that I could make no sound. I dreamed that enemies were surrounding me, and I was forced to defend myself. I guess—perhaps I scratched myself in my sleep. I was in quite a state when I woke up."

Durga's eyes narrowed to slits, but she said nothing. Had Darsh been right? Had she really kept the whole thing to herself, or did the queen know Aviama had been gone from the palace all night?

Sai gasped and smoothed out Aviama's skirts. "I'm so sorry to hear that, Princess. But the sleeves cover the scratches. You are a vision yourself, Your Highness."

"Thank you." Aviama smiled at Sai. "Luckily, the dream ended better than others I've had as of late. I was stronger than my attackers. And I did whatever it took to stay safe. They fell, in the end."

Aviama glanced Durga's way, and her eyes blazed with fire. The girl snapped her chin upward and clenched her jaw, but said nothing. A wise move. But as she lifted her chin, Aviama caught a glimpse of poorly blended powder along her jaw. Perhaps Aviama was not the only one covering scrapes and bruises from last night.

A knock came at the door, and Durga went to answer. Aviama tossed her towel on the floor next to the bath, and her stomach churned as Bhumi snatched it off the floor and returned for one more adjustment of the pillows. She made a mental note not to underestimate Bhumi and added an item to her imaginary to-do list: *Find out what side Bhumi is on.*

Durga spoke quietly to someone through the door, closed it, and turned back to the room. "Your Highness, Prince Shiva is here for you. He'd like to know if you are decent."

viama's jaw dropped. "Right now? Early in the morning? Are you saying he's in the hall, or that he sent someone to tell me he wants to see me?"

A strong voice from the hall definitively answered her question. "Is she decent? I need to see her. Now."

Aviama froze. This was it. He'd found out everything. She'd be dragged out by her hair and executed. The queen's hyena would rip her apart. He'd move up the wedding and marry her that afternoon.

All equally horrendous options. Durga, the weasel, curtsied to the person in the hall and threw the door wide open. Aviama clasped her hands in front of her and grimaced as Prince Shiva swept into the room. Breathless. His clothes were pressed and perfect, but his hair was disheveled. She'd never seen him with anything out of place.

She sucked in a breath. He ran forward and seized her by the arms, his deep umber eyes piercing her through. Aviama shrank back, and he lifted one arm gently by the hand, and then the other, as he looked her over. Was he looking for injuries? The frantic look in his eyes was so far from what she was used to from him, she wasn't sure what to do. Aviama furrowed her brow. "What's going on?"

The prince's chest heaved, eyes wild, and he stepped back. Durga, Sai, and Bhumi stood dutifully to one side, all in a row. He ran a hand through his dark hair, inadvertently offering a good look at his biceps, which she definitely shouldn't have spent so long noticing, and shot a glance in the servants' direction.

Without the cocky manipulative confidence slathering his demeanor like butter on bread, she couldn't help but see a troubled man whose pain she might alleviate. She hated herself a bit for caring, but why did he seem so *earnest*?

He's manipulating you, like always. His stupid little Lilac.

"I need the room." Shiva cleared his throat. "With my intended."

The girls filed out without a word, Bhumi taking the towel —and probably the servants' clothes—out with her. Shiva nearly melted around her the instant the door swung closed, his arms encircling her waist, his face turned into her hair. Her stomach twisted, and she stood stock still for a moment, her arms awkwardly out to the sides to avoid touching him in return as he held her.

"No one's watching. Humor me." His voice was thick.

Aviama hesitated, then gingerly placed her arms around him. "What's going on?"

Shiva pulled back and searched her face. "I thought you might be dead."

Her chest tightened, and she shifted her weight. *I thought you'd come to do the job.* "Why would I be dead? What happened?"

He gripped her wrist in his hand and tugged her to the sofa, sinking wearily into the cushions and pinching the bridge of his nose. He didn't let her go. She sat. "We received a note that the guard outside your door was dead and that you were missing."

Aviama's stomach dropped. Every muscle tensed. She wanted to respond. If she had, she probably would have croaked out something suspicious and weird. But her mouth went dry and her throat tightened, and all she could manage was a gaping stare.

Shiva continued. "The source is not verified as credible, but there is evidence of a break-in last night. They never should have gotten so close to you. I think Darsh and his radicals wanted to kidnap you and use you as leverage for their own ends. Darsh will stop at nothing to serve his agenda. But there's a rat in the palace too. Spreading fear. Rumor. Your guard from last night is alive, but he's not himself. I took him off your detail, and he won't be posted anywhere on the residence floors again."

Rendering Darsh's blackmail on the man worthless. Not to mention Shiva hit the nail on the head with Darsh's plan. The only thing he was wrong about was believing it hadn't happened already. Or that she wouldn't go willingly.

A shiver ran down her spine, and he glanced up at her. "We're postponing the dinner. Just one night, for a chance to restructure security. We're changing the guard pattern."

She swallowed. "I hope you catch them. I'm not happy to be your hostage, but I know you're motivated to keep me alive, so I trust you'll take care of it. And your announcement?"

The veneer snapped back into place. Shiva dropped her hand, straightened, and leaned back against the cushion—the professional, the royal, once again. She was sorry to see the softer side of him go. "The announcement matters more now than ever. *You* matter more now than ever." He hesitated as something off to the side caught his eye.

Aviama turned to see what he was looking at, and heat

flushed her cheeks. The easel with her sketches of Jannemari wedding gowns.

Shiva cocked his head, and the corner of his mouth twitched. "Dreaming?"

Aviama couldn't very well tell him the truth—that she'd sketched it as an excuse for what she'd been spending her time on in her room, and as evidence she might be willing to go through the whole wedding charade. But at the same time, if she *were* getting married, that was the sort of dress she might wear. And she'd never let another kingdom overtake her own heritage.

Long, flowing lines swept down the paper from a fitted bodice adorned with sapphires, a small reminder of her mother for a day she'd never see. Light strokes brushed gold accents in graceful rain down the skirt, the white backdrop fabric catching every shimmer in the light. At least, that's how it would look in real life. If she were getting married, that is. Wearing that dress. For a wedding she was swearing off.

Prince Shiva crossed to the easel and lifted the edge of the parchment for a closer look. "You did these?"

"Do you think your mother would have allowed something that looked so much like Jannemar? Yes, it was me."

"You really are something. These are good."

Aviama's cheeks warmed again, and she stared down at her feet. *You're a moron, Aviama. A compliment of useless art does not replace a laundry list of evils. He's probably manipulating you this very instant.*

Shiva sighed. "Mother is too focused on making you look Radhan for the wedding. Can I show her these? If I get support from a few nobles first, we might pressure her into allowing more Jannemari influence in your dress."

She shrugged. "Sure." *Don't say thanks. That's what stupid people say to their captors, who are the worst people ever.* Aviama winced. "Thanks."

Biscuits.

Surprise flickered across his face. Then Shiva smiled and returned to the couch. He took her hand. She started to pull away, but he held her there. "I meant what I said. We could work together. And before you say no, I want to give you something. Let's call it a token of my sincerity."

Aviama pressed her lips together. "It must be something astronomically significant if you want me to believe in your sincerity." Bold. Insulting. She shouldn't have said it, but she couldn't help herself. And he seemed weirdly measured today. Safer.

She held her breath, and Shiva examined her with a long, cool stare. But just when Aviama thought he might decide to be angry, he relented, and his shoulders relaxed. "Come and see."

Aviama's eyes narrowed, but she let him pull her off the couch and to the door. Shiva paused by the door and slipped her arm around the crook of his elbow. "We're still engaged to be married, and you will still be my wife. Please remember to act accordingly as we walk through the palace, where eyes follow us everywhere we go." His voice was soft, though firm, sounding more like a request than a threat. But she knew better than to mistake his meaning.

Aviama set her jaw and gave a curt nod.

What would Darsh think? Would he like that Shiva was trying to sweeten her up, because he might give her more allowances, more access, making her a higher quality of informant for the Shadow? Would he question Aviama's loyalty, since Aviama had not responded with exuberant willingness, and decide to kill her along with the Tanashai family when his plot came to fruition?

Aviama's gut twisted, and nausea rolled through her at the thought. Would it really come down to killing Shiva and his parents? Could they remove the Tanashais without killing them—maybe exile? If she recommended exile to Darsh, would he take it as rebellion against his agenda and make her a target?

Shiva led her down the corridor with Aviama staring ahead from hall to hall. Emeralds and blues and pinks danced in delicate patterns up scalloped archways and down gilded pillars, across every centimeter of the ceiling, through every new turn they took. The prince glanced at her several times, but she hardly noticed. They progressed down a staircase and out onto the main level without a word.

Shiva examined her again. "Are you worried about Darsh and the threats I mentioned? Did I just give you nightmares?"

Aviama snorted. "I've lived through my share of threats so far. Some of them even happened. My nightmares have nothing to do with kidnapping."

"What are they about?"

Liben staring up at me with a hammer by his head. My father in a cloud of smoke from the explosion. Limbs flying through the air. My mother with a knife in her chest. You and me getting married. Your family attacking mine, and me watching as the last of my family dies, because of me.

Aviama swallowed hard against the lump in her throat. Tears welled in her eyes, and she jerked her chin forward, blinking them away until she was sure they'd retreated. "None of your business."

"Fair enough."

They rounded another bend, and Aviama gasped as she realized where he was taking her. He wouldn't. Would he?

A pair of servants walked by, and Shiva passed the double doors Aviama couldn't stop staring at. Her heart sunk, but she shouldn't have been surprised. He never would have allowed her to go in there. Not after the arena.

But as the servants passed from view, he looped around, gestured at the guards at the doors, and escorted her through to the long room beyond. The smell of hay and fur mixed with the sounds of chittering, twittering, and calling reverberating through the space. Enclosures lined the room on either side, cage after cage of exotic animals and frightening beasts—birds and cirabas, monkeys and zegraths. And an aquarium jutting up next to the golden door of the king's private office on the far end.

Aviama turned to Shiva, wide-eyed, as the doors shut them in. He lifted a hand and twined a lock of her hair around his fingers before tucking it delicately behind her ear. "We're going to live a long life together, Lilac. I'm willing to give a little so that it might not be so miserable. I don't want you to be miserable. There are some things I cannot compromise on. But I will give you what I can. Today, I can give you this."

Her heart beat fast, and her lips parted as she surveyed the room she'd yearned to return to since the arena. The magnatreated walls muted her magic, its deadening effect leaving a tingling sensation along her skin. If anything happened here, she would be defenseless. But it was also the only place that felt like home. The one place she might have a friend who understood her.

Shiva stepped closer, and the unsettled frozenness worked its way through her body as he turned her chin toward him so that they stood nose to nose. He ran the fingers of his opposite hand up her arm, leaving a trail of goosebumps at the lightness of his touch. Slowly, he leaned in and kissed her. "I look forward to the day when I don't first kiss you—but when you kiss me. When you reach for me and want me, even in the absence of a crowd to appease, a show to put on at the edge of a knife."

He pulled back, scanned her face, and brushed his thumb over her lips, along her jaw, and down her neck to her collarbone, drinking in the sight of her as if he were parched, and she a goblet of fine wine. Shiva leaned in again, hesitating as his mouth touched hers. "You are a beautiful woman, Aviama. One day, you'll admit I have the same hold over you as you have over me. And one day, you will come to want me again. I am sure of it."

With that, he slipped through the side door, and it clicked shut behind him. She was alone in the menagerie.

18

T he bird of paradise lifted her graceful head in the enclosure nearest the doors, but nothing seemed to ruffle the impenetrable bird's feathers. Across from her, the monkeys raised as big of a racket as they always did when anyone entered, and Aviama wondered if they'd been placed there intentionally as an alarm system of sorts.

Aviama bit her lip. Shiva had left her alone in the menagerie. What did it mean? He couldn't care about her, though. Not really.

I won't let you marry him.

Why did she feel guilty for letting Shiva kiss her? It was survival. If she hadn't, Shiva would have been angry. All softness would have disappeared, overtaken by threatened authority and a sharp edge. The aggressive, dangerous side of him she liked the least. The scary side.

Chenzira could be scary too. She thought of the time she'd broken into the menagerie through the troll enclosure, picked the lock to King Dahnuk's office, and he'd shoved her up against the wall. Or when he tossed her over the half-wall like a sack, into the secret passage behind the painting inside the office. Or when he tackled the nobleman in the wealthy district, or he swung her off her feet and out of the way as the quakemakers opened up the ground to swallow the guard's body...

He was as strong as Shiva, if not more so, and certainly taller. If Chenzira was caught in the menagerie, his abilities quelled by the magna lining the room, he still had the capacity to protect himself. He had actual skills. Without her windcalling, Aviama had nothing. Moderate knife-throwing abilities at best.

But he could also be soft. The sort of soft she might come to believe. Images of Chenzira pressed unbidden to the forefront of her mind—him hugging the old woman in the hut of the slum, passing her tea, slipping his hand in hers to lead her through the dark. A little tingling shiver rippled down her spine. And the menagerie wasn't cold.

Aviama shook her head to clear it and curled her hands into fists. *Stop it. Shiva won't let you stay here forever.*

She hurried down the aisle past the fire lizards and snakes on her right and the massive cirabas on her left. Aviama supposed the menagerie also felt safe for another reason. It was honest. Radha saw her as a trophy, as belonging in one of these cages. Shiva had admitted it outright, and the king and queen had happily locked her here with Chenzira before the contest. She touched the bars of the empty enclosure between the cirabas and the zegrath where the two of them had been trapped, awaiting their fate, for hours.

He'd chosen not to kill her to save himself, though he had the skill to do it both in the cage and in the arena. Even without quakemaker melder abilities, Chenzira's experience with a weapon made him a formidable foe. Without her windcalling, Aviama was the orphan pawn princess. Nothing more. No actionable knowledge or practical skills. Useless.

But there was someone here who didn't deserve to be called an *it* or a *beast* or an *exotic creature* any more than Aviama did. Someone with magic *and* practical skill. Someone with a name.

Makana.

The Tanashais didn't call her a her. Even Chenzira had referred to her as an *it* last night when he told the story to the Shadow. Aviama knew better.

She doubled her pace as she approached the aquarium and slipped through the narrow path between enclosures out of sight of the main aisle until the trolls came into view. Sunlight from the window at the top of the wall eased into the trolls' cage enough to reach the door. The larger troll was frozen into statue form in the rays from the window. The smaller huddled in the shadow of a shack-like shelter in the corner. It bared its ugly teeth when Aviama approached, but she only smiled. It couldn't get to her without the sun freezing it in its path.

A school of striped red and yellow fish darted this way and that to avoid a larger fish as it dove after them, and Aviama couldn't help but think the scenario wasn't fair to the red and yellow fish. The aquarium was only so big. The predator would get them, eventually. Her stomach soured. It was not unlike the palace.

Aviama peered through the glass. Fish of every color swirled by in a mesmerizing display. Small rocks, sand, and marine plants filled the bottom. Seaweed waved in the water along the side. Aviama winced and ran a hand along the scar on her neck. But no Makana. Had they moved her? Did Shiva bring Aviama to the menagerie just to show her what happens to anyone who goes against the grain of the House of the Blessing Sun?

She turned to the troll enclosure, hiked up her skirts, and

climbed the crossbar of the cage until she stood a meter off the ground, her elbow looped through the bars to hold her upright and offer a better vantage point. A silver flicker on the far side of the pool caught her eye, and the knot in her chest eased. *She's here.*

Awe struck her as the graceful lines of a mermaid cut through the water, gliding as if made of glass. Silver scales glimmered along a powerful tail, white hair catching the light. Her skin glittered with an ethereal quality Aviama could not quite name as she broke the surface, draped her elbows over the edge of the aquarium, and pierced her through with an intense lavender gaze.

For a moment, Aviama wondered if perhaps she'd been wrong. Perhaps this siren, this daughter of the sea—*death* daughter of the sea, as the Shadow had called her—would shake off any belief in the goodness of man and kick Aviama back into the bucket of treacherous exploiters she'd experienced so far. The mermaid's stare was neither warm nor threatening. But as Aviama looked back at her, the solemnity that came naturally to Makana's face seemed to melt into a sort of curiosity.

Aviama cleared her throat. "Hello."

Makana tilted her head, but said nothing.

Aviama bit her lip and tried again. "I know you can do more than sing. You can talk. You told me your name. And I don't mean to pry. It's just that I'm so—" She paused. So *what*? Did she even know what she wanted from seeing the mermaid? What she hoped for? Aviama opened her mouth, closed it, then let out a shaky breath. "Lonely."

Aviama grimaced. "I'm lonely, and I'm sad, and I'm trapped. And I guess I thought maybe you would be too. And today is the first day they've let me come to see you."

The siren looked at her, her expression unchanged.

Aviama squeezed her eyes shut and passed her free hand over her face. The ache of hopelessness wormed its poisonous way up from her stomach and spread across her chest. Maybe she shouldn't have come.

And then a clear sound like the song of the heavens plowed through the dark, pulling at her heart as if a hand had broken through her rib cage and seized it. Aviama's eyes flew open, a sob hitching in her chest. Makana lifted her voice in a crystal song that was round, deep, and moving all at once, her eyes never leaving Aviama's face.

The melody wafted up to the ceiling, tugging at the hopeless pain in her chest, weaving in and out from sadness to comfort to ache to serenity. And Aviama's heart couldn't help but respond, the song wrapping around her like a blanket, the notes inviting her deeper in. Then, as quickly as it had begun, the song cut off.

Grief nearly overtook her at the loss of the melody. Aviama leaned out from her perch on the troll cage bars. Makana gave her a slow nod. "Now you."

Aviama gulped and shook her head. *No, thank you. When I feel like this and try to sing, I cry. I don't feel like blubbering in the menagerie, thank you.* Or in front of Makana, for that matter.

Makana's expression hardened, almost as if she could read her thoughts. She tilted her head and repeated herself. "Now you."

Aviama drew in a deep breath and let it out under the siren's scrutinizing supervision. She took two more breaths before getting up the gumption to sing, but something about Makana's cool, collected presence grounded her to this place, this moment, allowing her to block out the rest. Aviama opened her mouth and sang for the first time since the arena. It was a single note, soft and hushed, then swelling before falling again, low, lower, and up, in an uneasy minor key that perfectly translated the emotion she'd carried these last days.

The song dropped away, and Aviama let it die. She looked back at Makana, and the siren gave a sad smile. "When I sing, I learn. When you sing, I learn. You and I. One heart." The mermaid's voice was lilting, accented by a language of the heart Aviama had never heard. Makana extended her arm across the distance between them, palm up. "Tabeun sister."

It was the phrase and gesture Makana had used with Aviama in the aquarium of the arena before fighting off the guards. Aviama matched her movement, reaching across the gap and pressing her palm into the siren's. "Tabeun sister."

Makana nodded. "You are true."

The mermaid withdrew her hand, and Aviama tried to make sense of the exchange. Was it an extension of her siren magic that she could not only kill by singing a death lullaby, but learn about others by singing to them and hearing them sing in return? If so, what kind of things did she learn about people?

"Thank you."

Dummy. Why would you say thank you for that? Aviama clenched her teeth to keep from groaning at herself and wrinkled her nose in a wince. *Ridiculous.*

"You are melderblood key. I am sea. They cannot come to use both."

Aviama frowned. "You are the sea? Or a key?"

Makana dipped her head in assent.

What did that mean? Aviama took a breath. "How do we... how...what should I do?"

"I am Iolani. My father must not treaty. You must not marry."

She wasn't sure what Iolani was, but the next bit made more sense. "I don't *want* to marry. The rad—" Aviama stopped, then dropped her voice. Who knew what spiders might carry messages back to the queen, even here? She tried again. "I thought I might have a way, but now I'm not so sure."

The siren's pewter tail swished along the surface of the water and drifted down again. "If you marry, Radha have tabeun. We lose sea."

"I don't understand. Who loses the sea? How does me getting married impact the sea? And how could I stop it?"

"My family. My people. Iolani protect sea. Radha destroy. If Radha have tabeun, Iolani flee."

Aviama gaped at her. "You're telling me a community of mermaids protects the sea, and if I marry Shiva, Radha will have the power to take control of the seas?"

Makana dipped her head again. "Aeian Sea. Lose home."

Aviama's jaw dropped. "Are you what's keeping Radha's navy from attacking Jannemar by the cliffs? Are your people blocking the ships?"

Makana screwed her face tight in concentration, but only stared.

"Umm..." Aviama adjusted her grip on the bars, racking her brain for other ways to explain. "Ships. Do Iolani stop Radha's ships?"

The siren's face lit up. "Stop ships! Yes. Iolani stop Radha ships. Long history. Not good. Radha hate Iolani."

Realization slammed into Aviama like a sledgehammer. "Your father. You're not a prize exotic trophy. You're leverage. To keep the Iolani under control. And if they had melderblood power behind them, the Iolani wouldn't be able to fight them off."

Monkeys screeched at the far side of the room, and Makana's lip curled as she turned her head toward the sound. "Radha scum." She shoved off the side of the aquarium and disappeared just as elegantly as she'd come, leaving only a small ripple along the surface as evidence she'd ever been there at all.

Aviama uncrooked her elbow, slid her hands down the bars, and hopped down to the floor. The smaller hyland troll bared its stony teeth again, and she stuck her tongue out at it before hurrying out along the path to the aisle—and running smack into Shiva's broad chest.

He steadied her on her feet and pulled her hand back through his arm in the manner of a formal, traditional escort. "Nice chat?"

Aviama gulped, adrenaline rocketing through her veins at the sudden sight of him. When exactly had he entered? Had he heard anything? But they were quiet, and the monkeys were loud. There was no way he'd overhead them—was there?

"It was more me talking than her. But it was nice none-theless." She steeled herself, then said what she shouldn't have said to begin with. "Thank you." She shouldn't have said it before. Not when she did it out of reflex, out of manners and politeness to the man responsible for holding her hostage and plotting the hostile takeover of her home. Was this how Makana felt?

But now, a new era of survival presented itself. And the more she thought about it, the more certain she was that it was the right move. If Shiva came to believe Aviama might be open to a cooperative forced marriage, accepting her fate enough to at least stop openly fighting against it, he might trust her a little. Let her in more. Allow more privileges, like coming to the menagerie.

If Darsh came to believe Aviama was invested in his plan, in becoming queen, in training the melders in his radical Shadow caste, he might let her come and go more freely. He might share better ways in and out. And he might offer information he wouldn't offer someone who, say, insulted him to his face and stormed out of meetings in front of his underlings.

Oops.

And if Darsh had as many people stationed in the palace as he implied, Aviama could never know who was watching. At any moment, spies of Shiva, or the queen, or Darsh, could be taking notes and scurrying back to their respective masters.

The only result Aviama really cared about was getting herself free, getting word home to Jannemar about the situation in Radha, and as of sixty seconds ago, freeing Makana and keeping the Iolani from striking a deal with Radha.

Orphan girl Aviama, the princess pawn of everyone everywhere, needed to stop looking so troublesome. Troublesome people wound up dead. Useful pawns lived. How could she seem useful to them all, without letting any of them succeed, meanwhile working out her own ends?

Back to the box she would go. Back to the stuffy, prissy, over-decorated, beautiful prison rooms she'd been stashed in all her life. To a game she knew, playing an old role, to open new doors.

Aviama let out a long sigh. "I think I even mean it. Thank you. I hate that I'm here. But the fighting is wearing me out. Coming here, with no prying eyes or needling servants—well, it was good for me."

Shiva blinked back at her, and the corner of his mouth curved up into a smile. "I'm glad. I'll find a time for you to come again."

"I'd like that."

Shiva rapped on the double doors, and the guards opened them from the other side. He walked her back through the maze of halls and brought her to the courtyard with the pakshi-shaped pool beneath the guest residences where she'd stayed before the arena. A spread of meats, fruit, honey rolls, and lemon cakes waited for them under the shade of the trees. Her mouth watered.

The prince led her to a reclining chair, and she sat. He gestured to the food. "I'm sure you're hungry, so I've arranged for brunch. Unfortunately, I'll have to take my leave, but I told them we'd be eating together, so you can rest assured all the food is safe. I won't be able to make supper with you tonight, as we have a lot of security arrangements to deal with before the diplomatic dinner tomorrow night. But I'll have food sent, and if a lilac is on the platter, you can know it's from me and safe to eat."

Aviama's eyes widened. He'd thought out all the details.

Shiva turned to go, but Aviama grabbed his wrist. "Wait!" The prince turned, and she released him. "Um, earlier. You said there was a rat in the palace. I think it's Durga."

He arched an eyebrow. "That would make sense. I'll look into it. Thank you."

Shiva strode from the courtyard, and Aviama snatched a honey roll from the platter. Useful to Shiva, harmful to Queen Satya, and even more useful to Aviama herself. Only a thousand more moments like that, and she might just find a way out of this mess. She took a bite of the roll, and its sweetness melted against her tongue.

Next on her list: prove her loyalty to Darsh without compromising opportunities to prove her loyalty to Shiva.

Great.

19

Brunch was sublime, and by the time Aviama was done, she'd never been so stuffed in all her life. She leaned back on the reclining chair by the pakshi-shaped pool, breathing in the fresh air, and the sight of flowers and fruit trees. Fish glittered through the water here and there, and watching their movements eased the tension she'd been carrying.

The cherry on top of it all was that she was alone. Sure, a guard or two was posted somewhere in view of her, but not close. She couldn't feel them breathing down her neck the way the servant girls did. And now that Shiva had removed Ishaan, curse him, from her detail, the guards didn't bother her half as much.

She resolved to ask Shiva for daily brunch here, whether or not he joined her. She'd eat without worrying about poison, get out of her stuffy room, and breathe. Aviama liked breathing quite a lot. She wished other people wanted her breathing as much as she did.

The sound of claws click-clacking on marble drenched her in dread, ruining every calming effect the fish or the water ever had. Aviama used every ounce of strength to keep from jumping sky high from her chair, instead closing her eyes and pretending not to notice. Perhaps the queen and her horrible hyena would simply pass her by.

Click-clack, click-clack. Closer, closer. And then silence. Aviama opened one eye and nearly yelped. The ruby hyena's nose hovered over her skirts, its large eyes staring at her, two handbreadths away from her face. A long string of saliva dripped from the animal's open mouth, landing on the marmalade shades of her dress.

"Poor thing. He's hungry."

Aviama wrinkled her nose in disgust. She hoped the queen attributed the expression to her opinion of the hyena rather than her gut reaction to the sound of Satya's voice. She pushed further from the hyena, snatched a piece of lunch meat from the platter, and tossed it on the ground in Mrtyu's direction.

He didn't even flinch, his eyes still on Aviama. The queen barked a command in some language Aviama could not identify, and Mrtyu whirled and snapped up the meat from the floor.

Queen Satya came into view as her pet licked its chops. "Where is your accompaniment?"

Aviama stood and curtsied. "Prince Shiva had hoped to join me for brunch, but was called away. I'm sure you've heard of the latest threats."

Satya looked down her sharp nose at Aviama and sat on the chair next to her, posture ramrod straight, with the same severe glance she'd passed to Shiva. "Indeed. Tiring, is it not? All the worry of kidnapping and death?"

Aviama perched on the edge of her chair and folded her hands demurely in her lap, smoothing her expression into the sweetest she could manage. "Not at all, Your Majesty. Living in a royal household makes one acquainted with such annoyances. After hearing so many, threats lose their potency, wouldn't you say?"

"Naturally." Satya plucked a grape from the tray between them and popped it into her mouth. "Though the prudent person deciphers between the typical lackluster threat and the credible concern."

"I know His Royal Highness does not want anything to happen to me. His Majesty the king also values the advantages a union would bring. I trust they will take care of everything standing in their way."

Aviama smiled, and Satya's thin lips curved unpleasantly upward in response. "Even so. Every powerful person has their weakness. In these fragile days before the wedding, I'd advise you against being alone."

"In Jannemar, we love our servants like friends. The girls are tired. The guards can watch out for me while they get a break. And Durga seemed shaken today. Unsteady. Like she'd seen a ghost."

Like she'd seen a dead man walking again.

Satya lifted her chin just a hair, but a quick inhale betrayed her. She knew about the guard. Durga might not have told her everything, but she'd told her mistress about the dead guard outside Aviama's door. And her information had proved untrustworthy.

"I don't concern myself with every servant in the palace. I'm afraid I'm not sure I remember a Durga, in particular. But if you have any concerns, do take them to Amir."

Aviama inclined her head. "I'll be sure to do that. Thank you, Your Majesty."

They both knew Amir was favored by the queen, more loyal to her than to the king. Aviama didn't trust him to know what she had for breakfast, much less any matters of real importance.

Queen Satya stood, and Mrtyu came to her side, nuzzling her palm. The beast was closer to the size of a horse than a dog, and its head lowered to reach the queen's hand. Aviama stood also, trying her best not to stare at the hyena. Her gaze drifted to the animal just for a second, and it bared its teeth with a low growl that chilled her bones.

"Until tomorrow night, Your Highness. We look forward to hearing your public commitment not only to my son, but to Radha."

Aviama pressed her lips together in what was more a grimace than a smile and dropped into a graceful curtsy as the queen turned on her heel and swept from the courtyard, Mrtyu faithfully at her side. Satya disappeared, and Aviama flopped back onto the reclining chair. Okay, so there were certain disadvantages to escaping the four walls of her stupid room.

No sooner had the click-clack of Mrtyu's claws drifted from her hearing than Sai's slight form hurried over from the opposite side of the courtyard. "Your Highness! Is everything all right?"

Aviama groaned and flung her arm over her face. *Biscuits.* Where was the serenity of the morning? The twenty minutes of it or so that she got, anyway. Was there no place outside of the menagerie where she could be left alone?

"Your Highness?" Sai hesitated as she reached Aviama's side.

Aviama sighed. "I'm fine. I'm hounded all the time by people who tell me they just want to keep me safe. The same people who constantly tell me I'll die or get tossed in one dungeon or another if I don't do what they want. So, I suppose I'm about as *fine* as that situation sounds like I should be."

Aviama dropped her arm and squinted up at the servant girl. Her features were soft and concerned, eyes filled with some solemn emotion Aviama couldn't quite place. "Sorry. That was out of place."

Sai set herself on the chair the queen had recently vacated. "It sounds reasonable to me. Nobody likes a cage, no matter how gilded."

The words struck true to the core, and her chest tightened. Aviama turned her head to look at Sai. Her back was still straight, muscles taut, body poised. She wasn't lounging. She was on duty.

"We're practicing trusting each other, right?"

Sai tilted her head. "Yes?"

"Relax. Lean back."

The girl leaned back slowly, and the tension in her shoulders eased. Aviama nodded. "Which would you prefer— telling me where you got your bruise, or telling me you're a melder?"

All the tension flooded back. Sai's arm flinched, and she pressed her lips tight, but said nothing. And everything. Because she didn't deny it. Aviama lifted her hand and called a wisp of wind, gently nudging her skin, and sweeping up to rustle the leaves of the fruit trees next to them. Why else would Sai ask the questions she'd asked, but seem so sheepish? She hadn't just been curious, had she? Or was she as good a pretender as Shiva, and it was all part of some undiscovered ploy?

Aviama set her face forward and lifted her hand, but did not call the wind. "No one will know. Anyone looking will think it's me. You're right-handed, right? So, use that hand, hidden between us. Don't say a thing. Aim for the closest tree, with the blue fruit."

Nothing happened. Aviama shifted in her seat. *You're*

holding your hand up to nothing, and you look insane. Sai probably thinks you're crazy. After all, Aviama wasn't at all certain Sai was a melder. But acting like Aviama already knew Sai had powers was the best way to make her feel safe to reveal them if she did.

It would make sense, wouldn't it? With Durga's intentional placement with Aviama, and Sai's strange questions from the other day. The blue fruit wavered, then a burst of air blew the leaves back, and two pieces of fruit ripped free of the stem and fell to the ground.

Aviama squealed, then clapped a hand over her mouth. "Biscuits, I don't know my own strength! Good thing I'm practicing." She grinned and snuck a sideways look at Sai. The girl's eyes bugged out of her head, and Aviama thought she might be sick.

They had to try again before she lost her nerve. Practicing melder powers in the palace of the kingdom most bent on destroying them was not the wisest, after all. Aviama composed herself and focused on one of the fallen fruit.

"You asked me about uncontrolled powers before, about my training. And I told you I'd practice trusting you, just as you practice trusting me." Aviama swirled the wind in a tight circle at the tip of her finger and dispersed it. "You may fear the consequences of being found out. A reasonable fear. But do you fear the consequences of failing to practice? Uncontrolled powers also lead to death. Whether yours, or someone else's. Radha is right that we are dangerous. But we should gain such skill that we are only dangerous to those who threaten our lives, and not to ourselves or our loved ones."

Her voice was low, just enough for Sai to hear as they sat next to each other in the reclining chairs. The air was still, and every word fell on intently waiting ears. Aviama called another strand of wind and sent it after the second blue fruit, further than the first. The wind started to break up and waft away as it hit the small obstacle, but Aviama recrafted the strand and held it, drawing her finger across the space in front of her as she pushed the wind into the fruit once more.

"Wind can feel like a fickle chaos. But it has its rules, and when we learn what they are, they can help us. Air currents have greater strength to draw from than slower moving areas. Building on what you've already started to draw is easier than starting over from scratch. And sometimes small is better. 'The small wind carries the butterfly, but the great wind destroys it.'"

The little blue fruit rolled along the floor at the edge of her wind, scooting and bumping its way toward the edge of the pool. Aviama released it, and it rocked back onto a flatter side of itself. Something inside her ached to share the lessons she'd learned from Frigibar. But another part of her came alive, and a thrill of anxious anticipation worked through her stomach.

"Your turn. Take it into the pool. I'll cover you."

Aviama raised her hand, but did not call the wind. Sai snuck her hand up, just a tad, and Aviama could feel the change in the air around them as the girl beside her called upon it. The fruit began to shake, and then to move—and then the air around them burst outward, rocking Aviama's chair and nearly tipping her over.

In a reflex, Aviama lifted both hands and brought a dome of air down on them, containing Sai's escaping wind energy and letting it dissipate along the boundary. "Don't let go when you get frustrated. You added energy to it and then let it loose to wreak havoc."

She remembered only too well how her emotions built upon themselves. At her awakening by the smithy, the wind had gathered more and more strength when her terror had inadvertently whipped the air into a swirling gale and spun it into a whirlwind. Aviama shook her head, trying to shake free the image of Liben and the hammer, and glassy eyes staring up at her once again.

"A fruit does not need a storm behind it. Send a wisp. Aim at the center of the fruit. Again."

Sai took a deep breath and let it out, but the breath was shaky. Aviama shook her head. "Take a minute. Calm. How about this? As you breathe out, capture the breath and send that. It will be easier than creating something gentle as you start."

Aviama lifted her hand and took a steadying breath herself. Maybe this was a bad idea. Maybe Sai would destroy the trees and the courtyard and send them both flying backwards to the pillars, and the guards would tell the tale for years to come after they had both long since been beheaded.

But then, on a long exhale, Sai captured her breath and sent it after the fruit, nudging it along to the pool. It got halfway before the breath escaped, and she tried again, this time pushing the little fruit over the edge and into the water.

Aviama grinned. A big, stupid grin. She couldn't help it. She glanced sideways at Sai, and she was grinning too. "Beautifully done." Aviama stretched and dropped her hands at her sides. "Practice in your room on very small objects. If you aim small, and keep the energy small, the mistakes will also be small."

They lay there for several minutes, breathing in the stillness so rare in recent experience. A natural wind played through the leaves of the trees, and a fish tail burbled through the surface of the water of the pool at the edge of their chairs, sending graceful ripples flowing outward in concentric circles. In those few precious moments with Sai, and now sitting here in the quiet, Aviama didn't have to think about the threat on the seas, Makana or her people, Darsh or his radicals, Shiva or his mysterious announcement. For however short a time, she could just be.

She resolved to do it more often. They would come to the courtyard, whenever possible, to sit. If alone, excellent, she could be alone; if accompanied, perhaps she could come with Sai.

And if with Durga, by all things sweet in this world, Aviama would not come at all.

After an hour, Durga and Bhumi found them, and Durga's needle-like gaze and judgy, snappy movements sucked the enjoyment out of the courtyard faster than Aviama had believed possible. Aviama announced she was tired of sitting, and the three women trailed her as she walked aimlessly through hall after hall, terrace and veranda. She was sick of her room, but had no one to see, no one to visit, and nothing to do.

So sick of it as she was, she resigned herself to return to her chambers to draw. And wait. And wait some more. For something, anything, to happen.

But she needn't have worried. Because just as Aviama stepped out onto the east side veranda, shouts and screams rocked the air.

20

Aviama spun, and Bhumi ripped the door open behind them. Sai took her elbow and ushered her through the door, Durga taking up the rear. For the first time Aviama realized another advantage to having melder servants: Durga could keep her in the palace, but she could also act as a bodyguard. A wild, unmotivated one, maybe. But did this mean Durga had been instructed to keep Aviama safe? Or only that she would kill members of the Shadow if she saw them?

Bhumi flew along the hall, and Aviama broke into a run to keep up as the four of them navigated back through the corridor. Screams came from the left, and Bhumi hooked a right, away from the danger. But if Aviama didn't see it, she'd only ever know the story she was fed.

She caught up her skirts and took a sharp left, slipping free of Sai's grasp, and barreled down the path and into a wide-open room lined with pillars on one side and offset with meeting rooms on the other. A dozen guards surrounded a man on the floor. Two male servants and one female huddled around a large broken vase, picking pieces up off the floor.

Aviama came to a halt as a short Radhan man in fine, embroidered clothes strode in from the opposite side, barking orders. "Don't touch him! Take him to the queen."

A second man, the pakshi symbol of Radha emblazoned on the breastplate of his armor, swept into view from the meeting room. "No. The queen has no business here. He's the king's man."

"He was on the queen's detail, Captain."

"Whose seal approves your salary, Amir? Whose name signs decrees in Radha?"

Durga and Sai skidded to a stop next to Aviama. Bhumi ran up a moment later. Aviama craned her neck, not only wanting to see what had happened but also needing to see. Two guards broke from the dozen and seized the man on the floor.

A broad-shouldered guard stalked forward, leaving a gap in the line of guards. "What do they have over you? How much are they paying you?"

Aviama gasped. The detained man was the guard who'd been outside her door last night. The guard that had been dead, or so it seemed, and then not dead. The one Darsh had just started to blackmail.

Heads swiveled in her direction, and the man who'd stared up at her from the floor less than twenty-four hours ago curled his lip. His eyes darkened, and his face hardened. Someone yelled, and the guard's body sagged. A small sound skittered along the floor, like an object dropped or discarded from a meter high. And a knife protruded from the soft flesh at the base of his throat, though Aviama hadn't seen it fly. Blood dripped from the entry point, and the men on either side of him stumbled under the sudden weight. Light slowly faded from the guard's eyes—his stony gaze fixed on Aviama.

Bhumi let out a soft cry as men rushed forward, drawing

their swords as if any action would change the state of things now. Amir's face reddened as he stared at the body, but the sea of bodies around the corpse soon hid it from Aviama's view. Her mouth went dry, and her nails dug into her palms.

The broad-shouldered guard who had gotten in the man's face earlier turned to his superior. "Captain, forgive me. He drew a knife. The princess appeared, and he moved to strike."

The captain surveyed the damage, glanced back up at Aviama, and nodded. "Nothing to be done. Quick work. Good reflexes. Have the report on my desk by nightfall." He jerked his chin at Aviama. "Get her out of here."

The guard touched his fist to his chest and turned on his heel toward Aviama, leaving the man he'd killed spilling blood on the marble floor behind him. Aviama's lips parted. Arjun.

Arjun gestured at several other guards, and they arranged themselves around them. "Your Highness, you're not safe here. I'll escort you to your chambers."

Aviama set her jaw, but said nothing. She nodded in assent, and Arjun gave a slight bow and set a clipped pace forward. Sai and Bhumi took up either side of Aviama, and Durga fell in at the rear once more. Six guards fell into formation in front, on their flank and behind Durga, and Arjun led the way.

But the man was dead. What danger remained? How much investigation was required? What really happened? Aviama's stomach dropped. Had the guard really drawn his knife to kill her? Everyone had turned their attention from the guard to Aviama when she gasped. Everyone except Arjun, apparently. No one else saw. But she'd heard a knife clatter. It must have been true.

They wound their way through a service hall in a roundabout path to Aviama's chambers, the sturdy pace leaving

Aviama breathless by the time they reached her door. Arjun marched into her rooms, leaving four guards with her and her women in the hall, and the remaining two following him inside. After a moment, they reappeared, and Arjun placed himself in the doorway.

"Change clothes, Your Highness. We aren't risking anything today. We're setting up a decoy and taking you to a secure location."

Aviama raised her brows. "A decoy?"

Arjun nodded and scanned the three servant women. He pointed at Durga. "You. You're the right height; you'll do. Put on something from the princess's wardrobe. Both of you grab a mantle with a hood and pull it up. You other two servants will split up, each accompanying a princess."

Aviama swallowed. It was a good plan, but it sounded more serious than other interventions. How credible were further threats? Was Arjun here for Darsh, or simply following orders, maintaining his cover of the guard? She hadn't realized he was still part of the guard, but it made sense. If he fled with Murin to find Darsh, Darsh would have rather kept an already-established man in the palace as an informant.

"Okay. I'll take Sai."

Arjun's gaze flicked to Sai. "Why her? Do you favor Sai?"

"No, it's not that." Well, it was, but no need to make it more obvious to everyone. "She's just the other senior maidservant. She's more familiar with me, and Bhumi is excellent but has less experience."

"People who know you well might expect you to have Sai, then. She'll accompany Durga, and Bhumi will accompany you. Let's go."

Aviama hesitated, then nodded and turned into her chamber. Durga shut the door, and Sai and Bhumi rifled through the wardrobe. Sai shook her head at Bhumi's first suggestion. "Something dark, to blend in when night falls."

Bhumi pulled out two navy dresses a moment later. "Same color. In case we need to swap decoy and princess at some point."

Sai nodded, and Durga pulled the wardrobe door open wider to reach two long, hooded mantles. Aviama marveled at their speed and strategy. Her servant women might not be loyal to her, primarily, but they were smart. And tonight, at least, they seemed to want her to survive. Though Aviama did take some comfort in splitting up from Durga.

Sai and Bhumi quickly helped Aviama and Durga dress, and moments later, they both wore similar-style navy dresses and long hooded mantles on top. Sai tugged the mantle up over Aviama's blonde hair. Her fingers lingered on the hood, keeping them standing close together. She adjusted the edge of it and whispered, "Be safe."

Aviama smoothed her skirts and swallowed. "Try not to let anyone see. But if worse comes to worst, do whatever you have to do."

She scanned Durga, then walked to the vanity and pulled open a drawer. If she were going to pass for the princess of Jannemar, even at a distance, it should look as real as possible. Aviama snatched up three rings—not her favorites, but rings —and took hold of Durga's hand. "Don't lose these. And don't do anything stupid as me. The Tanashai family has a reputation to uphold."

Aviama slipped the rings over Durga's slender fingers. Up close, their complexions and features were far too different to be confused for one another, but as a silhouette or from a distance, with the hood up, their statures certainly could pass for each other. Durga curtsied, and Aviama gripped her elbow and pulled her back up, shaking her head. "Your Highness, you need only greet another prince or princess with a curtsy to pay respects to foreign dignitaries, and they should do the same to you. Always curtsy to the sovereign the first time in the day that you see them, and at public events. But never in deference to the same rank, in the same family. Hold your head high."

Durga eyed her, but her stony expression smoothed into focused attentiveness. She straightened and turned toward the door.

"Wait for a servant, Your Highness. Not because they are less important than you, but because it is their job. My mother told me if you take away their duties, you take away their dignity and their purpose."

It never stopped Aviama from helping from time to time, if something was spilled, or if she could make the load lighter. Her mother had taught her to value the servants and the work they did in the castle, often taking her around to watch their duties and talking through what they did and what would happen if it wasn't done. It felt strange to regurgitate her mother's lessons now—lessons she had only half-listened to as a child, but that she treasured now, as some small legacy of her mother. Saying them to someone like Durga was stranger still.

An ache set in her chest, but a strength wound through it as even the arrogant Durga followed her every instruction. The girl froze, stiffened, and waited. Sai followed Aviama's lead, inclining her head and offering a gentle curtsy to Durga as she pulled open the door. Durga looked truly uncomfortable for the first time, but she took a breath and marched through the door.

Arjun and the guards waited outside, and Aviama nodded at Sai as she held the door. "Follow your princess."

Sai dropped into another curtsy for Aviama, a deeper one,

and slipped into the hall. Bhumi took the door, and Aviama gave a slight inclination of her head to acknowledge her as she walked through to join the group in the hall. She didn't have to, and technically shouldn't have. But her life may well be in the hands of these people tonight. And their courage was not lost on her.

Arjun looked them over, then dipped his head. "Good. It's only afternoon, so the full light of the sun is still up. We're going to separate you now and take you to different locations until the threat is past. We've gotten wind of a potential threat, and the king has ordered us to take precautions."

Arjun assigned four guards to Durga and Sai, keeping two more guards besides himself with Aviama and Bhumi. To all appearances, from the right angles, a senior maidservant and a fuller detail were with Durga, not Aviama. But though he'd not revealed it here, Arjun was a melder. And so was she.

Did anyone in the palace know that both Durga and Sai were melderblood? The queen almost certainly knew about Durga. Did Shiva know about Sai? Did anyone?

Aviama lifted her chin and drilled Durga with an intent stare. "Durga. If it comes down to it, try to let others protect you. Do what princesses do. Stay in whatever claustrophobic room or box you're put in, and don't make a scene if you can help it."

Durga's jaw clenched, and the fingers of one hand curled into a fist, but she gave a curt nod. She was a smart girl. She should be able to read between the lines. *Your powers are chaotic. Don't blow the roof off a place when you don't have to.*

There were enough horrible reputations for melders in Radha already. No need to hand them further ammunition by demonstrating poor control, especially while dressed like royalty.

Aviama, on the other hand, had no such restrictions for

herself. Bhumi would not die because of her proximity. If the time came, she would call on the wind.

Durga and her entourage set off, her four guards in a square around her, and Arjun turned back toward Aviama. "We're going to work a triangle formation, but I won't be directly in front of you. So, we're going to need you to walk with purpose on your own, even as you follow me."

Adrenaline shot down her spine at the intensity of his tone, the seriousness of his voice. It had been a while since she'd been shuttled anywhere for her own safety, at least in as structured a manner as this, but she'd been through the drill a myriad of times. She lifted her chin. "I know what a triangle formation is. I'll do the best I can to keep the pace you set."

Arjun arched an eyebrow, but dipped his head and struck out down the corridor at a brisk pace. Aviama walked just slightly behind him so that he was offset slightly ahead and on her right. Guard Two settled in close on her left, nearly side-by-side, and Guard Three took the rear position, scanning in all directions.

Bhumi walked close at her right side, and Aviama looped her arm through the girl's to keep her closer still. Her heart hammered in her chest, and she pulled her shoulders back to offset the anxious feeling in her stomach. She was responsible for Bhumi now, a young girl serving a royal in someone else's game.

Aviama wanted to know precisely where she was if trouble arose. But if someone attacked from this position, Aviama's dominant hand would not be available, with Bhumi on her right side. Aviama grimaced, and as they reached the first corner, Aviama passed Bhumi to her left side instead, freeing her right hand for windcalling. Guard Two shifted wordlessly to the lead in response, and Arjun dropped back to cover the gap at Aviama's right side.

In her peripheral vision, Aviama saw Bhumi glance over, but Aviama kept her eyes fixed on the guard's movements. Bhumi took a jogging step to catch up as they rounded the corner and fell into a quick stride as the two of them moved down a service stair and through a series of corridors. Strangely empty corridors.

Bhumi leaned in toward Aviama. "I think you're very impressive. I know it may not be what you want, but—if you don't mind my saying so—I think you'll make an excellent queen."

Aviama's stomach knotted, and her mouth went dry. *Queen.* Her sister Avaya had wanted to be queen, and her ambition nearly destroyed her. Her mother, Sharsi, had been a remarkable queen and was assassinated.

What was so desirable about such an office? Perilous to the body, perilous to the heart. Especially when married to a prince bent on killing. What future was there with such a man? Could he really expect her to partner with him after everything? And without her mother to guide her...

Aviama bit her lip to keep it from quivering, and squeezed Bhumi's hand. If there really was a threat tonight, it would not be her mother's lessons she needed. It would be the lessons of an assassin. The lessons of her dragonlord sister-in-law.

"Don't walk like a victim. Don't look easy to overpower, even if you feel it. Walk like a princess, walk like a warrior."

A clamor came from the hall behind them, and the lead guard picked up his pace. Her heart dropped, and her tongue stuck to the roof of her mouth, but she drew herself up once more, running Semra's words through her mind.

"Show spirit, not deference. Show strength, even if your knees knock while you do it. Steal confidence from the show you put on, and wear it like a crown."

21

The palace shook, and a crash followed as Aviama hurried down the hall toward the south courtyard, Bhumi and the three guards hemming her in on all sides. The sun poured in bright through the windows, her satin navy skirts shining in its rays as they swept the marble floors. Guard Two led the way through double doors to where curated pools sparkled in the courtyard. Lilac trees dotted the garden, and the sight of them grated on her as a few soft petals from a blossom fell to the mirror of the water.

Boom.

A shout went up, and the sound of steel on steel rang out behind them. Aviama's heart lurched to her throat. Arjun grabbed her elbow and pulled her in against himself, shielding her with his large frame from some unseen danger and pushing her down behind a stone bench. Aviama turned just in time to see the archers high on the wall.

But the arrow had already left the string. Aviama threw a hand up and knocked the arrow sideways with a gust, but the arrow course-corrected in the air and turned again toward the guard. Fire ignited in her chest, and she rose from behind the bench, using both hands to throw a wall of wind at the archer.

The archer fell, and Guard Three moved to take hold of Guard Two. "Get underground! Go, go, go!"

Aviama whirled to the guards, but it was too late. The arrow had hit its mark. It protruded from the second guard's neck, the wound bleeding into the ground. His sword hilt rested in his limp, open palm. A lump rose in her throat. *He was protecting me.*

She scanned the wall, but no one was there. The archer had fallen to her blow, but he was a windcaller. He'd catch himself on the other side, even if he didn't have the precision to make it back to the top. And the third guard was still in danger.

Arjun pulled her from behind the bench and hurtled her toward a door in the wall on the far side of the courtyard. Aviama reached back for Bhumi, her fingers grazing the girl's hand, but couldn't reach. "Bhumi!"

Bhumi scrambled to her feet and leaped after Aviama just as another arrow pierced the ground at the place the girl had been a moment before. Aviama threw up a dome of air, and an arrow bounced off its surface. Arjun yanked her hood back into place over her hair and shoved her through the door in the wall. Aviama's hand found Bhumi's wrist and pulled her inside. She dropped the dome as the door shut behind them.

Aviama curled her lip and jabbed a shaking finger into Arjun's chest. "His blood is on your head. No one else dies."

Arjun held up a hand, his face solemn but unconcerned in the torchlight. "Your Highness—"

"I don't want to hear it. No one else dies, or I will respond with greater force against whoever strikes the blow." Aviama turned on her heel and stalked down the dark stone path inside the wall. Unbelievable. Darsh blackmailed a guard, and

Arjun killed him in the palace. Was it all a setup? An excuse to separate Aviama from her typical bodyguards and have time to get her away? How many would die to deliver Aviama to Darsh again—for however short a time?

Arjun cleared his throat. "It's this way."

She stopped and groaned. *Biscuits.* Aviama turned around and marched back to Arjun. She gestured down the path before them. "Lead on, then."

"Are you taking responsibility for a third party?"

Aviama gripped Bhumi's wrist and pulled her closer, glaring at Arjun. "If you're considering killing her for the conversation we've just had, in the name of your allegiance, you should consider what power I will have should I become queen."

Arjun quirked an eyebrow. "For someone who is demanding nobody die, you're making quite a threat."

Aviama lifted her chin. "She stays with me. I'll not be hearing of any accidents that occurred in the time following our separation. She gets to choose whether to stay and keep the secret, or go wherever she wants, free, when the day is done. Agree to my terms, or I march back out that door into the courtyard alone and show the palace how unnecessary it is for me to have a guard."

Bhumi's jaw dropped, and a small smile crossed Arjun's face. "I accept your terms. Keep up. We don't have much time."

Arjun led the way down the path, and Aviama went after him, pulling Bhumi along beside her. Her heart hammered in her chest, and her breathing quickened. She was going to get out of the palace. "Will the promised people be there?"

"You'll see Murin." Arjun pushed a panel in the wall, and the stone beneath their feet shifted, revealing an opening in the floor with a ramp underground. Arjun twisted back toward her, and the corner of his mouth twitched. "Ramta, too."

Heat flooded her cheeks, and an unstoppable warmth spread through her body. Murin and Chenzira. They were safe. And she'd get to see them, as promised.

I won't let you marry him.

Bhumi wanted to see her become queen. So did Darsh. So did everyone. Were Chenzira and the slimy Queen Satya the only people in Radha who didn't want to see her marry Shiva? What would they do to her if she didn't play along? What would they do to Chenzira if he tried to stop it?

Arjun led the way in the dark, and Aviama and Bhumi tripped after him. After running into a dirt wall a second time as the passage curved to one side or the other, Aviama stopped. "We're underground. No one can see us. Grab my hand or light a torch or something. This is ridiculous."

An orange-red glow jumped to life in Arjun's hand, warming the bronze tone of his skin and illuminating the tunnel. Bhumi yelped, and Aviama was grateful she wasn't the only one to startle for a change. The flame roared up high, licking the roof of the tunnel, and then died down again, nestled into Arjun's palm. Arjun grimaced and then smoothed his expression over. He looked up at her. "Happy?"

She pursed her lips. "Yes. You could have done that sooner."

Arjun continued down the passage, and Bhumi settled in beside Aviama once again as they followed after him. Arjun glanced back at them and slowed his brisk pace to a more moderate walk. "I'm glad you're here. We all are. Don't judge us so harshly."

Aviama's chest tightened, and a familiar ache weaseled its way back into her heart. "It's not so much that I judge you. Soldiers follow. It's what they do. But when the time comes to choose *who* to follow, perhaps for the first time, what then?" Her chest hitched, and she swallowed hard. "Why do people keep dying? Why is it so bad that I am sick of seeing mothers and fathers and friends turn into corpses? Does that make me weak?"

"It makes you human. You're optimistic. Maybe a little naïve. Control cannot be achieved without the use of power."

Aviama bristled. How many times would people call her naïve? "And power without control is just as dangerous. One tyrant for another, in a never-ending cycle. I've seen a few tyrants. Have you?"

Frigibar talked about this a lot. King after king, noble after greedy, high-aspiration noble had sought him out in time past. It had led him to setting up his home out of the way in a protected hidden space near Aurin's Spear at the Origin Well-spring, hiding from visitors and driving off any who got too close. Until Semra had come, dragging Aviama with her.

Bhumi leaned into Aviama's side as they walked. "I don't think wanting people to stay alive is weak. I think it's kind."

Something in Aviama's gut flipped upside down. She looked at Bhumi, her sweet face intent and earnest. Ice washed down her spine. "Bhumi. Why aren't you more afraid right now?"

The girl drew back, and Arjun's pace faltered as he walked. The truth knocked the breath from Aviama's body. She pulled her arm free from Bhumi's and clenched her jaw. "We have been attacked, one of the three assigned guards has been wounded or killed, the other is gone, and we are with one remaining guard who is clearly secretly working for a famous criminal mastermind, the radical melderblood leader. The foreign princess you serve apparently knows something about said extremist group, and you're heading there under her meager protection, with no guarantee you will live out the night. If you do return to the palace, and anyone finds out what happened, the crown may question your loyalty."

Aviama shook her head in disbelief, dumbfounded by her own stupidity. Anger boiled her inside out, and she dismissed the swirl of breeze wafting through her fingertips at the sudden emotion. She clenched her hands into fists and stalked rather than walked after Arjun in the passage. "So, I ask again. Why are you not more afraid?"

A beat of silence filled the tunnel, the air thick with tension. The comfort she'd felt at the innocent, peaceful presence of a young girl Aviama felt led to protect and care for evaporated, replaced by a swirling disquiet in every fiber of her being.

Bhumi started to speak, stammered unintelligibly, then tried again. "From what I've heard, Your Highness, your protection is hardly meager. My sister was serving in the arena. She saw you in the contest."

Was there no one left in life who could be kind for the sake of kindness, or care about her as a person outside of some greater cause? Were shadows of friendships too much to ask for, and strained alliances shaded with blackmail the best she could manage?

"Arjun, when did Darsh get a hold of Bhumi? Before she was assigned to me, or after?"

Bhumi touched her arm. Her fingers were cold. "I didn't join the Shadow because of him. I went to him because of you. I wanted to learn from you. To see for myself if what my sister had said was true."

Tears welled in Aviama's eyes, and she turned her face away from Arjun's fire, away from Bhumi's gaze, to stare into the dark, packed dirt on the sides of the tunnel. "And he accepted you because you had a sister serving in the palace, an in for placing you organically in a maidservant position. And because you're a melder. You must be. Admit it."

"I am a crestbreaker, Your Highness." Her voice dropped, and her shoulders slumped forward. "Though not a very good one. I'm not strong. I don't think I have much power at all."

Emptiness swept through Aviama like a wave. A tear spilled down her face. She wiped it away. No one was left to care about the orphan pawn far from home. Everyone who seemed to care had an ulterior motive. Even those who might like her in some sense and think she might be a good queen— even they, whether they realized it or not, sought only their own gain. They wanted some symbol, not a woman. The spearhead for a movement, not a human.

Her heart sank. She was only in the tunnel now, but Arjun was taking her to the belly of the beast. At least she'd see Murin. And Chenzira.

The ache in her chest tripled, and the comfort Murin and Chenzira's names brought to her transformed into hopelessness the longer she thought about it. They'd only put themselves in danger if they tried to help. What could they do against an army like Darsh's?

Arjun moved in silence, Bhumi creeping along beside Aviama in an uncomfortable, awkward sort of indefinite pause where Aviama had dropped the conversation and refused to pick it up again. Presently, the fire in Arjun's hand illuminated a rickety wooden panel door. He quickly extinguished the flame, jiggled the handle, and jammed his shoulder into one of the boards.

The door swung open with a jolt and a creak, and Arjun led the way into a dim stone room filled with large ceramic jars and wooden crates. The smell of thyme and roses filled Aviama's nostrils as she stepped from dirt onto a towel and then onto stone floors. Stacks of towels lined one side of the room; bars of soap and bottles of perfume lined the other. She squinted in the light, wiped her index finger against the corner of her eye to eradicate any residual moisture, and swallowed.

This was it. Time to be the product for Darsh to keep herself alive. Arjun swept his hand toward a solid oak door with brass handles and nodded to Bhumi. She took up a position next to him, each gripping the handle of one of the doors, and it was clear this was a less casual entrance. Aviama straightened, shoulders back, chin up, high head like she'd been taught since childhood before walking into a ballroom or feast hall or other high-profile political event.

And that's what this was. A political event. But with more at stake than ever before, and Aviama not just representing a royal family as she did back home, but as the center of a movement. The hope of a radical group she did not align with.

Everything was backwards.

Arjun and Bhumi pulled the doors open, and Aviama walked out. Stone floors flowed out for several meters, where pillars met a pool of water all the way around. Steps led into the pool from all directions, blue mosaic interrupting the larger slabs of sandstone in a border around the water. Bright sunrays filled the room from a vaulted ceiling surrounded by a series of scalloped archways, accented with various shades of blue. A bathhouse.

And on the opposite side of the pool, fifty people cheered at her arrival, whooping, hollering, and clapping their hands. Someone threw flower petals in the air, and every eye was fixed on Aviama's face. Her throat constricted.

She had no friends. She had fans.

22

Darsh rounded the pool and approached her, bowing with a flourish. He took her hand and kissed it, and Aviama's stomach churned at the polarity between the man who had broken into her room through the lattice window—cool, collected, and mysterious, tossing out orders, dictating to her what the future would hold and what deals would be struck—and the charming smile he had oiled on now.

Aviama allowed the gesture and painted on an answering smile, but did not curtsy in return. It wouldn't be proper. And Darsh was no king, no authority over her. The regality of their would-be queen only seemed to whip the gawking crowd across the pool into an even higher frenzy as she stood before them with their leader.

Darsh straightened and smiled again but kept his voice low as he spoke just for her. "Take down your hood, Princess, and give them a show. Something to remember you by. Something to be inspired by."

She returned a tight-lipped smile and allowed herself a

slight inclination of her head in acknowledgement. "I want to see Murin."

"She's here. Do this first."

Aviama set her jaw and turned to the fifty people across the way, lifting her hood from her hair and dropping it down her back. They dropped into bows and curtsies in response, and someone threw another handful of petals into the air. Aviama raised her hands and caught the petals in the air, pulling the wind and swirling the colorful fragments in a high arc over the pool. Holding one in the center, she sent the rest in a circle around it, then pooled the petals together in a ball before blasting air from the middle, sending them spiraling off in every direction.

The crowd oohed and aahed. Aviama winced. *Dance, monkey. Sing, minstrel. Entertain me.* A powerful urge overcame her then, not to be free from the palace but to be back in it, protected by its walls and finding small escapes to the menagerie, to Makana.

Beside her, Arjun straightened and angled toward her right. Aviama turned to follow his gaze, and her heart leaped for the first time in a long while. Murin.

Darsh offered Murin his arm and led her toward Aviama. Murin dropped into a formal curtsy, but she was grinning from ear to ear. Aviama's chest felt as though it would split open. *One safe person. My safe person.* Someone who cared about her for *her.* Someone who'd known her for years, encouraged her, heard her.

A lump lodged in her throat. *Biscuits, convention be tossed.* Aviama rushed forward and pulled her maidservant into a bear hug to the roar of the watching gaggle. Murin wrapped her arms around her, and they embraced for a long time. Aviama bit back tears and angled away from Darsh. He didn't deserve to see her face in a sensitive moment like this. And she had needed this.

Aviama squeezed Murin harder. "I'd hoped you'd gotten free and gotten home. I thought if you were in Radha, you'd be lost."

Murin pulled back and wiped tears from her face as she looked at Aviama with those familiar, sweet brown eyes. "It wasn't safe to get across the border. I tried to find a way to send word, but nothing was trustworthy, not after you learned the queen was in control of the messengers. So, we thought the best way to help you would be to stay nearby."

We thought. Aviama tilted her head. *We.* Murin glanced at Arjun, and her cheeks flushed with color. "I've been in good hands. Arjun wouldn't let anything happen to me."

Aviama stilled. She looked at Arjun, watching him intently, then shut her eyes and shook her head. This couldn't be happening. She'd lost everyone. Even Murin. Aviama opened her eyes, noted Darsh standing a respectful distance off, and looked deep into Murin's eyes, keeping her voice soft enough that he couldn't hear.

"Murin. Arjun is a good fighter. He can manage an axe and a sword. I don't know him well—he might even be a good man. But his loyalty isn't to you or to me or to freedom. It's to a criminal."

Darsh shifted his weight from his place out of earshot, and Arjun stiffened. He was close enough to hear what she'd said. But Aviama wasn't guaranteed an opportunity to speak to her friend privately. And Arjun's connection with Darsh made him dangerous. Which meant Murin couldn't rely on him to protect her.

Murin was a bargaining chip. An opportunity to keep Aviama in line, as long as she was in play.

Arjun eyed her from one side, dropping his voice to match hers. "I'm not a pawn. I can do both."

Aviama groaned. *He thinks he can serve Darsh and protect Murin. But what about when Darsh makes him choose?* If Arjun chose anyone other than Darsh, it would be the wrong choice. He'd be a liability. And Darsh would take them both out.

Because Darsh was a tyrant.

A spark lit in the back of her mind. Maybe that's why Chenzira had joined Darsh. Maybe he did know. Maybe he knew he had to feign loyalty to Darsh to get protection from the Radhan crown after being exiled after the arena. Maybe he, too, was only trying to survive.

But how could she tell? And to what lengths was he willing to go to secure his own safety? What vote did he cast about the guard they killed? Aviama swept the crowd on the opposite side of the pool. And where was he?

Her heart sank. *Alone, alone. Alone again.* She twisted a ring on her finger. Bhumi shuffled her feet on one side, and Murin and Arjun stood awkwardly waiting for her to do something. Everyone waited.

Do something.

Darsh clapped his hands and lifted his voice. "It's time for a demonstration. A lesson in the finer aspects of melderblood control. You saw the princess manipulate the petals. One inside another. Not raw power, not chaos. She didn't blow the roof off or knock Juni's hat from his head. To be melderblood is to be an artist. And today, we learn from the best. Princess Aviama of Jannemar."

Aviama hardly heard him. Her one friend in the world was trusting a lackey with her protection. A lackey with an allegiance to a dangerous man. Every moment Murin stayed close to Arjun was a moment she remained easy access for Darsh. Easy pickings.

Arjun seemed earnest enough. He might even believe it. But even if he did, and even if he tried to protect Murin, his control was lacking. It had to be. Why else did he wait so long to light the tunnel for their escape?

It was underground. It was dirt. It should have been safe. He was scared.

Darsh cleared his throat. "Your Highness. The floor is yours. Teach."

Teach.

She didn't want to teach them skills. She didn't want to teach them how to kill more people. But neither did she want their lack of control to create more collateral damage than they intended. And neither did she want to eliminate her usefulness to Darsh.

Where was Chenzira? Arjun had said he would be here.

Was he angry at her? She'd said some harsh things about the Shadow when she'd been with them before. Aside from generally stating that they were frivolous murderers as a group, she'd also accused him of being ungrateful, and selfish, and abandoning her. Aviama's mouth went dry. What if she'd driven him away? What if he wasn't coming?

You drive everyone away. You've lost Murin. You've lost Chenzira. You're alone.

But the extremist's command still lingered in the air.

Teach.

Aviama leveled Darsh with a long look, then turned to the people. If she was meant to teach, she would teach. And she would teach whomever she wanted, whatever she wanted.

Her nostrils flared, and an uncomfortable pressure built in her chest. Wind wrapped itself around her fingers, but she kept it in control. Could Arjun keep in control? How did he manage his emotions? What triggered his emotions?

Aviama lifted her voice and turned her attention to the

fifty waiting people. "Which melder powers have natural resources to draw from here?"

The answers came in staggered responses.

"Crestbreaking."

"Windcalling and crestbreaking."

She nodded. "Windcalling and crestbreaking, yes. But the sconces along these pillars tell me firebloods could draw from them in the evening, or that natural fire could be made rather quickly with materials in the bathhouse. Someone lights these. And what melder power is useless here?"

Silence stretched between them, then someone shouted across the distance. "Quakemakers!"

Aviama shook her head. "No. There is no visible natural ground to manipulate here, but a strong quakemaker could manipulate the foundation of the bathhouse. Which is why it is especially important for quakemakers to monitor themselves in here. A lot of people want to kill me, and I imagine you'd disappoint them if I died here in a pile of rubble instead of out there by their sword or hand or whatever other means they have planned." She said it casually, a sharp off-handed comment, but her insides still squirmed. A few of them exchanged glances. *Biscuits.* Why did she so often say what she was thinking?

Aviama grimaced and continued. "You'll eventually need to work together across powers, but right now we're focused on the minutiae. Quakemakers, stand over there. Then windcallers, firebloods, crestbreakers. Windcallers, you can add energy to a strong fire or snuff out a weak one. If you take on a large flame, you had better be twice as strong or have a plan for where you're going with it. Crestbreakers, you can help extinguish a flame. Quakemakers, you could swallow a flame in the ground. But not in here."

The choice of the bathhouse was more and more strategic

the longer she thought about it. The stone would contain a fire, the water was natural, and spills were expected. The tall, strong ceilings gave both playing room and a firm boundary for the wind. The quakemakers were the only ones without a good practice option. Maybe next time they could bring in a couple of crates of dirt and sod for detailed manipulation of their element.

"Your Highness. Why the focus on fire? Do you think fire-bloods are more dangerous than the rest of us?"

Aviama searched the faces for the speaker and found a lean young man leaning on a pillar. She smiled. "No. Only because my first demonstration will deal with fire. I have arranged to work with a volunteer."

Darsh cocked his head in his obnoxious way, and Aviama turned to Arjun. "Shall we?"

The color drained from his face. "Your Highness, I'm working."

Aviama arched an eyebrow. "I certainly hope so. Let's see how high quality your protection is when you're stripped of weapons."

Darsh shook his head. "He cannot lay down his weapons."

She ignored him. "Lay them down."

Arjun cast a sideways look at Darsh, but didn't move.

Aviama glanced at Murin. "The thing about loyalty is there's no room for opposing directions. One is always primary. And when the primary wins, the secondary dies." Aviama shrugged. "Fine. Keep your weapons."

She walked to the edge of the pool. Somewhere in the back of her mind, she wondered how long it would be until she had to be sent back to the palace, where she and her decoy had been separated and hidden from attack. Attack by the group surrounding her now. A group willing to kill.

A flash of Liben's glassy eyes intruded on her mind. How

could they practice without killing each other? How chaotic were their powers?

Aviama thought about the bubble of air she'd thrown up around them to protect Bhumi and the Radhan guard on their way out. The bathhouse was large, and creating and sustaining a bubble significant enough to protect someone several meters off took strength she might not have. Not after she'd been using her powers for the demonstration. Better to keep her people close.

She gestured to Bhumi and Murin. "Behind me, please. No powers. Just stay behind me."

Bhumi glanced at Murin, and Murin gave Aviama a questioning look, but they both obeyed.

Murin touched her on the arm as she passed. "He's good to me. Be good to him."

Aviama's heart wrenched. She nodded, but said nothing. Arjun watched Murin's every movement, then adjusted his position to stand on the first step of the pool, catty-corner to Aviama, the water lapping at the base of his boots. A fireblood standing in water. Not the move she would have expected. But the way he looked at Murin sent a pang to her gut. He looked like he'd rather have Murin behind *him* than behind Aviama.

Aviama raised her hands, pulling air to her palms. She moved her hands in circular motions, balling up the wind into a swirling sphere, and shot it across the space in Arjun's direction.

It was time to see what he could do.

23

S parks flew from Arjun's fingers, but there was no flame. He ducked, and Aviama shook her head. Fat lot of good that would do in protecting someone.

She pulled another ball of air into her palm, this time splitting it into two smaller spheres. Aviama sent the first, and he sidestepped the toss. Flame leaped to his palm in time for the second, but the wind blew through it, snuffing out the fire and hitting him square in the chest. He stumbled backward.

"Offensive, Arjun." Heat gripped her aching chest. *Where is Chenzira? Why has he left me again? And why has Murin attached herself to someone who can't protect her?* Aviama set her jaw and eyed him again, the man who had kept Murin safe when the world was normal, when there were no melder powers at play, getting her out of the palace—but had kept her from returning to Jannemar and embroiled her in twice as much danger outside the palace walls. With criminal radicals. Who used her as a pawn. Aviama lifted her chin and drilled Arjun with a cold stare.

"You can't create a barrier in here—not with stone on the floor and water all around you. You'll need to *send* the fire away from your body. Fire is a force in itself, with wind behind it when you throw. Elements work together. You can meet the wind with fire. Meet it and throw it off course, or strike first."

Arjun grimaced and dropped into a low stance. She'd seen the same positioning from Semra, or Zephan, or any of the guards or soldiers when they sparred in the outer ward back home. It was a good move—it should help brace him against the force of a gale. But he wasn't fighting a swordsman.

Aviama threw a blast of air at him, and fire sprang to both of his hands, stronger this time, taking the edge off her throw. She threw again, and he leaned his shoulder into the force, pushing the fire out, but it never left his hand. Her cheeks flushed hot, and she took a step forward. He wasn't invested. He wasn't fighting. He was defending—weakly.

Why wouldn't he try? Why wouldn't he throw the fire?

Aviama pulled the air from around them, whipping her hair and the fringes of her mantle as she gathered energy for a stronger blow. She drew the wind in towards her chest, pulling her hands into fists, then released the blast as she slung her hands out toward her opponent.

"Fight me!" The anger in her voice surprised her, and the added energy of her emotion built the blast stronger than she'd anticipated. Arjun's eyes widened, and he threw up a wall of fire against the onslaught, but he still fell back onto the stone, tripping over the lip of the pool and skidding across the smooth surface. A cry from behind her reminded Aviama that Murin cared about the man, and she sent a sheet of wind to cushion his skull before it cracked on the unforgiving bath-house floor.

This was everything she didn't want. Learning how chaotic Darsh's melderblood troop was. How insecure in their powers. Teaching melders to kill, to be more deadly, more confident in their abilities, without the principles to discern when and where.

Aviama threw her hands up. "Cowards! You'll set archers on the walls and cheat to find your mark. You'll kill fish in a barrel with no means to fight back, but you won't even spar with one of your own? Is it harder to be dangerous when your opponent has the same weapons you do?"

"Aviama."

Her bitterness faltered at the sound of the sweet voice, and she turned to Murin. It was the first time in all their years together that Murin had addressed her by her first name. Her eyes were glassy, and a lump lodged in Aviama's throat at the sight of her maid's stricken face.

Pleading eyes. Soft heart. Aviama's lips parted as the reality of what had just happened struck her. How long had she been in a position of authority before things went off the rails? Thirty seconds? Was she abusing her role so quickly, superficial as it might be?

How would she have reacted if Frigibar had treated her this way?

He *had* treated her this way at first. He'd had no kitten gloves for Semra, and even choked Aviama out and left her on the floor when teaching Semra. Frigibar had needed Semra to feel. To be afraid. To utilize her emotions and centralize her abilities. But his approach had been coarse.

It wasn't the way to make friends. And once he'd learned Aviama better, he'd been patient and measured. Not warm, exactly, but steady. He'd never berated her. And Aviama had just screamed at a crowd of young hopefuls. Human hopefuls.

This wasn't the way to win their hearts and gain their support or make them want to keep her alive if Darsh ever gave the order for them to kill her. She had to be better than this. Not just for herself, but for them. They had no concept of melder powers. Not really.

How terrifying must their awakenings have been?

Aviama swallowed, learning from the compassion and pain in Murin's face, leaning on her empathy and kindness. *This is the teacher I will be, for however short a time. Not the tyrant.*

She turned back to Arjun. He picked himself up off the ground and faced her again, his shoulders sagged, his eyes simultaneously hurt and hard. The watching crowd was still, hardly a breath heard in the vaulted space.

Darsh stepped forward, his hands behind his back, eyes sharp from their exchange. "I think our guard does not want to risk harm to our future queen, Your Highness. Perhaps this approach could use some finesse."

Aviama took a breath. She spun the rings on her fingers and eyed Arjun. He glanced at Murin twice as she watched. Yes, he was holding back to protect someone. And he didn't want to risk harm. But it wasn't about her. Because Aviama had been wrong, and Murin was right. Arjun's loyalty was to both Murin and to Darsh, but between the two, Murin might win. And from the expression on his face, Darsh already knew it.

Aviama nodded. "You're right. We need to simulate a protection scenario, like we had today when Arjun got me safely away from the palace. Thank you, by the way, Arjun. I'm sorry. I shouldn't have yelled at you. I'm afraid I'm rather stretched thin these days. Forgive me."

Arjun blinked back at her. Royals didn't apologize. But this one would, because not apologizing had clearly not done any favors to the haughty nobles and royals she'd known before. So, she waited for a response until the silence stretched uncomfortably long.

At last, Arjun nodded in acknowledgement. "Of course, Your Highness."

Aviama nodded, heart hammering in her chest. Time to change the game. "I think you're right, Darsh. We need a new test. Something with more urgency and opportunity to practice. Something immediate, but less focused on me."

She turned to Murin and Bhumi. "Bhumi, stand near Darsh, please." She dipped her head and walked to stand behind Darsh. Bhumi was in an important position as her maidservant and Darsh's informant in the palace. He would protect her.

Aviama gestured to Murin. "Go stand behind Arjun, please."

Murin walked forward, then hesitated as she rounded the corner of the pool toward Arjun. Aviama gave her an encouraging nod. "It'll be okay."

She continued to Arjun, and the tension in his shoulders seemed to ease as she approached. Murin said something to him as she passed, much like she had to Aviama as she'd come to stand behind her at the beginning, but it was too quiet for her to make out.

Murin took up her place behind Arjun and called back to Aviama. "If Arjun protects me, who will protect you? If things go sideways, I mean."

A deep voice cut through the air from behind her like steel through butter. "I'll protect her."

Aviama jumped and spun. Her stomach flopped, and she hoped no one noticed the heat that flew to her cheeks. Chenzira sauntered into the bathhouse as if he owned the place, lifting a hand to acknowledge people he knew in the crowd of melders to the side. Today, he wore the fine tunic of a nobleman, Radhan from the embroidery at the neck to the loose trousers falling to his leather footwear.

A prince the day she met him, a commoner yesterday, a nobleman today—Aviama could hardly keep track. But his ruddy, muscular arms, the cut of his jaw, the hand running through his trimmed black beard—the confident way he moved, not a slithering grace like Shiva had, but a storming strength, like a zegrath contained by a string—these she recognized with ease.

His searing gaze turned from the melder audience to Aviama. Her breath caught as he took her in, holding her there by some invisible force as he waltzed up beside her at the edge of the bathhouse pool.

Darsh laughed. "Ramta, you're a strong melderblood, but quakemakers will kill us all in here."

Chenzira's mouth curved into a thin smile as he pulled a battle-axe from a strap across his back. "I don't need powers to fight."

Aviama turned toward him, but when he looked at her again, adjusting his grip on an axe half her size, her mouth seemed to forget how to form words. He arched an eyebrow, and she swallowed. "The demonstration is for melder powers."

"Then let's hope I do as well as that prince you fought beside in the arena. The one without powers."

Right, that one. Without powers...

The fact that he'd survived the arena without revealing himself was a feat all of its own. Aviama knew she should be thinking about the demonstration, about what she wanted to learn about Arjun, and how to make that happen. But her thoughts were taken up by Chenzira.

He'd come. Had he always planned to come and been late? Why was he a noble today and a commoner last night? What did the radicals think of that? Maybe she *had* angered him, and he'd planned on leaving her, but changed his mind. What would have changed his mind?

Darsh crossed his arms. "I would hate for our host to renege on his agreement to let us use the establishment. We can't afford to damage it."

Chenzira whirled the axe in his hands and grinned. "Nonsense. The owner of the establishment is a reasonable fellow. I'm sure he'll accept mild damage—for a price."

Darsh's lips flattened. "For a price. Naturally."

Aviama glanced between them, but when she tilted her head at Chenzira, he only shook his head. *Never mind. Go on.*

Okay, fine. Aviama returned her focus to Arjun, Murin standing just beyond him. Chenzira stepped forward between Arjun and Aviama. Aviama squared her shoulders and lifted her hands. "Don't let me take Murin. If I take her, she comes with me today."

Arjun leaned into his combat stance, glancing once behind him to confirm Murin's placement before lifting his own hands toward Aviama. This time, flame leaped to his palms from the start, waiting for her to make a move. Aviama threw a ball of air over Chenzira's head and down on Arjun; he threw his hands upward, and the fire leaped to meet it, dispelling the air blast in a towering fire.

"*Yes!*" Aviama clapped her hands. Arjun stared above him in surprise, and a murmur rippled through the observers. Aviama drew more air toward her chest, whirling them into another ball. "Again!" She threw another blast, and again Arjun's fire met the air, though not as high as the first time.

Aviama tossed a light gust at Murin, and she stumbled backward with a soft cry. Aviama caught her with a wave of wind on the far side, but all Arjun saw was his ward falling. He whirled to Aviama, ran forward three steps, and rained down fire in a great torrent.

But Aviama's hands were still on the wind around Murin, stabilizing her from the fall. Heat washed over her in a blinding wave, knocking her to the ground. Pain rocked her body as she hit the stone, but the fire disappeared the moment her cheek connected with the cold floor.

24

Aviama squinted in the light, her eyes readjusting from the blaze of the fire. Her pulse pounded in her head, combining with the ringing in her ears. Her chest hurt. Searing pain shot up her left elbow. But there, three paces before her, Chenzira held two massive battleaxes crossed in front of his chest, keeping Arjun's stream of fire at bay.

Chenzira leaned into the blast, his feet slipping backward along the slick floors. His arms bulged with exertion, and the back of one heel bumped into Aviama's arm as she lay on the marble behind him. Aviama groaned and struggled to sit, but her head swam. Chenzira crouched, protecting her with his body as the fire still rained down against the metal of his axes.

"Control it! Pull it into yourself!"

Arjun shook his head. "I can't! I can't stop it!"

Aviama turned her head toward Darsh. He gave a signal, and four melders branched off from the sidelines.

Chenzira dropped his voice low and turned his head so Aviama could hear him. "Pull yourself up. Use me if you have to." He turned back to Arjun and called out to him. "The fire is yours. It's from you. Direct your palms to the water, and think of the calm you want."

Aviama reached up to Chenzira's shoulder and gripped it, pulling herself up to lean against his back as dizziness worked its way through her and her head cleared. She moved toward one side, but Chenzira shoved her back behind him with one elbow, never loosening his grip on the axes.

"Stay where you are. Work from there."

Aviama raised an eyebrow at the growl in his voice, but he was too focused to see it. The protective edge both surprised her and somehow warmed her through. *Sand and sea...*

She acquiesced, keeping behind him, but lifting her hands and reaching around Chenzira so that her arms touched his as he strained against the fire, and she called the wind to their aid. Air swirled at her fingertips, and she leaned into Chenzira's back as she thrust the energy of the wind out across the space toward Arjun's hands. Gently, gently—a firm, unrelenting, pressing in, but building in strength—she pushed his hands toward the pool. When his hands did not move, she shifted her attention to his feet. Arjun slipped, and his surprise interrupted the fury of his fire, turning his body and rocketing a stream of flame over their heads and sideways until it shot into the pool. Sparks clung to his hands, but the fire died out, steaming bubbles dissipating along the surface of the water where Arjun's fire had been.

Murin stared at the pool, at Arjun, and then at Aviama from behind her guard—eyes wide, lips parted. She was breathing hard, but seemed okay. Arjun was heaving, but his shoulders sagged forward, relieved. Chenzira's body was warm against Aviama's chest, and their closeness finally registered. Chenzira straightened and turned to look at her, and she pulled away from him, heat flooding her cheeks once again.

Darsh grinned and broke out in a clap. The rest joined in

until the room buzzed with excitement. He gave a signal, and the four melders he'd called out from the sidelines formed a line four paces off along the pool's edge. Aviama's mouth went dry. She dug her elbow into Chenzira's side and jerked her chin toward them, and he stiffened beside her.

The Shadow's leader rubbed his hands together. "An excellent start to a training day! Why stop there? Let's give a few more the chance to practice." He gave another signal, and the man who'd leaned against the column questioning her before flipped his palm up, sending a tower of water shooting toward the skylight from the pool. A bony woman in rags swirled air around herself, the gust of her summoning so strong and haphazard she knocked over the fireblood man on the other side of her. He fell into the water, the flame in his hand extinguishing with a hiss. A second woman summoned the force of the air and hauled her fallen friend, spitting and sputtering, back up onto the stone.

Darsh lifted his voice above the wind. "Crestbreaker, target Ramta and Her Highness's wind, not Her Highness herself. We can't send her back to the palace looking like a drowned rat. All of you—don't be afraid to push your limits, but stop your colleagues if they get out of control. See what it's like taking on one of your own—someone with experience and training."

Aviama winced. Giving wild extremist melderbloods near carte blanche to take her on however they wanted did not sound like a good idea. Even with Darsh supposedly invested in her survival, how could he manage the sort of catastrophic accidents this type of practice could bring?

Wind whipped through the bathhouse chamber, picking up the edges of Aviama's charred skirt hem as the women's windcalling powers expanded and contracted in pulsing, unsteady ebbs and flows. The tower of water bent, hovered, and then drove down toward Chenzira's head. Aviama squealed and threw up her hands, covering them both in a dome of air. The strength of the water knocked into her air shield, raining down around the dome like a glass ball and shoving her backward. Her shield burst, and the water splattered around them in a circular formation as she staggered backward. Chenzira caught her elbow and set her on her feet.

"I can't help here," he whispered in her ear. "I'd rip the foundations apart. But I'll try to draw their attention or block the fireblood like I did with Arjun."

Aviama threw up a blast of air to meet the windcallers' blows. The bony woman gritted her teeth. Aviama shook her head. "They're drunk on their newfound power, but they're chaotic. They don't know what they're doing. We can get close, and you can take them out one at a time."

Chenzira nodded. "Lead the way."

Aviama glanced back at Arjun only once to confirm he'd moved back off to the sidelines. Adrenaline flooded her blood as she formed a new bubble around Chenzira and herself. He walked in front, and she kept her arm touching his, so she knew his every movement. The fireblood had picked himself up off the floor and was trying to light a flame in his sopping wet hand. The pair of windcallers eyed Aviama and Chenzira, the two of them drawing near each other to combine their powers. And the crestbreaker slowly stepped into the edge of the water.

A smart move. The closer a melder was to a natural source of its element, the easier it was to manipulate it.

The three melders remaining on the side of the pool backed slowly away from Aviama and Chenzira's advance. Sparks flew from the fireblood's hands, but the fear in his eyes was signal enough of his struggle to produce a flame. Aviama pushed out the edges of the bubble, and Chenzira moved forward with her as one.

The windcallers threw blast upon blast at Aviama's dome, and she felt each blow as it struck and then wafted around the edges of the boundary, dissipating up into the vaulted ceiling of the bathhouse. The crestbreaker's mouth twitched into a pleased smile, and Aviama scanned his hands. Long fingers of water climbed up his body like vines and wrapped around his arms. Surprising control. Less of a one-trick pony than the others, who did nothing but blast after blast of air or fire. He'd be the one to watch.

Tssssss.

Fire rippled across the barrier, and the bubble wavered. Aviama snapped her attention back to the fireblood, but the windcallers were already working together to target the weak area. A punch of air knocked through the bubble. Aviama fell backward, her heart lurching to her throat as she threw her hand down to herself on a cushion of air before she hit the sandstone floor.

A second gust sent Chenzira skidding in the opposite direction, and her stomach dropped. *Biscuits*, they'd done it. They'd separated them. Chenzira lowered his center and leaned into the gust to keep himself upright. Something cold and clammy wrapped around Aviama's ankle. She looked down just in time to see a watery vine over her foot before she was yanked from her feet.

Aviama hit the floor with a thud, the wind knocked from her body as the pressure of the fall reverberated through her bones. Chenzira spun to look at her. The windcallers raised their hands toward him from behind his back.

Aviama gasped for air, her foot swallowed in the water of the pool. She opened her mouth to call out, but no breath came. She gasped again, and sweet, sweet air flooded her lungs just in time to shout a command. "Go!"

Aviama threw a shield up, blocking the windcallers' onslaught a handsbreadth from Chenzira's nose and setting a bubble over him as he ran forward to take them out. He swung the axe with a flourish and knocked the first windcaller to the floor with the butt of his weapon, blocking the fireblood's first meager flame throw with his second axe.

He slipped one of his axes back into place across his back and brought his elbow round hard across the second windcaller's chin, hooking her ankle for good measure and sending her crashing to the ground. He turned to the fireblood, and Aviama rolled away from the edge of the pool, pooling the air in her hands and slinging a gale through the bathhouse like a sword splitting satin. The blow plunged the crestbreaker into the pool with a mighty splash and knocked the windcallers sideways before they'd found their footing. Aviama stopped it just short of Chenzira, as he twirled the fireblood into a headlock.

Aviama rolled once more away from the pool, eager to be further from the surface of the water, and gathered her feet under her. She straightened, spreading her hands and nodding at Chenzira. Chenzira released the fireblood and stepped back. A thrill ran through her. The teamwork felt good. Natural. Like they'd been working together for years.

Her heart still hammered, and the melders stood gaping at her, ready for Princess Aviama to take charge of the room once again. She'd been presented as their instructor, after all. Chenzira glanced sideways at her, and she pressed her lips together to suppress a grin. Had she enjoyed this?

Chenzira's mouth quirked up at the corner, and she spun a ring on her finger. He'd enjoyed it too.

Darsh cleared his throat. "Nice work today, everyone. I

enjoyed seeing you work in groups, and I'm grateful you had the opportunity to see what kind of loss a lack of training can cost us. She wasn't even at her strongest today. This is child's play. We *have* to be the best." He turned to Aviama and gestured at the waiting melderbloods. "Your Highness. We run short on time. Any feedback for your students? Things to work on before next time?"

Aviama nodded and clasped her hands to stop them from fidgeting. "Stop trying to be grand and impressive. Can you make a tower of water or a windstorm? Good for you. Didn't we all, at our awakenings? Congratulations." She scanned the group before her, seeing a range of bedraggled discouragement, excitement, and skepticism. "You can threaten people's lives and homes and businesses, even without trying to. But can you send a handful of earth through a hole in a wagon? Can you pull water out of one glass and drop it into another one without spilling?"

Darsh tapped a finger along his chin thoughtfully. "Or unlock a door with the wind."

Aviama grimaced. She wasn't hoping to highlight overly useful ways to use melder powers, but he already knew about that one. "Correct. To aim higher, you must first aim lower."

One of the windcallers crossed her arms. "That makes no sense."

Arjun rolled his eyes. "It makes complete sense to anyone who knows a lick about combat."

The windcaller opened her mouth, but Darsh had clearly heard this sort of scuffle before. He held up his hand. "We don't have time. Our diversion has lasted long enough, and we are grateful for the princess's willingness to risk her life again to come to us. Practice, and we'll get her back again soon."

Aviama set her jaw. *Because I'm just so sacrificial, so willing to risk my life. No worries. Because I obviously had a choice in the matter.*

The crestbreaker smirked and sauntered off to rejoin the group. Murin walked back over with Arjun, and Aviama gave her another hug.

"It's good to see you. I'm glad you're safe." Aviama dropped her voice to a whisper and grinned. "I might even be glad of the person keeping you that way."

Murin blushed and smiled. "I know we want to see you safe too. It'll happen. And we'll find a way to get word home to Jannemar. As soon as we can."

Aviama nodded, a lump rising in her throat. The familiar ache returned to her chest, but she swallowed hard and pursed her lips against the emotion threatening to take her over again.

Chenzira and Darsh spoke for a moment, Bhumi standing awkwardly to one side, before all three of them approached a moment later. Darsh clapped his hands together. "Bhumi and Arjun will take you back now. There is a new tunnel opening that you should be able to use in the future to get out of the palace and here to the bathhouse. We'll send word when the time is right."

Biscuits, she'd almost forgotten Bhumi existed. How could she forget? One handmaid in the palace for every controlling interest in her life.

"Don't worry about your clothes. The damage only adds to our story."

Aviama glanced down in surprise at Arjun's words. Her hem was tattered where the fire had frayed its edges, and her shoe still looked stained where the crestbreaker's water had swallowed it.

Arjun offered what he may have meant to be an encouraging smile. "We were attacked by radicals. That's the story, and it's true. I hid you and Bhumi in the wall until it was safe to come out. The surviving guards can collaborate our story."

Darsh arched an eyebrow. "Surviving guards?"

Bhumi nodded fervently. "Oh, yes. Her Highness was most valiant. And strategic, showing her strength to Radha and providing more witnesses to the attack." The girl shot an adoring glance at Aviama, and Aviama wondered how much of it was put on. "She is so wise."

Aviama winced. In her peripheral vision, she saw Chenzira catch the expression, and from the look on his face, so did Darsh. His features darkened, but Chenzira whirled the remaining axe in his hands in a flourish and strapped it back into place with its twin before the leader could say a word.

"Right, well, no time to waste. I'll see to the tunnel and wait to leave until everyone is clear of the bathhouse. Do keep it in good condition for me."

Darsh dipped his head, and Chenzira swept his hand toward the exit. Arjun gave Murin a quick hug and led the way with Bhumi. Aviama trailed them, and Chenzira fell in step with her as they walked through the doors into the back room of soaps and perfumes and back into the dirt passage through which they'd come. Arjun mustered up enough fire to light the way and set off without looking back.

Aviama's throat closed, and a queasy feeling smothered her at Chenzira's closeness in the dimness of Arjun's flickering red-orange light ahead. They'd worked well together for the demonstration, almost like they had in the arena those weeks ago. Why was he late to the bathhouse? Why was he coming with her now, as she was led once again back to the belly of the beast? The one he'd sworn not to let her marry...

The minutes stretched on as the soft plodding of feet on dirt passed the time, each step bringing her closer to the House of the Blessing Sun—and the prison of the cursed room where she would inevitably toss, turn, and dream night-mares. At last, Aviama could take it no more. Chenzira was here beside her, and if she got to the palace without asking, she'd think of nothing else for the next week. So she steeled herself and spoke the words.

"When did you get to the bathhouse? What did you see?"

"You were yelling at Arjun and accusing all the melders of being bloodthirsty horrors." Bitterness dripped from his voice, and the warmth of their walk, the camaraderie of their work together, vanished like smoke. Her heart crashed into her toes, and for a moment, Aviama could hardly breathe.

She was alone again.

Forever.

25

Chenzira's voice was rough, the way it had been when he'd demanded Aviama stay behind him during the demonstration. "You need the melders. You'll die without them."

She could admit she'd been too harsh with Arjun. Things had gotten out of hand. But for him to criticize her, when he himself was who knows where, doing who knows what, and waltzing in just in time to see what she did wrong? Aviama lifted her chin, resentment hardening in her heart. "Just because you've sold yourself to Darsh doesn't mean I have to."

Chenzira groaned. "Sand and sea, I'm getting sick of your assumptions."

"I'm getting sick of you judging me."

"*Me* judging *you*? Are you joking?"

Aviama bristled. "You've been judgy ever since you thought I was lost in the palace when we first spoke."

He scoffed. "You *were* lost. You were just too proud to say it."

She pursed her lips. Arguing with someone was so much

more annoying when they were right. And he wasn't wrong now either. She *did* need the melders. They were her only defense against marrying Shiva, and if they cared to keep her alive, their hesitation to carry out an order to kill her would be her only leverage against Darsh if things got ugly.

Aviama racked her brain for what to say next, something to ease the tension, but Chenzira spoke first.

"Do you really think so lowly of people who have had to kill? You talk about it all the time. You mentioned it at the bathhouse and ranted about it at the last Shadow meet. But the brother you think so highly of is a warrior. Surely, he's killed before. And you seem to want to be like Semra, but she's killed too. Did you ever see her in action?"

Her chest tightened and her mouth went dry. Aviama had heard of Semra's expertise long before she'd seen it for herself. The assassin who'd graduated the secret program in the mountain at the top of her class and broken into the castle. Aviama had even gotten to help her sneak in once. It was how they'd first met.

Tales of Semra floated through the castle in whispers like wildfire, and the closer she got to Zephan, the more she was discussed. She'd saved them. Without her, Jannemar would have been lost. But it wasn't until Semra was escaping the castle with Aviama, protecting her from an old enemy, that she'd seen what Semra could do first hand.

A queasy feeling worked its way through her stomach, remembering. Even then, Aviama had asked Semra if the men who came after them had to die. Semra had assured her they did. She had no other choice. And Aviama trusted Semra. But even Semra was more comfortable with death than Aviama would have liked.

Maybe Semra had been exposed to it so much in her young life, trained to kill, sent on missions to murder, that she'd been desensitized to it. Or maybe Aviama was just weak, unable to stomach what she'd seen at her awakening. But Liben wasn't the first dead body Aviama had seen. Her own parents, for one, but there had been others. And hadn't Semra told her of the nightmares she'd suffered for so long? Perhaps the two of them were more alike than Aviama had thought.

Chenzira made a good point. Zephan was a man of war and had killed on the battlefield. So had Semra, as a necessary action where hordes of people were going to die if she didn't do what she did. Or was Semra overzealous with the sword? Was it really necessary, or was it the only way she knew?

"Aviama?"

Aviama snapped her head up to see Chenzira peering down at her as they walked, a troubled expression flickering across his face. What had she looked like as her memories carried her off back home to Jannemar? She swallowed. "I have seen it." She didn't like it. But she saw it.

The edge of Chenzira's demeanor seemed to shift, and he softened. "I'm sorry."

Ugh. Pity. It was the last thing she wanted, least of all from him. She grimaced, returning her attention to the dirt tunnel and the soft, plodding footsteps of Arjun and Bhumi ten paces ahead. She wondered briefly how much of their conversation the two of them could hear. Probably all of it. Aviama spoke quietly.

"I saw my mother bleed out on our ballroom floor with a knife in her chest. I saw a detached arm flying through the smoke of the explosion that killed my father. When I finally stopped getting shuffled off and stowed in some room or other to weather out the fighting, it was with Semra—she fought our way out of Shamaran Castle when the older dragonlord came.

"Semra without powers is still the most lethal person in a

room. Without mine, I'm nothing. Useless. With my combat skills, I'd die in two seconds flat. I'd never seen so much death up close. And then my awakening came, and the boy I saw dead there—the boy—"

Aviama shut her eyes and shook her head, but the image of Liben's glassy eyes still shoved its way to the center of her mind. "It was me. I did it. I killed him. Being a melder makes me powerful, but it also makes me dangerous. Chaotic melder power without control is just another form of reckless killing. And I'm tired. I'm tired of seeing corpses. I'm tired of seeing people die." She wiped a tear from her cheek and rotated a ring on her finger. "I didn't mean to be so accusing. I don't want you to think I—to think badly of me. But maybe it's true. Maybe I deserve it."

Chenzira tugged lightly on her elbow to guide her around a dark corner. His touch was gentle, and a knot formed in her stomach. The bend straightened, and he released her. "That's not what I meant. I didn't say you were bad. It's just that you can't accuse people and lose all hope of their help."

Of all the bridges she could burn, the thought of losing Chenzira sent a cold shiver of fear through her bones. Aviama put her hand on his arm, then snatched it back. "The power got to me. The authority of the position, of the room. Everyone listened to me. Even if what I had said was terrible, they would have listened. I need people to stop me when I'm making a mistake." She paused. *Just say it. Don't be proud.* Aviama took a deep breath and let it out in a gush. "You were right. I'm sorry."

Chenzira blinked back at her. The tunnel narrowed, and he bumped his head on a drop in the ceiling as he walked. Aviama laughed, and the sound bounced off the walls of the passage. Chenzira gave a grunt and rubbed the spot on his head, but when he glanced over at her, a twinkle lit his eye.

Warmth flooded her chest at the sight of it, and the next few minutes passed in ease. Arjun's firelight flickering through the passage felt more like a comforting glow than the eerie, sallow dread Aviama had felt before. Bhumi looked once over her shoulder at Aviama, but Arjun smacked her arm with the back of his hand, and she quickly turned around again, hurrying to keep up with his long strides.

Chenzira kept quiet, and though Aviama snuck glances over at him twice, she couldn't make heads or tails of his expression. She twisted her rings and bit her lip and told herself not to say anything, but it was probably only two minutes of the calm before anxiety won out and she turned to him once more. "Do you hate me?"

His step faltered, and he frowned. "Why would I hate you?"

Aviama shrugged, but her insides squirmed in a thousand directions. "I always say the wrong thing. I say things I shouldn't say. I used to think I was decent in diplomatic situations, but this—Radha has been different. And now I've yelled at people I shouldn't yell at, twice in as many days. Not to mention making the deal with Shiva. The one you said I was an idiot for making."

"Right. Well, it was a stupid thing to do."

Aviama's heart sunk to her toes, and she scuffed her feet along the dirt floor of the tunnel. Tears welled in her eyes; stupid, wet traitor tears that betrayed her stupid, obnoxious emotions, and she blinked them back hard until they rimmed her lashes but did not fall. A touch on her hand startled her, and she jumped.

Chenzira chuckled under his breath, then slipped his hand into hers, his large hand warm around her slender fingers. A tingle shot up her arm. "Stop fidgeting. I'm not mad." He hesitated. "I was, at first. I was angry. But I'm not sure what I expected you to do, exactly. And it's not like you would have killed me. You seem averse to killing a fly. But I wouldn't have killed you either. So, you're right. They would have killed us both. Yet somehow, because of you, we're both alive today."

Biscuits, the tears. Aviama snuck her free hand up to her face and turned away to the dark side of the tunnel to wipe them from her face.

After a moment of walking in silence, Chenzira stopped. Their linked hands halted Aviama beside him, and she bit her lip. She had to be the most ridiculous, dramatic woman he'd ever laid eyes on. The girl with nightmares that sent screams through the halls. The girl that couldn't kill, even when it might be the best option. The girl who blubbered at the drop of a hat.

But he didn't arch an eyebrow at her, or tell her to pull herself together, to be the princess she was. He pulled her into his arms and tucked her head against his chest, under his chin. And she went to him, a hitch in her own chest, fresh tears hot on her cheek.

"It's okay to cry. I wish I could do it as freely as you do. You're so much better at saying what's inside you than I am. I'm sorry you're in the position you are."

Chenzira's words fell like rain on desert sands, and if they hadn't been so tender, perhaps she could have dismissed them enough to muddle through without letting the dam break. As it was, to be so isolated and alone but to find someone to hold her in her pain, the fragile wall holding back the beast broke. She fell into him, her shoulders racked with silent sobs.

How had it come to this? She was only supposed to be in Radha for a few weeks, and then go home. With information to help protect Jannemar. Instead, she'd put Jannemar in even more danger, with no way to warn them, and had become embroiled in a double-blackmail scheme between a kingdom seeking to eradicate melders and destroy her home, and a radical extremist who could take the world by storm with his revenge campaign—with her as the face of his bloody endeavors.

Ahead of them, Arjun and Bhumi's footsteps stopped. Tears spent, Aviama stirred in Chenzira's arms, and they tightened reflexively around her. "I made you a promise the last time I saw you. But I have to know. You've been in the palace with him all this time. Could it be...are you sure you don't want to go through with it?"

She pulled back and glared at him. "Are you kidding?"

Chenzira sniffed, then winced. "He's not bad to look at. Charming, whatever. I see what women see in him."

Aviama's jaw dropped. How could he think she wanted to marry Shiva? "They see a shell. He's got a nice face, but the homicidal manipulative bit does put a damper on things."

"You didn't think he was so bad when you first met him. I saw how you looked at him."

"I didn't know him before. There are parts of him that are...I mean, he's human. He has moments that are kind. But I can't trust it to be real. And if I step a toe out of line, if something happens to tarnish the public persona they're spinning for the country...he is his mother's son. I'm not sure the limit exists on what he might do."

Chenzira tilted his head, and the movement caught her off guard. She reeled back, then resettled. Shiva was the one who normally cocked his head at her. But this was Chenzira, and his eyes were filled with something new. Something earnest, something genuine. He stared down at the ground, scuffing the dirt with his toe. "I thought...you looked...so close. In the processional. I wondered if maybe you'd changed your mind."

The feeling of Shiva's arms around her, the threats in her

ear as he claimed kisses for the crowd, made her stomach churn. Aviama placed a hand on his arm, calling his gaze back to her face. "Your promise is what has kept me going."

He scanned her face, then looked down at her hand.

Her breathing quickened. She dropped her hand. "I won't blame you if you can't do it. I'm not sure how you could. But you want to, and for today, that is enough."

Arjun cleared his throat. "We've got to get back. The door to the wall is just around this bend."

Chenzira coughed and folded his arms, then ran a hand through his trimmed beard before setting off again down the tunnel. Bhumi and Arjun avoided eye contact with them, but doubled the pace as they rounded the final bend. Aviama tried to stave off the weirdness in the air, but it was palpable. And the silence wasn't helping.

Biscuits. Did she have to fill every silence? But her mouth was already moving. "Is Darsh going to be mad you came with me all the way to the palace?"

Chenzira shrugged. "Don't care."

Arjun put his hand on a panel somewhere along the wall, and Chenzira dropped his voice low again, leaning in to whisper in her ear. "Don't change your mind. Whatever it is I do, it won't be able to be stopped halfway through."

A chill ran down her spine, the comfort of his desire to help and the fear of what exactly that help might entail striking a swirling contrast in her mind. "Don't do anything stupid."

He grinned. "That's your job. But me? Death-defying feats are my specialty."

She pursed her lips and rolled her eyes, but she couldn't suppress a smile.

Arjun waited until they stood right at the panel next to

him and Bhumi. He looked intently at Aviama. "I don't mean to be heartless, but let your tears die here. In there"—he jerked his head toward the other side of the wall—"don't let them see you cry. Be the royal. And as you step into your crown, we will follow you."

26

"Where is she? *Where is she?*"

Aviama adjusted the hood of her mantle and hurried across the marble floor, the swish of her skirts mixing with Arjun's heavy footsteps and Bhumi's feather-light patter. They'd exited the tunnel and wound through the wall and back to the main palace, making a brief stop in a secluded room so as to be seen coming out of it moments later, when Arjun heard soldiers patrolling outside.

"Send the decoy out to the courtyard. Draw the radicals and slaughter any you see. We need to know if they're still out there or if they found their prize."

Aviama's stomach turned. Durga needed to stay as far away from the Shadow as possible. They weren't out there anymore, probably, but was Shiva really so willing to kill a servant of his family?

Of course he was. Besides, Durga was his mother's informant. If the Shadow killed her, it could save Shiva the trouble.

Still, she jogged to the archway leading out into the pakshi courtyard and slowed just in time to make a more regal entrance. "Here! I'm here."

Prince Shiva spun at the sound of her voice, leaving the dozen soldiers behind as he strode to meet her and lifted her cold hands to kiss her fingers. "I was so worried. We found two of the guards assigned to your detail. Are you hurt?"

She shook her head. "I was in good hands."

Shiva glanced at Arjun and gave a nod. "You have my thanks. Jarun, is it?"

"Arjun, Your Highness."

"Yes, yes. Arjan. Many thanks. One of the men is in critical condition in the infirmary, and the other succumbed to his injuries three hours ago." Shiva looked her up and down, then paused at the hem of her dress. "You're hurt." He looked at Arjun again, this time with a cutting glare.

"I'm not. They had a fireblood, and I fell, but I'm fine. I defended myself, and I was in good hands. Bhumi was brave as well. She could have died in the attack, but managed to get out."

Shiva turned his attention to Bhumi, and she dropped into a deep curtsy. "Her Highness saved me. She created a barrier that stopped arrows. She was amazing, Your Highness."

Aviama frowned. She wished she could jab her elbow into Bhumi's ribs. *Stop giving him ideas on how to militarize melders.*

The prince's gaze fell on Aviama's face again, and his eyes were steel even as his lips twisted into a smile. "Impervious to arrows? How lucky a man am I! I'm glad to hear it. Let's get you to your chambers, dearest. You've been through quite the ordeal."

Locked up again, so soon. With the three maidservant informants of the three parties who cared nothing for her. Aviama shifted her weight. "I actually thought I'd go to the library or the terrace. Just to get out for a while. I'm antsy."

"If you're jittery, maybe you're in shock. Maybe you do have injuries that need to be assessed."

"I'm not in shock."

Shiva gave her a terse smile and a patronizing pat on the arm. "You'll be assessed, nonetheless. We need you healthy. I'll send the healer to your room."

Aviama set her jaw. "I'm fine."

"So you've said. Enough, Lilac. The healer will be there within the hour, or they'll no longer be employed by the crown. Jarun, see to it she makes it safely to her chambers, and have a report to your captain by sundown."

Arjun bowed, but said nothing. Bhumi clasped her hands demurely in front of her. And Aviama seethed.

Shiva turned away, snapped his fingers at the guards, and half a dozen of them broke off to escort her back to her quarters under Arjun's command. He barked orders to the rest to recall the order for Durga to be sent out to the courtyard and then swept out of sight beyond the pillars, leaving Aviama to her isolation once again.

———

THE HEALER CAME AND WENT, noting the various bruises Aviama had accumulated over the past couple of days, but ultimately determining she did not require the infirmary. Aviama asked if he also knew that the sky was blue and the grass was green, to which the healer responded that the sunset had actually been quite red that evening.

When the useless man was gone, Aviama dismissed Bhumi to rest and scoured her room for some place to form a secret cubbyhole in which to stow tools or weapons if she could find them—rope, for example, or a throwing knife. But the tiled floor was attached securely, the wardrobe boards were all tight and any damage would be obvious, and the latticework of the window was visible from the courtyard below. Ultimately, she gave up the search and flopped onto the sofa to think.

Rivulets of air currents wafted through her fingers, and she spun them around the legs of the low table in front of her until it lifted on one end. A knock came at the door, and she released it with a thunk just before her three women filed in. Durga still wore the decoy dress and mantle from Aviama's wardrobe, paired with an expression that crossed relief and annoyance. Rings under her eyes betrayed a haggard exhaustion, and from the slump in Sai's shoulders, Durga wasn't the only one. Water stains rippled across both their garments, with a splash of red dried across Sai's arm.

Aviama half-fell over the arm of the sofa in her haste to get up. "What happened?"

Durga unclasped her mantle and tossed it over the vanity chair, revealing goosebumps all up and down her arms. "Same thing that happened to you. We were attacked."

"Just now?"

Sai shook her head. "No, they had us in a back room of the servants' halls for the last couple of hours. Then they told us to do a walk to the stables through the outer ward, but sent us back here before we made it past the veranda."

It made sense. Both parties were probably attacked by Darsh's people at the same time, and then pulled back once they made their threat real and provided cover for Aviama to get out of the palace. Aviama nodded. "Melders?"

The girl gave a short nod, and a knot formed in Aviama's stomach. "Any casualties?"

Durga sank into the cushioned chair and popped her feet up on the table. "One of ours. One of theirs. Not sure if he died, but he's injured."

Aviama glared at her. How could she be so casual about the deaths of two people? But as Durga reached to fix her unkempt hair, her fingers shook. Maybe she wasn't so casual about it after all.

Aviama reached for Sai and examined her arm, but it was too dark to be blood.

"It's wine." Sai pulled free and crossed to the wardrobe. "They had a crestbreaker, and we were passing one of the pools. A tray of wine goblets stood a little too close to the water."

Running feet flew down the corridor outside, and all three of them froze. The door flung open without a knock, and Bhumi stood huffing and puffing in the doorway. "They found —melderblood. In the butterfly pavilion." Aviama's stomach dropped, and Bhumi gasped for breath. "He ran, but they caught him. Just now. Lotus pool."

The pool outside her window.

A shout rang out, followed by a scream coming from the window. Aviama flew to the lattice, the three women with her hot on her heels. But all she could make out three floors below, in the dimness of evening through the lattice of the window, were two torches, two guards, and a long shadow creeping along the edge of the lotus-shaped water. Trees obscured the pool on the side closest to the window. Whatever else was down there, she'd never know from here. And if she didn't see it for herself, she'd likely never know at all.

Adrenaline coursed through her veins like fire. Arjun was accounted for, but where had Chenzira gone after he'd left her? Hadn't he promised to do something stupid seconds before they parted? Something to save her from marrying Shiva. Something he wouldn't tell her.

Maybe he couldn't defy death after all.

A tremor ran through her body. Ice hardened around her lungs, an impenetrable wall making it impossible to breathe. Her vision swam, and a pain ached deep in her throat.

And then she was moving. Her legs carried her across the room and out the door before she'd hardly registered what was happening. The sound of her heartbeat hammering in her ears and the chaos in her own mind drowned out the dim awareness of someone yelling.

All the other melders were at the bathhouse, weren't they?

Oh, Chenzira, what have you done?

Whichever unfortunate guard had been left to stand at her door jerked upright as she whirled by, shaking off his surprise to tear after her. But Aviama barely noticed. She was already zeroed in on the stairs at the end of the corridor.

She'd saved his life in the arena and signed her life away to Shiva, all for him to get himself killed a few weeks later. But maybe he wasn't dead yet. Maybe if she got there in time...

The guard's hand closed around her elbow, but power was already circulating around her torso in a whirling wind. She threw a hand back without sparing a second glance, the air ripping the guard's grip from her arm and sending him flying who knows where. The stairs met her feet with a reassuring solidity, rushing up to meet her as she fled full-tilt down two flights and out across the open floor, under colorful scalloped ceilings, past torch after torch along the wall, to bronze doors with handles formed into pakshi heads.

A scream ripped her apart at the chest, but whether it was internal, or the sound made it out of her throat, she didn't know.

Don't be dead.

The knob of the Radhan national bird turned in her hand. She yanked the door open, darted through the narrow opening, and plunged forward past the line of columns and into the flickering torchlight illuminating the south side of the lotus pool.

The soldiers were gone, and the poolside was empty—

except for a long shadow creeping toward her across the edge of the columns. Two large, beady eyes glimmered at her from twenty paces off. Eighteen paces. Fifteen. Rolling fur moved smooth as oil over the high shoulder blades of the queen's hyena. For all her impulsive dashing from her window to the lotus pool where she found herself now, Aviama's muscles locked up as though they'd retired for the evening. The beast turned its head to stare her down over the corner of the pool, and the sallow orange-yellow light caught something dark dripping from its jowls.

No, not just dark. Red. Blood.

Aviama's scream caught in her throat, and no sound escaped. A low growl laced the air between them with an uneasy dread. The hyena's lip curled into an exaggerated snarl, revealing a full set of crimson-stained ivory teeth. Ragged breathing from the animal's deep chest mingled with the hollow clack of long claws on marble. Claws designed for shredding.

The hyena launched itself at her, closing the distance in a single bound and sailing through the air with the weight of a small horse. Aviama screamed and threw her hands up to protect her face as the red-brown blur flew at her fragile frame.

Smack! The hyena yowled like a cat with fire on its tail, snapping its teeth at Aviama against the solid barrier of wind suddenly swirling around her. The brute slid down the edge of her invisible shield, shaking its head and thrusting its nose into the current again and again.

"Mrtyu! *SSssss.*"

Aviama jerked her attention up to the rest of the room again, but the queen's silhouette was so dim in the opposite end of the opening that she could almost have been a mirage. But mirages didn't recall savage beasts. Mrtyu snarled his last spit-spewing snarl at Aviama before he slinked off after his mistress and disappeared into the labyrinth of corridors.

But just as Aviama dragged in a shaky breath in the isolation of the night, her gaze fell on something floating under the trees at the south end of the pool. Its back was ripped to shreds with long, talon-like strokes. Blood distorted whatever color its tunic used to be. Aviama's stomach churned as, at last, her brain accepted what her eyes were seeing.

The body of a man, face-down in the water.

27

Deep claw marks ran the length of the man's torso from shoulder to hip. A glimpse of crimson glinted in the torchlight in the water around him as the corpse's spilt blood tainted the pool. Aviama's lips parted, and her mouth went dry. The queen had murdered a melderblood.

Had Chenzira circled back and entered the palace on his own? If she turned the body over, would his glassy eyes haunt her nightmares next to Liben for the rest of her days?

Running steps edged into her consciousness, but she was rooted to the floor. The footsteps pulled up short as Aviama's women and the guard she'd slung behind her from outside her chamber door came up beside her and saw the scene in the shadow of the water.

"Oh..."

Bhumi raised a hand to her mouth, and Aviama lurched forward toward the edge of the pool. A wall of wind blew her back from the edge, and she stumbled into Sai and the guard, who caught her by the elbows. Durga lowered her hand.

"Don't touch him. We need to get out of here."

"I need to see...I need to see..." Aviama tugged against their grip, but Durga jerked her chin back to the hall, and the guard answered by hauling Aviama back from the pool and back through the double doors. Sai kept her hand firmly clutching Aviama's arm, moving with the guard so that they weren't separated.

A restless breeze whistled through Aviama's fingers, but she dismissed it. Bringing attention to herself with a dead man in the middle of the night was not a good idea. And she couldn't risk hurting Sai in the effort to get away.

The guard and Sai worked together to drag her back toward the staircase. The guard eyed her, but she did nothing to suggest a mad rush back down the hall to the lotus pool, so he set her on her feet.

All at once, a blanket of doom and weariness hit her like a hammer. This was it. The fate of melderbloods in Radha. The future of any brave enough to help her. Aviama's shoulders sagged, and the ache she'd been fighting all day swept through her body once again, weighing her down like a ball and chain. The image of the corpse in the lotus pool refused to leave her mind.

Please, let it not be Chenzira.

Sai squeezed Aviama's arm and tugged her up the stairs. Bhumi appeared at her other side, and Aviama let them pull her along, back down the hall and into her chambers. The guard took up his position outside the door once again, and the women wordlessly dressed Aviama for bed, braided her hair, and set her on the mattress.

The three women turned to go, and Aviama spoke for the first time in twenty minutes. "Your secret is out now."

Durga shrugged. "It'll all be public after tomorrow, anyway."

The door clicked shut behind them, and Aviama laid her spinning head on the pillow. Of course, that's what she needed right now. A reminder that tomorrow night Shiva's diplomatic dinner would come, along with his mysterious announcement. An announcement that Durga apparently already knew about.

Her hand shook as she pulled the blankets higher. The feel of the warmth of his arm, the strength under her fingertips—the way he'd looked at her as he asked whether she had changed her mind—whether she wanted to marry Shiva.

The dark look he'd given her that day at the processional, when she'd seen him looking up at her as she and Shiva rode the bahataal through the streets of Rajaad. Where Chenzira had watched Shiva slither his arms around Aviama's waist, whisper in her ear, press his lips to hers, to the cheers of the crowd...

Death-defying feats are my specialty.

Whatever it is I do, it won't be able to be stopped halfway through.

A shiver ran down her spine.

If Chenzira Bomani was dead, she'd never forgive herself, and she deserved whatever was coming.

A BRIDE DRESSED in the royal yellow garb of the House of the Blessing Sun stared back at Aviama in the mirror. *You agreed to this. You bargained for this.* Her stomach churned, and she swallowed against an impossibly large lump in her throat. *It didn't help.*

The door opened, and Shiva swept in, catching her up in his arms, sliding his hands around her body and pulling her against him. He claimed her mouth as he had claimed her future—with *forceful victory rather than love. He pulled back, smiling, and placed a dagger in her palm. For a moment, she thought perhaps she could kill him with it, but a voice called her attention back to the mirror.*

"I won't let you marry him."

The dagger moved then, Shiva's hand over hers, stabbing into the mirror as a scream tore from Aviama's throat. Glass shattered, and she fell through the mirror, landing on Chenzira's chest, falling, falling.

Sand kicked up in a cloud of dust as Chenzira's head hit the ground. A shout went up. The arena appeared around them, the beasts of the contest waiting on the fringes, poised to attack. Cirabas, zegraths, snakes, trolls—and Shiva himself, grinning ear to ear.

Aviama braced herself against Chenzira's chest as they landed, but his arms didn't curve around her, and he didn't try to get up. He was still. She pushed herself up, and her hand left a bloody print on his tunic. The dagger protruded from his chest, blood pouring from the wound. His throat made a gurgling sound, and his eyes stared up at her with the shock of betrayal as the color left his face.

A tremor racked her body, and her fingers shook. The life went out of his eyes, anguish frozen on his face. She reached for him, her hand brushing his cheek, but as she did, the body beneath her shifted into the form of her mother, the dagger still lodged in her chest. Aviama reeled backwards, and the body shifted again, to her father, to Liben, to the guard outside her door that first night, and back to Chenzira.

Shiva laughed, and Aviama looked up. He strode forward with another mirror and a fresh dagger. In the mirror, her brother Zephan held Semra in a loving embrace in the throne room of Aviama's childhood home. Cannons rocked the air, and smoke filled the throne room. Debris flew in every direction, and when she looked down, Aviama saw her own hand on a cannon that had appeared there next to Chenzira's dead body.

A blood-curdling shriek wrested Aviama from the dream, and she woke in a cold sweat.

"Your Highness? Your Highness, is everything all right?" It was Sai's voice, but memories of the shifting dead bodies in her dream still pulled at her consciousness. Aviama pulled awake like a fish dragged through mud and plopped flopping on a ship deck, clammy and breathless and cold.

"Open the door, or I'm opening it myself."

The door swung open, and three servants hurried in with platters of food. The clinking of silver and crystal reached Aviama's ears through the fog until the servants disappeared and the villain of her nightmare appeared only a handsbreadth from her face.

"Aviama?"

Aviama jerked away from him, the violence of her reaction so strong she plunged right over the edge of the bed and tumbled to the floor with a squeal.

Sai cleared her throat and spoke quietly to Prince Shiva. "The nightmares aren't going away, Your Highness. The stress of yesterday's attack seems to have made it worse."

"That wasn't the only thing that happened last night."

Aviama grimaced at the sound of Durga's voice, but made no effort to get up from the floor on the other side of the bed.

Shiva turned to Durga. "What do you mean? What else happened last night?"

"She heard they'd caught a melderblood. We heard a commotion downstairs. She threw the guard out of the way and outran us down the hall, down the stairs, and out to the lotus pool."

"And?"

"And saw a body in the water."

Biscuits. That's right—the maidservants hadn't gotten there early enough to see the hyena. But the corpse had claw marks across his back. It was obvious whose work the death had been. The guards may have caught him, but it was the queen who'd had him killed. If they'd only let her get to the body, to turn him over, to see his face…

"That's enough. She's getting up and eating. And she will be in the finest of clothes and appropriately prepared for tonight's dinner. Make sure of it."

The women gave their assent, and scurried throughout the room—one to the wardrobe, one to the vanity, one to the pitcher of water on the tray by the sofa. Aviama pulled her knees up to her chin and wrapped her arms around them, leaning against the frame of the bed. Everybody was dead or dying anyway. What was the point of delaying her fate?

Shiva rounded the side of the bed, seized her arm, and pulled her up in her nightgown. "Breakfast. Now. And stop blasting your guards away from you when they've been instructed to protect you."

Aviama lifted her chin. "I didn't hurt him. And I've never used it on you, except that time I saved your life from Darsh. You're welcome. A little gratitude wouldn't kill you."

Shiva's eyes flashed. "True, but *ingratitude* might kill *you*. I brought you breakfast, but now it's midmorning. We've made our plans for the evening. Nothing will delay our dinner tonight. If Darsh gets through our new security, we'll have our meeting in the rubble." Shiva pulled her to the couch and released her on the cushion. "So stop moping and eat."

Aviama made a face behind his back as he turned to pluck a goblet from the tray, and Bhumi's lips twisted into the smallest of grins. Sai came over, nudged her arm, and passed her a glass of water.

Bhumi caught Aviama's eye, lifting her chin and pulling her shoulders back. *Don't let them see you cry.*

She was right. And a maidservant shouldn't have to tell a princess to act like a princess. Aviama straightened on the couch, surveyed the trays of sweetcakes and fruit, and uncovered the large silver platter in the center of the nearest tray.

A severed head stared her in the face where a meal should have been. Traces of something red and squishy trailed from the base of the neck, the head propped up on a bed of lettuce. A face she'd known for years.

Aviama's lips parted, and nausea roiled her stomach. The glass of water fell to the floor with a crash. Sai gasped beside her, clutching at the arm of the couch.

Shiva groaned. "What's wrong now? I had it prepared alongside my own meal. Nothing's poisoned." The prince tossed back a gulp of wine and turned back toward her, but as his gaze landed on the tray, his annoyance darkened to barely restrained anger. The expression smoothed into ambivalence, and he took the platter lid and quickly re-covered the head on the plate. "Someone you know?"

Aviama stared at the platter, the reality of what she'd seen burned in her brain just as vividly as if Shiva had never replaced the lid.

"Isn't that the bodyguard she came with? The one who was with her from Jannemar at the beginning and then got sick?"

Aviama's hatred for Durga blossomed yet again as she flippantly described the man who had risked his life for her, and then apparently had given it, in her service. The queen had claimed to have killed him before, but Aviama had heard he had escaped and gone to Darsh. But he wasn't a melder.

She'd hoped he was safe in Rajaad, or even working to get word home to Jannemar. But he was too loyal to leave her here alone. What had he done to deserve this? Had he been working all these weeks to get her free? Was it his body she'd seen in the pool last night, or Chenzira's?

Aviama felt Shiva's burning gaze on her face. A wave of emotion battled in her chest. And from the shock and sadness, a new shoot took root. An angry, resentful root growing into something cold and dark. "His name was Enzo."

Because he had a name. Dead people still had names. Killing wasn't like pulling up weeds. It was ending a life. Of a person. A person with value.

Shiva took another look at Aviama's face, snatched the platter up off the table, and stalked toward the door. He yanked the door open and thrust the platter out toward the guard waiting there.

"Send this to my mother. Do not open it. Tell her it's from me, with warmest regards. Tell her I look forward to seeing her at the dinner tonight."

Aviama spun. "Why would she do this?"

"She's obsessed with proving her control over you. But more than that, she wants to tell me she can do what she wants. That me marrying, preparing you to bear an heir, and getting more and more ready to take over from Father one day will not shake her influence in the palace." Shiva's lip curled, and he snatched the lid off the other platter as if it burned him. Steaming roast duck filled the room with an appetizing smell Aviama could no longer appreciate.

Shiva tossed the lid onto the cushioned chair and stabbed a piece of duck with the fork provided on the platter. "My status will rise after we marry. I've been controlling what comes to your room. She apparently intended to let me know that I am not so in charge as I think I am."

Aviama swallowed, and he offered her the duck. She waved him off, and he ripped off a chunk with his teeth.

"Father is busy with military drills and plans. Our wedding

is none of his concern, so long as it gets done, and the box gets checked. 'Son marries, line secured, political position strengthened.' Check, check. So, he's left the details to Mother and me."

"Fantastic." Aviama blinked back tears and plucked grapes from the remaining tray to cover it. Sai picked pieces of broken glass from the floor and hem of Aviama's nightgown, and Durga wiped up the spilled water. Bhumi handed Aviama a fresh glass of water, and she sipped it.

Shiva swallowed the chunk of duck and drove the fork into the next piece like a javelin thrown into a target. "This was a tactical move. We're going to the dinner tonight. I don't care what happens. I don't care who dies. We're going. I'm making the announcement, and you're going to be happy about it."

Aviama gaped at him, her chest caving into a deeper, emptier cavern with every word he spoke. She set down the water glass to keep it from spilling and folded her hands to cover their quaking. "My husband, the tender partner any princess would die to marry."

The prince shot her a deadly glare. "You nearly did. You still might. Tonight, you're going to be as in love with me as you ever were." Shiva moved like lightning, capturing her by the back of the neck and yanking her head back by a handful of hair. His lip twitched in a hideous snarl, and his breath tickled her neck as he whispered in her ear. "And if I get even a glimmer that I am not the apple of your eye—if you do not *convince* me that I am your greatest dream, that you are obsessively, head over heels in love with me—I'll kill one of the women attending you."

Aviama's breath caught, and gooseflesh fled down her neck and arms. Shiva pulled away but held her looking up at him as he towered over her on the couch. He brushed his lips against hers and whispered his name for her against her mouth.

"Lilac." He kissed her for a long, squirming minute, and released her gasping onto the couch. "Convince me tonight."

He threw back another gulp of wine and strode for the door. "And pull yourself together. Eat something, and get all trussed up, and I'll let you go to the menagerie before the dinner."

28

E nzo was dead. And his head was on a platter. A literal platter. Served with salad. Her personal bodyguard from home, who'd hardly been in the palace before disappearing due to what the queen claimed was sickness. He'd eluded Satya all this time, gotten free, and for what?

"May I say something bold, Your Highness?"

Aviama turned to look bleakly at Sai, who had been standing in silence next to Aviama for half an hour. Aviama shrugged. "I'm not so important a person that you should care. Go ahead."

It did no use to say. Sai was in no position to treat Aviama as anything less than a princess, and speaking her mind freely was frowned upon in many royal circles. Even more so in Radha.

"Don't play what-if games, Your Highness. You did not do this."

Aviama scanned the room and wondered what the girls thought of her predicament. Shiva had never been so overtly domineering in their presence before. Not in a threatening, nasty sort of way. Not like he'd been before he left this time.

Sai had eyes full of pity. Or kindness. It was hard to tell the difference between pity and care when bitterness ensnared the heart. Bhumi was cleaning the window for the second time today, and Durga was reorganizing the wardrobe. None of it needed doing. They were keeping themselves busy so as not to stare at her in her distress and make her uncomfortable.

Don't let them see you cry.

Did any of them hear what Shiva had threatened her? No; if they had, they'd be more shaken. Aviama had no doubt the threat had teeth. But if he killed one of the girls, however convenient it might be to dispatch his mother's sneak, Durga, Aviama didn't like her, so the lesson in control might not land the way he wanted. If he killed Sai, whom Aviama did like, he'd be hurting himself, so long as she remained a useful informant. If he killed Bhumi, he lost nothing. In fact, he would be removing a dangerous spy for the Shadow.

Did he know?

Better not to cause panic. She would say nothing to them. But Shiva was right—she had to pull herself together. Now was not the time to snivel on the floor or bury herself in pillows. There would be time to grieve for Enzo later, when the shock wore off more fully and she was alone.

But right now, the queen had played a power move. That was all this had been to her. A move in a game. And Shiva had played a move of his own. What move did Aviama have?

If Aviama was going to be forced to live in the palace indefinitely, she couldn't let the queen believe she intimidated her. Especially if it was true. Aviama had to start sending her own messages, establishing herself in the palace as more than a sobbing strumpet or nervous nuisance. Maybe her best move really was to play along, get married, and create a web of her own. A web like Satya had built. A new spider for every silk thread, spinning new tales and tainted information to scurry back to their mistress.

Besides, she saw last night what happened to anyone who dared help her. Perhaps it was too great a request to make of any one person. Maybe she needed Darsh after all.

But could she stomach the cost of working with a man like that? Would accepting his help in exchange for training his people and providing information be the same as selling her soul, as she'd accused Chenzira of doing?

Aviama folded her hands in her lap and nodded. "Thank you, Sai. Durga, I was thinking of the coral dress for tonight."

Durga turned from the wardrobe and frowned. "Purple was requested, Your Highness."

"I thought that dress was sent off for repairs."

"It was, but with the delay of the dinner, it was found and repaired quickly enough for tonight. The prince ensured it."

"Biscuits." Aviama smoothed her skirts and set her jaw. "Fine. Find me all the most nauseating purple things you can, and swath me in the cursed color from head to toe. I'll be convincing tonight. So convincing he'll not know what to do with himself. I need to be *surprising*."

Bhumi wrung out the rag in her hands and grinned. "Can we dress you in Radhan style?"

"Yes. Perfect. Make me Radhan in every way possible, give me the most elaborate of hairstyles, and go overboard on everything. Make it look like a lilac bush threw up on me. I am a most devoted fiancée."

The women leaped into action, surrounding her with brushes, powders, and an assortment of gemstones to accessorize the lavender dress. Bhumi found a sash embroidered with gold and held it up. "Too much?"

Aviama smiled at her. "Not enough. Give it to me."

Bhumi's face lit like a beacon as she arranged the sash diagonally across her torso from hip to shoulder. Sai appeared with a pakshi-shaped broach and pinned it to the sash where it met a sweeping neckline beneath her collarbone. Durga brushed and perfumed her hair, twisting it back and away from her face into a half-crown around her head, pinning elaborate braids and accenting them with sprigs of lilac they sent out for.

Durga reached for Aviama's official Jannemari tiara she'd brought from home, but Aviama shook her head. "Tonight, I am Radhan, through and through."

The girl's sharp nose seemed sharper still as she eyed Aviama down its length, but she replaced the tiara in its velvet case and turned instead to a jewelry box that had yet to be cracked open during her stay. After a moment's rummaging, she found what she was looking for—a gold-plated headpiece to lie over the crown of her head, with an amethyst teardrop draped down her forehead.

Heavy earrings were produced from the box to match, along with bangles for her arms and a substantial gemstone necklace gracing her slender throat. The headpiece was adjusted over the crown of her head and braided portion of her hair, leaving the rest as blonde flowing waves spilling freely down her back. When at last they were done primping, applying powders, and painting her eyes and lips, Aviama felt several pounds heavier, but every ounce as dramatic as she'd hoped to be.

Aviama hoped never to hazard a guess as to how elaborately expensive the gems she wore on her body were, from those embroidered into the bodice of the dress, to the gold leaf twining around the pakshi on the broach, and the jewelry sparkling from her fingers to her arms, neck, ears, and head. She only knew that if she moved her head too quickly from one side to the other, Sai grimaced, and when she reached up to shift the headpiece, Durga swatted at her hand.

Preparations had taken several hours, and she'd eaten the brunch prior to having her lips painted. At last, the three maidservants stepped back to admire their work.

Aviama shifted under their gaze. "Well? How do I look?"

Bhumi beamed. "Like a queen, Your Highness."

"Absolutely beautiful," Sai agreed.

Durga snapped her open mouth closed and sniffed. "You'll do."

Bhumi lifted a mirror, and Aviama blinked back at her reflection. Bright eyes stared back at her beneath the glittering jeweled headpiece with the amethyst down her forehead. Gold chain with smaller amethysts mingled with her hair, twisted back into elaborate braids at the nape of her neck before falling freely the rest of the way down her back. The stones at her neck, cold and heavy, sparkled in the sun's rays pouring in from the window, drawing the eye up to her painted lips and eyes.

Gold embroidery glistened from the satin sash across her torso, the lilac bodice fitted through to the hips and then falling to the floor. Radhan and Jannemari influence blended together from head to toe in a surprising but pleasing array. The jewelry was a bit much—overwhelming and unnecessary —but over-the-top extravagance was the way of Radha, and Aviama intended to play the game.

A game of dress-up to combat a bloody chopped-off head on a platter.

It didn't seem like an appropriate comeback, but it was all she had. So, she would do it to the hilt.

The thought of Enzo, the memory of his frozen face, sent a rippling chill down her spine. The queen could not win. She could not be permitted to maintain a death grip on the palace. And Aviama was in a position now to weaken her hold.

But was it worth it to weaken Queen Satya if Aviama had to strengthen Shiva to do it? If she partnered with Shiva to weaken Satya, and partnered with Darsh to escape Shiva, was she really any better than the Shadow she had accused of selling their souls?

Aviama swallowed and looked away. "Thank you. You all did a great job. Now someone send word to Prince Shiva that it's time to uphold his promise. I'm ready to go to the menagerie. Alone."

Durga and Sai curtsied and disappeared, and Bhumi began straightening the room. Aviama perched on the edge of the sofa, careful not to muss her hair, wondering what Durga could be doing if Sai was running off to carry her message to Shiva. It wasn't a two-person job. What did she plan on spilling to the queen before tonight's dinner?

Bhumi finished organizing and dusting the vanity, then came around to fluff the pillows of the couches and chairs. She glanced twice at Aviama, furtively, as if unsure of herself. Then she swallowed and looked up at her again. "I know why you don't want to marry Prince Shiva. Don't worry, I won't tell anyone. But I understand...this is a great sacrifice for you."

Aviama's lips parted, and her chest ached. Someone understood her. After the terse, threatening exchange with Shiva, Bhumi had seen what a horrible match the two of them would make, what a miserable life they'd have together with Aviama only used for power plays and dominance.

Bhumi fluffed the nearest pillow and shot her a coy look. "Ramta. You're in love with him."

Her stomach plunged to her toes, and heat flooded her face. "What?"

The girl tried unsuccessfully to suppress a small smile.

"Don't worry. I won't tell anyone. But I think your work with the Shadow is admirable. I hadn't thought of how much you'd be giving up to be queen. Please know that I'll do everything in my power to make your situation more comfortable."

Aviama gaped at her. Bhumi wasn't thinking about her interaction with Shiva at all. She was hung up on her and Chenzira, as if some forbidden love with another man was the primary problem with her engagement. And even with this belief, Bhumi still believed Aviama had every intention of sacrificing herself and her supposed love of another man for the sake of being the melderblood queen. Her supposed love for a man whose corpse may have been floating in the lotus pool just that morning. If only she'd been able to turn him over...if only she'd seen his face...

She opened her mouth to object, but the door opened, and Sai peeked in. "It's time."

Aviama jerked up from the couch, the rustle of satin and clink of jewelry marking her movement, and smoothed her skirts. Bhumi dipped her head, and Aviama fled out the door toward the menagerie with Sai.

Sai flashed a letter with the royal seal at the guards outside the menagerie doors, and they opened them without a word. Sai curtsied at Aviama and disappeared down the hall. Aviama stepped inside the menagerie, a sense of calm washing over her the moment the doors swung shut.

An uneasy feeling always accompanied the tingling sensation the magna-lined walls of the menagerie brought. If Shiva were going to let her be alone anywhere, it was here, where her powers were useless. But at the same time, the animals didn't carry any agenda besides their next meal, and Makana was a kindred spirit.

Aviama wished she'd learned more about Makana's people since seeing her last, and about the hold the Iolani held over the sea, but between Shiva's demands and Darsh's, she hadn't had a moment to spare. Perhaps today she could learn what Makana knew about the king's plans and find out how to help.

The monkeys chittered loudly at her entrance, as if every lizard and troll in the place needed the warning of her presence. The bird of paradise across from the monkeys brought her head out from under her wing just long enough to see what all the fuss was about, and promptly returned to her dreaming. Aviama snatched up the folds of her skirts and hurried down the aisle between the cages, headed for the aquarium.

The ornately carved doors of King Dahnuk's private office stared her down from the opposite end of the large room, and for a moment Aviama wondered if she had time to pick the lock and snoop for information. But the longer she stayed in the palace, the more opportunities she'd have to bargain with Shiva for visits to Makana. She'd get into the king's office next time. Today, she needed to calm her racing heart and wipe Enzo's murder and Chenzira's possible death from her mind long enough to put on a show at dinner. She needed a friend.

Bursting yellows and azure blues flashed through the water in a school of fish along the side of the aquarium glass, and Aviama ducked into the path between the enclosures to follow them. Back through the narrow space, back to the troll cage, back out of sight of the main entrance or the king's office.

Aviama hiked up her skirts, climbed up the bars of the troll cage opposite the aquarium, and searched the water. Purple, orange, and pink fish swam past, parting in three different directions as a larger fish surged into their midst. Aviama thought of Makana's words to her last time they met. *You must not marry.*

Yes, well, she didn't *want* to marry. But the only other

person in the world who seemed to be on the same page was Chenzira, and he might be dead.

She needed every split second of time with Makana that she could have. And last time, Makana had required a song. But what melody could tell the siren that Aviama's position was more precarious than ever? That she was trapped between the queen, the prince, and the Shadow leader, and the people who tried to protect her were dropping like flies?

Aviama sang, hesitant and soft at first, the notes drifting into a Jannemari dirge for the dead. Her chest constricted, and her eyes welled as Enzo's and Chenzira's faces swirled to the forefront of her mind. No, she wouldn't focus there. She couldn't.

Her song broke off from the minor key, jumping up into a climbing tug-of-war tension between high and low, fast and slow—wordless, yet somehow more meaningful than any of the songs to which she'd dared put lyrics. Besides, the last one she'd penned was stupid and ridiculous. This one poured out the anxiety wrapping her chest like a chain, the danger pressing in from every side.

Silky white hair and silver scales caught the light from the window, as the mermaid, gliding effortlessly through the water, cut across the distance from halfway across the aquarium. Aviama's voice faltered at the sight of her, then pressed on with long, urgent notes until the siren breached the surface at the water's edge, and Aviama let the song die, unfinished.

Makana tilted her head at Aviama, glanced around, and reached one hand out of the pool toward Aviama. Aviama pressed her palm to Makana's, and Makana dipped her head. *Tabeun sister.* But she didn't say it out loud.

Aviama dropped her voice to a whisper. "What's wrong?"

"Not alone. Spear man here. Something happen."

"What do you mean? Who is the spear man? Are they keeping guards inside the menagerie now?"

Makana pulled back from the edge of the water, and Aviama leaned further out over the distance between them. "What have you heard? What happened? Shiva's making some announcement tonight, but I don't know what it is. And I don't know how long it'll be before I can bargain with him to come here again. How can I help you? Who can I trust?"

The mermaid shook her head. "Must not marry. Must not give Radha weapon for sea. Must not give him keys."

The key to the sea. The key to the melders. "I know, I know. I'm trying, but I need help. I'm alone out here, and everyone I think could be a friend turns out to be working for someone."

Makana shook her head again. "Not alone."

She'd said it twice, but it took two tries before Aviama realized what she meant. Someone was there, in the menagerie, watching them. Right now.

The mermaid glanced to one side again, and Aviama spun to follow her gaze. Her foot slipped on the bars, and she fell—just as the silhouette of a man emerged from the shadows.

29

Aviama's scream stuck in her throat as the shadow lunged to overtake her. She dropped like a rock, but strong arms reached out and caught her before she hit the unforgiving floor. Aviama's breath came in short gasps, her pulse thundering in her ears. Eyes of endless cedar brown with flecks of gold pierced her through, a mere handsbreadth from the end of her nose, her body gently cradled against his as though she were no heavier than a dove.

"You didn't scream."

"I'm getting better at that." Aviama bit her lip. "You're not dead."

Chenzira frowned. "Why would I be dead?"

"They caught a melder last night. The queen's hyena ripped him apart and left him in the lotus pool. I saw the body."

"Who was it?"

"I don't know. But my bodyguard from Jannemar, Enzo, wasn't a melder, and his head was delivered to me this morning with brunch. So, at least two people have been killed in the last twenty-four hours, and I thought—I thought it was you."

Chenzira pursed his lips. "You were worried about me?"

Aviama's midsection burst into a warm, weird squirmy feeling. But that wasn't right. She'd just talked about two dead people. "That's all you got from what I said?"

He sobered. "I'm sorry. I'm sorry that happened. That's horrible. You're right, I was being stupid."

Aviama shifted in his arms, suddenly aware of how close they were and how long he'd held her. "Um, you can put me down now."

"What if I don't want to?"

"What?"

"Nothing. You just have terrible balance, you know. You trip a lot. I'd hate for someone as important as you to hurt yourself."

Chenzira set her down, and Aviama rolled her eyes. He grew serious again as he looked down at her. "Are you okay?"

Aviama threw her hands up. "What about what I just told you could possibly give you the impression that I am okay?"

"I'm sorry."

Aviama crossed her arms. "Yes, well, at least you're not dead. And for the record, I think I've made it clear I don't like it when people die, so that shouldn't have been a surprise."

"What shouldn't have been a surprise?"

"That I didn't want you dead."

He leaned against the aquarium glass and folded his arms, each of them standing like mirrors of the other. "You wouldn't want me to think you cared about me specifically, is that it?"

"No, I'm just—I gave up a lot to keep you alive, you know?" Aviama winced and licked her lips. *Biscuits.* "I'd hate to see it go to waste. By doing something stupid and getting yourself killed. So, don't do stupid stuff, okay?"

"Don't do stupid stuff."

"Yes. Like sneaking into the palace to see me when they just murdered a melder last night for being here."

He quirked an eyebrow. "Who says I came to see you?"

A long tail smacked the glass next to Chenzira, and he jumped away from the glass. Above them, Makana perched her elbows on the edge of the aquarium and twined a piece of seaweed between her fingers. "Spear man ask me talk to you. Very important. Came for you."

Chenzira gaped up at the mermaid, and Aviama snort-laughed before she could stop herself.

"*She* says." Aviama grinned.

Chenzira's mouth twisted into a sheepish, answering grin. "Okay, fine, so I came for you. To get a message to you. I figured you'd come to see the mermaid eventually, and I hoped sooner rather than later." He paused, shooting Makana a look. "She didn't speak a word to me. Didn't even acknowledge I spoke. Just stared at me. Now, with you, she's a chatterbox."

Aviama shrugged. "What can I say? She is my sister."

A small smile broke across Makana's perfect, impenetrable features, and here with the Keket boy and the siren, Aviama felt safer and more at home than she had in weeks.

Further down the menagerie, monkeys chittered as some sound or other aroused their curiosity. Chenzira glanced around the corner, grabbed her hand, and tugged her further down the pathway between the aquarium and the trolls. "I did need to see you. I have news, and it's not good."

Every comforting feeling disappeared, save the softness of Chenzira's hand against hers. She hoped he wouldn't let go. He didn't.

"King Dahnuk is planning an attack on Jannemar, but he's moved up the timeline. He's got a force headed around by land. It'll take them time to get into position, but I just found out they already left. Two weeks ago. And he's got a fleet of ships slated to leave the harbor as early as next week. None of the crew knows where they're headed, but it's an impressive number. You'll be busy with whatever distraction Shiva cooks up for you, whatever this announcement is that he'll make tonight. But something is going down, and soon."

Aviama's lips parted. An army would be marching on her home before Zephan and Semra even knew she was engaged.

Chenzira continued. "Darsh isn't willing to wait. The bulk of Radha's military force, both by land and by sea, will be away from the palace in just a week. Shiva and Satya are so focused on their power grabs over you, and these plans with the wedding, that they're more distracted than we can ever hope they'll be again. And Dahnuk has been consumed with his war plans. All the variables are lining up, and Darsh doesn't want to wait. If we can't provide him a better time to sweep through, he'll skip the training phase and let the melders loose on the palace to wreak whatever havoc necessary to secure the throne."

Ice shot through Aviama's heart. "That's too soon. Too soon for everything. What happened to Darsh waiting for me to become queen first?"

Chenzira grimaced. "He wasn't impressed by your stunt at the bathhouse. He saved face in front of the others, but I think you're turning out to be more trouble than he thought. Darsh thought you'd be pliable, that you'd be grateful for the position and opportunities he offered. But the Shadow is talking about you in extreme terms. You're divisive. Some think you're salvation itself, and others think you're too slow and too careful. They don't want to work on moving dirt particles. They want to rip buildings apart at the foundation."

Aviama's stomach churned. "What do we do?"

His grip tightened on her hand, so hard her fingers hurt. He searched her face, solemn as the grave. "There's some sort of event tomorrow night in the grand ballroom. Don't be there. Be anywhere but there."

A lump lodged in her throat. Images started filing through her mind at lightning speed: debris flying in the smoke of explosives, a knife lodging in her mother's chest, blood pouring onto marble floors. Liben's glassy eyes, Enzo's severed head. The corpse from last night, floating in the lotus pool, his back torn to shreds by the queen's hyena. Aviama took a step back, and her voice trembled. "Chenzira...what's happening tomorrow night?"

Chenzira shook his head. "I can't stop it. I would if I could, but I can't. The Shadow isn't controlled enough to only hit their intended targets. I don't think they'll take survivors. I don't think they want to."

"They can't just...slaughter everyone. They can't." Aviama sucked in a ragged breath, shaking her head over and over.

No. No. No.

They couldn't do this. But Chenzira's face held the same answer she knew was true in her heart. They could, and they would. And they'd sleep soundly over the bodies after the massacre.

Aviama squeezed her eyes shut. If the Shadow succeeded, the wedding would be off. If Darsh still planned to use her as the face of his revolution, she'd still be bound to a tyrant, responsible for death upon death. And if he didn't plan to use her...well, then, she was already dead. Her utility had run out.

She opened her eyes, and as she stared up at Chenzira, a glisten in his eye betrayed a deep sadness she'd not seen before. Aviama clenched her jaw to keep it from quivering.

"Who would they make king? Darsh? The people know he's a criminal. They hate him. Rebellion will know no end. If he does this, he will be twice as bad as Dahnuk. He'll be just as genocidal, just with a different group to kill."

Chenzira spread his hands, took a breath, and let it out. "I don't know."

"Tell me you're not part of this."

"Sand and sea, Aviama, I didn't know. I came as soon as I heard. Darsh would kill me if he knew I was here."

Could she believe him? Or had Darsh sent him to feed her these lines because he saw what Bhumi and Arjun had seen— that she trusted him more than she should? Aviama ran a hand over her face, then adjusted the headpiece she had accidentally knocked askew. "I'll do my best to figure out what's happening tomorrow. I'll try not to be there, but you have to try to stop it from happening at all."

"I don't think I can."

"I don't care. You linked yourself with Darsh. Try." Aviama cleared her throat and smoothed her dress. "How do I look?"

"Like an overdone puff pastry. Too much decoration."

Hurt speared her in the chest, and she reeled back. "Excuse me?"

Chenzira grimaced and took a breath. "I just mean it's excessive. A little preposterous. Not you, just the stuff they've stuffed you into."

Aviama bored daggers at him, speechless. He stared back at her and finally took a breath. "I'm not sure why you're mad. You asked."

Her cheeks flushed hot, and her chest constricted. She lifted her chin. "I have a dinner to go to. If I don't convince Shiva I'm in love with him tonight, he's going to murder one of my women. He told me to dress appropriately, and I plan on doing so in as overstuffed a fashion as I can manage. And in case you didn't hear me just now, since you've been out wandering the streets alone without guards chasing you or

having decapitated heads of people you care about delivered
to your door, or having three different people blackmail you in
your waking nightmares, what I said was that my beloved
betrothed—the man you wondered whether or not I wanted
to marry—just told me if I do not physically demonstrate how
much I am in love with him, tonight, in front of his mother
and the dignitaries of the kingdom, he will murder someone.
If I have a hair out of place, my first impression will not be a
good one. I'm going to ask once more. How. Do. I. Look."

He gaped at her, stricken, then closed his mouth and swallowed. "You look perfect. Better than he deserves."

Aviama stared him down another full minute before
deciding whether to insult him again or beg him to spirit her
away from the madness here and now. After all, he'd gotten
into the palace somehow. But with her slowing him down,
they'd likely be caught, and then Chenzira would die, and it
would be Sai or Bhumi's head delivered to her room tomorrow
on a platter.

A soft ripple of water interrupted her internal debate.
Makana whispered from above them. "Someone here."

Their time was up.

Aviama started to turn away, but Chenzira said her name.
She stopped in her tracks and twisted back toward him. He
closed the difference between them in one long stride, his
fingers grazing her arm before falling to his side. His hand
flexed, and he leaned down toward her. She tipped her chin
up at him.

"Sand and sea." His voice was rough, a quiet murmur just
a hair above the sounds of the menagerie around them. Chenzira searched her face and inclined his head down lower still
until they were nearly nose to nose. Her heart pounded.

He was going to kiss her. He wanted to. He must have.

Aviama's heart skipped a beat as she soaked in the sight

of him, his dark, trimmed beard over a chiseled jawline, deeply piercing eyes set in warm almond skin. The memory of his muscled arms around her sent a shiver through her, though they did not touch. She could hear his breath as hers caught.

"To the depths with Darsh. I don't know if I can save you, but sand and sea, I'll try. Tell me you won't be there tomorrow night."

Aviama gazed at him, every line of his face cementing in her mind. The back of his hand brushed the back of hers, and she remembered he'd asked her something. "I won't be there tomorrow night."

She leaned into him then, but he was already moving away. She stumbled forward in the empty space where he'd been, while he melted into the shadows of the cages, and Sai appeared at the corner of the troll enclosure and the aquarium. Aviama's heart sank. But what had she expected?

Makana flicked her tail and dove back into the water with a silver flash, and Sai watched her go. Aviama sucked in a steadying breath, her hand still craving his whisper of a touch. Bhumi's voice echoed in her mind.

You're in love with him.

Aviama shook her head and backed away, nearly running over Sai in the process.

Sai offered an apologetic smile, as if she had been the one to bump into Aviama, and gestured back out toward the main aisle. "Did it help, Your Highness? Coming to the menagerie?"

"Yes. Thank you. It always helps."

"Good. I know today has not been easy for you. Or last night. Or really any of the last few weeks. I'm glad something can help to ease your mind."

But easing her mind was not in the realm of possibility, and as they left the menagerie and a guard detail fell in behind them outside the double doors, Aviama's world was spinning even faster than when she'd entered.

Sai reached up to adjust Aviama's hair, and a dark purple mark on her underarm caught Aviama's eye. A fresh bruise. What was happening to Sai?

Every new piece of information gathered today was like a punch in the gut. Enzo's head on a platter. Shiva's threat to kill Bhumi or Sai. Aviama's failure to help Makana, and the king's military campaign against Jannemar already underway. Not to mention Darsh's moved-up timeline and plan to cut her out in favor of a chaotic, melder-fueled massacre.

Mosaic tiled floors passed under her feet. Gold-leaf decorated designs glittered over blues and greens and reds on the walls and ceilings. How much of it would be standing in two days' time?

Strong pillars supported high ceilings, and the double doors of the grand ballroom turned on large hinges to usher her into her latest challenge: putting on a public show that she was in love with Prince Shiva, as the memory of Chenzira's arms around her still clung to her skin.

30

A sea of people seated at banquet tables stood as she entered, a wave rising up to meet her as her own world crashed down about her ears. Prince Shiva met her at the doors, sweeping his arm toward her with a beaming smile as if showing off a prize horse. Aviama smiled back, dropping into a deep curtsy before him. He bowed, took her hand, and kissed it as the announcer at the door raised his voice above the murmur of the gathered crowd.

"Her Royal Highness, Princess Aviama Shamaran of Jannemar, soon-to-be princess of Radha, our future queen!"

Over Shiva's shoulder, the king and queen clapped and smiled along with the rest. King Dahnuk exuded boisterous pleasure at the announcement, but Satya's lips flattened at the mention of a future queen. Aviama's stomach soured, and as her eyes locked onto Satya's, Aviama looped her arm through Shiva's and leaned in to kiss him on the cheek.

It was a bold move for court, but Shiva turned his head at the last moment and kissed her on the lips. Gasps and cheers went up throughout the room, and as they parted, Aviama pressed close against his side.

He led her across the room to their seats, the king at the head of the table, the queen on his left, and Shiva on his right. Aviama curtsied, and Shiva bowed to King Dahnuk and Queen Satya, and then Aviama was seated beside Shiva on his right. Various nobles wrapped in satin and dripping with jewels took their seats at their assigned places, positioned in order of importance, with the highest regarded closest to the king. Two men near Aviama's seat wore military cords and ribbons on their chest and the pakshi symbol of Radha blazing from the collar, but there were fewer commanders present than she would have anticipated at an event as important as this. But after the menagerie, Aviama knew why. The bulk of Radha's military leaders were already making the trek to Jannemar.

King Dahnuk raised a ruby-studded goblet, and the room fell silent. She'd seen little of him since the arena, busy as he was planning invasions. He'd come to threaten her and Chenzira when they were in cages before the arena, but seemed willing enough to let his son accept her proposal at the end and work out the wedding details. Tonight, he was all smiles.

"Esteemed guests, tonight is a marvelous night! This evening, we celebrate a new era. One in which melderbloods are not looked down upon, but welcomed. One in which chaos is not left to run uncharted through our streets, but channeled and grown, so that we, too, as Radhans, can grow with the times. We honor our sacred history, revering the sacred lessons of the blot in our record those six hundred years ago. But today, we protect ourselves, our people, and our neighbors, both by melderblood union and by kingdom alliances.

"Through Princess Aviama, laughing children and pattering feet shall fill the halls of the House of the Blessing

Sun once more, reminding my wife and I of a simpler time when our own children were small."

Aviama shifted uncomfortably in her chair, and Shiva placed a hand on her knee and squeezed. Hard. It wasn't comforting. It was a warning. Aviama turned her grimace into a smile and leaned harder into Shiva's arm. His grip on her knee lessened, and the pain eased.

The king wasn't finished. He lifted his goblet higher. "Tonight, our esteemed court shall learn the benefit of a strong monarchy. Renegades will always rise against mighty walls, but like water on rock, though the tide rises, the rock will stand as the waves break apart again and again. We've caught the attention of the latest rebels, as I'm sure you've heard. They don't want us to join with a melderblood princess, because they don't want us to evolve. They don't want us to take their young, their confused, their powerful, and give them a place to go. But we will give them a place to go, and the ant who fancies himself a ciraba will be stomped out.

"So, as they squirm this evening, we will drink. And dream. Of a new Radha, with expanded borders and continuity of rule throughout the southern and eastern regions. No more will there be division, conflict, or threat. Once and for all we will establish ourselves as the turn of the tide, the crest of the wave, the sun itself dawning on a new day. The sun shines on us and on our children. May the sun so shine on the apples of our eye, a young couple we look forward to seeing grow and lead us in uncharted waters. I call for a toast—to His Royal Highness, my son, the Crown Prince Shiva, and his bride-to-be!"

The room erupted in applause, and as Dahnuk eyed her and drank from his goblet, the entire table raised their goblets and drank in unison. Shiva made a show of raising his goblet toward his father's cup and draining it to the dregs in a single go. Aviama took a conservative sip and stared at him as her fiancé downed the beverage.

King Dahnuk laughed. "She is shy, this princess! Come now, we don't bite. I know you are more excited than that! You have the cream of the crop, the dream of women at your side!" He raised the glass in her direction again, and the eyes of the table bored into her like flaming arrows.

Queen Satya's mocking smile flashed from the corner of her eye, the courtiers a mix of polite attention and judgmental suspicion. Shiva nudged her playfully, but the message behind it was anything but friendly. Aviama smiled and laughed with what she hoped was a free-spirited, jovial laugh, but what she imaged was more likely a thin-lipped, awkward cackle, and gulped two massive gulps of wine from her own decorated goblet.

A roar of approval went up around the table, mostly from the men, and the noble seated to her right smacked the table so hard in his gaiety that she nearly jumped out of her chair. Warmth filled her belly, and a tingling sensation shot down her throat like a chaser after the wine. Had the alcohol reached her mind so quickly? What kind of wine was this?

But as the tingle hummed through her body from the inside out, she knew the answer. She'd felt it in the menagerie, though always like an external force rather than an internal dampening drug. Tabeun paralysis.

Aviama's mouth went dry. She smoothed her skirts beneath the table and reached for the wind, just a wisp of a breeze, anything to prove her wrong. But nothing came. She was defenseless. A melderblood without melder powers in the heart of the palace of melder killers.

It could have been poison. She was lucky it wasn't poison. Would Satya have merely dimmed her powers if she could have killed her instead? Who else would do this?

But the better question was, who *wouldn't* do it? Without her powers, Aviama felt even more helpless than before, and she'd have even less confidence with which to stand up to Shiva. Shiva preferred her that way—helpless and malleable.

Nearly all of Radha hated melderbloods, and plenty of nobles were against the match. How many of them were terrified of being in the same room with her? Were they afraid she might hurt them? But Dahnuk had been the one to encourage her to drink more. Was the king concerned about outbursts?

Dinner passed in course after course of food that shouldn't have tasted like straw, but did, and conversation that could have kept her interest, but didn't. Her mind raced as she nodded and smiled and leaned into Shiva and laughed at any and every joke he uttered, raising her goblet to her lips time and again, but never touching the liquid within it.

Nobles commended the king on military equipment upgrades issued to each soldier and on the diligence of the men at the most recently observed drills. Someone asked the king about a large shipment of *konnolan* that had arrived at long last after weeks of waiting, and whether it was true that the substance could down a dragon. Aviama's stomach turned, and she thought she might be sick. Tossing a coy smile in Shiva's direction, she plucked his goblet from its place and took a swig of clean, untainted wine.

Her powers were already muted. Why not her senses as well?

The man to Aviama's right asked her what she thought of Radha, and she mumbled something about vibrant colors and spicy food. The commander opposite her asked how many children she thought she might have, with a wink at Shiva. Aviama faked a sip of her own glass, set it next to Shiva's, and stole his the next opportunity she got. The magna was inert for anyone without magic. He wouldn't notice any change.

Dessert came in the form of a purple pudding-like substance with a lilac blossom set on its surface. Aviama grimaced at the color, then fixed her face as she felt the queen's glare settle over her like ice. Shiva leaned over. "It's not spicy. It's sweet, and made in your honor."

Of course it was. Aviama adjusted the amethyst jewels at her throat and swallowed. "What is it?"

"Lemon lavender cream with whipped topping and white chocolate shavings. Shall I take a bite of yours?"

Aviama leaned backward to give him room, and he scooped the edge of the gorgeously curated dessert onto the golden spoon he'd been provided with. He took the bite and smiled. "Incredible. The chef has outdone himself."

Okay, so the pudding was safe. Whoever had gotten to her goblet had meant to stop her powers, not take her life. Aviama picked up her spoon and dug in. Her best distraction from uncomfortable questions and eyeballs was food, and aside from the possibility of poison, it was really rather fantastic.

Shiva tapped his spoon on the crystal water glass used to cleanse the palate, and the buzz of conversation in the room hushed. He stood at his place, sweeping the room in his shining gold-embroidered yellow royal robes. Shoulders back, chin high, dark eyes roving over his audience, there was no question that this man was accustomed to authority. And when he opened his mouth, his voice commanded the large space. "My father knows how to throw a banquet, does he not?"

Cheers. Applause. One fool in the back of the room sloshing his goblet high over his head. Aviama's stomach knotted.

"The extremists have made a go of it the last few days, but we've caught and killed several of them in the last twenty-four hours. And one of them gave up critical information before he died. It's a mercy we got to him before Darsh did."

More applause. Raucous laughter. Praise for killing. Aviama shoveled in another spoonful of the lavender dessert.

Shiva surveyed the room, looking each noble in the face as he addressed them. "What do these melderbloods have that we don't? What do they want that we can't offer? Yesterday, melderbloods were purposeless wanderers. Today, they have a place to run from the crazy criminal at their helm. And we will welcome them with open arms, and they will use and not use their abilities according to *our* word. No more will these lost and vulnerable people taint our streets with the pandemic of their chaos! No, they will have a home where they can learn under *our* roof and under *our* restrictions. But how can they trust us? How can we trust them?"

Control. It's the only thing Aviama could hear pouring from his mouth. *Yesterday, melderbloods were outside our control and powerful enough to break into the palace. Today, we lure them in, keep our enemies close, and drug them with magna until they do what we want.* She took another sip of wine.

Prince Shiva turned toward Aviama, took her hand, and pulled her to her feet. She choked on her wine and side-stepped to avoid tripping on her own skirts. Heat flooded her face. Shiva kissed her hand and lifted it high in the air between them.

Aviama held her breath. Here it was—the crux of the evening, the anticipated announcement, the moment they'd all been waiting for. The demand Aviama must not deny, no matter how repulsive it might be.

31

P rince Shiva squeezed Aviama against him on one side and swept his free hand back to his audience. "Because a melderblood is in our house! When I become king one day, we hope a long day from now—long live the king—one of their own shall sit on the throne beside mine. A new era is here. Fresh perspective has arrived. And the turn of the tide comes with fighting fire with fire. What will the radicals do when we have melderbloods of our own taking *our* side instead of theirs?"

A murmur rolled through the room, a cocktail of excitement, anger, and uncertainty painted on the faces before them. Aviama shifted her weight, her reflexive, painted-on smile feeling more and more plastic by the second.

"My friends, not only does our union represent the strength of Radha, the alliances we shall increase, and the borders we will expand, but victory over melderblood rhetoric and a protection for your families and our people for years to come. The Return has served as a wakeup call for many of us. The world of the last three years has been a terrifying time, filled with death, destruction, and grief.

"Today, we set before you the plans to rectify this wave of tragedy rolling through our midst. Today, we say *no more* to the pain riddling our cities, the accidental deaths, the mass casualties of explosive power these melderbloods themselves cannot control. Because when I met Princess Aviama, she brought not only beauty and intelligence and wit, but partnership. She brought information we sorely needed, insight into a world that had been our blind spot for too long."

Aviama felt sick. *I told you how better to target and destroy my people.* The hum of the magna in her blood sent a dizzy spell through her, and she wavered on her feet. Shiva slipped an arm around the small of her waist and tugged her close against him, stabilizing her and illustrating his point at the same time.

"Princess Aviama was the first to show us that melderblood powers can be *controlled.* That she could use them *without* mass chaos. And that a melderblood heart could love this kingdom. Need I remind you that it was she who saved my life in the pit, putting her own life on the line in exchange for mine when Darsh could have killed me? She threw herself in harm's way for me, and now I put myself, my reputation, on the line for her. For you to hear me say this daring and new thing. That we will change, that we must change, to stay afloat in this novel current."

He paused, and Aviama stared at him. Confidence rippled off him in waves. His arm was strong around her waist, and his threat whispered through her mind again.

If you do not convince me that I am your greatest dream, that you are obsessively, head over heels in love with me...I'll kill one of the women attending you.

Sai stood against the wall with the other servants, and Aviama glanced in her direction. Her expression was neutral, professional, but her face was white. The question of her bruise came to mind again, but then Aviama saw Shiva turn in her peripheral vision, and she whipped her head back to him in time to meet his gaze.

She tried to summon a look of love, but felt more stricken than emotive in any way. A lump lodged in her throat, and Shiva's eyes darkened as he looked at her. The shadow of his disapproval melted an instant later, and his features softened into what could easily be mistaken by the casual observer as tenderness.

They were all casual observers. No one was so serious about their relationship as Shiva. And no one knew the truth of it all except Aviama. Terror seized her heart. Goosebumps ran up and down her flesh. If she didn't look convincing soon, one of her women would die.

Shiva watched her solemnly for a full minute before speaking again, and in the silence of that room, anyone could have heard a pin drop. When he spoke again, his voice was loud enough to be heard by all, but slow and purposeful, laden with oil and honey.

"I have fallen madly in love with the woman you see before you. I dare you to find a more stunning creature in all the land. And I know beyond a shadow of a doubt that she feels the same for me and will defend both me and my house, and therefore you and yours, as we work for the good of Radha for years to come." Shiva turned to face her head on rather than standing side by side and lifted a hand to graze her cheek. "Princess Aviama of Jannemar, my sweetest Lilac, you are my greatest prize. Will you accept publicly what you have already accepted privately in our conversation just this morning? Will you partner with me in training up a force of melderblood warriors for an elite protection squad in the service of Radha?"

Her lips parted, and the breath left her body. He wanted

her to train melders to fight against Darsh. Fire with fire. A silent scream stuck in her throat, and in that instant, Shiva's face began to change.

She had failed to convince him. In public, in front of everyone, appearances be hanged, she had failed to promote his agenda and fulfill his order. But try as she might, words would not come. And her death hung just a breath from Shiva's lips.

Aviama moved then, pitching herself forward, entwining her fingers in his hair and knocking the crown askew as her open mouth connected with his and their bodies collided. He staggered backward to catch her, but then his mouth moved with hers, his arms sliding around her—one around her waist and the other at the nape of her neck under her hair. She could feel him smiling in their kiss, a triumphant euphoria as his power over her cinched tight.

Her heart crumbled in her chest, and as she pulled away, and Shiva released her, the only need she felt at that moment was for survival. Shocked onlookers gathered themselves and applauded, but she refused to look at them. Aviama sucked in a deep breath and stared Shiva full in the face. She spoke quietly, for only the prince to hear, keeping her face tender and loving as she regained control of herself and cocked her head at him sweetly.

"I'm not a good teacher."

Shiva smiled back at her with an adoring expression twice as sweet as hers. "I don't believe you."

"I can't do it."

"I know you can."

"How would you know a thing like that?"

He couldn't admit to Sai informing to him, or he'd expose his servant spy. And he knew it didn't matter, because Aviama was clay in his hands to do with as he pleased. The pawn would obey or be cut to pieces. Shiva gave her another peck on the lips and dropped his voice to a guttural snarl in her ear. "Respond correctly, and loudly, right now."

Aviama smiled a tight smile and lifted her voice loud enough for the listening crowd. "I accept your offer and will train your melders. With the king's support, Radha is entering a new era indeed."

Shiva arched his eyebrow in approval over her nod to the king and embellished acceptance. He turned to the crowd, and after a beat of silence, the room erupted. Cries of support rose to the vaulted ceiling, the chandeliers swaying in the stamping and shouting.

"For Radha!"

"To a new era!"

"Long live the king! Long live the prince! Long live the House of the Blessing Sun!"

Shiva snatched Aviama's hand and lifted it into the air again, and King Dahnuk stood to his feet and thrust his goblet out toward the room.

"To my son and his bride!"

The room shouted back, eager to join with their king. "Hear, hear!"

Queen Satya clapped and drank to the couple along with the rest, but as Aviama met her gaze over the rim of the queen's goblet, murder lived in her eyes.

Aviama's chest tightened, and her mouth went dry. Nausea swept through her like an ocean tidal wave. She drained the wine in her goblet.

King Dahnuk held up a hand, and the excitement died down. Dahnuk clapped Shiva on the shoulder and kept his hand there as he addressed his guests. "I was elated when my son and his betrothed explained their plans to me. There is no greater partnership than one founded on a shared loyalty, a deeper purpose."

Aviama swallowed and fixed her gaze on the king, both to avoid the dark look of the queen and to ignore the frequent glances from every eye in the room. Shiva was his mother's son, but as she watched his father lie so easily to his people, she knew he'd inherited a strong dose of his father as well. Dahnuk's relaxed demeanor made for a convincing delivery, his assertion that Shiva and Aviama had approached him with a shared dream sounding just as believable as Shiva's statement that Aviama had already agreed to his proposal of training an elite squad of melder fighters for the Tanashai royal house.

Dahnuk dipped his head in her direction, and she instinctively bowed her head in return. "Tonight, you have heard these young people's dedication to you and to our kingdom and our safety in these troubling times. But I know newness is difficult to accept, and so we have arranged for a demonstration tomorrow evening in this very room. Tomorrow night, every noble in the region will have a front-row seat to Princess Aviama's exhibition of skill—and the melderblood students she will train. Don't worry, we will have safeguards in place, and you will see for yourselves how great power is not only an excellent tool, but a liability for the holder. How in these days, it is only with the partnership of trueblooded people that melderbloods prosper and stay safe.

"For the first time in history, we offer a marriage of melderblood and trueblood. Tomorrow night, we will show them off, and you will see them in action for yourselves. No one will miss this event. And now, toast with me once more—to the melderblood princess and the trueblood prince!"

Aviama spun the rings on her fingers, the throb of her heart setting a frenzied drumbeat in her chest as a sinking feeling rooted her feet to the floor. In one calculated final statement, the king had created a formal divide not only between the supposedly cursed melderbloods and the rest of Radha, but a separation between the two groups so stark they were almost different species. Melderbloods would be dependent on truebloods to survive, and truebloods would keep melderbloods in check, almost certainly with magna and konnolan as their weapons.

Aviama lifted her goblet to drink the toast, but it was already empty.

32

Musicians materialized in the corner of the room, striking up a romantic ballad. Shiva took her hand and led her out onto the dance floor in the center of the room. Melderblood and trueblood, side by side, hand in hand. A symbol of the control of Radha, the docile melder princess falling in line under the direction of her Radhan handlers.

Shiva led her through the familiar steps of the dance, and Aviama fell into the motions with practiced ease. He pulled her close and searched her face as the music offered an opportunity for private conversation. "You did well."

Aviama clenched her jaw, then released the tension. They were still in public, and appearances were everything. "Are you telling me there won't be a severed head in my brunch tomorrow?"

Shiva's mouth twisted into a lopsided smile. "The future is always uncertain, but it seems unlikely."

Not funny. Not amusing. Aviama chose not to dignify it with a response, so Shiva continued the conversation himself.

"Tomorrow, you will start early in the morning with a

group of four hand-picked melderbloods. You have all day to prepare a demonstration for the banquet. Be impressive."

Aviama gawked at him. "You say that as if it's a lot of time. It's not. Delay the banquet. There's no way I'll have anything prepared by then."

And anyone who's in this room tomorrow night will die. She'd promised Chenzira she wouldn't be at tomorrow's event, whatever it was. But how could she keep that promise if she was the star of the show?

Shiva pursed his lips. "You're not giving yourself enough credit."

"You're not living in reality. It can't be done. I don't even know who you have picked out, much less how wild their abilities might be."

"Enough." His voice was firm and final, and she snapped her mouth shut even as anger broiled inside her. Shiva twirled her away from him, then brought her back with a stronger spin than she expected, catching her as she stumbled her way back to him.

"We really did find the location of Darsh's people. You don't need to worry about any more attacks on the palace. We want you focused, so we're sending a platoon out to take care of it tonight. Everyone at the meeting place will be dead by midnight."

Stone-cold weight slugged her in the gut. "You're killing them all?"

He gave a nod, and she took a shaky breath. Murin. Chenzira. They'd all be dead. She let him lower her into a dip, chewing on what words she could say to stop the carnage. "Don't you think some of them could be turned? That you could use them? Won't killing them just tell the melders you're their enemy instead of the friend you claim to be?"

Shiva chuckled. "No, I think it will send a clear message

that extremist criminals will not be tolerated and that Darsh is not a legitimate option for melders. They'll soon learn that joining Darsh means konnolan strikes and death. That we are not defenseless against them. And when we offer an alternative, they'll be *begging* us for the chance to train in safety."

He was right. If melders really thought they'd die with Darsh, only the craziest would hold out for the Shadow. The rest would line up, falling over themselves for a way to avoid the terrors of their awakenings, for training and purpose and the promise of a prestigious job at the palace rather than the shame of their cursed blood they'd been living with so far.

Her head ached. She'd handed Radha the tools to harm melders when she'd been dumb enough to trust Shiva with the information about konnolan. Since then, she'd only managed to be blackmailed in every possible direction, hurt more people, and fail every person who dared see something good in her.

A quick rundown of her situation only made her headache worse. Darsh blackmailing her to train his radical melders. Shiva blackmailing her to train their own melders to fight Darsh. The queen wanting her dead, and the royal family killing any Darsh sympathizers they found. Enzo's head on a platter just that morning. Shiva threatening to kill one of her women. One of her women with a mysterious bruise. And a hostage siren who claimed that if Aviama married Shiva, Radha would have the final tool they needed to fight back against the Iolani and take control of the Aeian Sea.

Oh, and one more thing—Darsh planned to annihilate the royal family tomorrow night, along with anyone at the banquet. A banquet for which Aviama was the main event.

If the Radhan platoon killed Darsh's people tonight, Aviama would have no one to help her stall or avoid her wedding with Shiva, and Murin and Chenzira would likely die along with the rest of the Shadow. If they didn't kill Darsh's people, the Shadow would kill Shiva and his people, and Aviama with them, tomorrow night.

There was nothing for it. Aviama had to escape the palace again, tonight, and warn the Shadow. Maybe if she found Chenzira before the platoon did, she could save the people in the hidden underground room and find a way to convince Darsh to stop the attack on the banquet the following night.

But with Aviama scheduled to train all day tomorrow, she'd be closely watched every waking moment until the big event. The Tanashais wouldn't risk losing their star pawn. And without the Shadow's help, what were the chances she could really get away again so soon?

Aviama moved through the next steps with grace, facing Shiva at the next turn and giving a slight nod. "Okay. But I need to start preparing for tomorrow now. There is not enough time in the day. There's not enough time in a week. This demonstration is going to be awful. I need access to the open air and privacy. And time. Lots of it."

Shiva gave a slow, reticent nod as the music swelled toward its conclusion. "Very well. I'll excuse you for the night after this dance. That will give you the chance to slip away before all the nobles come to congratulate you and mob you with questions, and the evening will come to a close in your absence. Follow my lead, and I'll get you what you need. But rain or shine, war or peace, we *are* having the demonstration banquet tomorrow night."

The song ended four measures later. Shiva bowed to her, and she curtsied to him. Shiva thanked the guests and told them that Princess Aviama was so excited about her task for the next day, wanting it to be the best possible show she could manage, that she'd asked for extra time to get to work on it and would be slipping away to focus on her important task.

Aviama thanked everyone for the wonderful evening and the pleasure of their company, and assured them tomorrow would be a night they wouldn't forget.

She didn't mention it might also be the last memories they ever had before their untimely deaths.

Shiva escorted her to the doors, and Sai moved from her position on the back wall to follow Aviama out. With Sai on the move, no guard followed. Aviama hurried down the hall and around the first corner, doubling her pace and skipping the staircase toward her residence floor in favor of the way toward the guest hall and the pakshi courtyard.

No one followed. If she was fast enough, maybe she'd lose Sai. A twinge of guilt knotted in her stomach at evading Sai, but it had to be done. Aviama could worry about saving Sai's skin tomorrow.

The way toward the courtyard passed in shades of color after color in room after room as she wound through the halls and finally came into view of the bird-shaped pool and its accompanying flowers, fruit trees, and benches. The night was clear, and the silver light of the moon overpowered the orange of the torchlight and reflected off the surface of the water. Aviama cast a glance over her shoulder, but the place was empty. With the event going on in the main hall, and the army marching toward Jannemar, personnel must be running thin.

Still, she only had a matter of seconds before Sai or someone else would inevitably catch up to her and stop her. Aviama flew to the far side of the pool and into the shadow of the trees shading a bench next to a burbling fountain where the edge of the pool and the curated garden ran up against tile. The tingling effects of the magna still muted her powers, and if anyone found her, she'd be helpless to stop them from taking hold of her and dragging her away. And she wouldn't be able to use her powers to help find pockets of air beneath the floor to lead her to the entrance.

What if the tunnel had been found and stopped up? What if it led to the king's office behind the menagerie, but the Shadow hadn't built a way out from there to beyond the palace walls?

No, there had to be a way. Because if there wasn't, it wasn't Murin or Chenzira or Sai's neck she should be worried about, but her own.

Aviama dropped to her hands and knees on the tiled floor and searched the edges of each tile as it bumped up against the next. She'd only been in the tunnel once before, when Chenzira had helped her escape the king's private office before the arena, but they'd come *out* this way. Aviama never saw how to get *in*.

Her fingers flew over the smooth floor, searching for imperfections. She moved the rocks nearby in case they were somehow mechanical, but nothing happened. She tapped the edges of the panel—wasn't this tile the door panel?—and leaned her weight against each of its edges in hopes of a lever or weight-detection system. Nothing. Nothing but curious fish gaping their mouths open at her, begging for food, and the fountain softly bubbling.

The fountain. Aviama crawled forward and ran her hands over every inch of the back of the fountain, a stone pakshi with spread wings spouting water from its open mouth. All of it was one piece, without blemish or mark or—

The panel shifted beneath her, and she clapped her hand over her mouth to keep from squealing. Something underneath the fountain statue had pressed inward, and the panel slid aside to reveal the opening she'd been looking for. Aviama peered around the statue to the rest of the courtyard. A breeze wafted through the fruit trees, and the ripple of a fish disturbed the surface of the pool, but the courtyard was quiet. She dropped into the tunnel.

The tile slid back into place above her with a soft scraping sound, and she fled down the dirt tunnel, running into the wall three times before holding her hands out on either side to guide her flight. She ran into a fork in the tunnel, and remembered the way from which she'd come when she'd been in the menagerie, so she took the other one and followed it in the opposite direction as fast as her legs could carry her.

If Chenzira had thought she was crazy for running out into the streets of Rajaad before with the wealthy robes of a royal, he'd absolutely lose his mind with the dripping extravagance of what she wore tonight. But she hadn't had time to find a disguise or a mantle. She'd simply have to try her luck with the burglars of Waif's Garden, because the magna still hummed in her blood, and there was no turning back now.

Aviama ran on and on. Time seemed to slow, and she had no guarantee the tunnel would lead her where she wanted to go. The slum wasn't far from the palace walls, but who was to say that's where this passage was going? What if she had to turn around, and it was all for nothing?

She ran for over an hour, but just when she'd started to wonder if she'd ever come to the end of the tunnel, a flickering light winked through a crack in what looked to be a wooden door. Aviama came up short just outside the door, heaving in exertion, gasping for breath, legs burning. The night was hushed. No discernible sound came from the other side of the door.

Aviama ran her hands along its surface, but there wasn't a handle. She searched for a crack or lever, but there was none. Panic welled up inside her, and she threw her weight against the door. It didn't budge.

A cold sweat broke out across her forehead, and she wiped

clammy palms on her rich skirts. What kind of people might wait beyond this door? What would they do to her when they saw her—a blonde foreigner wearing enough baubles to pay their livelihood for years? The same foreigner that had been paraded through Rajaad riding on the back of a bahataal not long ago...But the alternative was worse. Oh, so much worse. Besides, if the tunnel was the Shadow's, it was likely everything beyond it also belonged to the Shadow.

Aviama banged on the door. "Help!"

Silence.

She tried again, banging on the door, and throwing her slight weight against it with all she had. "HELP! I'm trapped! Get me out!"

The tingling from the magna had dropped to a muted prickling feeling, but though Aviama could sense the air around her with better clarity, she still couldn't quite reach for it. "Help, please! Somebody!"

Aviama sagged against the door, warm blood running down her wrist where the wooden door had bitten into her fist. The light through the crack in the door leaped up, and a crackle broke the stillness. Aviama fell back just in time, eyes wide, as fire fell on the base of the door and started licking at its base.

33

F ire lit the tunnel, showing dirt in the cramped space around Aviama—except for several wooden support beams lining the passage at intervals. More wood. *Biscuits.*

"Idiot!" someone yelled.

"How was I supposed to know that would happen?" a second voice whined.

"It's a wooden door. What did you expect?"

"I only meant to make a little light!"

"Do us all a favor and make yourself scarce instead."

"But I want to see."

A slosh of water doused the fire, and a moment later, a sliding sound marked a bar removed from its place on the other side of the door. The door pulled open.

A teenage boy blinked around the shoulder of a slender young man blocking the way, taking her in with saucer-wide eyes. "Whoa."

Aviama grimaced and turned her attention to the man. With a start, she realized she knew him. He was the crest-breaker from the bathhouse.

He crossed his arms and arched an eyebrow. "Our intrepid leader, huh? How'd you find out about this tunnel, anyway?"

Aviama shook her head. "It really doesn't matter. What matters is a platoon of guards from the palace is heading to Waif's Garden right now to wipe out the Shadow. They know about the meeting place. One of the Shadows they caught talked before they executed him. We've got to get everyone out."

She lurched forward through the doorway, but the crest-breaker didn't move. She bumped into him and looked up in surprise.

His eyes narrowed as he looked down at her. "Who talked?"

"What?"

"Which of the Shadow squealed?"

Aviama threw her hands up. "I don't know. I wasn't there. But they're coming to catch you all. We don't have time for this! Take me to Darsh. Or Ramta. Or Arjun. Anyone. We have to go!"

How could he risk not believing her at a threat like this? How insane was this man? He turned from the doorway, and Aviama stepped through the opening into a cramped living area outfitted with a wooden chair, a long bench, and a three-legged stool. Two more closed doors interrupted the walls. An overturned bucket still dripped water onto the floor by the base of the door, and the kid grabbed a wool blanket from the bench and started working on soaking up the excess.

The man disappeared into one of the other rooms and reappeared with a large, rough-spun blanket. "I'll take you to Darsh, all right. But not like that, and not to the meeting place."

He tossed the blanket to her, and she caught it. "My hair?"

The man nodded, disappeared again, and came back with

a shawl. Aviama tugged it over her hair and headpiece, and wrapped the blanket around her shoulders, covering as much of her dress as possible, then turned to face the crestbreaker. "Let's go. We don't have long. If they're not dead already, they will be by midnight."

The boy, maybe thirteen, still gawked at her from the corner. He must be a fireblood. The crestbreaker cuffed him on the back of the head. "Don't stare. It's rude. Go tell the owner we've got company."

"Owner?"

"Owner of this shack." The crestbreaker waved a hand at the hovel around them. "Someone in the Shadow. Not a name I'll share. Let's go."

The boy grinned and scampered off, and the crestbreaker led her through one of the other doors into a cramped little room that doubled as a kitchen and an entryway. It had about a meter of counter space, a few buckets and baskets stacked on top of one another, and shelves against the wall opposite the door. The crestbreaker dipped out the front door, and Aviama followed.

The shack was connected to a long line of other shacks, occasionally broken up by little alleyways and strings of clothesline between the rows of houses. Three big, bulky boys crossed the walkway ahead of them, laughing and kicking at trash along the side of the dirt road. The crestbreaker paused in the shadow of one of the alleys, standing in front of Aviama until their boisterous noise faded down some other road. Side path? Neither road nor street seemed a fitting name for the packed dirt winding throughout Waif's Garden, but whatever it was, the boys traveled down it, and the crestbreaker set off again at twice the speed he'd set before.

Her legs ached from running down the tunnel, and twice she had to jog a few steps to keep up, but she still kept wishing the crestbreaker would move faster. They turned left, walked up a short hill, and left again at the end of a row. Aviama hurried to stay close. "Is Ramta here?"

"Don't know. He's been doing his own thing the past few days."

Was he trying to get Darsh to stop tomorrow night's attack?

The old woman's house came into view, and Aviama picked up her pace, but the crestbreaker held out a hand to stop her. "Wait here."

Aviama's pulse pounded in her ears as the crestbreaker spoke to the old woman at the door, went inside, and shut the door behind him. Approaching footsteps spiked her heart rate, and a woman came into view, gave her a look, and let herself into the house. Into the death trap. Into the target of the night.

Minutes ticked by, and still the crestbreaker did not return. What if the soldiers came, and they still had not heard the warning? What if the guards found Aviama in Waif's Garden? What if Darsh heeded the warning and took everyone out some back door, leaving Aviama hung out to dry by the front?

This last thought stopped her cold. It was likely. Darsh had already planned on ditching Aviama, and there was no reason he'd want to keep her around now if he'd decided she was too much trouble. She'd die here, and no one would mourn her passing.

Aviama whirled from the door and took off down a side street to who-knows-where. Could a blonde princess dripping in jewels hide from the king's men? With the elite working for the Tanashais and half the slum working for Darsh, what chance did she have to find new clothes and escape before someone snitched? Not to mention how conspicuous she was, even in new clothes. *Biscuits.* She was a dead woman walking.

And then she heard it, headed toward her from the direction in which she'd been running. Boots. Swords ringing free from scabbards. A dozen men, at least. She skidded to a stop and fled in the opposite direction, taking the first turn on her left and diving through two alleys. The waving silk threads of a broken spiderweb clawed her face as she shoved her way through it, and a shiver ran down her spine. Aviama yanked the threads from her face, wiping the excess on the blanket around her, and pushed blankets and tunics aside on the alley's clothesline to forge ahead to the other side of the alley.

More footsteps. More steel. From the opposite end of the alley. Aviama grimaced, her feet rooted to the ground. She called to the wind, testing her melder power, but the magna in her blood was still blocking her. A wisp of wind curled around one finger, mocking her. Two groups of soldiers now trapped her inside the alley, the rather conspicuous human blanket rolled like a croissant, clinking with gemstones and rustling in wealthy skirts every time she moved.

Aviama stifled a moan. The soldiers on one side passed, but the street was straight on that side for a long stretch, and she'd still be visible if she tried to get out that way. The second they started sweeping the streets, she'd be done for.

Her hand gripped the hanging tunic dress on her left, adjusting it to shield her from the open end of the alley. She froze, staring at the cloth in her hand. Did she have time? She wouldn't make it far in the cursed lilac dress Shiva had made her wear. And by now a thought was forming in her mind, as exhilarating as it was terrifying—she wasn't going back. She'd left the palace three nights in a row, and her only hope now was to warn the Shadow to save their lives, wait for the Shadow and the Radhan royal family to start ripping each other apart, and slip away when no one was looking.

A half-baked plan that would definitely get her caught and

killed one way or another. But if the half-baked plan might keep her alive for the next couple of hours, she'd take it. Aviama ripped the tunic dress off the clothesline and the matching pair of trousers that went under it, and peeled off the heavy gown. Shouts rippled through the slum just as the chill night air bit at her bare skin. Aviama shrugged into the coarse, rough-spun tunic and yanked the trousers up under it, shaking her sandals free of the dress once and for all.

"Pssst."

Aviama snapped her head left and right, her heart in her throat. The silhouette of a group of soldiers filtered in through the blanket against the light of the moon, but no one stood in the alley where she was hiding.

"Psssssst."

She looked up. Chenzira peered down at her from the rooftop of one of the houses in the row to her left. Her jaw dropped, and the safety of his nearness washed over her in a warm feeling from head to toe. "How did you find me?" she hissed.

He gestured her to be quiet and shrugged. He couldn't hear what she was saying. Chenzira motioned her up toward the roof, but how could she get to him?

Of course. He didn't know she couldn't command the wind.

Aviama snatched the shawl the crestbreaker had given her, secured it over her forehead and around her hair, and scanned the wall. A mix of wooden boards and run-down clay patch-worked the wall on this side. But though the wear on the wall did create some indentations, Aviama wasn't exactly an accomplished climber. And there wasn't much to work with.

She could pull down the clothesline and use it, but if she did, she'd also remove the clothing barrier protecting her from the soldiers' line of sight. Aviama grabbed the dress she'd just ripped off and hesitated. How long had Chenzira been watching from overhead?

Mortified, she rolled the dress into a ball and chucked it up toward the rooftop. It fell down again on her head in a wad. Aviama clawed through it and glared up at Chenzira.

"What?" he mouthed.

Aviama pursed her lips and gave an exaggerated jab at the dress and then at Chenzira. He furrowed his brow, but leaned forward toward the edge of the roof. Aviama threw it up again, and he caught it, freezing as he stared at the inside of the bodice as if he'd touched fire. Aviama waved her hand to get his attention and mimicked the motion of climbing a rope. Chenzira quirked an eyebrow.

Biscuits. This was embarrassing. She threw her hands up. "Toss it down!"

"After all the work you did to get it up here?"

She gritted her teeth, but he grinned, rolled the dress into a twisted rope, and lowered it over the edge of the roof, holding tightly to the top. Aviama gripped it with both hands and scrambled up the wall, making little progress, if any, until Chenzira started yanking at his end and hauling her up to the top. Her foot caught the lip of the wooden boards where they met the clay, and she pushed upward enough to catch the edge of the roof with her elbow. Chenzira pulled her over the side. She tried to stand, but he tugged her down, shaking his head. She'd be too visible if they stood.

Chenzira sniffed, then took a deep inhale. "You smell like wine."

"You smell like spices." Did she say that out loud?

"What?"

Biscuits. She had. Aviama cleared her throat. "And also like dirt. And maybe sweat."

"Yes, well, trying to keep you alive is a full-time job, so pardon me if I break a sweat now and then."

"Shiva told me they already know where the Shadow meets and they planned on killing them tonight by midnight, so I had to get out and warn you. But the soldiers are here now, and I guess I'm too late."

"Come on. We have to get to the house. We'll need all the help we can get. Stay low." Chenzira gathered his feet and perched on the roof in a crouch, but Aviama clutched at his arm as he turned away.

"Chenzira...I...I don't have my powers. They slipped magna in my drink tonight, and I can't do anything."

He stared at her, then cursed under his breath. "They knew. They knew you'd come to warn us."

"They want me to train an elite melderblood bodyguard for the palace. I'm supposed to practice all day with a few melders they've got and put on a demonstration tomorrow night. That's the event. I'm the show. I think they were afraid of how I would react."

Chenzira set his jaw, steel in his eyes. "Were you followed?"

"No."

"Are you sure?"

Aviama hesitated. Could she have been followed? Sai saw her leave, but Aviama had lost her in the halls before she made it to the pakshi courtyard. Hadn't she? And there were no guards trailing her...

Why had no guards trailed her?

Her heart sank. Chenzira swore.

"It's going to be a slaughter. We have to stop the soldiers before they get inside."

"Is that possible?"

"I don't know. If they have another squad, they could already be there."

Chenzira snatched an axe from its place on his back and whirled it in his right hand, then glanced at Aviama and paused. He took a sharp breath, and the look on his face made her think he was stifling an eye roll. "Turn around."

"What?"

Chenzira made a spinning motion with his finger, and she slowly rotated. He stuffed the axe under his arm and gently moved her shawl-wrapped hair to one side, cold night-bitten fingers brushing the skin of her neck. A chill ran down her spine, and she shivered. She was about to turn and ask him what he was doing when the clasp of her necklace released, and it slid from her neck.

"You're still not good at disguises."

"My options were limited."

Chenzira stuffed the amethyst necklace into a pouch at his waist and adjusted the shawl around her hair. Aviama unclasped her bracelets and passed them to him. She didn't have anywhere to keep them. She reached for her rings, but instead turned them in towards her palm and looked up hopefully at Chenzira. One of them was her mother's. She wasn't ready to let go.

He eyed her for a moment, then nodded. "Good enough. Let's go."

Aviama followed Chenzira at a low run across the rooftop and over what Chenzira clearly considered a reasonable bridge but what was really a narrow board placed between two rows of houses. Aviama gasped as she came to it, but Chenzira was already across. A breeze wafted over them, and the board rocked. *Great.*

The pounding of soldiers' footsteps grew closer. Aviama screwed up her face in a tight grimace and ran for it. Her foot slipped on the precarious board, and she stumbled onto the next roof, sending the board skittering its way down the wall and falling to the dirt below.

The soldiers' footsteps stopped. Aviama froze. Chenzira swore again.

Chink.

Aviama whirled toward the sound just in time to see an arrow fall from the roof where it had hit only a breath from her sandal. And then a wall of wind knocked her clean off the roof, sending her plunging to the ground to the sound of her own scream.

34

F ire lit the night in short, explosive bursts, and the ringing steel and shouts of exertion from men in combat filled the air. Aviama's trajectory slung sideways straight into the wall just before she hit the ground. It slowed her descent but slammed her forearms and body against the clay of a house. She couldn't see or hear Chenzira.

Her legs ached from running, her arms burned with pain from the impact, and her mind spun. If she'd come to warn the Shadow, why had they knocked her from the roof?

She didn't have long to wait. Two arms seized her, and a big, grimy hand clapped over her mouth. Wind wisped through her fingers, but stalled out there, like a current hoping for something to hold on to but finding nothing. The tingling effects of the magna still clung to her, and she settled for jabbing her elbows backwards into her captors instead. A grunt told her she'd found purchase, but the grip on her arms only tightened.

Darsh rounded the corner and strode toward Aviama, his hand up, a whirlwind hovering over his palm. The crest-breaker stood behind him, his arm cinched tight around a woman's slender neck. Sai. Aviama's breath caught, and she knew the moment she laid eyes on Sai that Darsh saw what he was looking for in Aviama's face.

Recognition. Fear. Fear for someone who worked for Shiva. All Darsh saw was a traitor to his cause, the face of his movement converted into his worst enemy. Her chest hitched, and even as Darsh's dark glare bored into her skull, it was the terror in Sai's wide eyes that weighed down Aviama's heart like a stone in water.

Like a pebble cast to vote on the death of a Radhan guard.

Where was Chenzira? The thought came and went, but he didn't appear. The hand over her mouth lifted, but the hold on her arms remained. Aviama glanced at the crestbreaker crushing Sai's windpipe and turned to Darsh. "Did he tell you? Did he tell you I came to warn you?"

Darsh swirled the little whirlwind in his palm, then hopped it over to the other hand, arching an eyebrow at her as he did so. "Oh, yes. He told me how helpful you'd been. How informative. How you took a tunnel you shouldn't have known about, escaping the palace at your whim, and led the prince's rat right to us. Should I be impressed that you predicted soldiers to arrive when it was you who brought them in the first place?"

Aviama's stomach churned. "No. I came to warn you. I didn't know she followed me—"

Darsh waved a hand. "I couldn't care less what words come out of your mouth. If you keep spewing them, I might be tempted to have your tongue cut out."

She stiffened, and goosebumps fled down her arms. Darsh walked forward again, favoring one leg just slightly. Her gaze drifted down toward his foot, and she raised her eyes back up to his. Darsh wasn't exceptionally tall, but his broad shoulders, powerful demeanor, and sweltering confidence more than made up for it.

Aviama tested the air again. It sprung to her fingertips at her call, stronger than before, but the energy wilted and died there. She lifted her chin. "If you want to appear as powerful as all your people seem to think you are, you're going to have to do a better job of hiding your limp. Do you remember how you got it? You were caught and nearly killed. Would have been, if not for me. I was the distraction *and* the leverage you needed in the arena. Is this how you repay me?"

One of the men holding Aviama shifted his weight. She couldn't see who it was, but any suggestion that she was getting in his head was encouragement enough.

Darsh's expression darkened, and he opened his mouth, but just then, four arrows whistled through the air. Aviama dove sideways as the hold on her arms loosened and one of her captors fell. She spun, only to see four soldiers with drawn bows and notched arrows as they let fly with another volley.

Aviama threw her hand up and called the wind as an arrow flew straight at her heart. But nothing happened. Until it did—a wind shield as wide as the alley flew up, dropping the arrows out of thin air. Aviama twisted, and Sai dropped her hand, shaking. The cat was out of the bag. Sai had revealed herself as a melder.

The crestbreaker holding Sai stumbled backward in surprise as three more soldiers sprinted into the other side of the alley, hemming them in on both sides. Darsh blasted two of them backward with a gust of wind, but the third dropped to the ground under the blow and threw a knife into the back of the crestbreaker's neck. He dropped like a rock.

Sai pitched forward, clutching Aviama by the arm. Tears streamed down her face. "I'm sorry. He'll kill my family. I'm sorry. But I didn't think you'd die too."

"Shiva?"

Sai nodded. Aviama's lip curled at the mention of his name on her lips, the bullying threat of murder he held over everyone's heads. Sai was a pawn. What choice did she have? But then again, Aviama couldn't afford to trust her, either.

Still, she didn't want to see her dead. And Darsh would gladly kill her, and at this point, just about anyone would gladly kill Aviama too.

A sharp whistle cut through the night, followed by two answering whistles from somewhere further into Waif's Garden. The scream of a grown man ripped through the air from somewhere nearby. The archers rushed Darsh and the remaining melder in the alley. Three more melders dropped in from the roof, one enveloping a soldier in fire but blowing the fireball beyond its target until the embers caught in the thatch of a residence on the far side. A windcaller threw a blast of air through the alley, breaking the neck of one of the soldiers, but knocking both Darsh and his adversary off their feet to boot.

Uncontrolled. Rash. Dangerous.

Aviama grabbed Sai's palm and yanked it up in front of them. "Make a bubble. Shield us."

"I can't! I don't know how!"

"Fine, settle for short bursts. Push them back. Push!"

A burst of wind shot forward from Sai's palm and swept two soldiers and a Shadow melder into the wall on one side, leaving a gap just large enough for Sai and Aviama to run through. Outside the alley, four men streaked by in worn, rough-spun tunics carrying swords, clubs, and daggers. Flames licked at one of the houses two rows down, the smoke rising into the sky, smothering the light of the moon with its billowing haze. The ground rolled unnaturally beneath their feet, sending Sai sprawling, and somewhere the sound of cannon fire added to the chaos.

Darsh's booming voice called out from behind her. "You don't have me fooled, Princess! You're *dead*! You will not live to see the dawn!

Air coursed along her palms. The magna was wearing off. She wasn't strong yet, but it was growing. Aviama yanked Sai to her feet and jutted her chin up to the rooftops. "Get us up there."

Sai shook her head. "I can't. What if we go too far and crash?"

Six more soldiers rounded the corner. Aviama groaned. "You can do this."

Aviama might not trust Sai completely, but she knew the girl didn't want her to die. And Sai had the power Aviama lacked. Sai threw her hands out, and Aviama grabbed them and repositioned them so the girl's palms faced downward. Aviama held tight to Sai's waist. "Just get yourself up there, and I'll come with you."

Sai nodded, and a gust of air rushed from her hands, lurching them up into the air a meter or so and then dropping them into the dust. The soldiers were only fifteen paces away now. Twelve. Eight.

"Halt! Halt in the name of the king!"

The first of the soldiers reached out to take hold of Aviama, but the ground beneath him opened up, and all six of the soldiers fell into a pit that materialized out of thin air. The house beside them pitched sideways, the wall collapsing into rubble as its foundation crumbled. Dirt flooded in around the soldiers' legs like a wave, solidifying around them until they were rooted in the earth like trees from the knee down, sticking up at two-thirds of their normal height.

A sharp whistle caught Aviama's attention, and she

whirled to see Chenzira standing on the rooftop next to the collapsed home, looking down at her. An arrow flew toward him, and he blocked it with his axe. "Hurry up! And leave the rat!"

Sai's face drained of color, but Aviama grabbed her wrist and pulled her along after her. She ran up the rubble, catching herself twice as she stumbled her way up the wood and clay and thatch. Chenzira extended his hand and pulled her onto the sturdy roof of the intact home, then shoved her behind him and held a hand out in Sai's direction.

"You stay."

Aviama shook her head. "She comes."

But Chenzira didn't bat an eye, and never took his gaze off Sai's face. "She'll get you killed."

Aviama put a hand on his shoulder. "They'll kill her too."

Chenzira snatched Sai's wrist and ushered Aviama ahead of them, away from the soldiers stuck in the ground and the blazing huts in the distance. "We'll give her a head start, and then we'll cut her loose. She's a liability, and we can't afford for her to know what happens next."

Her heart twisted at the ominous tone of his voice. "What *does* happen next?"

Chenzira's face turned to flint. "I can't afford for you to know it yet either."

Three short whistles and one long whistle came from somewhere below them, but Aviama couldn't see anyone on the dirt path to either side. Her aching feet flew over rickety roof after roof until, on the fifth roof over, Chenzira snatched her elbow to stop her and kicked at a darker-colored area of roof. With a start, she realized it was charred. The area fell through, and Chenzira swept his hand toward it. Aviama peered into the hole, and Arjun and Murin's ash-covered faces beckoned to her from below.

Murin! Aviama dropped into the hole without hesitation, and Arjun caught her and set her on her feet. Murin took one arm and Arjun took the other, quickly shuffling her away from the hole toward the pitch-black corner.

Murin pulled her into a hug, and Aviama hugged her back, tears pricking her eyes. Her lady-in-waiting for years of her life blinked back tears of her own as they parted. "Darsh is too extreme, and when he turned on you, we knew we were done with him." She glanced at Arjun, and he nodded.

"I joined him because I thought he could change things, rebel against the monarchy, and remove the dirty name of melderbloods from Radha. He was inspiring. But he's gone too far, and I didn't sign up for this. There has to be another way."

"Arjun has agreed to get me out of Radha and escort me home to Jannemar. We'll tell everyone what happened. Yesterday, Ramta helped us finalize a last-minute plan, but we're moving things up and slipping out tonight while the chaos takes over Rajaad."

Aviama hugged Murin, then turned to Arjun. She paused, then hugged him too. "Thank you. I'm sorry I didn't always trust you. Thank you." She turned back to Murin, her chest tight, tears welling in her eyes and spilling down her cheeks. "I love you. I'm so glad you're with someone like Arjun. Someone with integrity, not to mention skill. I can tell you care about each other. I'm happy for you."

Murin wiped tears from her eyes, and Arjun nudged her arm. "We have to go."

Aviama reached out to touch him on the arm. "Thank you. Take care of her."

He nodded. "I will. Take care of yourself."

Thump.

Chenzira landed on the floor through the hole in the ceiling and came to clap Arjun on the back. They embraced, parted, and stepped away from each other, Arjun next to Murin, and Chenzira next to Aviama. "Safe travels. Get gone. Don't forget to talk to my contact at the border."

He dipped his head. "We will."

The two of them disappeared through a door on the far side, and Chenzira grabbed Aviama's hand. "Our turn. Let's go."

Aviama didn't move. "Where's Sai?"

"She's safe. Just delayed. I think it'll take her five minutes to get free, and if you don't come with me, I'll toss you over my shoulder. I'm not taking her with us."

"She'll die!"

"She'll be fine. She brought the soldiers to the Shadow's hideout, and the whole battle and everyone dying is because of her involvement." He spat on the ground. "She'll be a hero. Let's go. We have an appointment."

35

Chenzira led the way through dark streets, stopping and starting three separate times to avoid squads of soldiers running through Waif's Garden. Aviama swallowed hard and ran to keep up. Chenzira adjusted his grip on his battleaxe, leaving one hand free and his second axe still fixed on his back. A woman's scream split the night as two more cannon blasts rocked the air.

Aviama turned to look back, but Chenzira gripped her arm and pulled her forward. "Don't look back. I need you fixed on what's ahead, not behind."

"Are they shooting up their own city?"

"My guess is they've stuffed the cannons with konnolan. That way, they can kill the Shadow without destroying the city. If we hadn't gotten out as quickly as we did, we would have been incapacitated by it."

"They might still hit this area. We're just farther from the palace walls than the first blasts."

Chenzira's mouth pressed together in a tight line. "Correct. Which is why I need you moving forward."

Aviama hurried forward, focusing hard on not tripping

over her own feet as the dirt path flew by beneath them. "How could we have an appointment if you didn't know I was coming?"

"Let's just say I had a feeling you might need a fast getaway and started making arrangements. But we're going to need them moved up. A lot. To tonight."

A blur leaped across the narrow path in front of them, a flash of silver interrupting the dark. Chenzira knocked Aviama sideways, spun, and buried his axe in the neck of a Radhan soldier. Aviama gaped at him as the soldier crumpled to the ground. Chenzira gripped the man under the arms and hauled him off the path into the deep shadows of one of the houses, then returned, took Aviama's hand, and tugged her down the street at a run.

Aviama's pulse pounded in her ears as her aching legs dragged themselves over more ground, the patchwork shanties of disrepair dropping away behind them as they left Waif's Garden and entered a district she'd only ever seen from the back of a bahataal in the royal processional with Shiva. The memory sent a shiver down her spine. Forced kisses, fake smiles, threats whispered into her ear as the crowds cheered below...

Could she really be free of it all?

Tall buildings four, five stories high lined one side, not exactly nice but not as disjointed as the slum either. Up ahead, quaint shops cropped up, and cobbles replaced the dust that still clung to her feet and ankles from the run through Waif's Garden. The streets of the shops were empty, but as Chenzira turned away from the shops and into the aged, overgrown cobbles of the tall buildings and free-standing establishments on the north-west side, figures began to slink from door to door and shadow to shadow.

Aviama pulled her shawl tighter around her shoulders and

pressed closer to Chenzira, his confident stride and secure hold on his battleaxe offering some comfort. A man with a neck twice the size of Aviama's arm and muscles rippling through every fiber of his shirt eyed them darkly as they passed, his hand on the hilt of the dagger at his side. Aviama gulped, but Chenzira ignored him and passed on toward the third row of tall buildings.

Chenzira slid his axe to its place on his back as the man went by, dropping her hand and guiding her with a hand at her side down the cracked road, past another two buildings, down a side street, moving toward the strip they'd walked through before. He glanced over his shoulder only twice, but Aviama couldn't shake the feeling that they were being watched.

Raucous laughter emanated from one of the few buildings with lights on inside, a wide establishment nestled in the middle of the stack of buildings, the center door of a row of doors on the first floor of a four-story structure. A signpost marked with a boar with an apple in its mouth swung in the breeze. The door opened, and the smell of cheap ale and cooked meat wafted out into the street, following a cackling man and woman who staggered their way outside. The man counted coins in his hand as the woman rifled through three satchels slung under her arm.

Aviama grimaced. "We're not going in there, are we?"

"Boar's Tooth Tavern? You have something against swindlers, drunkards, and gamblers?"

She bit her lip, and Chenzira chuckled. "It's a seedy place, which makes it perfect for finding seedy people. Tuck that bauble on your forehead up into your hair and pull your shawl down. Stay close to me. I know a guy."

Aviama pulled the glittering headpiece free from her hair at the front of her scalp and tucked it further back and out of sight under the shawl. "I'm pretty sure the phrase *I know a guy* generally ends in bad decisions, injury, or death."

"Luckily, we've already made bad decisions by coming here, and our chances of injury and death are already quite high, so we haven't got much to lose."

"*I* didn't decide to come here."

Chenzira shrugged. "Guilty by association. Get used to it."

He opened the door, and the buzz of conversation dulled for a moment as those sober enough to care took in the late-night stragglers. Tables filled the center of the room, and booths with curtains lined the walls. A long bar was staged to the right, with doors leading back to a kitchen and a staircase flanked by two lanterns in the far corner at the back.

Chenzira's confident stride melted into an unstable swagger as they crossed the threshold. Two women sauntered over from a table in the middle of the room, tight-laced bodices and low-cut necklines inviting looks from the front while the skimpy skirts slit almost to the waist ensured no one need rely on imagination when observing their legs or rear. Aviama tried not to gape, but she froze as the first woman stroked a long finger down Chenzira's chest, and the other offered a winning smile. Aviama was pretty sure she was offering more than that.

Chenzira threw his arm around Aviama's shoulders with a smirk and pulled her off balance under his weight as he drifted this way and that, swinging away from the women toward the bar as if he hadn't even noticed the girls. A strange relief ran through her as they passed without incident, and Chenzira walked into the bar and leaned halfway over it on impact. It was anyone's guess whether he was going to order or throw up.

The bartender finished wiping out a glass with his rag and set it on the bar in front of Chenzira. "You been betraying me for Jackal Draft again? Haven't seen you in for a fortnight, save yesterday."

Chenzira set two coins on the bar and the empty glass on top of them. "You know I don't like that scene, Tenzin."

Tenzin shot him a look, then leaned forward and dropped his voice. "What can I do you for, Taug?"

"I'm here for a ganda bartha."

"We're all out."

"No, you're not."

Tenzin's features darkened, and the grizzled indifference faded. He pulled the glass toward him, knuckles white on the glass, and when he lifted it, the money was gone. Aviama blinked. She hadn't seen him take it.

"Let me check the back."

Aviama leaned closer to Chenzira, his arm still slung around her shoulders. "I thought you said we had an appointment. Why are we drinking in the shadiest place in town?"

"Shhh, not so loud. If you compliment the Boar's Tooth like that too loud, it'll be overrun before the words are out of your mouth. I told you, we have an appointment."

"With the bottom of a pint?"

"Pshhh, never. My order doesn't come in pints."

Aviama frowned and reached for her rings to fiddle with one. She'd hardly noticed she was doing it when Chenzira placed a hand over hers and shook his head. *Biscuits.* It was bad enough walking into a place like this with metal bands on her fingers. But advertising she was wearing costly gems? Aviama wondered if there was a line the people wouldn't cross to get their take.

Her heart raced, and she pulled away, suddenly self-conscious. Chenzira pulled his arm back but stayed close, pressing his arm against hers from shoulder to elbow. The warmth of his nearness steadied her. She took a deep breath.

Tenzin reappeared, his face a shade lighter than she'd remembered, snatched up a sparkling-clean glass from the shelf behind him and wiped it clean—or would have, if it'd had a particle of dust on it. The man jerked his chin toward the booths at the back. "Third booth from the stairs. Don't get comfortable."

Chenzira slapped the bar with an open hand and grinned. "It's your sunny disposition that brings your regulars back, Tenzin. Don't let anybody tell you different."

He stood and gestured for Aviama to walk first, indicating the curtained booths wrapped along the back wall. No one seemed to care about them anymore. They'd gone back to their conversations. A group of men huddled over dice at the table nearest them, and a group of men and women on the far side clinked their mugs together and shouted something unintelligible before bursting into laughter. A man at the second table looked up from his drink and sneered at Aviama, sending a deck of cards dancing between his hands without removing his gaze from her face.

Aviama swallowed and hurried past, turning her face away. Chenzira shifted her to his right side, shielding her from the sightline of the room, and held open the rich green curtains of the third booth while she slid into the wooden bench within. The booths were small, just enough space for two reasonably sized people on either bench, with a table set between them. Chenzira slipped in beside her and adjusted the curtain closed behind them. He drummed his fingers on the table, glancing up at the empty seatback cushions opposite them, and then through a sliver of space between the curtains before snapping them shut more closely.

Chenzira drummed his fingers on the table again and knocked his knuckles against the wood.

Aviama groaned. "Stop that. You're making me nervous."

Chenzira folded his hands. "Keep your hands under the table. Don't talk. And don't cut any deals. Let me handle it."

Aviama rotated the gemstone of the ring she'd been fiddling with to the inside of her palm and folded her hands to mimic his. "What if you make a stupid deal?"

"What if you talk and you don't know what you're talking about?"

"Are you going to get us killed?"

"That's our specialty, isn't it? Trying to get killed?"

Aviama crossed her arms. "I don't think *trying* is a fair word to use."

Chenzira pursed his lips and glanced down at her posture. "Hands."

"Biscuits." She stuffed her hands into her lap under the table just as the curtain swept aside and the most unexpected character plopped himself onto the bench opposite them.

He slapped his hands on the table. "Good evening, friends. I hope I didn't keep you waiting. Did you hear the cannons? New design. Quieter. Smaller projectiles. But very impressive."

The man was dressed in a long, black leather jacket with gold embroidery, opening in the front to reveal a black vest with golden buttons and a fine linen shirt. His hair was just long enough to curl at the ends as it swooped over his forehead, but tasteful, and a short, trimmed goatee graced his sharp chin. His eyes were both arresting and concerning at once as he scanned his companions with interest.

He propped his head on his hand and pulled out a glittering sandglass, setting it between them on the table. It was small, easy to fit in a pocket, but looked to be formed of crystal and made with blue sand instead of the dusty yellow-gray color of dunes. It was a unique piece, and probably quite expensive. But why would he pull it out? Just to flaunt his wealth? He looked like a merchant. A good one, apparently. But he stuck out at Boar's Tooth like a pearl on a pig.

The man reached into his jacket again, pulled out a folding scale, and set it beside the sandglass. "You've found yourself a lady friend. Looks like someone with a story. Where'd you come from, missy?"

36

A viama shifted in her seat, and the stranger flashed her a smile. What did he think of her? How many people clocked her as *someone with a story* when she walked in—someone memorable, someone standing out? *Biscuits.*

Chenzira cleared his throat. "I need to double the passenger fee and move up our arrangements."

"If I had a creature as beautiful on my arm as you do on yours, I'd be tempted to sail away with her too. There's a rush fee for changing the departure time. When do you need to leave?"

Still the man kept his eyes on Aviama, even while he spoke to Chenzira. Aviama lifted her chin and stared back. What else was she supposed to do? But she remembered Chenzira's warning and said nothing.

Chenzira, on the other hand, spoke up just fine. "Tonight. I need a ship now."

The stranger laughed. "And I need a flying monkey with reliable solid-gold-nugget excrement, but here we are."

Tenzin moved the curtain aside long enough to drop off a

round of drinks for the table and pulled it closed again. Chenzira snatched his off the table and took a sip. He made a face, and Aviama left hers on the table.

"It has to be now. And no one can see us board."

The man across from them arched his eyebrows. "You have a lot of demands. They'll cost you."

Chenzira reached into the pouch at his waist and pulled out one of the bracelets Aviama had given him when she abandoned her amethyst gown. "Rush fee."

The man plucked the bracelet from Chenzira's fingers, dropped it on the scale, and eyed Aviama. "Rough-spun cloth takes some getting used to, doesn't it? People like us aren't made for it."

Aviama squirmed in her seat but said nothing, returning his gaze evenly.

He stuffed the bracelet in his jacket and stuck out his hand toward her with a grin. "Onkar Dhoka at your service, darlin'."

Not thinking, she reached her hand out to take his. Onkar seized it and flipped it over, revealing the gemstones littering her fingers against her palm. He glanced at Chenzira. "Rookie, eh?"

Aviama grimaced, and her heart sank. Chenzira swatted the man's hand away, covered Aviama's hand with his, and slid it back off the table. Wind wisped evenly through her fingers beneath the table, and a relieved thrill ran through her. The magna had finally worn off.

Chenzira leaned forward on the table. "Dhoka is just your name of the week. I can kill him and force you to start up a new one, which is easy enough for you. But what would you do if I killed off your most famous name?"

Onkar pursed his lips and leaned back against the cushion, propping his elbow up on the back of the seat cushion and leaning his head on his hand. "Went hunting, did you?"

"I did."

"And you think you've found the queen of the hive, do you?"

Aviama glanced between them, her stomach churning with every tension-laden word spoken in the small space. Onkar exuded relaxed, casual carelessness with his demeanor, but his sharp eyes told a different story. Aviama might have been a rookie in seedy taverns, but she'd been around enough diplomats to know a man was more than the persona he wore. And whatever she'd failed to learn of that fact in Jannemar, Shiva had taught her in Radha.

Chenzira rapped the table with his knuckles and tilted his head at Onkar. "You've never tried to fit in. You're not Radhan, obviously. But your real name is Frizzletwerf. I can't imagine I'd keep a name like that either, if I'd been born into it. Especially not one with a less-than-ideal, centuries-old legend attached to it."

Onkar flashed a beguiling smile and spread his hands, gesturing toward Aviama. "Can you believe this, darling? I said you were the rookie. Forgive me. It's Taug here who doesn't know his face from the seat of his pants." The man sipped at the mug the barkeep had brought him, letting a full minute pass before he set it down on the table again. He licked his lips and glanced up at Aviama. "How do you feel about your protector's black market dealings, Your Highness? Do you think it fitting a man of his station?"

Her lips parted, and Chenzira stiffened. He knew. He knew precisely who she was, and who Chenzira was too. Or at least had a guess close enough to the truth to set Chenzira on edge.

Onkar waved a hand dismissively. "Young men always want to feel confident. They always want to believe they're the smartest and most resourceful person in a room. I like you, boy. But you're inexperienced, and you don't know what you're doing. You think you can sniff around for a few rumors, and I'll bend over backwards to your demands? At least make sure your rumors are on the money before making threats."

Chenzira flushed red and set a fist on the table. "I don't think you understand—"

Onkar cut him off. "You ask me for favors. You approach me with a business deal. And then, when you are on the hook and about to die, when you're asking me to risk my business, my life, and the full weight of the royal house down on my humble endeavors, you insult me with bad information and manipulation tactics. Bold move. Stupid move. Would you like a do-over? Or should I have my boys kill you now?"

Aviama sucked in a breath. Wind pooled between her palms beneath the table, and she clenched her jaw to keep from biting her lip. The wisp of wind along her skin beckoned. She hadn't seen anyone accompany this Onkar Dhoka, but she took him at his word. A man like him would have henchmen. How else would he dare flaunt his wealth among a den of robbers?

His eyes fell on her. "Oh, I wouldn't do that if I were you, missy. You think the roof blowing off this place won't bring konnolan falling down on you like a hailstorm? What'll you do then, hmm?"

She froze. How did he know she'd summoned the wind?

Chenzira put a firm hand on her knee as if to stay her hand. A tingle shot up her leg at his touch. He snatched his hand back and focused on Dhoka. "We'll make it worth your while."

Someone brushed up against the curtain as they walked by on the other side. Aviama jumped, but Onkar only took another sip from his mug. "I certainly hope so. Does the girl have a voice box outside the House, or is she a pawn everywhere she goes?"

Anger broiled in her chest, and she shot him a glare. "I have a voice box."

"Excellent. I'm all for equality, so you wouldn't get a discount for having a disability. But I do like to know who I'm dealing with."

Aviama lifted her chin. "Sounds like you think you've got us all figured out. Not sure what else you need from us."

He smiled. "Young boy. Young girl. Both with such fire. If you're going to be stupid, it's important to have fire. Fire makes you more likely to survive stupidity and mature into more effective scoundrels. I'm proud of you."

Aviama frowned. How was she supposed to take that? She shook her head. "If you don't mind, we are in a bit of a hurry."

"You shouldn't be. There are soldiers in the tavern right now, looking for you. They know better than to get in the way of my men, though. We have a sort of understanding, so you're safe if you're out of sight and with me. But the minute I get up and leave you alone..." He brought his hands together and suddenly burst them apart, mimicking the sound of an explosion with his mouth.

Chenzira glanced at the curtain, then scooted away from it and closer to Aviama, and crossed his arms. "Get to it, Dhoka. What do you want?"

"The rush fee is barely acceptable, but I'll take it. You still owe a second passenger fee, a maladroit incidentals fee, and a treason fee, which I've added to your account as of this evening. Higher risk, higher cost. But I like you, so if you purchase a retainer for support services, I'll give you a discount on the maladroit incidentals fee, and I'll even waive the deadly peril fee. On account of the lady."

Aviama gaped at him. "Are you serious?"

Onkar Dhoka raised his mug in a mock toast and took another gulp. "As the grave."

She swallowed. "Maladroit fee?"

"Sophomoric. Clumsy. Clueless. You make more messes, you require more cleanup. Simple as that, rookie." He winked.

Chenzira exchanged glances with Aviama and sighed.

Onkar laid his arm along the back of the seat cushion again and grinned. "If it makes you feel any better, the confidentiality service is included in all price packages. And your chance of getting anyone else willing to roll the dice on you two instead of turning you over is less than zero percent. In short, I am your only hope, and I know you have the money. I also find you interesting, which is to your advantage. I'm tired of the same old thing, and there comes a time in a man's life when variety is the greatest spice. But if you'd rather die than cough up a few more coins, who am I to stand in your way?"

Chenzira dug in his pouch again and produced the layered amethyst collar necklace Aviama had been wearing that evening. Onkar whistled and reached for it, but Chenzira snatched it back. "Covers extra passenger, rookie fee, *and* retainer. Because I expect you to slow the departure of the rest of the ships in the harbor after us. Or leak bad information. We need them off our tail."

Onkar clucked his tongue and wagged a finger. "The retainer service is at my discretion. It's very good value, if I do say so myself. You pay for my experience, which means my ideas. I help. And I choose *how* I help."

Chenzira shook his head. "That's asinine."

Onkar shrugged. "If you'd rather die, it's none of my business."

Chenzira let out a slow breath and handed over the necklace.

Onkar's eyes lit up. He held the necklace up to the light, examining the stones, then gave a satisfied nod and stuffed his latest fortune into some hidden pocket or other in his jacket.

He rubbed his hands together and let out a contented sigh. "Pleasure doing business with you both. Do us all a favor and don't move a muscle until my boys escort you out. We'll get you out of here and down to the wharf quicker than a dog eats its vomit. Hold your peace and don't be stupid."

And with that, the rich swindler swept from the booth with all the pomp and flair of a man who'd added a lifetime's wages to his jacket—without having done a single thing to earn it.

37

Sweat beaded on Aviama's forehead. She dabbed at it with the edge of the shawl wrapped around her hair and shoulders, but it did nothing to assuage the nauseous feeling in her stomach. Chenzira took a sip from his mug. Aviama hadn't touched hers. The hum of conversation, sloshing drinks, and shifting chairs filled the tavern. But the curtain did not move again, and the emptiness of the opposite seat mocked them.

Chenzira tapped his thumb on the edge of his mug and pursed his lips, glancing at her fingers. "Stop fidgeting. You're making me nervous."

Aviama looked down at her hands, where she was twisting her rings in circles. She stuffed her hands in her lap. "You're the one tap, tap, tapping away over there. And maybe we *should* be nervous. What if he leaves us here? What if he skips town with the money? What if he takes the necklace, uses it to prove he knows where we are, and leads the soldiers right to us? Are there even really any soldiers in the tavern right now?"

"If there are, I'm not sure it would be a good idea to talk

loudly about how badly we don't want them to find us." Chenzira gripped the mug, his knuckles whitening against it, and he leaned forward to peer out through a slit in the curtain.

How well did Aviama know Chenzira? Sure, he didn't like Radha. She'd saved his life. He'd saved her life. Multiple times, probably. But it was easy to forget he was a runaway prince who'd got mixed up in a foreign kingdom's radical group. After tonight, she could add to the list that he had at least two aliases, between the one he used with the Shadow and the one the barkeep knew him by, and he knew exactly where to go to find the black market.

Her mouth went dry. Enzo was dead. Murin and Arjun were on their way out of Radha. Chenzira was her only hope of a friend left in the world. Without him, she would undoubtedly be dead. She owed him a certain amount of trust for that. But despite their shared traumatic experiences, she didn't know him that well.

Could Aviama really trust him not to make stupid decisions? Hadn't he essentially said he was exactly the type of person to *make* stupid decisions? Rash. Risky. Involved with slimy people. And now he'd sunk their only shot at getting out of Rajaad alive by banking everything on a gangster with no motivation to honor his commitments.

Aviama watched Chenzira sitting there with muscles tensed in strong arms and peering out through the curtain every few seconds. He ran a hand through his short, trimmed, black beard and took another sip from his mug. Piercing eyes, perfect skin, and a face she could stare at for an hour and still ponder over. Was he as worried about their situation as she was? Did he have a backup plan? How did he wind up leaving Keket for Radha in the first place?

He turned away from the curtain and froze as he caught

her looking. Her chest tightened as he held her gaze. She'd have given him her last coin to know what he was thinking in that moment. If she had any coins.

Aviama cleared her throat. "Well?"

Chenzira stared back at her another moment, then touched his finger to his lips and leaned close so that his breath tickled her ear, the feel of his whisper sending a warm tingle shooting across her skin. "Four soldiers. Two pairs. Coming our way."

Her breath caught, and her pulse rocketed upward. Chenzira's hand slowly lifted towards the axe at his back. Wind swirled in her palms.

Steel rang from a scabbard, and Aviama jumped at a crash on the other side of the curtain. Laughter turned to shouts, and sloshing drinks to mugs and glassware slammed against furniture.

Chenzira dropped his hand from the hilt of his axe and lurched for the curtain. "Time to go."

Aviama pitched forward after him, grasping at the ends of her shawl and half-falling out of the booth in her haste. A man staggered forward across their path, stepping over a knocked-over chair on his way, and threw a punch at a Radhan soldier. The first soldier caught his fist as a second soldier slugged the man in the gut with his free hand, lip curling in disgust. "Melderblood swine."

Her heart sank. She ducked in the opposite direction, keeping her head down as she hurried after Chenzira. A second pair of soldiers leaped over the bar, eyes locked on Aviama. By the time she looked ahead again for Chenzira, he was gone. Two Boar's Tooth patrons turned toward her, surly sorts with fists as big as her face. One wiped blood and spittle from his face with the back of his hand, then grunted and pointed.

"This the one with the bounty?"

One of the soldiers by the bar snort-laughed as he drew his sword. "Not if we get her first."

Aviama ran. Wind raced through her fingers, and a gust of natural night breeze snapped her shawl to one side. Five figures loomed in the gloom of the lantern shadows in the cobbled street. Three lunged toward her, and she sent a wall of air, knocking them backward. Chenzira was on the far side of the street, sinking his fist into the gullet of a man dressed in peasant's cotton but gripping a club. The cobbles beneath her feet rocked like a wave, and she fell.

Her hands hit the stone, one landing on the edge of her shawl, inadvertently ripping it from her hair as she twisted to see what quakemaker had caused the trouble. The two Radhan soldiers that had leaped over the bar crossed the threshold of Boar's Tooth Tavern and strode toward her. One waved long, spindly fingers at her and grinned.

The hairpiece she'd tucked into the shawl fell back into place over her forehead as she rocked forward and regained her feet. The two soldiers seized her by the arms and pulled her forward, and that's when she noticed—the armor on the soldier on her right didn't quite meet at the shoulder, and the pant leg only made it to just above his ankle rather than down to his shoe. Her throat constricted.

"Who do you work for?"

Ten paces away, Chenzira twisted away from his adversary, ripping his first battleaxe free and driving the hilt into his opponent's belly. The man flew back against the wall and collapsed in a heap. Chenzira whirled the axe in his hand and spun toward the soldiers dragging Aviama out of the open street and down the first of another web of alleys.

"Just don't blow me away, and we'll get you where you want to go." The soldier cleared his throat and adjusted his hold on the hilt of his sword. "I'd hate to have to resort to more drastic—and obvious—measures."

Aviama craned her neck around toward Chenzira, who followed at a run before a questioning look flickered across his face. He met her gaze as the men half-pulled, half-carried her along between them. She turned back around and focused on keeping her feet under her and muttering to her new supposed captors. "You wouldn't need the sword."

"The boss wouldn't like it if I destroyed the thoroughfare toward his business."

Relief swept through her. Her suspicion was correct. The first pair of soldiers may have been legitimate, but the second were Onkar Dhoka's men. "Where are the men you stole the uniforms from?"

The other soldier snorted. "None of your business. Keep up or you'll be harder to keep alive."

The first fraud soldier jerked his chin at an imaginary destination far off in the dark. "We'll get you to the wharf. After that, you're on your own."

Aviama nodded, but she needn't have bothered. Nobody noticed or cared.

Chenzira was behind her, the men on either side of her knew how to handle themselves and had been paid to deliver her to the wharf, and Chenzira had cut a deal with the swindler to arrange for passage on a ship. A ship going where?

But as the dark closed in around them, without a glimmer of lantern or torchlight to break up the night, and they rushed through street after street with only the light of the cloud-covered moon to guide them, hope began to blossom in Aviama's chest. Arjun and Murin had a hard road ahead, traveling by land after the footsteps of an entire army in hopes of passing by them unnoticed and slipping into Jannemar before war broke out.

And they were relatively unknown. For Aviama, getting out by sea was her best chance. Chenzira had thought it through. If she could escape by boat, she could leave Shiva and the queen and her hyena behind her. She could flee from a sham engagement and regain her life. She could be free.

Slanted multi-story buildings with broken roads eventually disappeared, replaced by near-perfect cobblestone streets, maintained buildings, and shops with awnings and flowers bowing to the moon above. Dhoka's men stopped outside a walled compound. One let himself in through a locked door in the wall and returned around the side with a horse and cart. Chenzira, Aviama, and the second man climbed into the cart, and the first drove the horse.

No one said a word as the cart rumbled through Rajaad toward the promise of liberty. The air grew salty and the ground dusty as sand mixed with bumpy, husky clumps of grasses. And then the buildings dropped away before them, and the masts of four large ships met the clouds in the distance. On the close side of the wharf, the ground was firmer, but on the far side, the ground transitioned to primarily sand as it ran off toward the northern desert running up against the beach. Aviama hadn't realized there was another wharf toward the southern side, perhaps in an inlet closer to Rajaad than the main dock for the Radhan fleet and visiting ships.

Onkar's man stopped the cart in the shadows of the last group of buildings. "Get out."

Aviama scrambled off the cart, and Chenzira followed.

The driver snapped the reins, and the man in the back of the cart called back to them as the horse carried the fake soldiers away. "The boss is on the dock. He'll get you on board. Don't forget the landing fee on the other side."

"Landing fee!" Chenzira shook his head, but waved them

off and turned toward the wharf. He glanced at Aviama, and she bit her lip.

Here they were, at the edge of a new adventure. On the cusp of escape. The beckoning metronome of water washing up in waves against the wood of the dock ahead and the sand of the beach to their northeast ticked away the seconds as they struck out over the dusty ground toward the ships. Cannon fire boomed in the distance, but as they approached the dock, moonlight still shone on the rippling water, and the breeze still kissed her cheek and played with the ends of her hair. They had nearly reached the dock now. She could see the water creeping up under the wooden platform, and the structure above the rolling tide going out to meet the ships. The konnolan assaulting Waif's Garden seemed almost like a dream.

Aviama's heart weighed heavily to think of it. Darsh may not survive the night. He didn't particularly deserve to, probably, but the Tanashai onslaught on the Shadow would still be a slaughter. It was wrong. And Aviama had brought them right to the Shadow's door.

Perhaps when she got home, she could find a way to reach out to melders in Radha. Perhaps she could—

A woman slipped over the side of the nearest ship and onto the dock. Aviama stopped cold. Chenzira stiffened beside her and dropped to the sands behind the nearest post holding up the dock. The wooden platform creaked, and the woman ran a hand up and down her arms from where she stood, perhaps a stone's throw from where Aviama and Chenzira crouched.

Wooden posts drove deep into the ground at intervals along the platform, and walkways branched off from there into deeper water where the ships were anchored. The woman squinted into the dark, then walked slowly down the dock toward where Chenzira and Aviama were hiding. The moonlight fell on her face as she turned, and Aviama swallowed hard.

Sai.

38

Aviama pressed further under the edge of the dock. Chenzira's chest rose and fell quickly beside her in the cramped space. Water lapped up against the sand less than a meter from where they hid. If Sai had been watching from the ship, there's no way she would have missed Chenzira and Aviama walking alone across the open space between the edge of Rajaad and the wharf.

Sai's light footsteps padded overhead, and Aviama sucked in a breath. Chenzira bent his head to keep from hitting it on the boards above them, and he silently slid his axe free from its position on his back. Aviama's eyes bulged, and her heart pounded wildly against her ribs. She shook her head. Chenzira grimaced, but said nothing, his gaze fixed on the shadow of the girl's figure through the slats of the wharf's platform.

Sploosh.

It was a soft sound, like a rock or large barnacle falling into the water, but Sai turned her head and retreated toward the ship. A swishing sound caught Aviama's ear, and she looked ahead and to her right. She couldn't see anything from this far under the wharf, but as Sai disappeared, Aviama crept along the sand under the platform to peer around one of the posts.

Two sand sleds were speeding toward them, pulled by the massive royal pakshi birds Aviama had seen when she first arrived. Behind them, six horses pulled the largest sled she'd ever seen. And surrounding them all, a small army of mounted soldiers.

Chenzira swore under his breath.

Going back now was suicide, with nothing but a long, wide-open space between the dock and the cover of the first city buildings. Sai paused, turning once more toward their position. Aviama froze. A shiver ran down her spine.

Was Shiva here? Or had Sai guessed what they were up to and come on her own? Maybe she came to apologize. To beg to come along, to escape from whatever kept giving her bruises.

But as the sleds grew nearer and nearer, and the *pthhh pthhh* of horse hooves in sand and the jingle of chomped bits and metallic jostle of royal guard armor mocked her waiting ears, Aviama knew Sai had told her the truth. She'd told her the truth when she was sorry. But she'd also told her the truth that very night, when she admitted she'd been blackmailed, and her family would be killed if she didn't inform on Aviama to Shiva.

Chenzira had been right to restrain Sai. But he hadn't counted on her getting so far ahead, and the enemy guessing their next move. To be waiting on the dock.

Aviama scanned the wharf. Where was Onkar? Was he even here? Or had he hidden like a coward when he saw Sai and decided to take the money and run after all?

A strong gust of wind swept through the space beneath the dock, knocking Aviama to the ground with a grunt. The edge of the water washed up over her ankles, and panic set into her chest. Aviama lifted her hands and summoned the wind, feeling the hum of energy in the air. Power split in two directions as she pulled at the wind, gathering first to her, and then to another. To Sai, standing on the dock.

Chenzira whirled his axe and set his back against one of the thick poles to cover him from another gust as it hurtled over them. "Cover me. We have to board before the guards get here."

Aviama threw her hands in front of her, creating a shield of air pushing back against Sai's power. "We don't even know what ship to get on! And at this point, I'm not convinced there *is* a ship!"

No way could they crew a craft this large. Not between the two of them, and not with the time they had to do it. Which was zero time. Thirty seconds, if she was being generous.

Chenzira set his jaw as Aviama gathered her feet and came to stand beside him. "Run to the first ship. Don't stop. And if I have to kill people to get you there, be mad at me later."

Aviama's heart lurched to her throat. "Please don't kill her."

But he only gritted his teeth and set out from their hiding place. "Move."

Aviama pressed the wall of air out before the two of them as they ran forward together, out from the cover of the dock and up and around toward the ramp. Sai spun and shot a blast of air in their direction, and Aviama felt the pressure of the hit as it dissipated against her shield and rolled over it. She doubted it was all the strength Sai had. What would happen when the girl got desperate?

Up ahead, the mounted guard let out a shout. The pakshi broke into a sprint and the horses into a gallop, sending their sleds careening down the dunes after them. Aviama leaped up the ramp onto the dock, gathering fresh air to bolster the barrier between her and Sai as Sai sent blast after blast against her shield.

Chenzira threw his hands out toward the coming entourage, and a spray of sand went up as a tall ridge rose into a high dune just in front of the approaching guard. Horses neighed in distress, and one of the sledges slipped over the edge, its passengers and contents spilling down the dune.

Aviama gaped at his work, and a crashing blow of air from above knocked them both to the platform.

Chenzira roared as he pushed to his feet. "Enough with the defense. Attack!"

She threw a blast at Sai, which the girl deflected, but Aviana countered with a sliver of air she sent wrapping like a vine around her ankle and yanking her off the platform into the sand. "I don't want to kill her!"

"I don't care! If you don't take her out, I will, and if I bring the whole dock down on top of her, she'll die anyway!"

Sai scrambled to her feet, and Aviama took off for the nearest ship. It wouldn't provide anything but shelter at this point, and it was only a matter of time before they found her and dragged her back out. But anything felt better than being out in the open for whatever was coming down the slope.

Aviama leaped for the rail, but the boards beneath her feet rocked just as she pushed off. Her balance thrown, she missed her mark, slammed into the side of the ship, and dropped into the water. Waves knocked the ship to and fro. Waves that shouldn't have been there. Not in the quiet, without a storm, when all had been still before.

Memories of the ground swallowing the Radhan guard in Darsh's hideaway filled her mind. What could a crestbreaker do out here by the water? Did the Tanashais have crestbreakers?

A mighty gale snapped at the sails above her, and a wave of

ice-cold water swept over her head. Aviama gasped as the frigid temperature bit through her clothes and into every muscle and fiber. Her heart pounded fast, her pulse reverberating in her ears. She reached up along the ship's side but found nothing to hold on to. The ship rocked again, and a swell of water flooded over her head with a *whoosh*.

When she came up again, Chenzira and Sai were both in the sand on the far side of the dock, and mounted soldiers were galloping down the slope. *Biscuits.* She tried to call to the wind, but with the water as choppy as it was, she needed her hands to stay afloat. Aviama sucked in a deep breath and shoved off the ship, this time diving below the dock.

She hit one of the posts of the dock, scuffing the heel of one hand, and followed it up toward the surface. Her hand stung on the heel and both sets of knuckles where the salt reached the cuts caused by punching at the wooden door at the end of the tunnel earlier that night. Aviama broke the surface of the water, but a swell knocked her under again just before she took a breath.

Her chest tightened, and her lungs burned. Was it a crestbreaker controlling the water, or a quakemaker moving the ground beneath her? Or a windcaller beating the sea with gales? Could it be a natural storm?

Why would Shiva need her to train melderbloods if he already had an army of them?

Maybe it wasn't Shiva. Her blood ran cold. She couldn't decide if that made her situation better or worse.

Aviama kicked hard toward the surface, but this time her head hit the underside of the dock, and she still wasn't free of the water. This was no natural storm. The burning of her lungs rose to a raging fire, her ribs aching as if they might cave in altogether. Aviama braced herself against the underside of the dock and lifted her hands in front of her from under the water.

Come to me.

She could feel a splitting somewhere in the atmosphere as something else pulled at the air beyond the surface. But there was plenty of air to call from, and when she turned to draw from another direction, it eagerly funneled to her waiting hands, broke through the water like a missile, and surrounded her in an air bubble under the dock. Aviama gasped, her shoulders racked with coughing fits in her desperate attempt to fill starved lungs.

But now, with the air around her, she could exit the water further down without being seen. Chenzira was still fighting Sai on the sand, presumably, and one of the two of them would end up dead if she didn't intervene. Aviama's money was on Chenzira winning that battle. But with more players in the arena...

Aviama grimaced under the intense concentration required to send the bubble of air rolling along under the water. Twice she bumped into a ship or a post in the dark, once bursting her focus enough to lose her air supply, forcing her to recreate the bubble. A roll of water swirled her into a third post. The air around her broke apart, and she kicked to the surface. She emerged from the water at last on the sand side of the dock opposite the ships, further down than where she'd entered.

Sai lay on the sand with her hand up toward Chenzira, sinking fast into the hole he'd crafted. Two dozen mounted guards pounded down the sand to the dock, their horses slipping as Chenzira lifted one hand from Sai toward the oncoming barrage. Three horses fell, their riders tumbling free of the saddle and running forward on foot.

Aviama ran for Chenzira, and he turned toward her. She

threw up a wind shield to repel a volley of arrows from archers on horseback up on the ridge to the north and let out a cry as something pulled at her ankle from underneath the sand. Her shield shattered, and her mouth went dry as her gaze fell on a new set of shadows moving toward them across the emptiness to the east. The ocean lined their west and south-west, hemming them in, and Onkar Dhoka was nowhere to be seen.

She yanked at her trapped leg, then plunged her fingers into the sand to dig herself free, but the ground did not let go. "Melders! They've got melders!"

Sai raked her fingers through the shifting sand, eyes wide with panic. "Those aren't with us."

Chenzira swore and pulled his attention to his own feet, lodged deep in the sand, and Aviama's. Sai bent her wind toward blowing sand off her, but it did little good. Chenzira bent his palms toward the sand around them, and Aviama fell as the ground rolled like a wave under their feet. It rose a meter higher than it had been before for a span of several meters around where he stood, freeing Chenzira, Aviama, and Sai all at once.

The figures running from the east let out a shout, hands raised, a few weapons scattered between them. Fire danced on several palms, and a stream of flame shot out from one of them toward the Radhan guards. Beyond the horses to the north, Aviama could just make out a group of people carrying something long and heavy, larger than a coffin, down toward the ships.

A wave rose up out of the water and crashed over the sand, scattering three of the carriers of the big heavy thing. One end of it dropped to the ground. In the other direction, fire enveloped the first of the guards to reach the melderblood militia, lighting the sky like a human torch. His scream sent a shudder down Aviama's spine. Three guards filled the gap behind him and skewered the fireblood from different directions.

Aviama drove a gale over the soldiers, sending several of them tumbling backward, as Sai blasted two arrows from the sky.

Chenzira tossed Sai a look. "Whose side are you on?"

Aviama grimaced, arms burning, as she threw up another shield. Maintaining a protective bubble from so many attacks sapped her energy, and short bursts seemed more sustainable. "I don't think she's going to kill us, so let's figure it out later." One of the melders turned aside from the Radhan guards and shot a ball of fire straight for Aviama's head. She ducked and popped back up, mouth agape. Were Darsh's men there to kill Radhan guards or to kill her?

One thing at a time. Aviama swirled her hands together, balling up energy from the air and whirling it back at the fireblood. "Sai, are you going to kill us?"

Sai set her jaw and raised a trembling hand toward the melders. "Never, Your Highness."

Aviama nodded. "Okay, it's settled. What do we do now?"

A horse galloped toward them, and Chenzira pulled at the ground under its hooves. A ripple moved in the sand, and the horse stumbled but regained its footing. The guard thrust his sword down at Chenzira, but he blocked it with his axe. The fireblood threw another fireball at Aviama, and Sai shot a burst of air toward him—overestimating and knocking the man beyond him off his feet.

Aviama threw up a short burst of air to block the fireball, but she could feel herself tiring. Another wave washed up past its boundary on the beach beyond the dock. It reached up like long fingers to grab at the ankles of the guards to the north, but it was another figure who caught Aviama's attention.

The cloud over the moon shifted, allowing moonbeams to

fall on a young woman striding toward her, both hands outstretched on either side, eyes glaring daggers down a sharp nose from the top of the sand slope. Fireballs cut through the dark on one side, the flash of steel on the other. Radhan guards had reached the melders, and blood stained the ground. A guard slit a melder at the back of the neck, then screamed as the sand beneath him split and swallowed him whole.

Chenzira embedded his axe in the neck of the mounted guard and shoved him off the horse. Sai blocked the fireblood again, but then a guard cantered by on his horse and seized her by the hair, yanking her off her feet, her body trailing behind him. Aviama spun to follow her, but her feet lifted from the ground.

Dread settled over her like a thick cloud, and a pit formed in her stomach. Aviama flailed in the air, her body lifted over the fighting, terror choking at her throat. Durga's arms wavered, and Aviama dropped a meter toward the ground before the girl caught her again. Spots floated in her vision, as the sensation of total and utter powerlessness took her by storm.

The fight continued four meters below, bodies strewn across the sand, the sounds of combat climbing to her unwilling ears. The box that was not a coffin had been righted and had reached the dock, though the boards of one side had broken apart and fallen into the water. Behind Durga, the unmistakable form of Prince Shiva sent Aviama's failing heart into a tailspin.

Aviama gasped for breath in the flurry of spinning air holding her aloft. Shiva met her gaze, eyes burning with fury, lip curled in disgust. He perched atop a pakshi, those massive birds emblazoned on every Radhan flag and shield. Beside him, the queen emerged from a crashed sand sled and climbed up onto another enormous beast—Mrtyu, the man-eating ruby hyena.

Sweat broke out on Aviama's forehead, the wind around her licking at the moisture on her skin. The knot in her stomach tripled, and an invisible weight crashed in on her chest. Durga's hold fluttered again as her endurance faltered, and Aviama's stomach lurched to her throat as she fell towards the earth, only to be caught once more in the air. This couldn't be happening. This couldn't be real.

And then she saw the cannon.

horn blew, and Durga dropped her arms. Aviama plummeted to the ground, throwing her arms out to cushion her fall. Her body reverberated from the impact as she slammed hard into a wall of air she pulled up a meter from the sand before falling the rest of the way and collapsing in a heap. She gathered her aching feet and ran at Durga, palms up, whipping the surrounding air into a whirlwind begging to be let fly. Heat filled her chest, legs pumping, rage boiling, feet pounding the sand as she crossed the space between them.

But Durga wasn't paying attention. She was reaching into a satchel, and—was that a flask?

Out of the corner of her eye, Aviama saw Sai toss something small to Chenzira down the beach. He caught it with one hand and slung his axe at a swordsman with the other. Durga threw her head back and gulped at the liquid in the flask. Aviama threw herself forward. She had to get to Durga before Shiva and the queen made it down the hill. She had to threaten their greatest weapon. She had to—

BOOM.

A cloud of powder fell like rain over the sand. Weakness slammed into her like a sledgehammer, and the wind swirling in her hands frittered away. Nausea rocked Aviama's stomach, and she clutched at her midsection as a dizzy spell sent her to her knees. Head spinning, body aching, her limbs moved as if she were back in the mud bog of the arena. She threw a hand out to steady herself, but fell sideways into the sand.

She could see Sai retching under the dock. Two dozen melders were strewn across the sandy strip of land to one side, and the beach on the other, joining in her misery. The surviving Radhan guards swept through, hacking helpless melderbloods to pieces. The sound of human shrieks assaulted her ears, just as loudly as the silence that followed— a slash and spill of blood, cutting off the screams of life.

Aviama lolled her head to the opposite side. Durga stalked toward her, head high, unaffected by the konnolan. Aviama squinted up at her. What had been in her flask? There was an antidote to konnolan?

A ghoulish, rattling roar shook the air. The hair on the back of Aviama's neck stood on end, and she stared wide-eyed, paralyzed, at the open, snarling mouth of the queen's hyena just two meters off. Blood and spittle hung down in strings from the creature's mouth as it turned away from the ripped-open corpse of a melderblood on the ground.

Aviama pulled herself up on her elbows and dragged her unwilling body away from the beast. But it only laughed a high-pitched, shrieking laugh that sent a shiver to her core as it slinked ever forward. Fish in a barrel. A treat on a stick. Aviama was as good as dead, and her flesh was as fresh as any other prey animal on the hyena's menu.

Queen Satya held out a hand toward Durga from the huge hyena's back, and the girl backed off without a second thought. The queen lifted her chin, eying Aviama down the steep slope of her nose. Her lips twisted into a thin smile, and she ran her hands up through the animal's fur until the queen leaned across him, her face almost to the top of Mrtyu's ears as he crept ever closer.

The hyena stopped a mere handsbreadth from Aviama's nose, breathing the stench of the dead into her face. Satya let out a low, rumbling chuckle and snapped her fingers to call Aviama's attention from the beast to herself, the royal brute on its back. Slowly, she dismounted and glided down to Aviama's level, where she wrapped her fingers through Aviama's long blonde tresses and yanked her head back, exposing the soft skin of her throat to the hyena.

The queen's whisper sent ice through Aviama's veins. "I told you what would happen if you didn't listen to me. I told you a melderblood would never marry my son. And I told you —I always win in the end."

Aviama's stomach dropped and twisted. Another wave of dizziness swept through her, and if it weren't for Satya's hold on her hair, she might have fallen. The queen laughed again and released her. "Mrtyu. Feed."

Mrtyu lunged. Aviama rolled to one side, wrapping her arms around her torso to protect vital organs. Something crashed into her, and she gasped at the weight of it on her rib cage. A taloned foot the size of her head plunged into the sand a hair from her nose, and she screamed. Her body yanked as a force tugged over her ribs. She felt the pressure of it, but no pain came. Her fingers found the wound. They came away bloody.

A hiss filled the air, and a flurry of feathers, fur, and steel swirled in her vision. None of it made sense. Was she dying? Is this what happened when a person died? Just an influx of stimuli until the brain shut off completely?

But in the next moment, she saw him: Prince Shiva,

swinging his broadsword at his mother's hyena. Satya was screaming, and the massive plumed pakshi struck at the animal with huge taloned feet, beating its wings and diving in with a long, sharp beak in jerking movements. Mrtyu's roar overpowered the hiss, but a swipe at the bird's chest only sent it into a frenzy. The hyena seized Shiva's sword in his mouth, and slung its head side to side to wrest it from the prince's grasp, but he wouldn't let go. Mrtyu drove forward, head down, and knocked Shiva to the sand before turning to sink his teeth into the pakshi's stately, slender neck.

Strong arms slid under Aviama's body and lifted her from the ground. "Are you hurt?"

Aviama's vision darkened, and she fought the urge to close her eyes. One hand clung frozen against her ribs, her fingers wet with oozing blood. Her head spun, her muscles still weak from the konnolan cannon. She groaned, but no words came.

Shiva cursed and started running, with Aviama held close against his chest.

Aviama grimaced at the bouncing motion as Shiva sprinted across the sand, leaping over melderblood bodies as he went. Dead Shadow melders. Dead Radhan guards. Dead. Dead.

The prince called out commands, and the living scurried to follow them. One guard scooped up Sai from the edge of the water and tossed her over his shoulder. Eight men strained to carry the box that was not a coffin across a gangplank onto the largest of the ships at the dock. They'd won the battle. No one pursued. But still they boarded.

Silver scales shimmered in the moonlight as the box tilted this way and that over the walkway. Aviama's lips parted. Makana. They were carrying Makana in a secured water-filled box. Onto a ship. The siren was going back to sea.

Makana's hands pressed against the glass, her lavender

eyes piercing the night as they met Aviama's gaze from her trapped position—the siren in her box, the princess sick and wounded in the arms of their common betrayer.

No, no, no. It was all wrong.

Chenzira had gotten them free. He'd made a deal. He'd secured them passage.

But what good was the word of a swindler to a dead man?

Aviama's chest tightened, her heart burning with the bitterness of defeat. More death, more carnage. Because of her. And still Shiva orchestrated every aspect of her waning life.

Shiva tripped over something on the dock, and Aviama's guts threatened to spill at the lurching motion. Then her eyes settled on the object—a crimson-stained battleaxe.

She scanned the dock. Soldiers. Blood stains. Bodies. Sailors she hadn't noticed before, coming off the ship. And then she saw it. A shadow in the water, half-hidden under the dock.

Shiva adjusted his grip as he cradled Aviama's body against his chest and called to men aboard the ship. A flurry of activity sprang to life at his word. Torches lit. Giant sails unfurled. An entire crew had been waiting below deck.

A seaman stepped to the prow with a torch, and a moment later, red flame filled the eyes of a giant skull figurehead from the inside. The skull glinted in brass, a helmet set on its helm and a breastplate adorning a set of open ribs fixed to the ship. The name of the vessel emblazoned the breastplate, glowing in flickering red and orange under the light of the skull's deep, empty eyes: *Wraithweaver*.

Another wave of dizziness washed over her, and Aviama moaned. Shiva touched her forehead, and she flinched away from him. Her gaze landed on the figure in the water under the dock, the light of the skull's blazing eyes just illuminating the curves of his face. Chenzira locked eyes with her, and her chest tightened at the sight of him.

Did she want him to leave her? Wouldn't that be best? What could one man do against a man with the resources Prince Shiva had—a prince with konnolan to incapacitate melders, when the melder's power was over land, and they were apparently heading for the high seas? But if he did leave, Aviama's last and final comfort would be gone forever.

A knot grew in her stomach. The men carrying Makana's box set it down with a hefty thud, her silver scales shining in the moonlight, her perfect face etched with distress. The sailors stared at her, mouths agape, and she curled her lip in a snarl. A seaweed bracelet wrapped around one wrist several times, and the sight gave Aviama strength.

Makana wasn't going down without a fight. She had managed to bring two weapons with her—her own voice, the song of the siren, if only she found a way to use it effectively from her little box aquarium cage—and braided seaweed rope to strangle enemies.

The mermaid had been a captive far longer than Aviama, yet still she would go down swinging. She would use what little she had at her disposal to her advantage. What leverage did Aviama hold? What was at her disposal to use to her advantage? How might she turn the tide...?

She glanced back at the place Chenzira had been just in time to see a hand grip the exposed rib of the figurehead's skeleton and disappear around the side of the ship. Shiva carried her across the gangplank to the main deck of the ship. Durga took up a sentry position next to Makana, eying the siren suspiciously. Sai was set down on a coil of rope, still woozy from the konnolan.

Someone shouted out orders, and more men came rushing up the stairs from below deck. Shiva set Aviama on her feet.

She wavered, and he wrapped his arm around her waist, tugging her roughly against his side. He shifted her out of the way to his left, using his right arm to clasp the arm of a middle-aged, long-haired, bearded man dressed in a long teal coat lined with pakshi-head buttons.

"Captain Samud at your service, Your Highness. It is our honor to fight and sail with you today."

"The honor is mine. You will be rewarded for your swift preparations moving up our schedule so suddenly."

"Shall we make arrangements for the queen? We hadn't planned on her coming, but we are more than happy..."

Aviama twisted away from the captain to see a group of sailors loading several last crates on board from the dock. Beyond it, Queen Satya glared at her darkly from the bristled back of Mrtyu. Four bedraggled soldiers flanked her, one on a pakshi, one on a horse, and two on foot.

Shiva turned to look at his mother and blew her a kiss from the rail, but his eyes were flint, and hers were ice-cold daggers. He turned away from Satya and squared his shoulders. "The queen has responsibilities at home and regrettably is unable to join us. Reserve the quarters adjacent to mine for Princess Aviama. I intend to keep her close. And I need one of your men posted at her door every night."

Leverage be cursed. Aviama ripped away from his hold, staggering to clutch at the rail as her splitting head spun with new fervor. "I will never marry you."

Prince Shiva smoothed his coat jacket, using a fingernail to scrape at a speckle of dried blood at its hem. "It no longer matters. I will get what I want by other means." He looked back at Samud and raised his voice for all the crew to hear, scanning the men with pride. "I have yet to disclose our heading. But if you are on this ship, you have been hand-picked to my specifications. The glory of this voyage will be told for generations to come. Our quest is nothing short of legendary, and each man on board this ship will soon see things with his own eyes that our forefathers only dreamed about. It's time for this ship to own up to its name. Children's stories will come to life, and the proof of our destination will come with the plunder of the Aeian Sea."

Silence reigned on board the *Wraithweaver* as the weight of the prince's words settled over the crew. Shiva lifted his chin, resolve hardening in his deep umber eyes. A chill shot down Aviama's spine at the prince's next words: "Captain. Set sail for Ghost's Gorge."

Aviama's lips parted, and her pulse pounded in her ears. She couldn't allow Shiva to get what he wanted—to leave her helpless yet again, to do to the Iolani what he had done to her. The time had come. He may have gotten her on a ship full of people, he may have kidnapped a siren, he may have killed every melderblood radical who dared stand against him. But as soon as her strength returned, she would find a way to make a stand.

BOOK 3: WRAITHWEAVER

Continue the adventure with the third book in the series, *Wraithweaver...*

The enemy kingdom of Radha has set their sights on the sea. All hope of alliance is lost. And a forced concoction is limiting her powers.

Click here to learn more on Amazon!

THANK YOU FOR READING!

Thank you so much for reading *Shadow Caste,* book 2 of *The Melderblood Chronicles*! I hope you enjoyed reading it as much as I enjoyed writing it.

If you did, would you be willing to leave a review? Reviews help enable authors to continue doing what they do, and help other readers to find books best suited to them.

If you'd like to leave a review on Amazon, **click here.**

ABOUT THE AUTHOR

Author of *The Forgotten Stone* and *The Blood and Flame Saga*, E.A. Winters loves pouring a hot chai tea latte and delving into creating epic fantasy worlds for you to enjoy.

Erin lives in Virginia with her husband and two boys. When she's not writing, she sees clients as a Licensed Professional Counselor, and spends time with her family. She loves playing board games and reading, whenever the elusive "free time" opportunity arises.

ABOUT THE AUTHOR

ALSO BY E.A. WINTERS

Blood & Flame Saga

Book 1: Dragon's Kiss

Book 2: Broken Bonds

Book 3: Noble Claims

Book 4: Crimson Queen

The Melderblood Chronicles

Book 1: Melderblood

Book 2: Shadow Caste

Book 3: Wraithweaver

Book 4: Riddleborn

Book 5: Reaverbane

Stand Alones

The Forgotten Stone

Made in United States
Troutdale, OR
06/04/2024